LION OF TWILIGHT

A MEDIEVAL ROMANCE
SONS OF CHRISTOPHER DE LOHR
PART OF THE DE LOHR DYNASTY

BY KATHRYN LE VEQUE

KATHRYN LE VEQUE
NOVELS

ARE YOU SIGNED UP FOR KATHRYN'S BLOG?

You'll get the latest news and information on exclusive giveaways, exclusive excerpts, coming releases, sales, free books, cover reveals and more.

Kathryn's blog followers get it all first. No spam, no junk.

Get the latest info from the reigning Queen of English Medieval Romance!

Sign Up Here

kathrynleveque.com

The Lion Cubs are about to take charge!

Richard "Roi" de Lohr is the second son of Richard the Lionheart's champion, Christopher de Lohr. Roi was raised in the finest homes and with the finest training. Emerging as a powerful and intelligent knight, he married the woman he wanted and enjoyed the life of prestige he had earned. When his wife gave birth to a son, Roi's life was complete.

Until tragedy struck.

When Roi's wife dies in childbirth with their third child, he is devastated. But he's a de Lohr, and de Lohrs don't crumble. He focuses on his son, his eldest, proud that the lad promises to take his place among the great de Lohrs. He even arranges a marriage for his son with the daughter of a prestigious lord, an heiress of great wealth. Everything is going as planned.

But tragedy strikes again. Roi's son is killed in a freak accident, leaving Roi shattered beyond repair. The prestigious lord, however, has no sympathy and demands that Roi fulfill the marriage contract or risk losing a strong alliance. With Roi's son gone, that means Roi, a widower, must marry the young heiress he's never even met.

Lady Diara le Bec is that heiress.

From one of the finest families in England—though that prestige masks a problem—naturally vivacious, and charming,

Diara has earned herself a scandalous reputation that Roi wasn't told about. He's rather reserved by nature, serious and deliberate, and when he finds himself married to a woman who can light up an entire room with simply her smile, he's taken aback. There are whispers of Diara's flirtations and the men she has conquered. Roi suspects he has gotten himself into a miserable marriage. But that soon changes as he comes to know the lightning bolt known as Diara. *Deedee.*

And so begins a love story for the ages.

Treachery and deceit, it seems, aim directly for Roi and Diara as their relationship deepens. Join them as they navigate the turbulent waters of a romance that was never supposed to happen… and a joy that they could have never dreamt of.

HOUSE OF DE LOHR MOTTO

Deus et Honora
God and Honor

AUTHOR'S NOTE

I can't tell you how excited I am to finally be writing about Christopher and Dustin's sons. If you've read *Rise of the Defender* (and I hope you have), then you're already familiar with the House of de Lohr. If you haven't read it yet, I suggest you do it right away. While you don't need to read it to make sense of this book (all of my books are standalones), it makes the story—and characters—that much more endearing. I love me some de Lohr men!

Let's start off talking about the offspring of Christopher and Dustin de Lohr. There are several, so here's the list of kids and their stories:

Peter (Christopher's son with Lady Amanda) (The Splendid Hour)

Christin (A Time of End)

Brielle (The Dark Conqueror)

Curtis (Lion of War)

Richard (Lion of Twilight)

Myles (Lion of Hearts)

Rebecca

Douglas (Lion of Shadows)

Westley (whose middle name is Henry and he was sometimes referred to as "Henry" when he was young) (Lion of Thunder)

Olivia Charlotte (the future Honey de Shera from the Lords of

Thunder series)

Now, there's always been a question about Douglas de Lohr. I've mentioned before that he was killed in my novel *Tender is the Knight*, but that's not true. That was a mistake on my part (after 147 novels at this point, I'm allowed a mistake or two). Seriously, I do keep detailed notes, but some of them are twenty-five or thirty years old in some cases. I went back to my original notes on *Tender is the Knight*, and although I had intended Douglas de Lohr to be Christopher's son, I changed the timeline in the story that made it impossible for *that* Douglas to be Chris and Dustin's son. Instead, I made him the grandson of Baron Lohrham of Lohrham forest, Philip de Lohr, who was Christopher's uncle. We met him in *Rise of the Defender*. However, Philip wasn't really Christopher's uncle—but a cousin—which is why Christopher was never in the line of succession for his ancestral home of Lohrham Forest. So—the Douglas de Lohr in *Tender is the Knight* is a cousin to "our" de Lohrs. He's not a son. Thankfully. That means "our" Douglas will, indeed, have his own story told.

Something more to note in this novel—remember that Christopher and Dustin had their children during a spread of several years. Their eldest child, Christin, for example, is quite a bit older than their youngest child, Olivia Charlotte (Honey). Dustin was only nineteen years of age when she had Christin, who also had her children quite young, so in this novel you will see—gasp!—Christin's grandchildren. Also, you'll discover that Honey married before some of her older siblings, so the ages of the grandchildren are all over the place as well. Note that they call Christopher "Taid" and Dustin "Nana," which are basically the Welsh words for grandparents.

The Executioner Knights play a small role in this tale, too. Mentions appear in this book, as do second-generation

Executioner Knights. Keep in mind that when the main Executioner Knight series was written, it was back in the time of King John—about forty years or more before this book is set—so the original Executioner Knights were in their thirties or so. In this novel, they are considerably older but still alive. Just keep that in mind when you read about their children. Life goes on!

And speaking of "older," Christopher is incredibly old in this book. He's healthy and he has a secondary role, but if I told you how old he really is, you'd probably freak out. According to the year he was born—1156 A.D.—he's eighty-nine years old. I think I mentioned on a Facebook post once that in figuring how long Christopher and David, his brother, really lived, using all of the clues I'd given in books like *Shadowmoor* and *Silversword*, I discovered that Christopher had died in 1249 AD at the age of ninety-two and David lived to the ripe old age of one hundred. Seems that the de Lohr boys have longevity. Was that possible in Medieval times? Absolutely. It would have been excessive, but it wasn't out of the realm of possibility. Life spans were shorter, of course, but there was the odd few who lived to a ripe old age.

And with that, I'm not sure there's much more to be said. No pronunciation guide because all of the names are familiar with the exception of the heroine, Diara—it's pronounced "Dee-AR-uh." She's quite a lady. And I have to say that I think Roi is one of my new favorite heroes. See if you don't agree.

Happy Reading!

PROLOGUE

Year of Our Lord 1243
Chateau de Montreuil Bonnin, France

"I'LL NOT SPEAK one word to you unless you tell me what sort of dowry your daughter has."

The rain was pounding, the lightning flashing, and the knights from the army of Henry III of England were up to their knees in mud and blood, in that order. The entire field of battle had turned into a quagmire of sludge, and when one was trying to swing a heavy broadsword, it was difficult to keep one's footing.

Knights were sliding onto their arses all over the field.

But not the man who demanded dowry information. Sir Richard de Lohr, son of Richard I's greatest knight, Christopher de Lohr, had managed to keep his footing and his dignity as he engaged enemy knights, but the man following him around was covered in so much mud that it was in his ears and nose. But that didn't prevent him from trailing after a man he very much wanted to bargain with.

In spite of the muddy ear canals, he could hear very clearly when he wanted to.

"She is very wealthy, Roi," he shouted over sounds of the storm. "Will you at least stop to discuss it?"

Richard, who had gone by the nickname Roi since he'd been a young lad, paused and turned to the man with a grin.

"I am supposed to stop what I am doing?"

"Aye!"

"We're in the middle of a battle, Robin."

"I am well aware."

"Did you not think this might not be the most opportune time to discuss a marriage between our children?"

"It was the only time I could get your attention, you bullish man."

Roi let out a peal of laughter, but it was cut short when a knight bearing the colors of the Count of Poitiers charged at him through the sheets of rain. He was on foot, as Roi was, as the knights had long ditched the horses because the mud was so bad that equine legs were in danger of breaking. The French knight's movement wasn't really a charge so much as it was a slip-sliding attempt to get at him, but Roi was ready. After a nasty battle with broadswords swinging beneath the stormy sky, Roi managed to undercut the knight and slice him behind the right knee. Tendons and muscles were cut.

The man went down for good.

Roi walked away.

"Why do you not kill him?" Robin demanded, looking at the downed knight. "You are in a perfect position to do so!"

Roi glanced at the knight who was writing in agony. Then he turned to the chatterbox next to him. "Because he is an excellent knight," he said. "I knew him before Henry and Alphonse decided to battle one another. Men like Etienne do not deserve to be killed, but I have disabled him. He will not follow us."

"He was your friend?" Robin asked, shocked.

Roi looked around the field of battle. "Not a friend, but I know most of the knights out here," he said. "I know them on sight. Chances are I have fought with them or against them. You forget who my father is and who my uncle is. You must further forget who my family is."

"I have not forgotten anything." Robin le Bec, also known as the Earl of Cheltenham, wiped the mud out of his eyes. "I know who your family is and who you are. I know you come from a great line of knights and your father is mayhap the most powerful warlord in all of England. Well do I know this. Why do you think I wish for my daughter to marry your son? She deserves a de Lohr legacy."

Roi grinned. "You know that you are not the only father who has been asking after my son," he said. "I only have one. He is very much in demand because of who his father and grandfather are."

"I am highly aware of this," Robin said. "Christ, Roi, stop taunting me. Tell me what you want to hear in order to ensure that this betrothal happens."

Roi turned away from him and headed west, where the English army was starting to gather because the battle was waning. The French, suffering a massive siege at a Lusignan property of Chateau de Montreuil Bonnin, had made the grave mistake of opening the portcullis in the hopes of charging the English and chasing them off after three days of being bottled up in a relatively small castle. It had been a foolish move by an amateur. The French, led by one of the Count of Marche's men, had underestimated the English resolve.

And the English numbers.

Now, the English had the beautiful castle of Montreuil Bonnin and about two hundred French prisoners, including knights who had fought bravely. But for Roi, the man whose nickname translated to *king* in French, it was simply one battle in a long line of battles in France as Henry III fought against the Count of Poitiers in an attempt to keep some of his Angevin properties. Roi had been in France for a solid year.

He just wanted to go home.

But he would return to a dozen fathers hounding him about his eldest and only son, Beckett, a fine lad with all of the de Lohr characteristics that fathers wanted for their daughters. He was handsome, skilled, of good character, educated, and strong. He was also wealthy. Roi had been fielding demanding fathers for the better part of three years and now, with Beckett approaching his nineteenth year and already in line to be knighted next year, that gang of eager fathers were pestering Roi like vermin, le Bec included.

"What do I want?" Roi repeated the man's last question. "I want to know how much of a dowry you intend to give my son. I want to know what virtues your daughter has that makes her better than any of the other daughters I've been offered. What makes her so special?"

Robin was right on his heels as they made their way to the east side of the castle walls.

"Because she's *my* daughter," he said firmly. "She's bright and brilliant and obedient. She would make an excellent match for Beckett. They would produce powerful, intelligent sons to carry on the de Lohr name. Does that not appeal to you?"

"Nay."

Robin's bushy eyebrows flew up in outrage. "It does not? What kind of man are you?"

Roi glanced at him, his eyes twinkling with mirth. "One that knows you want something badly enough to pay well for it," he said. "Let us be honest, Robin—marriages are based on wealth and importance, not on beauty or obedience. You have an adequate army and your proximity to the marches and my father's empire is desirable. I will be honest when I tell you that you have that advantage over many others. But you've yet to tell me what your daughter's dowry is. Don't you even know?"

Robin reached out and grabbed him by the arm, forcing him to stop. "You have a mercenary soul, Richard de Lohr," he growled. "You want to know what my daughter's dowry is? Then here it is—she is the heiress to Cheltenham. If your son marries my daughter, he shall inherit my lands and titles when I die. Through her mother, who is a de Bermingham, she will inherit a small fortune. I have nearly a thousand marks of gold in my treasury at home and nearly as much here, with me, as I travel with my army. I will give you half of that for a dowry today if you agree to a betrothal, and if that is still not good enough for you, then I hope you choke on your own arrogance and I hope your son ends up marrying a pauper."

He was genuinely angry by the time he was finished, leaving Roi biting his lip to keep from laughing.

"That is quite a dowry, Robin," he said, resuming his walk. "Why did you not tell me all of this before?"

Robin was still peeved. "Because the moment I start talking about all my daughter will inherit, I can see the glitter of gold in men's eyes," he said. "Do you think my daughter is not much pursued? She is, you know. She is a much sought-after heiress, so do not think your son is the only one in demand. My daughter has her share of suitors."

"Yet you have hounded me about a match."

"Because I want a de Lohr. That is what Deedee deserves."

"Deedee?"

"Lady Diara Elizabeth Esmerelda Julietta le Bec," Robin said. "That is my daughter's name. But she will answer to Deedee."

Roi came to a halt. They were nearing the field where the English were gathering, and overhead, more rain was starting to fall. His gaze drifted over the destruction before them, the burning castle, the red mud, the injured men, the general status of warfare.

The mood of the conversation suddenly changed. Where it had been feisty banter, now it became serious as Roi's expression took on a distant cast.

"I have been looking at this chaos for almost a year," he said. "I have told Henry that I am returning home at the conclusion of this particular battle. I've given the man a year of my life and more besides, and it is time for me to return home and resume my life. My father is quite elderly, and the truth is that he will probably not be with us much longer and I would like to spend his last years with him. Henry has agreed. But when I go home and see my family, I will take home news of my son's betrothal to the Cheltenham heiress."

Robin was gearing up for another round of verbal battle, but Roi's statement had him sputtering.

"You *will*?" he said, eyes wide. "But of course you will! My dear friend, I am delighted!"

He threw himself at Roi, kissing the man's cheeks, literally clapping and cheering in both relief and happiness in a gesture sorely misplaced among the litter of a battle.

"Aye, I will," Roi said, wiping his cheeks where the man had kissed him because his breath smelled like sour wine. "When you return to England, you will send me word so that we may arrange a meeting for our children and families. I think it is only right."

"Of course, of course," Robin said eagerly. "I will be returning home very soon. My wife and daughter will be thrilled with this news."

"How old did you say she was?"

"She is two years younger than your son—she has seen eighteen years."

"I'm assuming she fostered in a fine home."

"One of the finest," Robin said. "Carisbrooke in Devon."

"Ah," Roi said. "With de Redvers. Then she knows something of politics if she's been at Carisbrooke."

Robin nodded. "I've not seen her in a year, but the last time we met, she was able to carry on a very astute conversation about the political climate of England," he said proudly. "Your son will not be disappointed, Roi. Diara will make a fine wife."

Roi simply nodded before resuming his march toward the gathering English. "Beckett has been at Selbourne Castle in Hampshire," he said. "That is the home of the Sheriff of Hampshire, you know. My son has been well educated in law and order, which was the main reason I sent him there. He is to be a proctor in the king's council when he comes of age, so his education in the laws of the land has been intense. I received the very same education."

Robin was rushing after him again. "I know," he said. "Why do you think I have pursued this betrothal? I know your background. I know that the king relies on you for law interpretation and order. I know that is why you are here, Roi. You are not simply a knight sworn to the king. You help him create the laws and treaties and you have advised him, legally, throughout this campaign. You are a very important man."

Roi grunted, glancing up at the castle again. "And this one went awry," he said. "We tried to solve it with negotiations, but the French would not listen. Poitiers' men seem to be under the impression that they can win this battle."

It didn't appear that they could, given the state of the castle, but Robin didn't comment. He had what he wanted, and that was all that mattered to him at the moment. He ran to catch up with Roi and tried to put his arm around his neck, a difficult task considering how tall Roi was. He settled for putting it around his shoulders.

"Forget the French," he said. "We have something to celebrate tonight, you and me. I shall finally have the son I have hoped for in Beckett de Lohr, and you... you will have a daughter you can be proud of."

Roi glanced at him. "I already have two daughters I am proud of," he said. "But I know what you mean. We shall welcome Diara with open arms."

Robin was beside himself with glee. A de Lohr husband for his only child and a legacy that would continue with the de Lohr name behind it. Six months of pestering Roi de Lohr had finally come to fruition, and he was thrilled to death. He needed to have a contract drawn up as quickly as possible and executed because he didn't want Roi to change his mind. Men had a habit of doing that if something more attractive was presented, and Roi had made no secret of the fact that he wanted a prestigious marriage for his son. Diara le Bec brought the Cheltenham earldom with her as well as lands in Bedfordshire, so she was as good as it got. At least, on the surface.

If her reputation didn't reach Roi's ears before the contract could be signed.

Robin had every reason to rush the contract.

And he would.

CHAPTER ONE

Pembridge Castle
De Lohr outpost, Welsh marches
Two years Later

"WHERE IS HE?"

A knight with a growth of dark beard and pale blue eyes asked another knight a question in a tone that conveyed pain. At Pembridge Castle, the last day had been one of excruciating pain and agony. No one was spared.

It was a castle on edge.

Pembridge was the southernmost outpost of the de Lohr empire, a castle built halfway down a slope amongst the verdant hills of the Welsh marches. Oddly, it didn't see much action from rebelling Welsh or English feudal wars, but when it did see conflict, it had historically been heavy and long. The situation it found itself in at the moment wasn't a conflict between adversaries, but rather an emotional conflict that was going to become worse before it became better.

If it ever became better.

The knight who had asked the question knew that. They all knew that. Sir Kyne de Poyer, a big knight with big hands and an immovable spirit, had asked the question of his associate, Sir Adrius de Gault. A mountain of a man with a shiny, bald head and, strangely enough, gold earrings in both ears had listened to the question with great sorrow.

"In his solar," Adrius replied quietly. "Why do you ask?"

"Has anyone spoken to him this morning?"

"Haven't you?"

Kyne shook his head. "Nay," he said. "He was so drunk last night that I thought he would sleep longer than he did. I was going to seek him now, in his chamber, but he was gone."

Adrius nodded his head, sighing heavily. "I saw him go to his solar," he said. "He has the missive in his hand, still."

"He slept with it."

Adrius simply shook his head sadly, his gaze moving to the castle around them as he pondered his thoughts. "Christ, Kyne," he muttered. "What are we going to do? What is *he* going to do?"

"There is nothing he can do," Kyne muttered. "There is nothing we can do, at least between the two of us, but help is arriving."

"What do you mean?"

"I sent word to Lioncross Abbey yesterday after we received the news," Kyne said. "Our scouts spotted a contingent from Lioncross Abbey on the perimeter of our lands."

"The earl himself?"

"Aye," Kyne said. "I'm sure Christopher de Lohr is coming along with his wife and one or more of Roi's brothers. The entire family is coming, and I was looking for Roi to tell him that. He will not be alone in this."

Adrius pointed in the direction of the solar. "Go," he commanded quietly. "Go and tell him before he starts drinking again and is a drunken mess before midday."

Kyne didn't have to be told twice. He passed through a shadowed portion of the bailey, cool and damp from morning dew, before continuing into the keep, which was part of the outer wall. Pembridge was built from the red sandstone so prevalent to the area, a solid and imposing castle that guarded the main road out of southern Wales into the midlands of England. The castle had belonged to Roi for many years, ever since his father's army had wrested it from a Welsh prince who wanted to use it to launch raids deep into England. Once de Lohr captured it, he had to wrest it further from the Earl of Gloucester, who made the argument that it was closer to his lands than it was to de Lohr. But that wasn't the truth.

De Lohr got what de Lohr wanted.

Yet the beautiful castle set within the bucolic hills of the marches had not been an entirely happy place for Roi. He'd been delighted when he was appointed the garrison commander. He'd brought his wife and son there, and both of his daughters had been born there. But his wife had also died there.

And now this.

Pembridge had become Roi's personal monument to tragedy.

The interior of the keep smelled of smoke and rushes, familiar smells in most castles. Kyne made his way to the solar door, which was in the entry, listening carefully to what might be on the other side of the door before rapping on the panel softly. When he received no answer, he rapped again and pushed the door open.

Even though it was midday, the chamber was mostly dark. No fire in the hearth, no glowing lamp. The only sounds were those from the bailey, filtering in on the soft spring breeze.

Kyne finally spied Roi sitting near the darkened hearth, his head in his hands.

Kyne cleared his throat softly.

"My lord," he said quietly. "Our scouts report a party from Lioncross Abbey on the approach. They should be here within the hour."

Roi didn't stir. Unsure if the man had even heard him, Kyne took a few steps in his direction and tried again.

"My lord?" he said gently.

Roi twitched, which at least indicated he was alive. After several long moments, his head finally came up.

"My father?" he asked hoarsely.

"I would assume so, my lord," Kyne said. "I sent him word yesterday about the missive from Selbourne. I thought you would want him to know."

Roi sat back in his chair, staring at the wall. He just sat there, staring, his ashen face set like stone.

"My father has never lost a son," he finally said. "He will not know how to comfort me."

Kyne was very careful in what he said, unwilling to provoke the man at this time. Roi was known for a quick temper, and Kyne didn't want to find himself on the wrong end of a grief-driven sword.

"Would you prefer he not come, my lord?" Kyne said. "I can ride out to meet him and tell him to return to Lioncross if that is your wish."

Roi simply shook his head. "Nay," he muttered, sounding defeated. "Did you tell him what happened?"

"That is your privilege, my lord," Kyne said. "I simply sent word that there was an accident and your son had been killed."

Roi sat there for a moment, still staring at the wall before falling forward and putting his head in his hands again.

"An accident," he said, muffled. "My brilliant, strong, noble son was killed by falling from a horse. We've all fallen from a horse. All of us. I've fallen off or been thrown off a hundred times in a hundred different ways, only Beckett landed on his head. And that is the end of my son's future. It is the end of everything."

Kyne watched him as he suddenly stood up and went to the table behind him, the one that contained wine and cups. It was always in the solar. But it had been drained yesterday, along with several other containers of wine, and the servants hadn't yet filled it. Realizing this, Roi hurled the pitcher against the wall, shattering the earthenware. Kyne backed away, toward the door.

"I'll have the servants bring you wine, my lord," he said. "Do not fret. I'll have it brought right away."

The wine was immediate.

A little more than an hour later, the gatehouse of Pembridge opened the wooden and iron portcullis, heaving it up on the old ropes that held it. When the party from Lioncross Abbey Castle, seat of the mighty Earl of Hereford and Worcester, passed beneath the opening, Kyne and Adrius were there to greet them.

Leading the Lioncross group were two big knights who turned out to be sons of Christopher de Lohr, brothers to Roi. Curtis de Lohr, his eldest brother, was astride a massive silver charger, while his youngest brother, Westley, was riding a muscular blond warhorse that kept tossing his head and throwing froth. There were about fifty soldiers with them, all of them mounted, all of them circled around a big carriage that came lurching into the bailey of Pembridge. It was a fortified carriage, one used to transport the family comfortably, but it was also virtually impenetrable. It was like a fortress on wheels. As the carriage came to a halt, Kyne and Adrius went to meet Curtis and Westley.

"My lords," Kyne greeted both men as they began to dismount from their steeds. "We did not expect you so soon, but I am very glad to see you nonetheless."

Curtis de Lohr, the heir to the earldom, was an enormous man, like his father, with a blond beard and shoulder-length blond hair he pulled into a ponytail. He removed his helm, handing it off to the nearest man who had also taken the reins of his horse.

"We came as soon as we received your message," he said, his sky-blue eyes dull with anguish. "What happened, Kyne?"

Kyne wasn't keen to answer him. "I told your brother that it was his privilege to tell you, but I am not entirely certain he will," he said. "The man has been drinking heavily since we received the news from Selbourne."

"Then you tell me. How did Beckett die?"

"Thrown from a horse, my lord," Kyne said quietly. "The new one that your brother gave him for his birthday. The white one."

Curtis suddenly looked at him in horror. "The white beast with the black mane?"

"I would assume so, my lord. We were told he was thrown from his new horse."

Curtis looked as if he'd been hit in the stomach. "Christ," he gasped. "I sold him that horse. It was too much horse for me, and I did not have the patience to… He gave it to Beckett?"

Kyne nodded, seeing the guilt sweep across Curtis' face. "Aye, my lord," he said. "Beckett was here a few months ago for his birthday, and the horse seemed to like him a great deal. The lad begged for it, and Roi gave it to him."

Curtis closed his eyes, tightly, realizing what had happened. He put his hand over his mouth in dismay as his brother, Westley, walked up beside him. Shorter than most of the unusually tall men in the de Lohr family, he was nonetheless built like a bull, with flowing blond hair that had enraptured many a maiden. Westley de Lohr was a god among men. He'd caught the tail end of the conversation and looked between Curtis and Kyne curiously.

"Who begged for what?" he said. "What are we talking about?"

"Beckett," Curtis said, muffled through his hand. "The white Belgian warmblood I sold Roi."

"I know the horse. What about it?"

"He gave it to Beckett."

Westley wasn't following him. "*And?*"

"The horse threw him and killed him."

Now, Westley was getting it. His eyes widened and his jaw went slack as he understood what happened. But an older couple was walking up behind them, and he kept his mouth shut as the Earl and Countess of Hereford and Worcester made an appearance. Having come from the overly cushioned carriage, Christopher no longer rode his warhorse for longer distances. As he told everyone, he'd earned the privilege to ride more comfortably in his twilight years, but the truth was that he had an affliction of the joints, age-related, that made it difficult for him to ride astride or grip the reins for long periods of time.

Christopher was in his eighth decade of life, a massive man with blond hair that had long gone to gray and a beard that was snow-white. He was fixed on Kyne, who bowed his head in respect as the mighty earl came before him.

"My lord Hereford," he said. "We are honored by your visit. I wish the circumstances were better."

Christopher sighed, conveying the depth of his grief. "You will tell me what happened to Beckett."

Kyne glanced at Curtis, who was still struggling. "He was thrown from his horse, my lord," he said. "According to de Nerra of Selbourne Castle, they were departing the stables and the horse spooked. He did not know why, but Beckett was tossed on his head and broke his neck."

Christopher was old, that was true, but he'd never truly shown his age until that moment. Suddenly, he looked very old and very sad as Curtis spoke up.

"The horse I sold him, Papa," he said grimly. "The white Belgian, the one that was difficult to handle. He'd already thrown Arthur, if you recall. I did not want him any longer, but he was well bred and expensive. Roi purchased him, but I did not know he'd given the horse to Beckett. I had no idea."

Christopher looked at his firstborn and could see the shadow of guilt all over the man's face. "Roi knew the horse was difficult when he bought him, did he not?" he said. "You never made any secret of that."

Curtis shook his head. "I did not, but that does not matter now, does it?" he said. "The horse *I* sold him has... My God... What have I done?"

"You did nothing." Dustin, who had been standing quietly next to her husband, spoke softly. "Curtis, you did nothing. You sold your brother a horse. That was all you did. 'Twas the horse who threw Beckett, not you. You had no hand in it."

That might have been true, but Curtis was wrestling with unbelievable horror. He turned away from his parents and struggled to reconcile himself with what had happened. His parents watched him go, concerned, but Christopher soon returned his focus to Kyne.

"Where is Roi?" he asked quietly.

"In his solar, my lord," Kyne said. "He… he has been drinking. You should be prepared."

Christopher simply nodded. Reaching out, he took Dustin's hand, and the two of them began to head toward the keep. When Westley tried to follow, Christopher held him off.

"Nay," he said quietly. "Stay with your brother. He may need you while he regains his composure. That will give your mother and I time to speak with Roi alone."

Westley agreed, watching his mother and father continue their walk of sorrow toward the keep. But it was more than sorrow that they were feeling—the sense of loss was tremendous. While Curtis had eight sons, Roi, their second-born son, had only been blessed with one. Beckett had been his shining star.

Roi, their son named for Richard I, had been Christopher's close friend. When he'd been quite young, the family called him Richie until he decided that was the name for a baby. The name "Roi" came from a close friend, a man who was Roi's godfather. Marcus Burton, a great northern warlord, had once called Roi "*Petit Roi Richard*" because of who he was named after, and the name "Roi" stuck. He'd been about seven years old at the time.

He'd gone by Roi ever since.

Their quick-tempered, blindingly brilliant son whose keen intellect could outshine everyone in the family was suffering through yet another tragedy in a life that had seen several. Roi fought hard, loved hard, played hard, and grieved hard. It had taken him ten years to recover from Odette's death fourteen years earlier.

But they both knew he would grieve Beckett to his grave.

There was no overcoming the death of a child.

"Let me speak to him first," Dustin said as they neared the keep. "If he has been drinking, he will be more emotional than usual. Let me talk to him before you do."

"Why?" Christopher looked at her. "I am capable of dealing with my son."

"I know," she said. "But he was always attached to my apron strings more than our other children. I know we are not supposed to have favorite children, but if we did, Roi might be mine. You had Curtis and Myles and Douglas and Westley all worked up to be men among men, and Roi always thought of me first, came to me first. Just... let me speak to him first. Give me a few moments before you come in. Please?"

They had entered the keep by that time, and Christopher shrugged, letting her continue on to the solar. The door was shut, but she quietly opened it, sticking her head in and immediately spying her big, auburn-haired son near the hearth with his head in his hands.

Silently, she entered.

For a moment, Dustin simply watched his lowered head. He was sniffling. She could also see a pitcher on the table next to him, the wine he'd undoubtedly tried to find solace in. Roi had been such a sensitive child who had grown into a sensitive man, feelings he'd learned to keep well hidden. Sometimes Dustin felt as if Christopher had been too hard on Roi because he perhaps felt that his son wasn't as strong, emotionally, as he needed to be. It had been an age-old disagreement between Dustin and Christopher when it came to Roi—she thought Christopher should have shown more compassion with him because he was so sensitive, and Christopher thought he simply needed to toughen the lad up.

And that was why she needed to see Roi first.

She needed to see her sensitive son.

"When your father and I were first married, I became pregnant almost immediately," she said softly, watching his head lift at the sound of her voice. "I was not quite midway in the pregnancy and I had a terrible accident. I fell down a flight of stairs and lost the child, but I nearly lost my life in the meantime. The entire time, however, all I could think about was the son I had lost. It was indeed a boy. Before Curtis, there was the child your father and I never speak of. But sometimes I think about him and wonder what he would have been like. Would he have been strong and noble? Or ruthless and ambitious? I have always wondered."

Roi turned to her, relief in his eyes at the sight of her. "I did not know that."

Dustin smiled faintly. "I know," she said. "There was no reason for you to. But now... I thought you should be aware that your papa and I know what it is like to lose a child. We lost ours before he had a chance to breathe, and we never got to know him. But you... you knew your son. You were able to raise a fine and strong young man. I will not go as far as to say what happened to Beckett was God's will, but it was most certainly an accident, and Beckett would not want you to grieve overly. He would want you to remember his life with pride and joy."

Roi was looking at her with doubt and grief, combined into a cloud that hung over him. It was in everything about him. He breathed it and bled it.

"I do not know if I can, Mama," he finally said, standing up to face her. "I do not know if I can survive this."

Dustin went to him and took his hands. "I know how you feel," she said softly, squeezing his big fingers. "I know that this shocking loss seems insurmountable. But I promise you that it is not. Beckett was a man to be proud of, and we were all proud of him. You must honor your respect and love for him by being strong. It would destroy him if you were to collapse."

Roi's eyes were filling with tears. "I miss him."

"I know, sweetheart."

"I miss his laughter," he said, breaking down. "I miss the way he would grab my head and kiss me and then taunt me when I tried to swat him."

The tears streamed down his face, and Dustin put her hand to his cheek, trying very hard not to weep right along with him. "Then speak of that," she said tightly. "Speak of those humorous stories or those annoying stories. Speak of your memories and of the good times. That is how you keep him alive, Roi. As long as you continue to speak of him and remember him, he will never truly die."

Roi sobbed as the tears kept coming. "I do not understand why this happened," he said. "I cannot understand why God would take my only son. Were it not for him, I would not have survived Odette's death."

Dustin was wiping away his tears with her hand. "There is your answer," she said. "Don't you see? He has gone to take care of Odette now. He took care of you all of these years after she left us, and now it is time for him to take care of her. She is no longer alone, Roi. What a joyful moment that must have been in heaven when Beckett appeared to her. She was waiting for him, you know. He'd not seen his mother in fourteen years. Can you imagine her happiness? Can you imagine his?"

Roi shook his head, looking at his mother in a way that utterly broke her heart. "I know he missed her."

"Of course he did."

"But I was not ready to lose him."

Dustin smiled as she continued to wipe his face. "You did not lose him," she said, putting a hand over his heart. "He is here, with you. He will always be with you. You take a piece of Beckett with you everywhere you go. But now, he shall take care of Odette, and they shall both watch over you from heaven. Instead of one guardian angel, you now have two. Rejoice that they are together, Roi. You will see them someday, but until you do, you must continue to watch over Adalia and Dorian. They need you very much. We all need you very much. You still have great things to accomplish in this life."

Roi had stopped openly sobbing. Now, he was just standing there as his mother wiped away his tears.

"I have seen forty years and three, Mama," he said. "I think I have accomplished everything great that I was ever going to accomplish. I always thought of Beckett as my greatest accomplishment, and now that is gone."

"He is still your accomplishment," Dustin said. "His death does not take that away."

Roi took a deep breath, trying to compose himself after his outburst. "I suppose," he said. "You know, he was to be married this summer. He was very much looking forward to it. Now I must send word to le Bec that there will be no marriage."

There was a knock on the door, interrupting their conversation, and they both looked up to see Christopher sticking his head in the door.

"May I come in?" he asked.

Roi nodded. "Come in, Papa, please."

Christopher stepped inside, moving straight to Roi as Dustin held the man's hands. He essentially pushed her out of the way so he could hug his son tightly.

"Above all else, I love you and your mother loves you," Christopher murmured into his ear. "We are here to help you, whatever you should need. But know how very sorry we are that we have lost Beckett. He was a remarkable young man."

Roi was back to tearing up. "Thank you, Papa," he said as his father released him. "Mama and I were just speaking of Beckett and how he has now gone to Odette. It gives me comfort to think of them together."

Christopher nodded, his hand still on Roi's shoulder. "I hope so," he said. "Odette loved her son deeply, and he loved her. It was very hard on him when she passed on."

Roi wiped at the remaining moisture around his eyes. "It was hard on all of us," he said. "But Beckett... Papa, I am not certain I can overcome this. I will try, but right now, I feel as if all hope is lost for me. I feel... empty."

Christopher simply patted his shoulder, quietly instructing Dustin to sit him down. As Dustin directed Roi into the nearest chair and then sat beside him, Christopher went to the open door and summoned a servant for food. When the servant went running off, he returned to the solar.

"Where is the missive de Nerra sent?" he asked.

Roi pointed to the table, a large table that was neatly arranged except for an open vellum envelope lying on the top. Christopher picked it up and read it carefully, twice, before sighing faintly and setting it down again.

"He says that he is sending Beckett home," he said quietly. "I would assume he meant immediately, which means he should arrive in a couple of days. He cannot be too far away."

"I think so," Roi said. "Papa, may we bury him at Lion-cross?"

"You do not wish to bury him with his mother?"

Roi shrugged. "When Odette passed, her father begged to bring her home, and I allowed it," he said. "I do not wish to be buried in Cumbria, and I do not know why I allowed her to be, only that her father seemed so desperate about it. But Beckett should be buried at Lioncross. It is where he was born."

"Whatever you wish, of course," Christopher said. "I will send West back to Lioncross tomorrow to make the arrangements."

Roi looked at him with as much curiosity as he could muster. "West is here?"

Christopher nodded. "He and Curtis came with us," he said. "Roi... I must ask before Curtis comes in, but the horse that Beckett was riding when he was killed... Curtis fears it is the one that you purchased from him."

Roi nodded. "The big Belgian warmblood," he said. "I gave it to Beckett for his birthday."

Christopher lifted his eyebrows, an expression of regret. "Your brother is outside punishing himself over that," he said. "He fears you may hold him responsible. Whatever happened, Roi, I hope you understand that it was not Curtis' fault."

Roi stood up immediately. "Of course not," he said. "I must go to him. Where is he?"

Christopher held up a hand. "He will be in shortly," he said. "I just wanted to make sure there would be no bad blood between you two."

Roi shook his head, genuinely perplexed. "Between Curtis and me?" he said. "No brothers are closer than we are. I would never blame him for something that he had nothing to do with."

"Good," Christopher said sincerely. "You will tell him that, please."

"Of course I will."

Christopher was clearly relieved. The last thing he needed was for his sons to be at war over an accident. As they waited for the food, he went to see if there was anything left in the pitcher.

"Where is the horse, by the way?" he asked. "Is he returning home with Beckett?"

Roi shrugged. "I would assume so," he said. "I don't really know. But if you are thinking to ask for it, the answer is no. I am going to sell that horse to someone I do not know and be rid of it. I do not need a constant reminder of what has happened."

Christopher couldn't disagree with him. As the door to the solar opened and servants began entering with trays of food, Christopher moved over to sit with his son as Dustin went to direct the servants.

"Is there anything else I can do for you?" he asked. "Anything else you need?"

Roi shook his head. "Nay, Papa," he said. "Just having you here is a great comfort. But mayhap... mayhap you can have West arrange for a fine crypt for my son, something to bury him in. I'd like to place him in the back of the chapel at Lioncross, where the windows are. I would like some light to fall upon him in the morning when the sun rises."

Christopher smiled faintly. "I think that can be arranged," he said. "But mention of the chapel brings up something else."

"What is that?"

"You asked if Beckett could be married there this summer."

Roi nodded. "I mentioned that to Mama," he said. "Robin le

Bec was adamant that our children marry this summer, and now I have the unhappy duty of telling the man there will be no marriage. While I am certain he will be grieved, he will also be furious. He has been counting on this marriage for two years."

Christopher held up a hand. "I will handle le Bec," he said. "I know the man. He is greedy, but he is not heartless. It is possible that I can appease him with another de Lohr offspring."

Roi frowned. "My son's memory is so easily pushed aside with another de Lohr son?" he said. "Is that a reminder that I only had one son and Curtis has several? That Myles has…?"

Christopher shut him down quickly. "I did not mean it the way it sounded," he said. "Forgive me for being clumsy. I simply meant that I would be willing to offer the man whatever he wishes in order to keep our alliance. I hate to sound callous, Roi, but that must be considered."

Roi knew that, though he didn't like to hear it. "All I care about is the loss of my son, not some damnable alliance," he said. "Nay, Papa, I will send word to Robin myself. This must come from me. It was my son, after all. I am his father. I will do my duty."

Christopher didn't press. Roi had always had a strong sense of duty, and he wasn't about to shirk it, even in his moment of grief. That showed his strength of character, and Christopher was proud of his son in an overwhelmingly difficult situation. But he also thought that the man was rather calm for someone who had just lost a son—until it occurred to him that Dustin had spoken to him first. In private. Mother to son. Like salve to his spirit, she'd apparently worked wonders.

He was glad.

As Christopher pondered life for Roi now without his son,

and without a wife, Dustin brought over a couple of bowls with bread and cheese and stewed fruit. She gave one to Roi first, then to her husband, as the solar door opened again to admit Curtis and Westley. While Westley went straight to Roi and put his arms around the man, Curtis hung back, mired in uncertainty.

Curtis and Roi were born so close together that it had always been the two of them, like twins. They'd even fostered together. He'd never been without his brother in his entire life, except for the times when Roi had gone off to fight for Henry. But even then, Roi would return and it was as if they'd never been apart. The bonds were unbreakable.

So Curtis hoped.

Roi sensed that. He didn't even have to see his brother to know the man was there. He lifted his head from Westley's embrace to spy Curtis over near the door, looking at him with apprehension and grief. Gently pushing away from Westley, Roi went over to Curtis as the man stood there and trembled.

"Roi," Curtis breathed softly. Then his face began to crumple. "I am so sorry. Forgive me, brother. Forgive me for my role in all of this. If I could…"

Roi put his hands on his brother's face, stilling him. "This was not your fault," he said huskily. "It was no one's fault. That beautiful horse is simply a dumb animal that had no ill will towards Beckett. I do not want you to feel guilt over this, Curt. If you do, that will end now."

Curtis simply nodded, but there were tears in his eyes. "As you wish," he murmured. "But I am still so very sorry."

Roi put his arms around his brother, and they hugged one another tightly as Christopher, Dustin, and Westley looked on. In fact, all Christopher could do at that moment was whisper a prayer of thanks—thanks that there would be no animosity between his eldest sons, thanks that they could move forward and grieve Beckett as he deserved to be grieved without any additional drama with the situation.

It was bad enough as it was.

Little did Christopher know that it was about to get much, much worse.

CHAPTER TWO

Cicadia Castle
Cheltenham

"WHAT DID YOUR father say?"

The question came from a young woman far too eager for information that didn't concern her in the least. But it concerned her cousin, and in her mind, that made it her business, whether or not it actually was.

She was addressing a young woman in a pale shift with a surcoat of thin, yellow wool over it. The young woman was ethereal in her beauty, with long blonde curls to her buttocks and a face of perfect porcelain. For certain, tales of the beauty of Diara le Bec were far and wide.

For good reason.

"Hush," Diara said as she entered the chamber and shut the door. She went so far as to grab her cousin and slap a hand over her mouth, dragging her to the other end of the chamber, where a cushioned window seat overlooking the small bailey awaited them. Only then did she remove her hand from her cousin's mouth and shove her onto the seat.

"Well?" her cousin said anxiously. "What has happened?"

Diara appeared genuinely distressed. "Terrible news, I am afraid," she said. "It would seem that Beckett de Lohr was killed in an accident a short time ago. My father has just received word of it, and he is beside himself."

Her cousin's eyes widened in shock. "Nay!" she gasped. "It cannot be!"

"I am afraid it is."

Diara spoke grimly, but genuine grief wasn't there. She spoke of the incident in an almost detached manner, which gave her cousin pause when responding. In truth, she reacted the only way she could.

With polite pity.

"I am so terribly sorry," her cousin said. "Is that what your father wanted to speak with you about?"

"Aye."

"But what happened to him? What kind of accident?"

Diara sighed sharply. "A horse threw him," she said, putting her hand to her head to stave off the headache that was coming on. She suffered from them regularly, sometimes so powerful that she couldn't rise from her bed. "Please do not ask any further questions, Iris. I cannot answer them right now. This news… it is devastating."

Lady Iris le Bec was about to disobey her cousin's request, but she could see by the look on Diara's face that the woman was serious about no more questions.

Devastating? Perhaps.

But to whom?

The betrothal between Diara and Beckett de Lohr had only been sealed for a couple of years, but in that time, she'd met the handsome Beckett only once. They'd spent some time together. Beckett hadn't been particularly attentive, but Diara was certain she could change that with time. He seemed to be a dreamer, too—he wanted to travel and do great things, things that didn't include a wife, and he'd told her so. Diara hadn't told her father about those conversations, mostly because it would have enraged the man, so she kept it to herself. She was convinced she could change Beckett's mind once they were married, and she'd clung to that hope, though deep down, perhaps she wasn't entirely certain she could make the man into something he didn't want to be. But she was determined to be a good wife because that was what her parents wanted.

And now this.

But knowing all of that... *why* was she speaking of devastation at the news?

Iris wondered.

"Deedee, I must ask you a question," she said. "Mayhap it is not a kind question, but I feel I must ask."

"What is it?"

"Did you feel something for him that I was unaware of?" she asked. "I am certain your father is upset, and I know why, but it seemed to me that he was more excited about this marriage than you ever were."

Diara looked at her sharply. "That is a terrible thing to say."

Iris averted her gaze. "As I said, it was not a kind question," she said. "I do not mean to be cruel, but Uncle Robin always seemed much happier about the marriage than you were. He spoke of it so frequently, while you... you were less inclined to speak of it."

Diara knew she was right. It was certainly a terrible thing to say, but it wasn't untrue. She couldn't hold up a front any longer because Iris, who had lived with her family for years, knew everything that went on. She knew the players, she knew the nuances, and she knew the situation.

She knew what Diara thought of her intended.

There was no use denying it.

With a sigh, Diara sat heavily opposite her cousin on the window seat.

"Two years ago, my father came back from France crowing about the betrothal he'd made with the House of de Lohr, a marriage he'd practically sold his soul for, or so he said," she said wearily. "He'd arranged a contract with the Earl of Hereford and Worcester's second son, Richard, the man named after the Lionheart. According to my father, Richard de Lohr will replace his father as the greatest knight in the realm once his father passes away, and his son would enjoy all of the benefits of such respect. That means his son will enjoy the same prestige."

Iris was watching her cousin closely. "I know."

"Then Beckett came here with his father."

"I was here."

"And you saw what went on."

Iris nodded slowly. "I saw a man who was arrogant and apathetic towards you," she said. "Beckett was not kind to you in the least."

Diara put her hands over her face. "It was worse than that," she said. "You saw what happened. He would mostly ignore me, but the moment I spoke to any man other than him, he would glare at me."

"But he hardly spoke to you himself!"

Diara threw up her hands in despair. "He called me a whore before he left," she said, verging on tears. "Do you remember that? He told me that he'd heard all about how I had dozens of men following me around, and he said that only a whore would have such a following."

Iris went to sit next to her, putting her arm around her shoulders. "He did not know you," she said softly, with encouragement. "He did not know that you are bright and witty and men are naturally attracted to you. You are a happy, sweet woman, Deedee. Beckett could not see that through his suspicion and jealousy."

Diara flicked a tear from her eye. "I've never even been kissed," she said sadly. "How can I be a whore?"

"I know," Iris said, giving her a hug. "But it is not for lack of trying. From men, I mean. Some of your admirers are here at Cicadia, and they hang on every word you speak. They would gladly give you a kiss if you would let them."

Diara snorted softly. "My father's knights?" she said, smiling weakly at something she didn't find particularly humorous. "One of them has probably never taken a bath in his life, another one is simply a good friend, and the last one is too, too old. I have known him since I was a child."

Iris removed her arm from the woman's shoulders and clasped both of Diara's hands in her own. "Though I am sorry for Beckett's death, because surely it is a terrible thing for his family, I do believe it is a good thing for you," she said. "You were going to be miserable with him, Deedee."

Diara wouldn't look at her as she shook her head. "That is not true."

"It is," Iris insisted. "I have watched you try to convince yourself for two years that this will be a good marriage. We both know it would not be. Beckett made it clear he does not want a wife, and he made it very clear that he was unhappy his father had forced him into a betrothal. He would have made you miserable."

"I would have been a good wife."

"To a man who did not want one?"

"He was young," Diara argued weakly. "That's all I really saw in him—immaturity. He would learn to appreciate a wife as he grew older."

Iris sighed sharply. "That is your mother talking," she said. "Aunt Annie was trying to convince you that all would be well if you would only be patient. But she was wrong."

Diara looked at her then. "She had no choice," she said, suddenly firm. "I had no choice. Truth be told, I was not happy my father forced me into a betrothal either, but there was nothing I could do about it."

"There is now."

Iris was right. Diara knew she was right, and as she thought on that, she began to nod her head. "Papa has been trying to marry me off for years," she said. "He told me that I would only marry the highest bidder, and Beckett's father must have bid dearly. But now there is no longer a betrothal…"

"*And?*"

"And I can tell my father just what I want in a husband."

"What would that be?"

Diara stood up, moving to the window and gazing over the fertile landscape of the softly rolling hills around Cheltenham. Overhead, birds rode the drafts as the clouds began to roll in from the west.

She could smell the rain.

"I do not want a boy," she said. "Beckett was a boy, hardly older than I. I want a grown man."

"Handsome?"

"Of course," Diara said. "Handsome and strong, mature, responsible. Someone who wants a wife and is prepared to treat her like… like…"

"Like *what*?"

"Like she is important." Diara turned to look at her. "Like she matters to him. Iris, I spent years at Carisbrooke with the pages and squires as my friends because the girls were petty and would not talk to me. Lady de Redvers was the worst of them, and so were her awful daughters. Because the boys were my friends, I was accused of being unladylike. I was accused of teasing them. But you know I did not; never did I tease anyone. Had they not been my friends, I would have had no friends at all. But my father thinks I was a harlot because of that vicious gossip from spiteful women."

Iris shook her head. "He did not think that," she said. "He did not listen to the gossip of fools."

"He listened to a countess and her forked tongue," Diara said, torn between the sadness it provoked and the anger. "But it does not matter. I will tell him that I will not accept a child as a husband. I want a grown man who did not listen to Lady de Redvers' gossip, who does not even know de Redvers and the politics of London. Someone who is far away from that kind of thing so he will not have a preconceived notion about it. I simply want a fighting chance to have a good marriage, Iris. Is that too much to ask?"

Iris shook her head. "Nay," she said. "I will support you, whatever you wish. I will tell Uncle Robin that Lady de Redvers was a jealous liar. She only did it because you were more beautiful and kinder than her two daughters. They are trolls, those two."

Diara's eyes glimmered with mirth and gratitude. "How do you know that?"

"Because I saw them," Iris said. "Remember? I fostered at

Thetford, and whenever de Redvers would have a gathering, I would come with Lady de Warenne. I saw de Redvers' daughters at least three times. They were wretched creatures."

Diara laughed softly. "I know you saw them, but you never spent any time around them," she said. Her smile faded. "I wish I hadn't. I dislike women as a whole, Iris. I dislike them intensely. I have never had a good experience with any woman other than you and my mother."

"That is because we're not jealous of you," Iris said. "We're proud of you."

That brought a grateful smile from Diara, but Iris could feel the woman's pain. She'd been so persecuted by her own sex that she didn't trust, nor did she like, women as a sex, just as she'd said. Iris had heard it before.

It was a lonely way to live.

Outside, the rain was beginning to fall in widely spaced, fat droplets. They hit the windowsill now and again, causing Diara to reach up and grasp the oil cloth that was hanging from the top of the window. Securely fastened, it would keep the rain out. But just as she unrolled it, she caught sight of one of her father's knights down in the bailey, motioning to some of the soldiers. It was clear that he was giving orders, and Diara paused, watching the tall, dark-haired knight as he moved about. Iris walked up beside her to help, also seeing what she was seeing.

There was a commotion going on down there.

"What's Pryce doing?" Iris asked curiously. "It looks like he's sending men to the stables."

Diara was watching her father's captain as he sent more men on their way with orders. Pryce de la Roarke had been with her father for many years, an older man who was more like an uncle to Diara than a mere knight. He was wise, but he was also strict. The man didn't have a humorous bone in his body. If someone was looking for understanding and compassion, they more than likely wouldn't get it from Pryce. He was, however, quite efficient at his job and could show kindness when he wanted to.

But that was rare.

"I do not know," Diara said. "He's issuing commands. Men are running."

Horses began to come around, out into the bailey, and Iris leaned on the windowsill to get a better look in spite of the rain.

"It looks as if men are preparing to leave," she said. Then she looked at Diara. "Who is leaving?"

Diara shook her head. "No one that I know if," she said. "Papa was down in the solar yelling about the betrothal and how…"

She stopped suddenly, and Iris peered strangely at her. "How *what*?"

Diara blinked as if startled by the answer she was about to give. "How he would go to Hereford himself and demand restitution," she said. "My God… do you think he is actually going to ride to the Earl of Hereford and Worcester and demand that I be allowed to marry a dead man?"

Before Iris could answer, Diara was rushing from the chamber, taking the spiral stairs of the keep far too quickly as she made her way down to the first floor where the main rooms of the keep were. There were two solars, one for her mother and one for her father, plus a small hall and a collection of other smaller chambers. But Diara was heading for her father's solar, where she last saw the man, and she heard his raised voice before she ever burst into the chamber.

Startled by his daughter nearly ripping the solar door off its hinges as she entered his solar, Robin looked at his only child in shock.

"Diara?" he said, both puzzled and annoyed. "What is wrong, lass?"

Diara didn't even look at the other people in the chamber. She was completely focused on her father as she rushed toward him.

"Why is Pryce ordering horses to be brought forth?" she demanded. "Papa, are you going to see Hereford?"

Robin had been in the middle of a raging sentence, but was now forced to calm himself simply by the expression on his daughter's face. He took a deep breath and turned away from her.

"That is none of your affair," he said. "You will leave, please."

Diara didn't obey. In fact, she began to follow him.

"Papa," she said. "You cannot blame the House of de Lohr over the death of a son. Don't you think they are sick with grief over it? You cannot go there and make it worse. You will make an enemy of them."

Robin glanced at her. "I appreciate your concern, but it is unnecessary," he said. "If you must know, I am indeed going to Lioncross Abbey, but I am going to express my condolences to Hereford. You needn't worry."

Diara wasn't sure why she didn't believe him, but she didn't. She took a moment to look around the chamber, seeing her mother and the remaining two knights in the chamber. Her father had three, and with Pryce outside, Sir Eddard de Vahn and Sir Mathis de Geld were inside the solar, perhaps awaiting further orders. Diara might have actually believed that had she not heard her father ranting as she ran down the stairs, so they were merely there to take the brunt of his rage.

So was her mother.

Lady Ananda Maxwell le Bec was looking at her daughter with some apprehension. Unlike most husbands, Robin sought his wife's counsel. She sat in on any business or anything that had to do with Cicadia Castle or the Cheltenham earldom. She was a brilliant woman, wise with her advice, and that was something Diara had inherited from her. But Diara was the life of any party, whereas Ananda was quite reserved. Reserve wasn't what Diara saw in her mother's expression, however.

What she saw, she didn't like.

"Papa," Diara finally said. "Should I not go with you, as Beckett's intended? I should like to extend my condolences also."

"Nay," Robin said flatly. "I will go. It is my duty. You will remain here with your mother."

"She is not going?"

Robin's jaw flexed as he looked at her. "If you have come here to ask foolish questions, then I will again tell you to leave," he said. He pointed to the door. "Go, please."

There was so much that wasn't being said. Diara could feel it. However, not wanting to argue with her father in front of people who served him, including her mother, she quit the chamber.

But she didn't go far.

Diara sat on the spiral steps that led to the upper floor, just out of sight. She could still see the solar door, however, peering around the bend of the staircase, and she could hear more of her father's shouting, but she couldn't really hear the words. The thick walls of the keep muffled them. But she waited him out, knowing something would happen at some point, until the door opened and one of her father's knights spilled out.

Mathis quit the solar, quietly shutting the door behind him. He turned for the entry, but hissing from the stairwell caught his attention. Diara was waving him over, and he headed in her direction.

"What are you doing?" he asked.

"Waiting for you," she said. "He's not going to Lioncross to convey his condolences, is he?"

Mathis was a good man from a good family. He'd been in love with Diara since nearly the moment he met her, so talk of betrothals didn't sit well with him. He'd offered for her hand, more than once, only to be told that although he was an excellent knight and Lord Cheltenham appreciated his service, he wasn't suitable for the earl's daughter. Worse still, Diara only viewed him as a good friend. Therefore, he had to stand by and watch someone else take what he wanted.

It was a difficult position for him.

"Nay," he said after a moment. "He is not."

"Is he going to demand that they consider the betrothal a marriage by proxy?"

He knew what she meant. Sometimes, betrothals were considered just as good as a marriage. The church considered it binding, so, for all intents and purposes, Diara and Beckett were already married. In theory, anyway. But Mathis shook his head.

"I do not know," he said honestly. "He paid Roi de Lohr five hundred marks of gold, which was half of your dowry, when the betrothal was agreed upon, so I think he is going to demand the return of the money."

Diara sighed heavily. "I wonder if they'll return it?" she said. "I was thinking he was going to demand that I be considered

Beckett's wife and all of the benefits that would entail."

"Like what?"

"Like anything he would inherit from his father, I suppose," she said. "I don't really know. All I know is that my father does not seem the least bit concerned that a young man has died. He only seems to be concerned about the marriage that will never happen now."

Mathis was watching her as she spoke. Those sweet, slightly red lips that he'd dreamt about kissing. But he shook himself mentally before those thoughts took hold.

Thoughts that would do him no good.

"Whatever he is going to do, he seems to want me and Pryce with him," he said, looking away and feeling the familiar stab of disappointment. "He is leaving Eddard here in command."

"When is he leaving?"

"On the morrow."

Diara thought about her father riding all the way to Lioncross Abbey Castle, the largest castle on the Welsh marches with an enormous standing army. A castle he wanted very much to be allied with by marriage, as he'd told her many times.

That gave her an idea.

"Mathis," she said. "Do you suppose he is going to Lioncross for another reason?"

Mathis glanced at her. "What other reason?"

She looked at him thoughtfully. "What if he does not want the money returned?"

"Of course he will. That is a good deal of money."

"But what if he allows them to keep it in exchange for another de Lohr husband?"

That thought hadn't occurred to Mathis. "The House of de

Lohr has many sons and grandsons," he said. "That may be a distinct possibility."

Diara thought so, too.

And she hated it.

Slowly, she stood up.

"It would be nice if my father looked at me as his child for once and not something to be bartered with," she said, turning to mount the steps. "If I had any sense, I'd simply run away."

She wandered up the steps as Mathis watched her go. When he was certain she was out of earshot, he craned his neck around in time to see her right foot disappear as she continued to the next floor above.

"With me?" he whispered. "If you would, I'd leave this minute."

It was a sweet, if not heartbreaking, thought.

And a foolish one at that.

CHAPTER THREE

Lioncross Abbey Castle
Welsh marches
Several days later

"I'VE NEVER SEEN Papa so angry," Westley said. "Thank God you've come. Cheltenham is causing an uproar."

It was sunset on a day that had been cold but sunny as spring began to transition into summer. The ride from Pembridge Castle, for Roi, had been a smooth one, and he'd reached Lioncross in record time at the summons of Curtis. But it was Westley who had met him at the gatehouse.

"When did he arrive?" Roi asked. "Christ, Papa has only been returned from Pembridge for a few days. Robin must have received my missive and immediately raced here."

"Raced?" Westley repeated in disbelief. "I believe he flew. You should have seen his horse when he arrived—the poor thing is still recovering, and Cheltenham has been making a nuisance of himself ever since."

"I do not know what that man wants from me," Roi growled as he turned his horse over to the nearest soldier. "I no longer have a son to marry his daughter. What in the hell does he want from me? Blood?"

Westley eyed him with uncertainty. "I probably should not tell you this, but I heard them arguing," he said. "Cheltenham wants his five hundred gold marks returned, the dowry he'd already paid you when the betrothal was signed. Or…"

"Or *what*?"

"Or he wants another de Lohr son," Westley said grimly. "One way or the other, that man wants his daughter to marry a de Lohr. He doesn't care who it is. He's going around asking every man he sees if he's a de Lohr. He asked Curtis and then demanded to know if Curtis was already married. Curtis nearly took his head off. Papa has kept me out of the solar for that very reason."

Roi looked at him, aghast. "Cheltenham wants *you*?"

Westley grunted, perplexed. "He wants one of us—any one of us." He shook his head. "I have no desire to marry Beck's betrothed. No offense to Beck or the girl, but I will choose my own bride, thank you."

Roi stared at him a moment, processing the outrageous situation, before heading off toward the keep with Westley by his side. He'd ridden at a hard pace, concerned with the information in his brother's summons, but now that he knew the details of Robin's appearance at Lioncross Abbey, he was growing more furious by the second. How dare the man come and harass his elderly father? How dare the man behave so abominably in the face of their grief? Roi was going to take the five hundred gold marks he brought with him and shove them down Robin's throat.

After he told the man what he thought of him.

They reached the wide steps that led into Lioncross' keep, but before they could pass through the doorway, Roi held out a hand to Westley.

"Stay here," he said. "If the man is spitting venom, I do not want you in his range. In fact, I want you to stay well clear of what I am about to do."

Westley looked concerned. "What are you going to do?"

Roi's response was to crack his knuckles before heading into the keep.

Lioncross Abbey's keep was only a keep in the literal sense—it was the center of the castle and where the family lived—but it wasn't round or even square. It was a building, like a palace with many rooms, built atop the ruins of an ancient Roman temple, which was why they called it the "abbey." But the structure itself was vast and wide, with wings and floors, and it was a most fitting residence for the Earl of Hereford and Worcester. In fact, Roi thought he could hear his father's voice as he approached the man's solar. But he also heard another voice, talking over him.

Robin.

Roi burst into the chamber.

The first thing he did was point at Robin standing a few feet away from Christopher, who was sitting in a chair with a hand on his head. Seeing this, and the strained expression on his father's face, Roi boomed.

"You!" he said. "*Sit!*"

It was perhaps the loudest shout anyone had ever heard out of Roi, but he was positively enraged. Robin, shocked at the man's appearance, stumbled back as Roi came toward him.

"Roi!" he said in surprise. "You... you have come!"

He didn't sit fast enough for Roi's liking, so Roi charged the man and shoved him back into the nearest chair. He shoved him so hard that the chair tilted sideways, nearly toppling to the ground, but both Roi and Robin stopped it from falling completely. As Roi righted it, he got in Robin's face.

"That will be enough out of you," he snarled. "Do you understand me?"

Robin was truly taken aback. "What do you—"

"Shut your lips," Roi barked. "For once, shut your bloody lips. I had to listen to you for two solid years, you and your eternal yapping, never listening to anyone but always making sure your voice was the loudest. I will tell you now that your assault of my father will not be tolerated, and I do not care if you are an earl. One more word out of you, in rage, towards me or my father, and I will gut you where you sit and dump your body out on the road for the birds. If anyone asks, you were killed by outlaws. Do you understand what I am telling you? Your bullying and insults will no longer be tolerated."

By the time he was finished, Robin was looking at him with both fear and outrage. "Say what you will," he said after a moment. "But I am still an earl, and you cannot threaten me."

"I just did."

"Roi," Christopher said quietly. "Back away from Cheltenham. Go."

Roi let his furious gaze linger on Robin for a moment to emphasize that he meant everything he said before moving away, over toward his father. He tore his gaze off Robin to look at his elderly, exhausted father.

"Are you well, Papa?" he asked. "I am so sorry he came here, though I do not understand why. He should have come to me at Pembridge."

Christopher put his hand on Roi, his emotional son, and pulled him closer as if fearful Roi would break away and throttle Robin right in front of him.

"Cheltenham is a valuable ally," he said simply. "This situation is… difficult. He came to offer his condolences, but he also wants to know what we intend to do about the situation now that it has happened. He paid for a husband. He wants one or he wants his money back."

Roi's jaw twitched furiously as he looked at Robin still sitting in the chair. "I shall give him his money back," he rumbled. "I will shove it right down his contemptible throat."

"Roi," Christopher snapped softly. "I realize you are upset. We are all upset. But I told you that this was an important situation to us all. Cheltenham would like to be allied with us by marriage, and whoever marries his daughter will inherit the earldom. That is quite a prize, and one I intend to keep, so this is not all his doing."

When Roi realized that his father wasn't all for kicking Robin from Lioncross, he looked at the man sharply. "What do you intend to do?"

Christopher sighed heavily. "I have other grandsons," he said. "I also have other sons that are not married. That is what Lord Cheltenham and I were discussing."

Roi's brow furrowed. "Then you do not want me to give the money back?"

Christopher shook his head. "Nay," he said. "For the good of all of us, I would like to provide Cheltenham with a de Lohr son. He will be the next Earl of Cheltenham."

Roi stared at his father, understanding what the man was saying. One way or the other, Robin would get his de Lohr husband and Christopher would have an alliance with Cheltenham. That was what all of this boiled down to—he could see that both of them were in on it. Both were determined to have an alliance, no matter the cost. But in this case, Christopher was determined that the earldom would have a de Lohr name. One more feather in the cap of the de Lohr empire. But the problem was that his father hadn't made the bargain in the first place.

Roi had.

This was all his doing.

At that realization, he began to feel sick. It occurred to him what he had to do, what the most logical choice in this situation would be, though he was loath to do it. The more he thought on it, the sicker he felt until he finally, and reluctantly, opened his mouth.

"You needn't select a de Lohr son or grandson, Papa," he said, suddenly sounding quite resigned. "It is not your responsibility to shoulder the problem that originated with me. I made the bargain. I would not ask anyone else to assume the burden."

Christopher looked at him curiously. "What do you mean?"

Roi's gaze lingered on his father for a moment before finally turning to Robin.

"You want a de Lohr husband?" he said. "Then you shall have one. Not a grandson of the earl, either, but a son. A son with wealth, reputation, property, and title. You can have me, Robin. It is only right, since your daughter was to marry my son. I shall wed your daughter in his stead, and then you can have everything you want."

Robin shot to his feet. "You?" he said. "*You* will marry her?"

"I am the best candidate. And the moral one."

He was right, and they all knew it. If the son could not marry the daughter, it was not only expected, but preferred that the widowed father marry the daughter in his son's stead. That had been the one solution neither Robin nor Christopher had suggested, given the fact that Roi was undoubtedly mourning his son. Adding a new wife on top of that would have been too much for any man.

But Roi made the offer.

Robin's jaw went slack as he took a few steps toward Roi, absolutely stunned by the offer.

"But you…" he said. "Are you serious, Roi?"

"I am."

"You're twice her age."

"I have seen forty years and three."

"She has only seen twenty."

"That does not matter, and you know it," Roi said steadily. "Age has no bearing here. I have more money than you do. I have property, prestige, and political position, and a family name that is respected throughout England. I have proven that I can father children, and, quite honestly, I am sure you would rather have your daughter married to a man who knows how to treat a wife than some young lord who has no concept of how a marriage should be conducted. I understand how to treat a woman. What more could you want?"

Nothing. That was the point—there was nothing more Robin could want. It was the perfect solution. The more he thought on it, the more thrilled he was.

"Roi," he said with sincerity in his tone. "I am truly at a loss for words. I never expected to marry my daughter to the second son of the Earl of Hereford and Worcester. That is a great and noble destiny for any woman."

"Then you accept?"

"I do. With God as my witness, I do."

"Good," Roi said, turning back to his father. "Papa, have your cleric draw up the agreement. I will sign it."

Christopher was looking at his son with great concern, trying to see how Roi really felt about this. It had taken the man years to get over his first wife's death, and he'd never, in that time, expressed interest in marrying again.

Until now.

Until he was given no choice.

"Are you sure?" Christopher asked softly. "Roi, are you absolutely sure?"

Roi nodded, but it was with effort. "Have the contract drawn up, please," he said. "I would appreciate it."

Christopher didn't make a move to summon his cleric, a man who happened to be married to his youngest sister. Gowen was his name, a scholarly man who had aptly helped Christopher manage his empire for years. But he didn't want Gowen at the moment. He stood up and went to the table that held wine and cups, pouring measures for them all. Roi got the biggest measure. He handed the drink over to his son and watched him drain the cup in two swallows.

That told him just how strained Roi was over the situation.

What the man did in order to save an alliance.

Sadness gripped him.

"It did not have to be you," he said so only Roi could hear him. "I nearly had Curtis convinced that it should be William."

William de Lohr was Curtis' second son, a good and noble lad, but he was also quite young. "Nay," Roi said, feeling exhausted and defeated now that the anger had drained from his veins. "William is not ready for marriage yet, and if Robin's daughter is abused or neglected in any way, it will sour this alliance faster than if there had been no marriage at all. You know that. If you want this alliance safely made, then this is the only way."

Christopher could hear his words reflected in Roi's statement, how he'd insisted the alliance with Cheltenham was something to be upheld in this matter. The way Roi made it sound, it was perhaps the most important thing to Christopher. But it wasn't—Christopher felt guilty that he'd evidently hammered that into Roi's brain too hard. It had caused Roi to make an offer he didn't want to make, but what was done was done.

It was finished.

"I apologize if I was hard on you, Roi," Robin said, breaking the silence in the chamber. "I realize you just lost your son, and I am greatly grieved for you, but you must understand that my primary concern is my daughter. She is involved in this whether or not you like it. I must look out for her best interests."

After his burst of anger, Roi couldn't even muster the strength to discuss it with the man. But he needed to make his position perfectly clear because he'd just committed to marrying the earl's daughter in his son's stead.

Their relationship was going to change.

"And I must look out for mine," he said, turning to Robin. "Understand I am only doing this in place of my son. It is my duty. I am not doing this because I want your daughter or her money or your earldom, but those things shall be mine now, and you and I are going to come to an understanding."

"Of course, Roi," Robin said, oddly compliant now that he had what he wanted. "What is it?"

Roi's gaze was intense. "Firstly, you will apologize to my father for harassing him," he said. "Do not deny it, because I hear it for myself. Apologize to this legendary man for your abominable behavior in a difficult situation."

Robin looked at Christopher, clearly regretting the temper tantrum he'd been pitching since his arrival. "My lord," he said. "I did not mean to disrespect you. As I said, the situation had me on edge. My daughter's future was of the utmost concern to me. If I was abusive, then I beg your forgiveness."

Christopher finished the cup of wine in his hand and poured himself another. "I have done verbal battle with men far greater and far more annoying than you," he said in a subtle insult. "Your alliance is valuable, le Bec, but sometimes you are difficult to stomach."

He went back over to his big table, a heavy oak table that had been built by some of the finest craftsmen in London. The de Lohr crest was on each side of the table, perfect in presentation, except for one side where Curtis and Roi, when they'd been small boys, had tried to carve their names into the shield. They'd received a fatherly beating, but Christopher still smiled when he saw their juvenile marks. He ran his fingers over those marks, reminding himself that the young boy who had carved them was now making a man's sacrifice.

"What must I do to gain your forgiveness?" Robin said, following from a distance. "I do not wish to be at odds with you, my lord."

Christopher held up a hand. "There is nothing to forgive… this time," he said. "But come at me again with your petulance and I will not be so forgiving a second time. Is that clear?"

"It is, my lord. Thank you."

Christopher pointed to Roi. "And thank my son, who has made a great sacrifice this day," he said. "He had no intention of marrying again, but because we value the Cheltenham alliance and because he felt that he must personally honor the betrothal contract in Beckett's stead, he has made a most noble sacrifice to keep our relationship intact."

Robin looked at Roi. "You know I am grateful," he said, sounding deeply sincere. "I know that Diara will have the finest husband in England. She is a good girl, Roi. She is kind and obedient. She will make a fine wife."

Roi simply nodded his head. Then he set his empty cup aside and quit the chamber because he simply couldn't look at Robin anymore. The more he realized what he had done, the more regret he felt. Nay, he didn't want to marry, but that didn't matter anymore. The only thing that gave him just a hint of pleasure was the fact that perhaps now he could have more children. Another son. It seemed that he had failed his family in that respect, so now he felt that he could at least fulfil his family obligations and procreate.

Maybe that was the only good thing that would come out of this.

As he headed out of the keep to get some fresh air and rec-oncile himself to his new future, he tried to remember what Diara le Bec looked like. He'd met her face to face only once, when Robin had brought her to Pembridge so that she and Beckett could become acquainted.

Roi remembered that she was somewhat tall and willowy, with long blonde hair and a beautiful face. That much, he did remember. She *was* a beautiful girl, and even Beckett had commented on the fact. He also seemed to recall that she had the bluest eyes he'd ever seen, the color of periwinkle. But beyond that, he had no real impression of her because he'd not spent any time with her. Beckett had. Roi had spent all of his time with Robin while their children became acquainted under the watchful eye of Lady Cheltenham.

"Well? What happened?"

The voice came from behind. Roi turned to see Westley standing there along with another brother, Douglas. Douglas de Lohr was big and blond, like most of the de Lohrs, with straight, pale hair that hung down over one eye and a faint growth of beard on his face. He was three years older than Westley, known as the quiet brother due to a slight speech impediment. He was more of a follower than a leader, but he would carry out any order, any time, without hesitation or question. When one was entering into any kind of armed conflict, Douglas de Lohr was the knight everyone wanted. The first man into a fight and the last one out.

He was a knight's knight.

"Well?" Douglas said. "Did you give back to Cheltenham what he's been dishing out since his arrival?"

Douglas' speech impediment manifested itself as a slight lisp, which made him self-conscious although no one else really noticed. But Roi shook his head.

"Not as much as I should have," he said. "Had he been bellowing at Father like that since his arrival?"

Both Westley and Douglas nodded. "Why do you think Curtis sent word to you?" Westley said. "Cheltenham was yelling the moment he rode in through the gatehouse. What happened in there?"

Roi sighed heavily. "I told him to apologize to Father."

Westley and Douglas grinned in approval. "Good," Douglas said. "The arrogant bore. What else? Is he getting his money back?"

"He is not getting his money back."

"Is his daughter marrying William?"

Roi shook his head. "Nay, not William."

"Praise the saints," Westley said, looking at Douglas in relief. "I told Papa about the girl, you know. He must have taken that to heart."

Roi looked between his brothers. "What girl?"

"Cheltenham's daughter," Westley said.

"What about her?"

"It seems that the girl has something of a reputation."

Roi blinked slowly. He didn't like the sound of that at all. "What *kind* of reputation?"

Westley slapped Roi on the arm. "'Tis a good thing Beckett did not marry her," he said. Then he froze. "I'm sorry, Roi. I did not mean that the way it sounded. I did not mean what happened to Beckett was a blessing. Not at all. I shall miss my nephew desperately. I simply meant—"

Roi waved him off. "I know what you meant," he said. "But what about the girl?"

Westley, still feeling bad about his slip, threw a thumb in an easterly direction. "Sometimes Cheltenham men come to the Rose and Crown in Hereford," he said. "Passing through, you know. It's on the road from Shrewsbury, and Cheltenham has a sister in Shrewsbury."

He was speaking of a tavern in Hereford that the knights liked to haunt because it had a surprising variety of ales from ships offloaded in Chepstow and brought north. Roi knew the place because he'd spent a good deal of time there himself.

"*And?*" he demanded.

"And the Cheltenham men have spoken of the earl's daughter," he said. "She is evidently quite… friendly."

Roi frowned, as he thought he knew what his brother was alluding to. "She's unchaste?"

"Nay, not that," Westley said. "But she has many men who have fallen in love with her. She's a beautiful girl and will evidently speak to anyone. They say she spends time tending the poor and seems to not have an aversion to the lower class. But women like that are fodder for gossip. That's all I meant."

Roi still wasn't sure how he felt about the news. "If she tends to the poor, then she must have a compassionate heart," he said. "As for the rest—her father told me she had other suitors, but he did not tell me she had a reputation for being overly friendly. Does she tease men? Is that what she does?"

Westley shrugged. "I do not know," he said. "But better to avoid someone like that, I suppose. Let her marry someone else."

Roi shook his head at the irony of it all, running his fingers through his hair. "We have *not* avoided someone like that," he said flatly. "In order to spare any of you marriage to Cheltenham's daughter, I assumed the role myself. With Beckett gone, the most logical replacement is me. I am fulfilling the contract."

Westley and Douglas' eyes widened to epic proportions. "You?" Westley said. "You are marrying that girl?"

Roi was starting to lose his patience. "I am marrying the Earl of Cheltenham's daughter," he said. "When the earl passes on, I will inherit the title and the lands. Cheltenham will be mine. This is a marriage of political and strategic importance, and it is *my* marriage, so if I ever hear you repeat those stories about the earl's daughter, I will throttle you myself. Am I making myself clear?"

Westley nodded, fearful of his older brother even though he was an equal match for him in a fight. "Aye, Roi, of course," he said. "I am sorry I said anything at all. I am sure she is a very nice lady. I hope."

Douglas slapped a hand over Westley's mouth and pulled him out of Roi's range, but Roi had no intention of taking a swipe at his youngest brother. In fact, he had very much the same thought.

I'm sure she is a very nice lady. I hope.

He had the distinct feeling that his life was about to change—drastically.

"It is of little matter," he muttered. "It is done. We have the alliance, and I will have the money and titles and the hope for more sons from my new wife. No one can replace Beckett, of course, but it would be nice to have sons to pass my title and wealth to. A man needs a legacy, after all. I thought mine had died at Selbourne Castle, but it seems that it has not. I am being given a second chance."

"That is a good way to look at it, Roi," Douglas said. "If there is anything we can do to help…"

"There is," Roi said, turning to him. "Beckett is supposed to be arriving at Pembridge any day now. I've told Kyne and Adrius to send him straight to Lioncross, so would you ride to Pembridge tomorrow and await my son's body? I would consider it a personal favor if you could give him an escort to Lioncross because I intend to remain here, at least while Cheltenham is here."

Both brothers nodded. "Absolutely," Douglas said. "We will leave right away. Mama is still at Pembridge with Adalia and Dorian, is she not?"

Roi nodded. "I left her there with the girls," he said. "We are fortunate Pembridge is less than a day's ride away, especially where Papa is concerned. He has done much traveling in the past several days. I do not want it to wear him out."

"He's strong," Douglas said. "But you… I am worried about you, Roi. First the death of Beckett and now an unexpected marriage? That is a great deal to happen to one man in such a short amount of time."

Roi smiled weakly at Douglas. "I will survive," he said. "There is nothing I can do about Beckett except mourn him for the rest of his life. As for the marriage… the more I think on it, the more I am pleased with the opportunity to have more children. That is how I must view the situation. I must see something positive in this horrific circumstance."

Douglas smiled sadly, patting him on the shoulder. There wasn't much more that either one of them could say. The wheels were in motion, and Roi was committed to fulfilling the contract his son could no longer fulfil. As a good father, it was his duty. They all knew that, and it made them respect him all the more. Through his pain, Roi was doing what needed to be done.

That was the sign of the strongest of men.

As Westley headed off to the stables to prepare for the journey to Pembridge, Douglas remained with Roi, following him into the chapel of Lioncross Abbey, where Roi selected just the right spot for his son's final resting place. Near the rear of the chapel, behind the altar, there was a spot near the lancet windows. As Douglas stood off in the shadows, Roi stood in that spot, seeing the view his son would see for eternity. Feeling the air from the windows that Beckett would feel.

Or not feel.

For a moment, Roi forgot about the new wife, about Robin and his petulance, and about his world that had so suddenly and brutally changed. He thought of his son, from the little boy who liked to collect bugs to the young man who was so skilled at combat. Roi had the privilege of fighting a battle with his son, just once, a small skirmish that was not worth mentioning, but he'd experienced that father's pride that he would never feel again with Beckett. All of that was lost when Beckett had been unseated from his horse and landed awkwardly on his head. Roi knew he wasn't the first father to lose a son, but, by damn… it certainly felt like it.

It felt as if his world had ended.

At least, the old one had.

Standing in the spot where Beckett would be spending eternity, he finally allowed himself to feel the grief that he'd been wrestling with since he first received the news. For Beckett, he wept. For the son he lost, he let the agony fill him. Just this once, he let it wash over him. It was a farewell on the most basic parental level, and it was the most painful thing he'd ever experienced.

From the shadows, Douglas wept with him.

CHAPTER FOUR

Cicadia Castle

D IARA COULDN'T BELIEVE her ears.

In fact, she plopped down onto the bed behind her, staring at her mother as if the woman had just grown another head.

Stunned was an apt word.

"I… I'm *what*?" she stammered.

"Marrying Richard de Lohr, Beckett's father," her mother repeated patiently. "Your father has sent word ahead. He and Richard are traveling to Cicadia as we speak, and they should arrive shortly. This is a much better match for you, Deedee. Sir Richard is a son of the Earl of Hereford and Worcester. No longer will you have to marry *only* a grandson. You will be marrying the second son of the earl, a man who has position and prestige. He is an advisor to the king, in fact. You will be an important woman. Are you not pleased?"

Ananda seemed very happy about the whole thing, but Diara could only feel shock. As Ananda began rattling on about what to wear when she was introduced to her betrothed, Diara labored up from the bed and wandered over to the window seats overlooking the bailey. She was trying very hard to accept what she'd been told, though it was difficult. She'd only just had some hope that she could actually have a husband she wanted, and now this. Now, she was to marry the father of her dead intended.

I am to marry an old man.

The realization was sickening. She'd gone from a young pup to an elderly man in the blink of an eye. From one future to quite another. She tried to remember Beckett's father, a man she had only briefly met when she was introduced to Beckett.

He was big.

That much, she remembered. He was a very big man, broad-shouldered, and she remembered he had a big neck, something some of the knights tended to have because they wore heavy helms and heavy protection around their necks and shoulders. Men without muscular necks and shoulders would collapse under such weight, so Beckett's father had muscles all over his upper body. She remembered the size of his hands because he'd reached out to greet Robin, and she'd caught sight of hands that were the size of a trencher.

Big.

That was all she could recall about him.

Leaning against the window as the breeze lifted her hair, she thought hard on the man's face. He had hair that was auburn, with a hint of blond around his face that might have actually been gray. She couldn't really remember. He had to be more than twice her age. However, the more she thought about it, the more she remembered that he was nice looking and that Beckett had looked a good deal like him. Beckett, in fact, had been quite handsome, something he surely got from his father.

So, he was big and handsome. And old.

But she couldn't remember anything else.

For the rest of the afternoon, she had to listen to her mother discussing wardrobe issues. The marriage to Beckett had been coming in the summer, which was about three months away, so although her trousseau had been planned and the fabric purchased, the seamstress hadn't yet begun the garments. She listened to her mother talk about sending word to the seamstress to hurry up with the dresses that had been ordered so that all of it could be packed away and taken with her once she had married.

Her mother seemed to think the marriage was to take place immediately.

Truth be told, that was a little intimidating. Diara had been given two years to become accustomed to the idea that she would be marrying Beckett, and she had taken all of that time to prepare herself for what was to come. Now, in just the space of a few days, her world had been upended, and not only had she lost one fiancé, she had evidently gained another.

Everything was happening in a blur.

As Diara stood at the window and looked out over the bailey, she could hear her mother issuing orders to the servants. They were to bring in trunks and capcases and, already, the packing for the new marriage had begun. Ananda wasn't wasting any time. Of course, every woman wanted her daughter to be married and to marry well, but in this case, Ananda had lost hope over the past few days due to Beckett's demise, so the missive from her husband that another husband for their daughter was on the horizon had the woman worked up into a frenzy.

Diara simply let her mother run with it.

In truth, she was still too stunned to get involved with her own future. She didn't feel like packing or talking about wedding plans. She'd always assumed that she would live with her husband once they were married, which meant they would be returning to Selbourne Castle, a place she'd never been. She had prepared herself for that. But now, she had no idea where she would be living, only that she would no longer be living at Cicadia. When she had been introduced to Beckett, it had been at his father's castle near Gloucester, so she had to assume that was where she was going to be living from now on. A chatelaine of her own castle. Not just any castle, but a de Lohr marcher castle. That was a massive responsibility.

She wasn't entirely sure she was mentally prepared for it.

Certainly, Diara had been trained to run a household just like every other noble daughter in England. That was simply part of their education. She knew how to manage a kitchen, purchase supplies, manage money, manage the servants, and every other task that was normally performed in a noble household. Chatelaines had to know the jobs of every person they supervised, and she knew how to do just about everything. Her training at Carisbrooke had been, if nothing else, complete and thorough. Lady de Redvers was a taskmaster when it came to training her young charges, so in spite of whatever gossip there happened to be flying around, all of that was pushed aside when training was in session.

Now, all of that education was about to be put to the test.

Diara turned to watch her mother as the woman had her trunks neatly lined up so that the packing could begin. Ananda did not seem to have any concerns at all about her daughter becoming the chatelaine for a major castle on the Welsh marches. Either she was so happy to get rid of her daughter that the thought hadn't crossed her mind, or she simply had faith that Diara could effectively accomplish the task. All of that fine training in a fine household was about to pay off.

Her daughter was marrying a de Lohr son.

Still trying to reconcile herself to her impending future, Diara returned her attention to the bailey. She was rather young to be married to a seasoned knight, at least one as old as Beckett's father, because a man like that needed an equally seasoned wife. A man like that had royal connections, and he had seen much in life, so she could only imagine what he must have been thinking about marrying a woman so young, hardly out of fostering herself.

She suspected how it all came about.

Diara knew her father had gone to Lioncross Abbey to demand a new husband to replace the one that had passed away, but she never imagined he would demand the father of her former betrothed. The more she thought about it, the more she realized that Robin must have gone straight to the Earl of Hereford and pitched such a fit that the man had no choice but to give him what he wanted. She could just hear her father demanding one of the earl's own sons to fulfill the contract. She supposed it made the most sense that Beckett's father, whom she knew was widowed, should be the chosen one.

She could only imagine what a nuisance her father must have made of himself.

Diara was certain that did not bode well for her. Already, her soon-to-be husband was probably greatly aggravated by her cantankerous father, so she could only pray that annoyance didn't cross over to her. The poor man had just lost his son, and now he'd been forced into a marriage that she was quite certain he did not want. She didn't know who she felt sorrier for—her or him.

The afternoon passed as Diara continued to sit near the window and pondered her future. Her mother continued to busy herself by packing her daughter's trunks, grateful for the fact that Diara wasn't participating because she preferred to do everything herself. That suited Diara just fine, and she remained in the window, watching the bailey, rather pleased that Iris hadn't joined her in her vigil. Her cousin was down in the kitchens today, helping supervise the baking. Ananda insisted that the young women under her charge, including her husband's niece, actively participate in the management of Cicadia, which was rather interesting considering the woman was one of those people who always liked to be in control of everything.

But she also didn't like lazy young women.

The long and moody afternoon passed into evening. Most of Diara's trunks were packed, and her mother was doing inventory on her collection of combs, scarves, and products like cream for the skin and perfume that she felt would be alluring enough for a new husband. Iris had joined them near sunset, when her chores were mostly done and before the evening meal commenced, and she mercifully sat in silence once the situation had been explained to her. None of the usual questions or pestering, probably because she could see the expression on Diara's face and realized this was not the time for her usual interrogation. Therefore, they sat quietly while Ananda virtually ignored them so she could finish her tasks.

Then came a knock on the door.

"Who comes?" Ananda called.

"Eddard, my lady."

Ananda waved her hand at one of the servants, who went to open the panel. Eddard stood there, the knight Diara often accused of never bathing, a hairy young knight who seemed to wear the same clothing for weeks at a time and sometimes looked, and smelled, as if he lived in a hole in the ground. He focused on Ananda.

"A contingent is approaching, Lady Cheltenham," he said. "It is Lord Cheltenham, accompanied by a rather large escort of de Lohr soldiers. Mathis and Pryce have ridden out to meet them."

Ananda clapped her hands together. "Excellent," she said, swishing her hand in his direction. "Go, now. Prepare for my husband's return, and he has a very special guest with him. You will show Sir Richard de Lohr all proper respect."

Eddard hadn't known who was approaching with Lord Cheltenham, but considering he'd gone off to Lioncross Abbey to discuss the death of de Lohr's son, the fact that Richard de Lohr was coming to Cicadia made some sense. With a swift bow, he rushed back down the stairs, leaving Ananda in a state.

"Pack up these trunks," she snapped to the servants. "Leave the blue silk hanging on the peg. That is what my daughter shall wear for her wedding day. Diara! Come here, quickly!"

Diara sighed heavily and, with a long look at Iris, begrudgingly stood up and went to her mother. She'd barely reached the woman when Ananda was reaching out to pull the clothing from her body.

"You shall wear the pink brocade," she said, spinning her daughter around so she could get to the ties on her back. "Pink is such an alluring color on you."

Diara was being buffeted back and forth by her mother's hurried attentions. "It is an ingenuous color," she said. "I do not like it. I would rather wear the sapphire wool or even the red silk."

Ananda glared at her. "*I* will tell you what to wear for your betrothed," she said. "He must see you as fragile and beautiful. Show a man a delicate flower, and I will show you a woman he wishes to protect. Let him be glad for this betrothal."

"Dress me in pink and I will look like a child."

"Shut your lips and do as I say."

Diara rolled her eyes as Ananda continued to strip her down, calling for rosewater to wash with. Diara simply stood there, shaking her head at her mother's eagerness, until a servant came from the hall to ask about housing the incoming soldiers. That divided Ananda's attention until she could no longer handle both—dealing with the de Lohr soldiers as well as dressing her daughter. Leaving her daughter to the servants, she headed for the chamber door.

"Finish dressing and I shall see you down in Papa's solar," she said. "You and your betrothed should be introduced in private, not in the hall for all to see. Be demure and obedient when you meet him, Deedee. Do not chatter at him as you usually do."

Diara didn't have a chance to reply. Her mother had already flown from the chamber, slamming the door shut behind her.

"God's Bones," Iris muttered as she came over to stand with her cousin. "Aunt Ananda is in quite a state."

Diara's gaze lingered on the closed panel. "Aye, she is," she said. Then she turned around in time to put her hand out to stop the servant who was preparing the pink garment. "Not that one. Bring me the red silk. The one with the angel sleeves."

The servant hesitated fearfully for a moment, but quickly put the pink down and ran off to the wardrobe. What she returned with was an exquisite red dress that Diara had made last year without her mother's knowledge. She'd been given permission to engage the seamstress in town with the garment of her choice and fabric of her own choosing, and she chose a red silk that had been made into a body-hugging garment that was as obscene as it was gorgeous.

Ananda had forbidden her from wearing it.

Unfortunately, it had cost a small fortune to produce, so Ananda wouldn't dispose of it or give it away, either. It was a dress made for a queen, and Diara fingered it as Iris giggled in support of the rebellion. One servant put a featherweight linen shift over Diara's head while the other servant lifted the red dress. Diara shimmied her way into it as it fell gracefully down her body.

Standing in front of the polished bronze mirror, Diara watched the servants smooth out the dress. It had a modest neckline that was high on the chest, but open enough that it hung slightly off her shoulders. The sleeves were what was known as angel's sleeves, meaning they were long past her hands, belled out at the bottom. The bodice was cinched up just beneath her breasts, with crisscrossed red silk ribbons that the servants tightened up to give her a daringly small waist.

Meanwhile, Iris had picked up a comb and set about combing out Diara's blonde locks, which went to her buttocks. It had a natural curl to it, wavy and thick. She braided the front of her hair, pulling it back and securing it with a gold ribbon, while a circlet of gold and rubies went on her brow. The last item to go on was a big, heavy gold cross on a golden chain that had belonged to Diara's grandmother. It was a spectacular piece against the backdrop of the red silk. Truth be told, nothing could compare with Diara in that red dress, for she outshone any woman in England when she wore it. The trouble was that her mother would never let her wear it.

But perhaps her new husband would.

She wanted to look like a bride fit for the son of the greatest warlord in England.

"Well?" she said when everyone was finished fussing over her. "Do I look like a bride that a man might be proud of?"

Iris nodded with approval. "Aunt Ananda will be furious, but you look like a goddess," she said. "If Aunt Ananda becomes angry and makes you give the dress away, can I have it?"

Diara giggled at her bold cousin. "Nay," she said flatly. "I will burn it before I give it away, so be ready to light the fire when I give the word."

"I will steal that dress before you can get it near a flame."

Diara started laughing, twirling in the dress as one of the servants brought over the perfume that Ananda had been picking through. She settled on an oil that smelled strongly of roses, putting it on every bit of exposed skin and rubbing it in. After that, she simply stood there and looked at herself, wondering if she was truly brave enough for the change her life was taking.

Ready or not, it was upon her.

"What is it?" Iris said, standing behind her, watching her. "What are you thinking?"

Diara shrugged, fingering the big gold cross at her chest. "After we received news that Beckett had been killed," she said, "do you remember the kind of husband I told you I wanted?"

Iris thought on that. "You said you wanted a man, not a boy."

Diara nodded. "It seems that I am to get my wish," she said. "I met Sir Richard when I was introduced to Beckett, but I do not remember much about him other than he was a very big man."

"Are you afraid?"

"Not afraid. But a little nervous. What if he does not like me?"

Iris turned her around to face her. "He will love you," she insisted quietly. "Be yourself. Do not listen to your mother and be demure and obedient. You've managed to charm nearly every man you've ever met, Deedee. Now you must charm the only man that counts—the man you are to marry."

Diara nodded as if trying to convince herself of the very same thing. "I remember Beckett telling me that his mother had been dead for many years," she said. "Sir Richard has not married in all that time. If he had wanted a wife, I am sure he would have."

"Whether or not he wants a wife is not of issue," Iris said. "He has you now."

"I am certain my father bullied him into it."

"You do not know that. You cannot assume the worst."

That was true. Iris was wise when she wanted to be. Diara took one last look at herself in the mirror before squaring her shoulders.

"Then I will go down to the solar and meet the man I am to marry," she said. "I can only hope he will be pleased."

"Should I come?"

"If my mother is furious about the dress, then she will be even more furious if you go where you are not wanted," Diara said. "Retreat to the hall and wait for me there. Please."

Iris nodded, walking Diara to the door but going no further. The last vision she had was of that deep red dress heading down the stairs. She couldn't help but think that Diara was walking as if going to her own execution—there was no joy in her movements. Only duty.

Only dread.

Iris found herself saying a little prayer.

Please, God. Let this betrothal be agreeable to them both.

 C3

ROI WASN'T QUITE sure what he was seeing.

Having ridden hard from Lioncross Abbey for two days, he and Robin and one hundred de Lohr soldiers arrived at Cicadia Castle just after sunset on the second day. It was a dark night, but hundreds of torches lit up the grounds of the castle, illuminating everything in a festive sort of way.

Cicadia was prepared to greet her returning liege in style.

Roi was weary from the ride, not paying much attention to his surroundings as he and Robin dismounted their horses, greeted by Robin's three knights, two of which had ridden out to escort them the last few miles to the castle. He knew all three of them, distantly, but he was understandably preoccupied. He was also thirsty, and hungry, and Robin led him into the keep with the promise of wine and some food before the evening meal was served.

Therefore, Roi entered Cheltenham's solar with the mood of an unhappy and weary man, removing his gloves and taking the time to look at the richly furnished chamber. He'd spent two days reminding himself that everything he saw would eventually become his, and what he saw did not disappoint him. Not even the wine that Robin gave him, which was quite good. So far, everything had been good. He liked what he saw and his mood was starting to lift, just a little.

Then a woman entered the chamber.

That was when he wasn't quite sure what he was seeing. An

exquisite creature with long blonde hair floated into the room, wearing a dress of red silk that emphasized a figure the curves of which Roi had never seen before. She evidently hadn't known her father was in the chamber, along with his guest, and she quickly dropped into a low curtsy. Roi had no idea who she was until Robin extended his hand to pull her to her feet.

"My lord," he said to Roi. "You remember my daughter, do you not? This is Lady Diara, my daughter. Diara, this is Sir Richard de Lohr, Beckett's father. You have met him once before, at his home of Pembridge Castle. He has come to Cicadia because he has graciously agreed to fulfill the marriage contract and marry you in the place of his son."

Diara dropped into a curtsy again before their eyes even met. "My lord," she said. "You honor us with your presence. Welcome to Cicadia."

Now, Roi was starting to realize what he was seeing. His bride. The truth was that he didn't remember Diara le Bec looking like this. He wouldn't have been able to pick her up out of a crowd. Somehow, in the past year or so, the lady had grown up and matured into magnificence he'd never seen in his entire life. And her voice... soft, gentle, soothing. He could have listened to her all day.

Stunned, he set his cup down.

"This is your daughter?" he said to Robin. "*This* is Diara?"

Robin nodded proudly. "This is."

Roi looked between Robin and Diara, clearly baffled. "This is the same young woman you brought to Pembridge last year?"

"The same," Robin said, though he was starting to think that something was wrong. "Why? What is amiss that you should ask that question?"

Roi shook his head. "Nothing is amiss," he said, his focus

fully on Diara. "I was simply… I will admit that I did not remember her well because she spent all of her time with Beckett, but this glorious young woman is not whom I remember. My lady, you honor me."

Robin was back to beaming, looking at his daughter, who smiled timidly at the compliment. "I should like to, my lord, very much," she said. "But before we speak further, I should like to extend my condolences on Beckett's passing. I was so very sorry to hear of his loss. I was wondering… mayhap it is too much to ask, but I was wondering if it would be appropriate for me to attend his funeral. I should like to pay my respects to him and to your family, if I should be permitted."

Roi stood there a moment, rubbing his hands together, unsure how to respond to her very polite request. He realized he was stunned rather speechless by the whole thing, but there was something he knew for certain—he wanted to speak with her without her father hanging over them. He had a feeling their conversation would be stilted and superficial with Robin around because he had, from the beginning, gripped the reins of control tightly in this situation. He'd worked very hard to manipulate everyone into doing what he wanted them to do, Roi included.

He finally turned to Robin.

"Would you permit your daughter and I to have a few moments alone?" he asked. "I swear upon my oath I shall not take any liberties that I am not yet legally entitled to take. I simply wish to speak with her, if I may. I believe that is my right."

Robin nodded quickly, before the words were even out of Roi's mouth. "Of course," he said. "I will leave you, but I shall remain right outside the door. Summon me when you are finished."

With that, he darted out of the chamber, shutting the door behind him. Roi waited until he was gone before returning his attention to Diara. There were two big chairs before the hearth, which was burning weakly with a flickering flame, and he indicated the cushioned seats upon the elaborate wood frames.

"Will you sit and be comfortable, my lady?" he said. "I am sorry if my request was bold, but given these peculiar circumstances, it is probably best that we have some time to speak alone."

Diara quickly moved to one of the chairs, perching on the end of it and sitting straight because she didn't want to wrinkle the silk by sitting back. Roi took the other chair, finally lifting his head to look at her.

He couldn't seem to stop staring at her.

"It was not bold, my lord," she said. "I am glad you asked. Otherwise, my father might not allow me to get a word in."

"I was afraid of that."

"Then you know him well."

"Unfortunately."

He saw her fight off a smile, an utterly charming gesture, and it bolstered his courage. Oddly enough, he felt as if he'd never been alone with a woman in his life, and it was a struggle not to laugh at himself for it. Sitting with this magnificent creature made him feel the least bit giddy.

"I am not sure how to start, so forgive me if I am tactless," he said. "Do you know why your father went to Lioncross Abbey?"

Diara could see that he was nervous. Perhaps even on edge. He'd done nothing but stare at her with big blue eyes since she entered the chamber, so she was starting to feel uneasy. She sensed that perhaps her appearance did not impress him. In fact, she thought that he may have wanted to tell her that he wanted nothing to do with this marriage and simply couldn't. She knew very well why her father had gone to Lioncross.

There was no use playing stupid.

"I am very sorry, my lord," she said, sounding deeply sincere. "He told me he was going there to offer his condolences on Beckett's loss, but I know he did more than that."

"You do?"

"Aye." She nodded. "He wanted the marriage with Beckett badly, you see. My mother could never have more children, so he was stuck with a daughter when he desperately wanted a son. I am very sorry if he went to Lioncross and forced you into assuming your son's place. It was a terrible thing for him to do, so please know that I had nothing to do with it. I did not tell him to go."

Roi could see how distressed she was by it, but even in her distress, he was so fascinated by her that he could hardly think straight. But he was coming to suspect that this marriage wasn't something she wanted, either. He had to admit that he was disappointed. Now that she'd seen him, she didn't want an old man for a husband.

He didn't blame her.

"Of course you didn't," he said quietly. "You are a beautiful young woman and it is only right that you should like a strong, young husband. Truly, I did not mean to offend you by offering to marry you in my son's stead. That was never my intent. But your father was quite insistent that he either be given a de Lohr husband for you or that your dowry be returned. I thought offering to marry you in place of my son was the more honorable thing to do, but now I see that it was wrong. You have my apologies."

Diara, whose clasped hands had been fidgeting in her lap, suddenly stopped and looked at him curiously. "You... *you* offered, my lord?"

Roi nodded. "I did," he said. "But I can simply give him back your dowry and you can find a husband more to your liking."

Diara blinked, puzzled by the conversation. "That is not what I meant, my lord," she said, hastening to reassure him. "I am sorry if you thought I did not... that's *not* what I meant at all. I was simply apologizing that you felt you had to placate my father by offering yourself. Surely you do not want to marry me."

"Surely you do not want to marry *me*."

"Not if you do not want to marry me."

Roi's eyebrows lifted. Then he started chuckling, rubbing a hand over his cheek and mouth. "I think we are going in circles," he said. "Do you want to marry me, my lady?"

"If you want me to. But only if you truly want me to."

More circles. Roi suspected she was going to defer to him in all things and leave the decision up to him, so he put up a hand to ease her. "Let us proceed in another way," he said. "May I?"

She nodded eagerly. "I wish you would, my lord."

"Then I suggest that we take this evening to get to know one another," he said. "This is all very new and mayhap even shocking to the both of us, so I think we should take a little time before we make a life-changing decision. If, at the end of the evening, you decide that I would not make a good husband to you, you simply need say so and I shall return your dowry and your father can find you a husband more to your liking. Is that satisfactory?"

Diara seriously thought on that. It was a shockingly generous offer, considering what a marriage to her would bring to him. But he was giving her some choice in the matter, something she was quite touched by. No one, not even her father, had ever given her a choice at all when it came to her own life.

But Beckett's father had.

She had to admit that, in her eyes, that was just the least bit endearing.

"It is," she said. "But I must say the same thing to you. If, by the end of the evening, you decide you would not like to have me as your wife, you simply need tell me. I will not be offended. But I do ask that you be honest with me, my lord, as I will be honest with you."

"I can ask for no better request."

Diara smiled hesitantly. "Good," she said. "When I came to visit Pembridge last year, I did not have the chance to speak to you, so I look forward to the opportunity."

"As do I," Roi said. "But the last time we met, you did what you were supposed to do, which was spend time with Beckett. He had good things to say about you."

"That is kind," Diara said. "I found him polite and full of dreams of adventure."

"I think most young men his age have those dreams."

"Did you?"

Roi was feeling a little more relaxed with her as he settled back in his chair. "Certainly," he said. "Though I cannot tell you exactly what they were. I'm sure I had dreams of battling the French, of killing in the name of the king, of being much decorated, like the gladiators of Ancient Rome."

Diara's smile grew. "Did you wear a wreath of laurel leaves after your first battle?"

Roi laughed softly at the cute question. "I did not even think of it," he said. "But if I had, I'm sure I would have. Now I feel as if I have missed something."

Diara laughed because he was. It was a surprisingly pleasant moment in a conversation where neither one of them was sure there would be such a thing.

It was encouraging.

"Then mayhap after the next battle, I can make you a wreath of holly and plant it right atop your head," she said with an accompanying gesture. "That would make a bright display."

He winced. "And a painful one," he said. "Can we not find a better leaf than holly?"

"Oak, but that can be quite dirty."

"True."

"I could always weave a garland of roses, but that might not suit you too well."

He rolled his eyes. "Thankfully," he said. "I am not entirely sure I could show my face wearing a garland of roses. But if you made it, I would wear it."

She smiled, displaying a big dimple in her right cheek. "Ah," she said. "A man who knows his obligation. If a woman makes it, he wears it. No matter if he likes it or not."

Roi was grinning, swept up in her obvious charm. "Only a fool would not do as a woman asks," he said. "I learned that many years ago."

Diara was smiling openly at him. "And you have carried that knowledge into your adult years."

"Indeed," he said. "Beckett's mother taught me that, in fact. If a man wishes to make his wife happy, then he does as she asks. Truly, it is not difficult, though some men are simply stubborn. But they all learn in the end."

Diara chuckled. "My father still has not learned," she said.

"If he feels like obeying my mother, he will do it, but mostly, he insists she obey him in all things."

Roi's smile faded. "I think your father insists that most people obey him in all things."

He was referring to the marriage contract and the commotion he'd caused. Diara knew that, and her smile faded.

"Will you tell me truthfully, my lord?" she asked quietly. "Was he terrible to you? If he was, I cannot apologize enough."

Roi thought her concern to be quite sweet. "Nay," he said softly. "He was not terrible. I suppose if I had a daughter I wished to marry to a fine husband, I might have behaved the same way."

Diara shook her head in regret of her father's behavior. "But he should have waited," she said. "You have only just lost your son. It was too much of him to expect you to fulfill your son's obligations."

Roi shrugged, propping his right foot onto his left knee and brushing the dirt off the heel. "It is done," he said. "I was the most logical choice, so let us speak no more about it, shall we? I do not want you to think your father tied me to a pole and beat me until I agreed."

Diara burst out in soft laughter. "If you must know, that was what I envisioned," she said. "I had this image of my father, who is half your size, wrestling you to a pole and taking a switch to you. Do you mean to tell me that did not happen?"

Roi was back to grinning. "It did not," he said. "But I had some help in resisting him, to be honest."

"Who?"

"My elderly father, for one."

Diara was still laughing. "I have heard tale of Christopher de Lohr," she said. "Elderly or not, I am certain he could take on an army all by himself and still emerge the victor. Men like him are made of legends."

Roi appreciated her respect for his father. "They are, indeed," he said. "And where did you hear tale of him?"

"I fostered at Carisbrooke Castle," she said. "The House of de Redvers is always in the middle of whatever is transpiring in England. There is not much I haven't heard through them."

Roi's eyebrows lifted. "Did you get on well with the family?"

Diara hesitated. In case Roi happened to be friends with the House of de Redvers, she didn't want to disparage them, even though she had enough reason to do so. But she forced a smile.

"Lady de Redvers was a great teacher," she said as neutrally as she could. "I spent several years there. I do like Devon."

"The House of de Winter has property near Carisbrooke. Do you know them?"

She nodded. "I do, my lord."

He held up a hand to give her pause. "Wait," he said. "Before we continue, I would consider it a favor if you would not address me so formally. In private like this, I would be honored if you would call me Roi."

An expression of warmth flickered across her face. "I would be honored," she said. "But... I thought your name was Richard?"

He nodded. "It is," he said. "I was named after my godfather, King Richard. When I was young, I was even called Richie, but somewhere around my eighth year, a family friend called me *petit Roi Richard*, and from that moment forward, everyone addressed me as Roi."

She nodded in understanding. "Roi," she repeated in that soft, soothing tone he found so alluring. "I like that. I would be greatly honored if you would call me Diara."

"Your father called you Deedee."

She grinned. "Like you, I inherited a childhood sobriquet."

"What do you prefer?"

"Whatever you choose," she said. "I will answer to either."

He smiled because she was, but there was something more to it. As he gazed at her, he could feel the warmth from those eyes. They were the color of periwinkle, as he remembered, but he hadn't remembered them being so magnetic. As if he couldn't look away from her. That giddy feeling he'd been experiencing was only getting worse, which was quite surprising, considering the last time he'd felt giddy was probably back when he was courting Odette. He couldn't decide whether it was thrilling or foolish.

He settled on just a little bit thrilling.

"Then I shall decide how to address you depending on the situation," he said. "And thank you for giving me permission."

"It is my pleasure, my lord. I mean... Roi."

He laughed softly, and she joined him. In a private meeting that could have turned out so badly, they had found common ground and a surprising bit of honesty. Roi had to admit that the conversation—and Diara—had been nothing as he had expected. Frankly, he was flabbergasted by the whole thing, but not in a bad way.

In a way that gave him hope.

"I'm assuming your mother has a grand feast planned for this evening," he said. "I'm further assuming that your father is on the other side of that door, his ear pressed against it, wondering what we're speaking of. Now that we have briefly spoken, it would be kind to let him in."

"Must we?"

Roi snorted. "Of course not," he said. "If you do not wish it, then he can remain out there as long as you desire."

"Good," she said, suddenly looking around the chamber. "But I do not see any wine. I would pour you some because you must be weary from your journey."

"I am, a little."

She rose from her chair. "Then I am afraid we must open the door to allow the refreshments in," she said. "I do not wish for you to suffer."

She was standing in front of him in that glorious red dress, and Roi had a difficult time not looking at what was straight in front of him. He struggled to look her in the eye.

"Trust me when I tell you that I am not suffering," he said. "But opening the door to let the servants bring food and drink would not be unacceptable."

Diara scurried over to the door, putting her hand on the latch. But she didn't open it right away. Instead, she paused and looked at him.

"You said earlier that we should take this evening and decide if we truly want to enter into this marriage," she said. "I... I do not think I need all evening to decide."

His eyes glimmered faintly. "Nor do I."

"I have decided that I am agreeable if you are."

"I decided that the moment you walked into the chamber."

With a smile that set Roi's heart to thumping, Diara opened the door to an impatient father.

CHAPTER FIVE

"WELL DONE, MY lady," Roi said, lips twitching with a smile. "Where did you learn to shoot with such skill?"

Diara still had the bow in her hand. "Contrary to popular belief, I wasn't only taught domestic things that are expected of women," she said coyly. "Carisbrooke was a wealth of learning opportunities, and archery was one of them."

"I can see that."

"If you need me upon the battlements the next time the barbarians attack, I am at your disposal."

Roi laughed softly, reaching out to take a bow from Eddard. It was a warm afternoon, two days after his arrival to Cicadia, and he was finding out just what kind of woman he was about to marry. He and Diara had spent nearly every moment together since he arrived, and the archery competition was the latest event in days that had been full of such things.

And he'd enjoyed every single minute of it.

In fact, he couldn't remember when he'd enjoyed anything more.

"I will take that into consideration the next time I need

archers in battle," he said, selecting an arrow as stable servants removed the arrows from the targets several dozen yards away. "Not to slander your skill, I will say that hitting a moving target is slightly different than hitting a bale of hay."

Big targets had been raised against the castle wall near the stables as Diara, Roi, Iris, and Pryce competed for the title of Supreme Archer. Or Queen of the Archers, as Diara so charmingly put it, because she was convinced that she was going to win. Truth be told, Roi was happy to let her because he very quickly realized that he loved to hear her laugh, and she did a lot of it. She was a smooth-talking, sweet flatterer and brilliant conversationalist, something he'd never before seen from a woman.

But it wasn't just with him.

She teased and laughed with her cousin. She did it marginally with Pryce, who mostly stiffened up and seemed nervous when she did it. She called out to the servant moving the hay bales around, taunting him without making it seem mean-spirited. She even talked to the dogs that would wander into their range. As Roi was coming to see, she was just a very friendly person, and a happy one as well.

But he remembered what Westley had told him.

She is evidently quite... friendly.

Absolutely, he could see that she was. It simply seemed to be her personality, and it was clear at Cicadia that she was well loved. He'd spent two evenings with her, chatting nonstop during supper, and never once did her banter suggest anything inappropriate. No ribald comments, no sexual innuendos. Nothing. She was, quite simply, the most charming woman he'd ever met, and he couldn't believe Beckett had never mentioned it. His son had only spoken of her in passing, and only rarely, and he'd never mentioned what an enchanting creature she was, which Roi found odd. But not so odd, considering Beckett hadn't wanted to marry at all.

Aye, Roi knew that.

He'd ignored it, however. No young man wanted to marry at an early age, and Beckett had been no exception. There was a whole world out there, as Beckett had put it, that he wanted to see. He wanted to see and experience everything he could. There was no crime in that. But the reality of a wife didn't sit well with him, so in a sense, Roi didn't blame the lad for not speaking favorably of a wife he never wanted.

But, God's Bones... what his son had missed out on.

As he was pondering the situation and the woman a few feet in front of him, he suddenly realized that servants were gripping the hay bales, moving them from side to side. He came to stand next to Diara as she tightened up the string of the bow.

"What, pray, is happening with the targets?" he asked, fairly close to her ear. "Have you decided to use men instead of hay?"

Smiling, Diara looked over her shoulder at him. "You said that hitting a moving target is quite different," she said. "I will prove to you that I can hit a moving target."

He fought off a grin. "What shall I do if you hit one of those men?"

"Give him a proper burial."

He lowered his head, laughing low in his throat. "Mayhap you should not hit him and save me the expense."

"I will try. But no promises."

He continued to laugh. "You are a cruel, cruel woman, my lady," he said. "Look at those men—they are positively terrified."

She stopped fussing with the bowstring. "They must show

courage," she said, selecting her arrow and lining it up. "I do not mean to be rude, but do not speak to me while I am trying not to hit those men. If I do, it will be your fault."

Smirking, Roi backed away, and after a couple of seconds, Diara let the quill fly. It sailed straight into the center of the hay bale, even though it was moving back and forth, and the men who had been witnessing the competition from the wall above erupted in cheers. Beaming, Diara turned to Roi.

"Well?" she said. "What do you have to say to that?"

He clapped lazily, still smiling at her. "I say that my betrothed is the most skilled, the most brilliant, and the most beautiful woman in all of England," he said. "I say that I am a very fortunate man."

The big grin on her face turned to one of genuine warmth, and he could see her cheeks growing pink.

"Do you really?" she said, sounding as if she didn't believe him. "Or are you simply saying that because I bested you?"

Eyes riveted to hers, he reached out and took the bow from her. "I most assuredly mean it," he said softly. "I do not say anything I do not mean. You *are* the most skilled, brilliant, and beautiful woman I have ever had the honor to meet."

Diara let him take the bow. She was so pleased by his kind words that she was feeling a little flushed. And the way he looked at her... sweet Jesus, the man had a gaze that could cut through steel. She felt as if he was looking right down into her heart, for if he really could, he would see just what these past two days had meant to her.

Everything.

They had meant everything.

"You flatter me, my lord," she finally said, lowering her lashes. "I do not know what to say."

"Say that you are pleased with this betrothal."

She lifted her gaze. "I am very pleased," she said. "Do you not know that?"

Roi's gaze never left her face as he held out the bow for someone to take from him. When Pryce reached out to grasp it, fully aware that Roi couldn't take his eyes of Diara, Roi simply held out an elbow to her.

"Walk with me," he said quietly.

Diara latched on to his arm with both hands, and the two of them headed off toward the center of the bailey, where they could have some privacy. At this time of day, it was the least crowded part of the yard. Leaving Pryce and Iris to pick up the bows and arrows from their game, they wandered in the direction of the kitchen yard. Diara clung to Roi's big arm, feeling the strength and firmness beneath her grip. On the wall overhead, she could see Mathis near the gatehouse, watching them.

She knew why.

Truthfully, she was surprised he hadn't tried to interfere over the past couple of days. Mathis had been offering for her hand since before she went away to foster, but her father had turned him down repeatedly. Mathis was a friend and nothing more in her eyes, and he knew it, which made the situation worse for him. Diara could only imagine how difficult it must be for the man to watch her show affection to someone else, and there had been times in the past when he'd deterred or otherwise intimidated suitors that had come to call. But not with Roi; Mathis knew he couldn't get away with anything. The man would probably squash him like a bug.

But she wondered if Roi had sensed anything from the quiet, moody knight.

"Well?" she finally said. "Where shall we have the crowning ceremony?"

He looked at her. "What crowning ceremony?"

"Because I am the Queen of the Archers."

He chuckled. "I see," he said. "I suppose we can do it in the hall tonight. I will put you on a table and insist all worship at your feet."

"Including you?"

"Especially me."

Diara broke down into soft laughter, indicating she wasn't at all serious about the crowning. Well, not really. But it was fun to tease him.

"May I ask you a question, Roi?" she said.

"You do not have to ask permission to ask a question," he said. "Simply ask me. I will answer if I can."

"How long are you going to remain at Cicadia?" she asked. "And when you leave, will I go with you?"

Roi nodded. "Your father wishes for us to be married right away," he said. "Did he tell you that?"

Diara shrugged. "My mother has," she said. "Have you agreed?"

He glanced at her. "That is your decision."

"Why is it my decision?"

"Because I want to make sure this betrothal is agreeable to you," he said. "Why do you think I have been here for two days? I wanted us to come to know one another a little. I want us to be certain."

She came to a stop and looked at him. "I told you that I was certain the first night you were here," she said. "But if you feel you need more time to make your decision, then I will go along with whatever you wish."

He looked at her, his eyes glimmering. "And I told you that I was also agreeable on that first night," she said. "That has not changed."

"Then why do you feel we must wait?"

"I simply want to make sure you've not changed your mind."

"I haven't. Have you?"

He shook his head. "I shall say it again," he said. "I am the most fortunate man in the world. When you become my wife, I shall be the proudest one as well."

She smiled, once again flattered by his compliment. "I was wondering if we may speak on something," she said. "I know it may seem silly, but I have never been married before, and I was wondering what your expectations of me are. As your wife, I mean. Are there certain things you expect from me? Things you expect me to do? I see other married folk, like my parents, and I see how they are with each other. How each person has a role. I was wondering what you expect from us. From me."

She was rambling on a little, as if she didn't know, exactly, how to ask the question. But it was a legitimate question as far as he was concerned, and an astute one. The woman wanted to know what she was getting in to.

"That is a reasonable concern," he said. "But there is no simple answer. Being my wife will require all of the usual things—tending my home, tending to me. We've not discussed this, but I have two daughters. Did you know that?"

Diara nodded. "Beckett told me," she said. "Adalia and Dorian."

"That is correct."

"Are they fostering?"

"They were, but they returned home a couple of years ago,"

he said. "They had been fostering since they were young, and I simply wanted them home, with me. They live at Pembridge."

"Are they your chatelaines?"

Roi snorted. "Nay," he said. "Though they are involved in the management of the house at my mother's insistence. Dorian is fourteen years of age, and all she wants to do is tend to her horses. She has four of them. She cares nothing for managing a household, but my major-domo does require her to do chores. She must help manage the stores, and she hates every minute of it. Adalia, on the other hand, understands the duties more."

"How old is she?"

"She has seen seventeen years."

"Then she is a woman grown."

Roi half nodded, half shrugged. "Nearly," he said. "She is much more adept at doing things around the keep, but she has a terrible head for figures. I am constantly having to fix her sums. If there are ten onions in a bag, she'll count seven. She always has. But she has other talents."

"Is she betrothed?"

Roi shook his head. "She is not," he said. "Men terrify her. She is of an age where I must think about seeking her a husband, but every time I bring it up, she weeps. She says she would rather go to a convent."

"Is that a choice for her?"

"I suppose," he said. "But I am hoping she outgrows this fear. I do not think it is normal for a lass to feel that way."

"Mayhap she hasn't met the right man yet."

"Mayhap."

The conversation lagged a little, but it wasn't uncomfortable. Roi was aware he hadn't fully answered her question, so he reached out and took her hand. Holding it tightly, he began to walk again.

"As for you," he said. "I suppose my expectations would be that we always try to understand one another, that we always be kind to one another, and that we always be truthful. A marriage is nothing without truth."

Diara liked the feeling of her hand in his big, warm palm. It made her feel safe. "I will agree completely," she said. "Sometimes the truth is difficult, but it is better to know than to not know. Nothing solid can be built on a foundation of deceit and secrets."

"Very wise," he said, smiling at her. "Who taught you such things?"

"I had to learn for myself."

"Where?"

They were on to something she really didn't want to talk about. She wasn't sure how they got here, but she'd opened the door when she made her comment—*I had to learn for myself.* She supposed that she should tell him before someone else did. The man traveled in the first social circle and knew many warlords, including de Redvers. He hadn't been oblivious to what his wife and daughters did to Diara, so she thought that perhaps it was time for a little of the truth she just spoke of and hope she didn't offend him.

"You mentioned that you knew the House of de Redvers?" she said.

He nodded. "Of course."

"Do you know the family well?"

"Well enough."

"What do you think of them?" she said. "Are you a good friend?"

At this point, they'd reached the kitchen yard. There were a few goats and chickens scattered about, and servants as they moved about on the course of their duties. Coming to the gate, Roi paused again and faced her.

"I'm assuming you're asking for a reason."

"Aye."

"You fostered at Carisbrooke," he said. "Are you a good friend of Lady de Redvers?"

She hesitated a moment before slowly shaking her head. "Nay," she said. "She did not like me very much."

He scratched his head, clearing his throat as if he wanted to say a good deal, but instead, he was searching for the right words.

"I had wondered," he muttered. "Aye, I know them well. Am I a good friend? Nobody is good friends with Richard de Redvers and his wife... She's respected, but not well liked. She is a shrew of a woman, from what I've seen."

Diara felt a great deal of relief with that statement. It would be easier to be honest with him about her time at Carisbrooke now. "I would never disparage them because they taught me a great deal," she said. "But you should know that Lady de Redvers and her daughters were not very nice to me. If we are speaking truthfully, they were horrible to me. It wasn't bad in the beginning, when I first went to foster when I was about twelve, but as I grew into womanhood, they became quite... unkind."

Roi wasn't without sympathy. "How so?"

Diara showed some reluctance. "I do not wish to complain."

"You are not complaining by telling me the facts."

"I do not wish for you to think I am a gossip, or worse."

"By speaking of your experience at Carisbrooke? I would not think that."

She took a deep breath. "The daughters did not like me because the pages and squires would pay attention to me and not to them," she said. "I do not ignore people. I like to talk to them because I find people interesting, but there was a squire that one of the daughters was sweet on, and he did not like her. He would only talk to me."

Roi nodded in understanding. "And that is when the trouble started."

"Aye," Diara said timidly. "They told the other wards not to speak to me, and soon, none of the women would. The only people I had to talk to were the other pages and squires, and even some of the knights, because the women shunned me. Lady de Redvers would punish me for what she considered inappropriate behavior, all because the only friends I had were the boys around me. It only grew worse as I got older, and finally, I had to beg my father to let me come home. The other woman had resorted to stealing my things and cutting my hair while I slept. I am telling you this not to complain, as I said, but should you ever encounter Lord de Redvers and his wife, and they only have terrible things to say about me, I want you to know the truth. You can ask any of the men or boys at Carisbrooke about me and they will bear witness that I was never immoral or sinful. They will tell you that I was quite persecuted."

There was not one part of that rather painful statement that Roi didn't believe implicitly. He knew the de Redvers. He knew that they were petty and ambitious. The House of de Lohr didn't have a close relationship with them, but the House of de Winter did, and de Winter was a great friend to Hereford. Roi had been in the politics of England too many years not to know of the disdain most had for the de Redvers. Diara's story was probably one of many emerging from Carisbrooke, stories of poor treatment and shame. He felt a great deal of pity for her.

"I would never believe what they told me, even if I did not know you," he said. "But you should know that before I came to Cheltenham, I was told that you had something of a reputation for being… friendly."

As he watched, her eyes filled with tears. "I am so very sorry," she said. "I know those rumors have been going around, but I did not know you had heard them. I swear to you on all that is holy that they are not true. I've never let a man touch me, and I swear upon my very life that I have never even been kissed. I would never let a man I was not betrothed or married to do such a thing."

The tears were falling, and he grasped her hands, holding them against his chest. "Listen to me," he said softly as she sniffled. "I know they are not true. I am a good judge of character because, quite often, my life depends on it, and I can tell that you are a woman of good and noble character. You are sweet and friendly, and that can rouse jealousy in the hearts of those who are not. They wish they were like you. They envy your spirit and your beauty. Those are the people who have started those rumors, without merit, and I do not believe any of it. Please do not weep. I will defend your honor to the death, my lady, I promise."

That only made her weep harder. "No one has ever said that to me," she said, pulling a hand free out of pure necessity and wiping the tears from her face. "Not even my father. He is ashamed of me."

"I am not. And I am the only one who matters."

She nodded, overcome by his support, and he smiled at her. Lifting the hand he still held, he kissed it sweetly, twice, before reaching out to smooth a few stray pieces of hair from her face.

"Stop your tears," he said gently. "There is no need. I will take care of everything from this point forward, and woe to the man or woman who repeats anything unsavory about you. They will have to deal with me."

She was trying to regain her composure. "Thank you," she said. "But I am very sorry my burden will become yours."

He kissed her hand again. "I'm not," he said. "My shoulders are very big for such burdens, in case you've not yet noticed."

She took a deep breath, stilling herself. "I've noticed," she said. "I've noticed everything about you, and it's all quite nice."

He smirked. "Thank you, my lady," he said. "I am flattered that you should take notice of an old knight like me."

She cocked her head at him, wiping the last of her tears away. "You are not old," she said. "You are ageless."

"I have bits of silver hair about my face."

"Those are merely bits of steel from your sword," she said. "When you fight in battle, the slivers fly off your blade and into your hair. They become part of you."

He laughed softly. "I like that," he said. "I shall tell everyone that from now on."

They smiled at each other for a few moments, joy and warmth filling the air between them. The past two days had seen such happiness overtake them, such giddy happiness, that it was difficult for others not to see it. If there was any question lingering that this betrothal was not agreeable to both of them, that had been summarily dashed.

It was more than agreeable.

"My lord!"

A shout came from the gatehouse, and they turned to see Eddard heading in their direction. He was moving at a swift pace, jogging intermittently, and Roi let go of Diara's hand for propriety's sake. They were betrothed, but he didn't need to be seen pawing her in public.

"What is it?" he called.

Eddard held up something in his hand, and as he drew closer, they could see it was a vellum envelope. He handed it to Roi, who looked at the seal.

"From my father," he said, casting Diara a quick glance as he broke the seal and unfolded it. After reading the message quickly, he folded it back up. "I must speak with your father."

He took Diara's hand, and they headed back to the keep.

☙

"YOU WILL BE married here, before you leave, if you want to take her with you."

Roi wasn't pleased with that response. "My son is not even in the ground yet," he said. "I do not intend to marry the woman he was betrothed to until he is properly buried. That is where I am going—back to Lioncross on the morrow to bury my son, and I would like to take Diara with me."

"Marry her first."

"Nay."

It was a standoff in Robin's solar. Roi had just received word from his father that Beckett had arrived at Lioncross and the family was preparing for his funeral. It would take Roi two days to return to Lioncross, and he didn't want to delay. He also didn't want to leave Diara behind, but he didn't want to marry her before he went. He didn't feel that was particularly appropriate when his son wasn't even properly buried yet. Everything had its order, and the order was to honor Beckett before he could take the woman who had been intended to be his wife.

But Robin didn't see his perspective. In fact, he was being quite mulish about the entire situation. He sat at the expensive table in his solar, wine in hand and a stubborn expression on his face.

"I will not permit my unwed daughter to travel with you to Lioncross Abbey," he said frankly. "What if you get there and decide not to marry her? How could you even think to compromise her like that when she is already... Well, it would be unthinkable."

Roi cocked an eyebrow. "When she is already *what*?"

"What do you mean?"

"You were about to tell me that your daughter is already talked about in such ways, weren't you?"

Robin bolted out of his chair, instantly furious. "In what ways?" he demanded. "What are you saying?"

Roi didn't rise to the man's anger. "I am saying that you were not honest with me in the least when you were not forthcoming with the rumors regarding your daughter's reputation," he said. "Do not deny it, for it would be a lie. You never told me that the House of de Redvers spoke unkindly of her. I had to hear about it from someone else."

Robin was taken aback. "So that is why you feel it is appropriate for you to escort my unwed daughter to Lioncross?" he hissed. "Because her reputation is already compromised? It is a two-day trip. What were thinking of doing with her when night fell, de Lohr? Did you think it would be a simple thing to damage her because she is already spoken of in such a way?"

That unfounded accusation had Roi's dander up. "You have said many things over the past several weeks that have been slanderous and ugly," he said. "You have bullied and annoyed my father, you have bullied and annoyed me, and now you are accusing me of immoral intention. I am telling you now—one more word from you that even hints at insult or petulance and you'll not like my reaction."

Robin wasn't used to being challenged. He didn't like it when anyone fought back against his tirades, so he stiffened with rage. "You threaten me in my own home?"

Roi jabbed a finger at him. "I make you a promise," he said. "Any more of this bad behavior from you and I will tell my father to dissolve whatever alliance you may think you have with the entire de Lohr empire. We will no longer tolerate your childish tantrums, Robin. I am warning you."

Robin was angry, but not angry enough to fire back at him. He didn't want the de Lohr alliance removed, but he was coming to see that he couldn't control Roi. More and more, he was coming to realize that. The man would do as he pleased no matter what Robin wished for him to do, and that awareness made Robin's blood boil.

"No alliance, no marriage," he said, trembling because he was so angry. "If you are serious in your promise, then I will dissolve the betrothal at this very moment. I'll find a husband for my daughter who will bring me a strong alliance elsewhere."

Roi hadn't forgotten that Diara was standing back by the doorway, hearing all of this. Before another word was said that would see his betrothal broken, he took a deep breath. He found that he had more at stake than he thought he did.

He didn't want to lose Diara.

"See if you can understand my position, Robin," he said, struggling with his composure. "Think back to the days when you had some compassion and understanding. My son is in a wooden box at Lioncross Abbey, waiting for me to return so he can be buried. I do not want to marry Diara before I put him in his crypt because she was his betrothed before she was mine. It would be in extremely bad taste to marry her now and then show up to my son's funeral married to the woman that had once belonged to him. Furthermore, if I marry her now, my focus will not be on her. It will be on my son and the grief that is tearing at me. That is completely unfair to her. Can you understand that in the slightest?"

Robin was still in verbal battle mode. "It will make no difference to your son if you are married to her or not," he said. "Beckett is dead. He is not going to crawl out of his grave and berate you for marrying a woman he did not show much interest in marrying to begin with. It will not affect his ability to lie in that grave and rot."

That was all Roi could take. He took three steps and lashed out an enormous fist, catching Robin squarely in the face. The man fell backward, immediately unconscious, as the blood flowed from his mouth and nose. But Roi didn't even check to see how badly he'd hit him; he simply turned for the door, where Diara was standing with her hand over her mouth in shock. He marched right up to the panel and put his hand on the latch, pausing to look at her before he opened it.

"If that upset you, then I apologize," he said through clenched teeth. "But I will let no man speak to me so callously about the son I lost. He should be thankful you were in the chamber, or I would have done much worse."

With that, he yanked the door open and headed out of the keep. Diara, however, wasn't going to remain behind. She ran after him, catching him as he descended the stairs into the bailey.

"Wait!" she cried, rushing down the stairs. "Roi, please

wait!"

He came to a halt at the bottom of the steps, turning as she came up behind him. Her eyes were wide with concern.

"Where are you going?" she asked.

He took a deep breath, struggling to calm himself. "I am going to prepare my horse," he said. "I am also going to tell the de Lohr troops to prepare to leave immediately. I must return to Lioncross."

"May I go?" she said eagerly, putting her hand on his forearm. "Please? I should very much like to go with you."

He sighed. Looking into that anxious face, he was starting to feel some remorse for what he'd done. He knew it was the end of the betrothal, and he deeply regretted that.

"I do not think you should," he said. "I am certain that when your father awakens and realizes what happened, our betrothal will be no more."

"Why?" she said. "You did nothing to warrant such a thing."

His brow furrowed in confusion. "What do you mean? You just saw what happened."

She was very calm as she spoke. "I saw my father trip and hit his face on the edge of his table," she said evenly. "I saw you move to try to catch him, but he still injured himself. That is all I saw."

Roi's eyes widened. "You... you saw *what*?"

She smiled at him. "I saw my father trip and fall," she repeated patiently. "Now, I am going to tell my mother that Iris and I will be going to Lioncross to attend Beckett's funeral. Iris will make a good chaperone, don't you think?"

"But your father did not give permission."

"He did," she said. "Before he hit his head. He simply will

not remember."

With that, she winked at him and turned around, heading back up the steps and disappearing into the keep. It took Roi a full minute before he realized that he was standing there with a stupid grin on his face. Every hour, every minute, saw him learn more about this woman he was about to marry.

And positively loving it.

CHAPTER SIX

H E DIDN'T TRIP and fall.
He knew he didn't trip and fall, no matter what Diara and Roi had attested to. They'd both sworn he tripped on the rug under his table and pitched forward, knocking himself silly. Two witnesses with the same story.

But Robin knew differently.

While Roi gathered his troops and departed for Lioncross Abbey along with Diara and Iris, because Diara had convinced her mother that he'd given his permission, Robin had remained in his solar and sulked. He didn't even bother seeing them off because they'd all gone against him and he'd lost control. It was as simple as that. Somehow, Roi had taken over his daughter, his niece, and finally his wife because Ananda was so thrilled her daughter was finally to be married that she didn't care that the man had assaulted her husband.

In fact, she didn't believe he had.

That was the worst of all. Ananda believed that her husband had hit his face on the table because, in the past, he'd been known to get drunk and fall. He'd fallen in the hall several times, down the stairs of the keep, in the bailey, in his solar—

aye, he'd fallen before, so when Diara told her mother what had happened, Ananda believed her. That left Robin nursing a swollen nose and three loose teeth, drinking away his sorrows as his daughter completely disobeyed him.

Everything was going wrong.

The night the de Lohr party departed, he was up most of the night drinking and feeling sorry for himself, falling asleep just before dawn only to be awakened in a couple of hours by Mathis announcing a visitor. He was still drunk when his knight entered, going so far as to berate the man for not having stopped Diara from leaving, but Mathis didn't have much to say to that, and Robin kicked him out of the solar.

In his place stood a man.

It took Robin several long seconds to realize who it was.

"Cirencester?" he gasped. "What are you doing here?"

Riggs Fairford, otherwise known as Lord Cirencester, came into the solar with a lazy grin on his face. A tall man with a crown of bright white hair, he had big lips, a big nose, and a big voice. He stepped into the chamber and put his hand on Robin's shoulder as the man tried to rise.

"Nay, my friend, stay seated," he said. "Do not get up for me. I came to offer my condolences and see how you are faring, but by the look of you, I can guess. I can see how heartbroken you are."

He sat opposite Robin, who stared at him dumbly. "Over what?"

"The loss of your daughter's betrothed, of course."

Still quite drunk, Robin took several moments to realize what he was talking about. "You mean the de Lohr boy?" he said. "That loss?"

"Aye," Riggs said. "The de Lohr lad. I have just heard of his passing."

"How?"

"Because the escort taking him from Selbourne to Lioncross passed through Cirencester a few days ago," he said. "The road they used passed right through my lands. Knowing he was to be your daughter's husband, I loaned them an escort to the boundaries of my property. I thought you would want that."

Robin just looked at him, blankly, before grabbing the pitcher on the table. He realized this was a social visit, but not one he particularly wanted to speak of.

"The death of the de Lohr lad does *not* have me heartbroken," he said as he poured himself more drink. "But I do wish he'd not gotten himself killed. His foolishness has forced me to deal with his father, a contemptible bastard if there ever was one. I hate him."

Riggs frowned. "Roi de Lohr?" he said. "But I thought he was your dear friend."

"He is *not* my dear friend," Robin announced firmly. "I hate the man. I'm sorry you have wasted your time coming here to give me your condolences. They are unnecessary. One less de Lohr in the world does not trouble me."

It was a rather harsh thing to say, but it lent itself toward the purpose of Riggs' visit. He'd come for a reason, and it wasn't to convey only his condolences.

He had quite a different reason in mind.

Riggs and Robin had been neighbors for many years, as the southernmost part of Robin's land bordered the northernmost part of Riggs'. It was just a tiny border, but one nonetheless. Their families had long been allied, though more of just a pleasant association than a strong alliance.

But that was about to change, if Riggs had anything to say

about it.

"It is a large and powerful family you speak of," he said, reaching for the pitcher himself and looking around for a clean cup. "I remember there was a time when you told me how much you needed to be a good friend of Roi de Lohr because there was something you wanted from him."

"That was true, then."

"It was something you denied me."

Robin stopped toying with his cup and looked at him. "Ah," he said, the light of understanding coming to his eyes. "I see now. You came here because you thought my daughter no longer has a betrothed."

Riggs smiled as he poured himself some wine in the only cup he could find. "You are not as drunk as you look," he said. "With the de Lohr lad gone, your daughter is without a marriage contract. Let us be frank—a lady as lovely and wealthy as Lady Diara will not remain unattached for long. I came to see if you would reconsider a marriage between your daughter and my son."

Robin almost said no. He almost threw his cup of wine in Riggs' face and ordered him to leave. Riggs' visit had less to do with actually extending his sympathies than it did with pressing his own agenda. But something stopped Robin from tossing the man out on his arse. Somehow, he could feel his control coming back. He liked it when he could command and manipulate men, and if Riggs wanted something badly enough, he'd do whatever he was told.

"I do not know," he said as he carefully regarded Riggs. "Tell me what qualities your son has that I should consider."

Riggs shrugged. "He will inherit the Honor of Cirencester," he said simply. "He will inherit Totterdown Castle and everything my father and I looted in France when we were fighting wars for Henry. His great-grandfather on his mother's side was the Duke of Burgundy, for God's sake. Mayhap de Lohr has ties and wealth and property, but I have that, too, plus royal blood. Flavian has more elite blood flowing through his veins than any de Lohr can claim. Will you still deny him?"

Robin was struggling to push away the drunkenness and focus on what Riggs was saying. But even he knew, at this point, it was a lost cause. He waved his hand at Riggs in a careless gesture.

"If it were within my power to agree, I would," he said. "But it is not. Though the de Lohr son may be dead, his widowed father has stepped in to replace him. Diara is still betrothed, only now it is to Roi de Lohr himself."

Riggs' eyes widened. "She is?" he said with surprise. "How did that come about?"

"Me!" Robin shouted, smacking himself on the chest. "It was my fault. I did this. When I received word of Beckett's death, I rode to Lioncross Abbey and demanded another de Lohr husband for my daughter. It was Roi who agreed to replace his son."

Riggs was greatly disappointed. "I see," he said. "Then there is no hope?"

Robin snorted. "No hope unless Roi has an accident like his son did."

For a moment, they simply sat there, wallowing in disappointment, until Riggs spoke softly.

"That is always a possibility."

"What is?"

"An accident."

Robin, suddenly, was listening when he realized what Riggs

was saying. He looked at the man in shock before leaning toward him in a curious but restrained manner. "Life is full of possibilities," he said, his eyes glittering. "Do you mean what I think you mean?"

Riggs shrugged. "I simply said that an accident was possible."

"Do you have any ideas, then?"

"Not unless you promise me that my son will marry your daughter."

Robin let his gaze linger on him for a moment, mulling over the mere suggestion. It hadn't even crossed his mind that there was a possibility of ridding himself of Roi, but having a partner in crime—someone with the same goals—then, indeed, there might be every possibility. More than that, there might be a real chance. Perhaps he'd wanted a de Lohr husband and had bullied himself into a corner because of it, but he was not a man to sit around and lick his wounds. Wounds would heal.

But death would be permanent.

Perhaps he didn't want to be allied with the House of de Lohr after all.

"Given the change in circumstances, that is a promise I would be willing to make," he said, sitting back and collecting his cup again. "But to arrange such an event—if it could even be done—would be very difficult. Roi is a seasoned knight in the prime of his career. It would not be a simple thing to be rid of him."

Riggs shook his head. "Not by any common method," he agreed. "But for the sake of argument, let us think about the perfect situation for such a man. He is a knight. He fights in the heat of battle. Didn't you say that you spent two years in France with him?"

Robin nodded. "Two very long years," he said. "But Roi was always the first man into battle. If there was fighting going on, he was in the middle of it. He fights with the power of his father and grandfather. He is a great knight."

"Indeed," Riggs agreed. "He would not be where he is today if he was a weak man. But all men do have weaknesses. Mayhap they have a blind spot, or they become too distracted in a fight. It happens."

Robin snorted. "Not with Roi."

"You know this for certain?"

"I do."

Riggs simply nodded, mulling over an idea that was slowly coming to him. He saw something he wanted in the form of Lady Diara. The only obstacle between her and his desires was, in fact, Roi de Lohr. He knew the man, distantly, but they didn't travel in the same circles, mostly because Cirencester, an old title, had once been a distinguished family but now was mostly associated with thieves and cheats. Wealthy thieves and cheats, but thieves and cheats nonetheless. Their army wasn't particularly large, either. Riggs didn't do much with his army other than use it to protect his properties and occasionally hire it out. He'd been known to take money from the French for the use of his men.

But the opportunity to be allied with Cheltenham was one he'd long coveted.

"I'm simply thinking aloud, so do not take any of this to heart, but if I were a man who wanted to be rid of someone like Roi de Lohr, then I might, mayhap, speak to an ally with similar ambitions," he said. "Let's say it's me. Knowing that de Lohr would come to your aid should you need his sword, I would arrange for someone like me to attack your property. Not a real attack, but enough to draw de Lohr into the fight because if he is married to your daughter, then it is his duty to fight for you."

Robin was back to listening closely, practically hanging on Riggs' every word. "Aye," he agreed. "And where should such an attack take place?"

Riggs was very casual about it. "Your property border and mine end near the village of Colesborne," he said. "To me, that might be the perfect—and most reasonable—place to raid. In fact, the area has been in dispute between our families for years. What could be more natural than a skirmish there?"

Robin shook his head. "I do not dispute it," he said. "It *is* mine. But let us say we choose that location. What then?"

Riggs shrugged. "At some point, you would send de Lohr to Colesborne and make sure he was either unprotected or alone, or both," he said. "It would be a simple thing for your ally to ambush de Lohr and make sure he was quite dead. Men die in battle all the time. Once he is dead, the ally would simply pack up and go home, leaving you with a widowed daughter who would bring de Lohr wealth and property with her to a new marriage. But, as I said, I'm simply thinking aloud. It must be the wine talking."

He chuckled, taking a big swallow of wine, when they both knew he wasn't drunk enough to concoct such a wine-nightmare story like that. What he'd suggested had been very calculated.

He knew exactly what he was saying.

"That is a fine story," Robin said, grinning. "One I like very much. Let de Lohr marry her, then. I do not care. But it would be a fine thing for you to send your army to Colesborne sometime very soon. Roi will surely come to defend my lands, and then my daughter shall marry your son by the autumn.

Will he wait that long?"

Riggs' smile was nothing short of pure evil. "He will wait as long as it takes," he said. "But the sooner, the better. I should like your daughter to start providing me with grandsons to carry on the Fairford name."

"She would be honored."

Riggs lifted his cup to salute their scheme, causing Robin to loosen up quite a bit. He'd been drunk and distressed when the man arrived, but now... now, he was far more at ease. Happy, even. Control was returning to him, and that was all that mattered. Roi used to be a friend, but he'd outlived his usefulness when he stopped bending to Robin's will. Now, the man was on borrowed time.

The loss of another de Lohr was in Robin's future.

And Diara's.

CHAPTER SEVEN

Lioncross Abbey

B ECKETT'S FUNERAL WAS surreal.
That was the only way Roi could describe it.

Upon their arrival to his ancestral home, Roi immediately went to the abbey in the sub-levels beneath the keep. It was in the dark recesses of the abbey portion of the castle where they stored things, mostly foodstuffs or other things in need of cold spaces. But the truth was that they also stored bodies down there, if needed, because it was the perfect environment. It was cold and surprisingly dry.

This was where Roi found his only son.

He left Diara and her cousin in the great hall of Lioncross and proceeded to visit his son alone, something Diara had encouraged him to do from the onset. He was coming to see, if nothing else, that she was a very understanding and compassionate individual, more than likely because she'd received none of those things whilst fostering during her formative years. In fact, Diara seemed to be quite sensitive to what he was feeling or what his needs might be, as she had demonstrated on the entire journey from Cheltenham.

It had been a two-day journey that passed pleasantly enough in spite of what they had left behind and what they were moving toward. They had only discussed Robin twice, and that was shortly after they left Cicadia. Roi was half expecting the man to send his knights out after him, but no army and no knights were forthcoming. That was both a relief and a concern to Roi, who was more than certain Robin had not completely surrendered. At least he could see the knights and fight them accordingly, but he worried about what he couldn't see. He suspected the worst was yet to come where Robin le Bec was concerned.

And then there was Diara.

Taking her away from her father and her home, Roi presumed that he would begin to see what she was truly made of. The past two days had been spent in the comfort of her own home, a place that she was familiar with, so taking her on the road with him was a big change for her. He wondered if it would be a dose of reality for them both about this marriage and what they were truly about to face, but over the course of those two days of travel, he saw nothing that indicated any kind of change in heart with her.

In fact, he saw quite the opposite.

Diara seemed to blossom away from her father. Astride a small gray palfrey and with her cousin at her side, she kept up a running stream of chatter that was quite enchanting. It passed the time beautifully, so much so that Roi was sorry when the day of travel ended and they had to find shelter for the night. They found it in a small tavern on the edge of Hereford, a place he had been to before, since it was within his father's lands, but he quickly discovered that Diara had never been to a tavern in her life.

He quite enjoyed watching the situation through her eyes.

She was someone who was truly interested in people. She didn't look at them and see the rich and the poor, the slovenly and the well dressed, but rather she looked at them as individuals. As she had commented to Roi more than once, everyone had a story, and she liked to hear of other people's perspectives and their experiences. Even when they were sitting at the table in the tavern, enjoying their supper, she ended up talking to a merchant at the next table because the man was wearing exotic robes that were quite lovely, and she was curious about them. The man ended up at their table, buying their entire meal for them, as he told her about his travels from the Holy Land.

It was enough to nearly keep her up all night, but just after midnight, long after most people had gone to bed, Roi finally forced her to end the conversation so she could get some sleep. He had done it in a kind way, and she was very sweet about it, but she had been sad for the evening to end. He was coming to see that she was simply naturally curious about everything, and hearing of the merchant's travels had given her more perspective of the world in general. For someone who had spent her life at essentially only two locations—and one of them had not exactly been pleasant—Roi could see that she hungered for knowledge and the world at large.

And that had given him an idea.

Since he didn't have anything terribly pressing in the near future, he decided that he would take her on a wedding trip after they were married. He had traveled to many places over the course of his lifetime, so the thought of travel wasn't of great interest to him—but he knew it would be to her. He wanted to take her to France, and he wanted to take her to a beautiful lake known as *Lac du Lausanne* that was surrounded by soaring mountains and beautiful scenery. Knowing how much she seemed to like new and interesting things, he decided she would love such a place.

If she was by his side, so would he.

Spending time with her had given him some respite from his grief over the loss of Beckett. When he was with her, she lightened his heart in so many ways. It was only when he was alone that he thought about his son and the future that would never be. When they arrived at Lioncross and he went straight into the undercroft, he sat next to Beckett's casket for a full hour before he even made any attempt to look at his son inside. He sat there and thought about the young man that he'd never fully come to know, or the more mature man that he would never witness, the great knight and the husband and the father that would never be.

He missed those things he would never know.

He knew his son was young and arrogant and had dreams of grandeur. That had never been a question. Beckett had been heavily trained at Selbourne Castle in the laws of the land, hoping that he would follow in his father's footsteps. Beckett seemed to think that his knowledge of the law would set him aside from other men, and, in truth, it did to a certain extent. He assumed that there was no reason that he would not be as great as his father and grandfather, and that had reflected in his manner. Lord de Nerra, his liege and mentor, had commented on that fact to Roi more than once. They both knew that they were dealing with an extremely bright and extremely prideful young man, and they both assumed that age and wisdom would temper his pride somewhat.

Now, that would never be.

It was all of these things that Roi grieved over as he sat next to his son's casket. When it finally came time to lift the lid and look at his son's face, he did it without hesitation. What greeted him was nothing horrific; Beckett looked as if he was sleeping, except for the fact that he had a giant bruise on his forehead and his skin was as white as snow. However, it also had a greenish cast to it, as did his ears, his fingers, and the tip of his nose.

That was the only hint of death.

Roi wept softly as he put his hand on his son's head. He could see exactly what had happened and exactly how Beckett had broken his neck. The proof was in front of him, and it was a difficult thing to accept. He stood next to the casket for another hour, his tears falling on his son as he spoke to him softly and told him just how much he was going to miss him. He also told him of Diara and how he hoped Beckett would wish him well. He asked Beckett to take excellent care of his mother, who had been alone these many years. Roi rejoiced in the knowledge that Beckett and Odette were finally together again.

To be truthful, it was the only thing that kept him from collapsing into complete despair.

With the lid of the coffin still removed, he went to sit down again because he was emotionally and physically exhausted. He couldn't see Beckett's face from where he sat, but he could see his son's hands, as they were placed over his chest. Somebody had tied them together to keep them from falling away. He lost track of time as he sat there, lost in memories, until he heard faint footsteps approach.

"Roi?"

It was Christopher. Roi took a deep, ragged breath and looked up to see his father standing a few feet away. When their eyes met, Christopher smiled faintly.

"Your mother has sent me to see how you are faring," he said quietly. "She wanted to make sure you did not require anything."

Roi returned his gaze to the open casket. He shook his head unsteadily, finally lifting his hands in a gesture that suggested he didn't know what he needed.

"Nay," he said, his voice dull with grief. "I do not require anything. But tell me something, Papa."

"If I can."

"How would you feel if you were sitting in my place and I was in that casket?"

Christopher sighed heavily. "Distraught," he said. "I would feel what you are feeling. Utter agony and distress."

Roi knew that. He really didn't even know why he had asked, only that he was looking for some commiseration.

"Mama told me about the child you lost before Christin was born," he said. "Other than that, you've never really lost anyone close to you, have you?"

Christopher moved to sit down next to his son, on a stone bench that jutted out from the wall. "Nay," he said truthfully. "But only by God's grace. I've lost knights and friends. I've lost my parents. But I have never lost a living child or even a brother, thankfully. I have been very fortunate."

Roi was still looking at his son. "How do I recover from this?" he asked. "I told Mama that I did not think I would survive this, but I will. I know I will. But survival is not recovery. How do I *recover* from this?"

Christopher put his hand on the man's shoulder. "By remembering what you do have as opposed to what you have lost," he said. "You have Adalia and Dorian. They are upstairs right now, and they need you. And you have a kind young woman who is about to be your wife. Lad, sometimes when God takes something away, he gives us something in return. He would not leave you completely alone in your hour of pain."

Roi thought on the ray of sunshine he'd brought with him, who was up in the hall at this very moment, and he could feel his heart lighten at the mere idea.

"Mayhap," he said. "You have never met Diara before, have you?"

Christopher shook his head. "Nay," he said. "But your mother likes her already. That is a good sign."

Roi smiled weakly. "It is," he said. "Mama is very selective about the women she likes."

"True," Christopher said. "Especially those marrying her sons. I feel some pity for them, to tell you the truth."

Roi's very nearly chuckled at the thought of his tough-as-iron mother inspecting women meant for her sons. "Diara can hold her own against Mama," he said. "She is a very amiable person."

"I know," Christopher said. "I've seen it. I've spent the last few hours speaking to her, and before I realized it, I told her nearly everything about my time in the Levant. She managed to get it out of me, and I did not even know it."

That made Roi laugh. "You do not easily speak on those things."

"I do not."

"She has a way about her, doesn't she?"

Christopher nodded firmly. "She's enchanting without being pretentious, and that, my son, is a gift," he said. "King-doms go to war over women like that. Cheltenham knows what he has in her, but I must admit, I cannot believe such a woman is Robin le Bec's daughter. A man like that... I should not expect such an affable child."

Roi's smile faded. "I have not had the opportunity to tell you what happened when we left Cheltenham," he said. "Robin was not—"

Christopher held up a hand to stop him. "Say no more," he said. "Lady Diara told me everything."

Roi looked surprised. "She did?" he said. "What did she say?"

"That Robin tripped and hurt himself just as you were preparing to leave," Christopher said. "That is why he did not come."

Roi realized that Diara probably had to tell his father something about Robin's absence, so she gave him the same story they had both agreed upon. With regret, he sighed and averted his gaze.

"She had to tell you that," he said. "She was protecting me."

Christopher frowned. "Protect you from what?"

Roi cleared his throat softly. "Robin was being difficult," he said. "I wanted to bring Diara to Beckett's funeral, but he demanded I marry her first. I told him I did not wish to because, until my son is buried, my focus will be on him, and that is not fair to a new wife. But Robin did not see it that way. He said some fairly distasteful things about Beckett, so I struck him."

Christopher wasn't surprised to hear that, but he still shook his head with regret. "Hard?"

"Hard enough to knock him cold," Roi said. "When he awoke, Diara told him that he tripped and hit his face on the table. I am sure he does not believe that, but Diara told her mother the same story, and, as you have seen, the lady can be quite convincing when she wants to be."

"She does not want her father to know you struck him."

Roi shook his head slowly. "Nay."

"He could have you punished."

"Possibly."

"Then I like her already, because she has tried to protect you," Christopher said. "Not that I condone striking Cheltenham, even though the man undoubtedly deserved it, but I like that she would do what is necessary to protect you from his wrath. That is a good woman."

Roi nodded. "I think so," he said quietly. "Papa... I have spent the past four days with her, and I have come to a conclusion that makes me feel quite guilty."

"About what?"

Roi stood up and went to his son's casket, looking down at that pale face. "About the fact that I do not think Beckett would have been a good husband for her," he said. "She is far more mature and responsible than he was. Mayhap he would have grown into it, but he simply wasn't ready for marriage. He lacked the sense of maturity that it requires, and poor Diara would have been married to a man who was not as sensible or wise as she was. That would have made for a sad marriage, indeed."

"But why do you feel guilty?"

Roi looked at him. "Because I am glad he didn't marry her," he said. "She is a much better match for me."

A smile tugged at the corner of Christopher's mouth. "Can I assume that you are pleased with this betrothal?"

"Very much so."

"You were not so certain when you told Robin that you would assume the contract in Beckett's stead."

"I did not know her at the time. She is perfect."

"As perfect as Odette?"

Roi shrugged. "Odette was completely different," he said. "We were both young when we married, and there were times I was more like her father than her husband. She would not make a decision without me. She would hardly make a move without me. She was kind and educated and accomplished, but she was very much a helpless creature. Diara is most certainly not a helpless creature."

Christopher sat back against the stone wall behind him. "Does she remind you of someone in that respect?"

"Who?"

"Your mother, mayhap?"

Roi thought on that for a moment. "A little," he said. "I am not ashamed to admit that the older I have become, the more I like a woman who is not a poor, fragile flower. I like a woman with a little fire and the sense to control it."

"You see that in Diara?"

"I do. And I think she and Beckett would have made each other miserable."

Christopher stood up and went to him, standing next to his son as he gazed down at his grandson.

"Mayhap," he said. "But it is nothing you should feel guilty over. Everything happens the way it should in God's good time. Not to say that Beckett's death has been something welcome, because it most certainly has not been. I'm simply saying that it was God's will, and he is infinite in his wisdom. Knowing how distraught you would be, he has given you someone to ease your pain. It is up to you what you do with her."

Roi knew what his father was trying to say. He was trying to see something good in all of this. Roi wasn't sure if he could, but he could try. He *would* try. There was nothing more he could do, as his father had said, than look at what he had as opposed to what he had lost.

He had Diara.

"Thank you, Papa," he said. "For your wisdom and advice. I would be lost without it."

Christopher patted him on the shoulder and began to head back the way he'd come. "Your mother wishes to know if you will be attending the meal this evening," he said. "I can just as easily have food sent down to you."

Roi returned to the stone bench. "That would be best," he said. "I am going to spend the night here with my son. We shall bury him in the morning."

"The grave is already dug."

"Thank you," Roi said. "But I should like to complete this vigil alone, please. I know my brothers mean well, but I do not want any company."

"Understood."

"And the horse that threw Beckett—did it return with him?"

"It did."

"If Curtis does not want it returned to him, then please sell it. I do not want it."

"As you wish."

As his father turned to walk away, Roi stopped him. "Papa," he said. "Please have Diara bring the food down to me. I may like to have her sit with me for a while."

But Christopher shook his head. "She will not come."

Roi looked at him, surprised. "Why not?"

"Because your mother already suggested she bring some food to you after we arrived, but she refused," Christopher said. "Politely, of course, but she would not come. She said that this is your time with Beckett, and she has no intention of encroaching on that time. She said that this day belongs to just the two of you."

Roi smiled faintly. "She is a considerate woman," he said. "One of the many things I am coming to appreciate about her."

Christopher smiled in return. "Me too."

With that, he headed back up the stairs that led from the abbey's undercroft. Roi continued to sit there, hearing his father's footfalls fade away, before returning his focus to Beckett.

But his thoughts were lingering on Diara.

It was enough to keep the smile on his face, at least for a short while. The fact that she should be so considerate was something he simply wasn't used to. Someone who was thinking of his feelings, of his thoughts. Instead of insisting she be the center of attention, even in a situation like this, Diara was perfectly happy to be in the background while Roi dealt with a life-changing situation.

He would never be able to thank her enough for it.

That would have to wait, however, because today, as she'd said, was only for Roi and Beckett, and he was content with that. Roi remained in the undercroft all night, sometimes speaking to his son of memories past, sometimes praying for his soul. Once, he even spoke to Odette to ask her to take good care of Beckett. He hoped she was proud of their son for what he'd accomplished in his short lifetime. Certainly, he was positive that she was.

When morning finally came and his brothers appeared to help him take Beckett into the chapel of Lioncross Abbey, Roi was at the head of the casket as Beckett's uncles carefully carried him across the bailey to the old chapel, where a grave had been dug in the spot that Roi had selected. Roi himself helped lower his son into his final resting place, and he even helped replace the dirt that had been disturbed, covering the casket up.

Sealing Beckett away for all eternity.

The entire time, Diara had been well to the rear of the group, making sure the family was close to their young son and nephew and grandson without her getting in the way. She simply stood back and let the de Lohr family grieve. If Roi hadn't been falling for her before that time, seeing how she conducted herself at the funeral had him thinking that he never wanted to be without that woman by his side, not ever. He was starting to get a glimpse of just how decent of a human being she was.

Beckett's funeral changed everything.

CHAPTER EIGHT

"GOOD HEAVENS," DIARA said, throwing her hands up into the air. "I swear to you that I am not armed, my lord. I have no weapons. May I pass?"

She had just walked into the ladies' solar of Lioncross Abbey and straight into an ambush. She'd made the mistake of traveling alone because Iris wasn't feeling well, so she'd left the woman in her bed. That meant she was moving about unattended, and currently, she was being held hostage by three small boys, sons of Roi's middle sister, Rebecca. The boys had wooden swords in their hands, all of them pointed at Diara, and they were unfortunately being egged on by older cousins, sons of Roi's youngest sister, a woman known to the family as Honey. Diara had met most of the de Lohr family over the past few days, with all of them coming to Lioncross for Beckett's funeral but now remaining for Roi's marriage.

That was where there was some trouble.

Not with Roi's siblings, for all of them were very kind to Diara, and she felt happy and comfortable with them. It had taken her about a day to endear herself to the brothers with her sweet manner and witty conversation, and the women followed closely. Roi had four sisters—Christin, Brielle, Rebecca, and Honey, but Diara hadn't yet met Brielle. The others, however, were positively delightful. Christin had seemed particularly difficult to win over because she was very protective of Roi, but in the end, even she gave her approval.

Then came the grandchildren of Christopher and Dustin.

There were quite a few of them, from toddlers up to grown men. It was the grown men that Diara was having some difficulty with, in particular, Honey's sons. Gallus, Maximus, and Tiberius de Shera were close to Beckett's age, and the boys had all grown up together, meaning they weren't very happy about Uncle Roi marrying Beckett's intended. They'd been grumbling about it, something most of the adults except their mother had ignored, and Honey had told them to shut their lips or feel her wrath.

That wasn't exactly how Diara wanted to win them over.

Now, she was standing in an unexpected position in the ladies' solar with Rebecca's young sons trying to ambush her. She could see Gallus, Maximus, and Tiberius back in the shadows of the solar, drinking and snorting at the antics. Diara was fairly certain she wouldn't get any help from them, so she tried to reason with the three hooligans in front of her—seven-year-old twins and another boy who had seen five years.

Vaughn, James, and Westley had her cornered.

"You may not pass!" Vaughn barked. "What do you have?"

Diara had a spool of thread in her hand, and she held it out so they could see it. "I've come to look for red thread," she said. "Your grandmother told me she keeps it in here. May I go and find it?"

Vaughn frowned and took the spool from her, inspecting it. "Don't you have any money?"

Diara shook her head. "I am sorry, I do not."

That seemed to confuse the older boys, who looked at each other. "But we need money," James said. "Bring us some money and we will give you back your spool."

Diara shook her head. "I'm afraid I have no money," she said. "May I have my spool back?"

The boys weren't sure what to do at this point. They looked at one another, puzzled, and the five-year-old finally set his sword aside and started picking his nose. He'd quickly grown bored of the ambush. As he wandered off, leaving the twins to decide Diara's fate, one of older cousins emerged from the shadows.

Diara recognized Tiberius de Shera on sight. He was tall and slender, with gleaming eyes that always suggested he was in on a joke. She'd been introduced to him prior to Beckett's funeral, but he hadn't spoken to her since that time. In fact, he seemed to make a point of staying away from her. He reached down to pick up the wooden sword that the five-year-old had dropped before looking at Diara in a rather appraising manner.

"I think she does have money," he said, speaking to the twins. "Her father is the Earl of Cheltenham. He's very rich."

The twins looked at Diara in surprise. "You *do* have money?" Vaughn asked, outraged that she would lie to him. "Where is it? I want some!"

But Diara shook her head. "I do not have any with me," she said. "I did not bring any money, so I'm afraid I cannot give you any. Moreover, I would not give you money to reward you for your thievery. It is a naughty thing that you are doing."

"So is stealing another husband," Tiberius said, the gleam in his eyes fading.

"Ty," one of the men behind him said. "Enough."

"Nay, it is *not* enough," Tiberius said, his eyes fixed on Diara. "You *do* know that Beckett was supposed to be your husband, don't you?"

Diara was immediately on her guard with what sounded like an accusation. "Of course I do."

"Then why take his father?" Tiberius demanded. "I heard what happened. I heard that your father came here and demanded Uncle Roi marry you in place of Beckett. Why did you do it?"

Diara could have flamed at the young knight, who was quite a bit taller and larger than she was, but she kept her composure. She didn't want to fight with an emotional young man who clearly misunderstood the situation.

"I did not do anything," she said evenly. "It was my father's doing, without any prompting from me. I know you are asking because you loved your cousin, and I respect that. It must be wonderful to have family and cousins that you love so dearly. But I did not have anything to do with the marriage contract or what happened with it. Women usually don't."

Tiberius hadn't been prepared for that polite answer to his nasty query. He turned to look at his brothers seated behind him, but they gave him no indication of what they were thinking. In fact, one of them simply looked away as if he wanted nothing to do with whatever was going on. Seeing he had little support in the matter, Tiberius returned his attention to Diara.

"Didn't you love Beckett?" Tiberius asked seriously. "How could you even think of marrying someone else, much less his father?"

"That is none of your affair, Tiberius."

Roi was suddenly in the doorway, looking at Tiberius in a

decidedly unfriendly fashion. Behind Tiberius, his brothers stood up and came forward, rallying around their brother now that their uncle, and Beckett's father, was in the room. They all had a healthy fear of Uncle Roi, and for good reason.

"He did not mean any disrespect, Uncle Roi," Gallus, the eldest, said quietly. "But it's what we're all thinking. I am sorry if that is upsetting, but it is."

Roi's piercing gaze moved to his sister's eldest boy. "So you think to corner her and interrogate her?" he said. "Over something that is none of your affair? How rude and arrogant of you to assume she owes you any answers at all. She doesn't owe you a thing, and I am ashamed that you should think so."

"But... but she belongs to Beckett," Tiberius said before Gallus could stop him. "How could you... *Why* did you... She belongs to your son!"

Roi would have been extremely angry except for one thing—he knew that Beckett and Tiberius had been close. He'd seen Tiberius weeping at the funeral, heartbroken by the loss of his cousin. Taking that into account, he went to Tiberius and put his hand on the young man's shoulder.

"Ty," he said, considerably softer. "I know you are over-wrought with Beckett's death. I understand that completely. But your grief is making you lash out at someone who does not deserve it. Lady Diara was indeed pledged to Beckett, but she is not his widow. She was never married to him at all. With Beckett dead, surely you cannot expect her never to marry at all. But there is indeed a marriage contract, and her father asked if another de Lohr male would fulfill it. Since I am Beckett's father, it is my duty to marry her in my son's stead. But let me be clear—she had nothing to do with my decision. She is innocent in all of this, so you will treat her with all due respect.

For my sake."

Tiberius had backed down considerably. After a moment, he hung his head and nodded. Roi patted him on the cheek before looking to his brothers behind him.

"That goes for all of you," he said. "Lady Diara is worthy of our respect and love. If you spend any time around her, I think you will see why."

Gallus and the middle brother, Maximus, simply nodded, looking to Diara, who was standing there with an anxious expression on her face. Gallus looked at Maximus, feeling that perhaps they should apologize to the lady, when Vaughn, who was still in the chamber, came up behind Roi and tugged on his tunic. Roi looked down to see his nephew pulling on him.

"What do you want?" he asked. "And why are you in the ladies' solar?"

Vaughn held up the wooden sword in his hand. "We came to find money," he said. "Do you have money?"

Roi took the sword out of the child's hand, turned him for the door, and spanked him right on the buttocks with his big, hard hand.

"Not for you," he said as Vaughn yelped. "Get out of here before I beat you, you little thief. And I'd better not catch you trying to steal money anymore. Do you hear me?"

Vaughn fled the chamber in tears with James on his tail, but not before he handed the spool of thread back to Diara. They could hear the boys wailing as they ran down the hall, which brought giggles from Tiberius and Gallus. They were always in approval of anything that made the younger boys weep. But Roi looked at them, and their smiles instantly vanished.

"As for the rest of you," he said, "unless you have any further business here, leave the ladies' solar. You do not belong here."

Properly rebuked, the three of them departed the solar without another glance to Diara. Once they were gone, their footsteps fading away, Roi finally turned his attention to Diara.

"I do apologize," he said, smiling weakly. "They were attached to Beckett, particularly Tiberius. I had a feeling they might say something to you."

Diara shook her head. "They are grieving," she said. "I know that."

"You are gracious, my lady."

"It is simply a matter of understanding why they are asking such questions," she said. "It is not because they are wicked. It is because they loved your son. I understand that."

She smiled, and Roi felt himself grow weak in the knees. Every day that passed saw him drawn more and more to Diara until he couldn't think of anything else. It had been a very strange week, burying his son and preparing for a wedding. Part of him grieved Beckett's loss on an hourly basis, but part of him was also excited for the coming nuptials to a woman who seemed to occupy his thoughts constantly. With his mother planning everything, a wedding of vast proportions was coming together at the end of the week. Cheltenham had been notified and invited, but he had yet to arrive. He even had yet to respond. But Roi wasn't going to let that put a damper on things.

He hadn't been this happy in years.

"Ty and Beckett were very much alike," he said, moving in her direction. "I know Ty did not mean to be disrespectful, but I could not let him speak to you like that. I hope you understand."

Diara's smile grew as he drew closer. "I do," she said. "But I was not offended. Thank you for coming to my rescue, however. It was quite noble of you."

Roi reached out and took her hand as he came near, bringing it to his lips for a gentle kiss. "I told you that I would defend you to the death," he said. "I meant it. Even against nosy nephews."

Diara let herself feel the thrill of his lips against her hand, something she'd been indulging in since he'd done it the first time back at Cicadia. He never went any further, however, though the pull between them was more than either one of them could bear. In fact, at this very moment, that magnetism was causing Diara's breathing to come in unsteady gasps. She was focused on his soft lips, wondering what they would feel like against hers.

"Roi?" she said softly.

His lips were still against her hand. "What is it, angel?"

"Do you remember when I told you that I'd never been kissed?"

"I do."

"I am ready for that moment whenever you are."

He stopped kissing her hand and looked at her, a smile playing on his lips. "I have been ready for quite some time," he said. "But therein lies the problem."

"What problem?"

"I am afraid that if I kiss you, I will not be able to stop."

She bit her lip to keep from smiling. "Then you never intend to kiss me?"

He shook his head. "I intend to kiss you several times a day once we are married," he said. "But it is the same reason why I will not take you in my arms right now. I know that if I do, I will never let you go."

"Never?"

"Never," he confirmed. "It would, therefore, be best if we waited until our wedding before I kiss you or hold you. Because once I have you, dear lady, you are mine forever and I will never, ever release you. God himself could not pry you away from me."

"Then you are concerned for your self-control."

"Absolutely," he said. "I do not wish to compromise you before I am entitled to do so under the eyes of God. Are you agreeable to wait? It will only be another day."

Diara wasn't. Truly, she wasn't at all. One day wouldn't make a difference to her because the man made her knees weak and her heart race. There was nothing about him that didn't make her entire body feel like jelly, feelings no man had ever given her. And he wanted to wait? She was positively averse to the idea. Nay, she didn't want to wait. Everything in her body screamed for the man. Even her never-before-kissed lips. They wanted to know what they were missing. Therefore, her answer was to throw her arms around his neck and slant her lips over his.

Diara had thrown herself at him so hard that Roi grunted with the force of it. She'd essentially slammed her body against his, and, unprepared, he staggered a little as she latched on to him. But his surprise was only momentary, for the moment her lips touched his, he was lost as he knew he would be.

Instinct took over.

His arms went around her, holding her against him as he feasted on her. All of the restraint he'd shown in the past few days, fighting off urges that were reawakening deep within himself, were blown to cinders the moment she touched him and he knew that his fears had been immediately confirmed.

He couldn't let her go.

She was soft and sweet and delicious in his arms. She was also very eager, but it was clear within the first few moments that she was inexperienced. All she'd ever known in her lifetime had been chaste kisses, from relatives. She'd never known anything passionate, kisses the way a woman was supposed to kiss a man, so Roi took his time with her. She was new to this and clearly wanted to learn, so he kissed her gently, suckling her lips, showing her what was pleasurable, and then delighted when she mimicked him.

Introducing his tongue into the mix was something different. Men and women tasted one another because it enhanced the passion and power of the gesture, so he showed her what it meant to be licked in between kisses, something very gentle and discreet, before prying her lips open and snaking his tongue over hers. She didn't pull away, but she was unsure at first. He felt her tense. But it was for only a brief moment until she realized that she liked it.

Then she couldn't get enough of him.

Roi was fully prepared to pull her into a corner and ravage her, but he began to hear voices—female voices—and suddenly let her go, pointing in the direction of the sounds, and she quickly understood. Staggering over to a chair because her knees were so wobbly, Diara nearly fell into it, landing on her bottom, giggling uncontrollably because she was so lightheaded from their encounter. Roi grinned, putting a finger to his lips in a silencing gesture, as he put distance between them. It was just in time, too, as Dustin and one of her daughters, Christin, entered the solar. They were followed by two very young girls who happened to be Christin's granddaughters, children of her eldest son.

"Diara!" Dustin said in surprise. "I thought we'd lost you, lass. Where have you been? Did you find the thread?"

Diara realized she was still holding the spool, and she bolted up from the chair. "I am afraid I was prevented from doing so, my lady," she said. "When I arrived, three young boys demanded money from me, and it was a standoff until Roi came to my rescue."

It was then that the women noticed Roi at nearly the other end of the chamber. As the small girls began to run toward the table with the paints on it, as they loved to paint with their grandmother in the sunny chamber, Dustin looked at her second-eldest son with concern.

"Who was it?" she asked unhappily. "Wait—let me guess. Vaughn and James, wasn't it? They did the same thing to Honey yesterday, and they actually poked her with one of those swords."

Roi stepped out of the shadows, toward his mothers. "If Rebecca does not do something about those thieves now, she is going to have trouble with them when they grow older," he said. "But it wasn't only them. Gallus and Maximus and Tiberius were in here, as well. Ty was rather... rude to Diara."

Dustin's eyes widened, and she looked to Diara, who immediately shook her head. "They were not exactly rude," she assured her quickly. "At least, I did not think so, but Roi's opinion differs. It is simply a matter of perception, truly. They were... They spoke of..."

"They wanted to know how she could marry me after being betrothed to Beckett," Roi finished for her. "Really, Mama, they were asking questions that were none of their affair. You had better tell Honey to curb her boys before I do. It would be less painful coming from her."

Dustin sighed heavily and shook her head. "Ty has been rumbling about that all day," she said, looking to Diara apologetically. "I did not think he would actually speak to you about it."

Diara shrugged. "I am sure that he spoke from a place of love for Beckett," she said. "I sense that he somehow views me still as Beckett's property."

"It is none of his affair," Christin stepped in, eyeing her mother. "Ty has a loose tongue. Roi, I do not blame you if you take him to task over this. And what was he doing in the ladies' solar, anyway? This is not a place for him. It must have made Diara feel terribly uncomfortable."

Diara looked at the eldest de Lohr sibling, a beautiful woman with dark hair and her mother's gray eyes. Her husband, Alexander de Sherrington, had been Christopher's right-hand man for many years, a man of great reputation and talent. Sherry, as he was called, was in the north with two of their sons, trying to broker some kind of peace treaty for Henry between two warring barons, leaving his wife and remaining children and grandchildren at Lioncross. Truth be told, Christin was firm, unapologetic, and had a strong way about her. She was no shrinking violet, a strong woman for an equally strong man.

Diara smiled at her when their eyes met.

"You are kind to worry over my feelings, but truly, it was no trouble," Diara said. "I think it is a natural question. Beckett is gone, and, suddenly, I'm marrying his father. It is puzzling."

"That is true, but it is still none of their affair," Christin said. "You are gracious for not being angry about it."

Diara's smile broadened. "I am trying to get along with all of the de Lohrs and their offspring," she said. "Anger has no place until I know them better and can back that anger up with a club."

Christin started laughing. "I have no doubt that you would," she said. But then she looked at Roi. "Speaking of clubs, did Curtis tell you what has been planned for your wedding celebration?"

Roi frowned. "Christ," he muttered. "Do I want to know?"

Christin was grinning. "You should probably be fore-warned," she said. "I heard him speaking with Douglas and West about having some games to celebrate. The usual games, with balls and sticks. You used to be fairly good at them."

Roi rolled his eyes. "I am still good at them," he said. "But I will be a new husband, and I do not want to be crippled when I have a new wife, and those fools will try to take me out by the knees and laugh because they will have ruined my... Well, it will be difficult to be a husband. In the usual way."

He was digging himself into a hole trying to describe how difficult it would be to make love to his new wife with busted knees. He started to snort, unable to go any further, but Christin and Dustin knew what he meant even if Diara really didn't.

"I would not worry," Dustin said, smiling at her embar-rassed son. "Your father will not compete, so it will only be Curtis, Douglas, West, and a few of the others."

Roi pointed a finger at her. "It is those 'few others' I worry about," he said, counting them off on his fingers. "Ty, Gallus, Maximus, Chris, William, and Arthur. Thank God Myles and his sons are not here and that Sherry and his sons are up north. And Cassius... If Brielle and her brood were here, including her beast of a husband, I would not play altogether. Cass will go for the kill."

Dustin and Christin were laughing, but Diara looked at him

curiously. "Brielle is another sister, isn't she?" she asked.

Roi nodded. "The one you haven't met," he said. "Christin is the eldest, followed by Brielle. Her husband rode the tournament circuit professionally for years, and he's positively unbeatable in nearly everything. He's also a de Velt, which means he comes from a dynasty built on blood lust."

"And you have many nephews that could compete in these games?" Diara asked.

Roi shook his head sadly. "Many," he said. "Too many to name. Trust me when I say that there are too many de Lohrs, and all of them love to best one another in games of competition. If Curtis has games planned for our wedding celebration, I can promise you that they are out to do damage."

"But why should they want to?"

"Because you don't know my family. We would kill for one another, but we are also quite competitive with each other."

"He is making it sound worse than it is," Dustin said. "Do not listen to him, Diara. In fact, let us speak on something more pleasant. I was hoping you could go up to my chamber and ask my maid for the Dublin lace. I wanted to show it to you. Will you fetch it and bring it back?"

Diara nodded, already heading for the door. "Of course, Lady Hereford," she said, pointing to the ceiling. "On the top floor?"

"Aye," Dustin said. "Roi, go with her. Help her navigate this enormous place."

With a smile playing on his lips, still thinking about bruised kneecaps and gloating brothers, Roi took Diara's hand and led her out into the corridor. She beamed at him, holding his big hand with both of hers, gazing up at him adoringly. Roi was so busy watching her and not where he was going that he nearly

ran into a wall. As they laughed softly at one another, completely caught up in the romance that had become their lives, Roi
caught sight of his eldest brother near the entrance to the keep.

"Can you find my mother's chamber on your own?" he
asked, eyes on Curtis. "I should like to speak with my brother."

Diara could see where his attention was. "About the wedding celebration?"

"Aye," Roi said, kissing her hand before letting it go. "I feel
the need to make a few things clear to him about his plans. No
clubs, no targeting my knees. Or anyone else's."

Diara giggled. "Go," she said. "I will see you later."

He glanced rather seductively at her. "You surely will."

He winked at her and was gone. Diara watched him go,
sighing rather dreamily. But she shook herself of the day-
dreams, so deliriously happy for the first time in her life. It was
as if Roi de Lohr had opened up an entirely new world to her,
one with a big family of people who were kind to her, and most
importantly, of women who were kind to her. That was
something of an anomaly in her world. A marriage she was
dreading, at least at first, had turned into something she was
looking forward to more than she could express. Everything
about Roi made her sing.

Especially her heart.

The stairs in the keep of Lioncross were wide, at a rather
low angle, so it seemed to take some time to make it from floor
to floor. She wasn't paying much attention to her trip up the
stairs, still thinking about Roi, still daydreaming over him. She
eventually reached the second floor, knowing Lady Hereford's
chambers to be on the top floor where there was the best view,
but as she headed up the next flight of stairs, she could hear
voices in the stairwell below her. She wasn't entirely sure, but

she thought it might have been Tiberius again. She was coming to recognize his voice.

"… and I am telling you that she has bewitched Uncle Roi," he was saying. "You saw how he scolded me. You saw the look in his eye. That Cheltenham chit has done something to the man. He was prepared to kill me."

"It is quite possible that he is simply happy," another voice said. "You cannot blame the man. He's been alone for so long, and now he has a pretty young lass to warm his bed? Of course he's happy. You should be happy for him."

"Uncle Roi loved Aunt Odette deeply," Tiberius said, sounding snappish. "She is the only woman for him. The only wife he ever needed, a fine and gentle creature. And now that le Bec bitch has schemed her way into his bed. Uncle West told me that she has a loose reputation, if you know what I mean. Apparently she is not a stranger to spreading her legs."

"Is that what you think she did to Uncle Roi?"

"It has to be," Tiberius said. "Why else would he want her so badly? She ensnared Beckett somehow, and when he died, she went after his father. Let us face the facts, lads—Uncle Roi is marrying a whore."

The voices faded away after that. Diara was frozen on the stairwell above them, her eyes filling with tears. Ashamed and horrified, she went back down the stairs and down another corridor, running blindly in a castle she wasn't familiar with. All she knew was that she had to get out of there.

She found a stairwell and rushed down the stone steps, too fast, and ended up slipping at the bottom and scraping her hand. Those stairs led to the kitchens, and she rushed through the steamy room, past people she wouldn't look at, and out into the kitchen yard beyond.

But she kept going.

The stables were attached to the kitchen yard, and she entered the stables from a small door at the end of the block. Immediately, she was hit with the smell of horses and hay and urine. But she kept moving, weeping, wiping at her face, until she came to the other end of the stable block and could go no more. There was a ladder here that led up to the loft, and she climbed up into it, shielded from the world around her.

Plopping down into the hay, she sobbed.

It wasn't enough that Roi's nephews were opposed to her marrying their uncle, but it was like a stab to the gut to hear that Roi's own brother had been speaking on the rumors that had followed her ever since her days at Carisbrooke. How were she and Roi supposed to start a life together if his family thought she was a whore who had ensnared him? Surely Lady Hereford and her daughters had heard the rumors, too, and although they were friendly to her, what on earth were they saying behind her back?

It was just so incredibly hurtful to hear such things. Diara was beginning to wonder if she simply shouldn't leave for home and stop dreaming that a marriage to Roi was even possible, because no matter where she went, the rumors would follow. No matter whom she married, surely, they would hear such things.

It simply wasn't fair.

As she sat in the hayloft and sniffled, a head suddenly popped up at the top of the ladder. Startled, Diara found herself looking at a young girl.

"Are you well?" the girl asked timidly. "I saw you run through. Are you hurt?"

Diara knew Roi's youngest daughter, Dorian, on sight. She

had been introduced to both Adalia and Dorian when she arrived at Lioncross, but the girls had made themselves scarce and she hadn't seen them since. Adalia evidently liked to spend all of her time tending to the youngest de Lohr grand- and great-grandchildren, and Dorian had spent all of her time in the stable. Roi had mentioned that the lass was mad for horses and the stable was her favorite place in the world, so rather than force the girls to get to know their future stepmother, he'd simply left them where they were the happiest. They'd just lost a brother, and he wanted them to remain where they were most comfortable for now. Time with Diara would come later, when they were ready.

Diara understood that, and she agreed with him, but the result was that she didn't know her future stepdaughters at all. She didn't even know how much she should say to them, or not say to them, so she quickly wiped at her face and tried to force a smile.

"I am well, thank you for asking," she said. "You are Lady Dorian, are you not?"

Dorian nodded. She was a tall girl for her age, with dark hair and her father's blue eyes. "Aye," she said. "Are...are you hiding up here?"

Diara sighed faintly. "Mayhap a little," she said. "Do you ever feel like that? Like hiding?"

Dorian shrugged, sort of, as if unsure how to answer. "I will leave you if you want to hide."

"Nay," Diara said quickly. "Please do not go. Will... will you come up here and sit with me? We've not had a chance to talk since I arrived."

Dorian debated on that request for a couple of moments before finally climbing to the top of the ladder and into the loft.

She sat down near the ladder well, crossing her legs and looking at Diara with some uncertainty.

"Your father told me that you like horses a great deal," Diara said, trying to make conversation. "Do you have a favorite horse?"

Dorian nodded. "Her name is Hildr."

Diara cocked her head curiously. "That is an interesting name," she said. "Is she named for someone?"

"A Valkyrie."

"You know about Valkyries?"

Dorian nodded. "I learned about them," she said. "When I lived at Pelinom Castle, they had many books, and I was taught to read. I read about the old gods and the Valkyries."

"Are you interested in reading about things like that?"

"I am," Dorian said, seemingly warming up to the conversation a little. "I like stories."

"Do you have your own books?"

"Some," Dorian said. "But I… I like to tell stories, too. I like to write them down."

Diara smiled faintly. "What do you write about?"

Dorian shrugged. "Things," she said, either embarrassed or shy about it. "I wrote a story about a fae named Flit."

"Flit? I like that name."

"She lived in a bluebell and rode on the back of a bee."

Diara's smile grew. "I think that's lovely," she said. "Will you read it to me someday?"

Dorian looked at her, shocked. "You want to hear it?"

"I would. But only if you want me to hear it."

Dorian seemed encouraged by that. "I wrote another story about a lass who falls into a well and shrinks to the size of a bug," she said. "She lives in the well with the other bugs, and they crown her the queen of the well."

Diara laughed softly. "How wonderful," she said. "Was she happy there?"

"She loved the well, and when it rained, she would dance on the water like the other bugs."

"What is her name?"

"Echo."

"That is an interesting name."

"It's because her voice bounces off the sides of the well when she talks."

"I think that is very clever," Diara said. "Your father did not tell me he had such a clever daughter."

Dorian's smile faded. "My father does not know about my stories," she said. "I do not think he would like them."

"Why not?"

"Because he is very busy," Dorian said. "He does not have time for things like that."

"Have you ever asked him if he would like to hear your stories?"

Dorian simply shook her head and averted her gaze, and Diara sensed a very timid and lonely girl. Diara didn't know what Roi's relationship with his daughters was like, and, truthfully, he didn't seem like a disconnected father, but she did notice that he let his mother take charge of his girls. He had since Diara had known him. Perhaps it was because he simply didn't know how to raise girl children, or perhaps it was as Dorian said—he was too busy. Whatever the reason, Diara felt a little sorry for quiet, lonely Dorian.

"Well," she said briskly, "I will listen to your stories whenever you wish. I would like to know what happened to Flit and Echo. Will you tell me sometime?"

Dorian nodded. "I will," she said. "If you really want to hear."

"I do, very much. Do you have more stories you wish to write?"

Dorian was flushing, having difficulty looking at Diara because they were on a subject she never spoke of for fear of ridicule. "I… I want to write a story about a lady who rides lightning and chases horses in the clouds," she said. "I even drew a picture of her, once, but the priest found the picture and told me it was wicked to draw such things."

Diara's smile faded. "What priest?"

"At Pelinom Castle," Dorian said. "That is where I fostered. He came to give mass every Sunday, and he spent hours talking to us. Some of the other wards fell asleep, but I drew a picture. The lady who rides lightning is called Helen. If I ever have a daughter someday, I want to name her Helen."

"A true and lovely name," Diara said. "And the priest was wrong. It is not wicked of you to draw those things. It shows that you are bright and extraordinary. Would you like for me to send him a missive and tell him so?"

Dorian's eyes widened. "Are you not afraid of priests?"

Diara shook her head. "They are simply men," she said. "And, between you and me, men can be wrong sometimes."

She giggled, causing Dorian to grin. After a moment, Dorian moved from where she'd been sitting next to the ladder and came over to plant herself next to Diara. As they gazed at each other, Dorian slipped her hand into Diara's.

"Would you like me to tell you about Helen and her cloud horses?" she asked.

Diara squeezed her cold, soft hand. "I would, indeed. Please tell me."

Dorian, the lonesome little de Lohr, did.

CHAPTER NINE

Cicadia Castle

T HE MESSENGER HAD been wearing de Lohr colors.

Ananda happened to be crossing from the stable area toward the keep when she saw the messenger at the gatehouse. It was about midday beneath a fine and clear sky, and she had been busy inventorying the livestock in preparation for future meals. It was a mostly normal day in a series of abnormal days that had been clouded with the departure of Diara and Roi. That entire situation was still a mystery to Ananda, mostly because her husband seemed so upset over it.

To her, that didn't make any sense.

Robin was the one who had pushed the de Lohr betrothal. He had been the one who hounded the family after the death of Beckett. Everything that had happened was because he had orchestrated it, and God only knew, he liked to control everything and everyone around him.

That was the husband she had come to know.

But ever since that evening when he had fallen and hit his face, something had been eating away at Robin. He was normally a social man and tended to get out quite a bit, but ever since that day, he had mostly stayed in his solar. Whenever Ananda tried to speak to him or bring him food, he would snap at her and tell her to get out. He wasn't in any mood for conversation, and he certainly wasn't in any mood to explain his problems to his wife.

Therefore, she had no idea what was wrong.

Ananda wasn't the plotting sort. She wasn't the type of wife who schemed or tried to trick her husband. She and Robin had always had a good partnership, or so she thought, but the de Lohr betrothal had changed something in him, and she wasn't sure what it was because he wouldn't talk to her.

There had been, however, an interesting visit from Lord Cirencester the day after Roi and Diara had left for Lioncross Abbey Castle. Riggs Fairford made an appearance, something the man did on occasion, since his seat wasn't far from Cicadia, but this visit seemed to be different. It didn't seem to be a social visit because he had entered Robin's solar to talk to the man and ended up spending about twelve hours in the chamber. When he had finally emerged, it was simply to get on his horse and leave. Normally, he would have remained for a few days, indulged in Robin's fine wine, eaten his share of good food, and departed for home when his gluttonous body could take no more.

But this visit had been different.

Ananda had no idea what to make of it.

So, she simply went about her business, and that included doing an inventory of the livestock on this day. As she crossed toward the keep, she noticed the de Lohr messenger at the gatehouse, and, curious about his appearance, she changed directions and headed toward the gate. As she drew near, Mathis left the messenger and approached her.

"My lady," he said, holding out a vellum envelope. "A missive from Lioncross Abbey. It is addressed to both you and Lord Cheltenham."

Ananda looked at it. It was a big yellow envelope with the blue wax de Lohr seal on it. She flipped it over to see that, indeed, her name was on it.

"I wonder what it is," she said. "Did the messenger say anything?"

"Nay, my lady."

"My name *is* on it."

"It is, my lady."

Even so, she was hesitant to open it. Robin opened all of the missives that arrived to Cicadia, but this one did have her name on it. She supposed that it was her right to open it before her husband did.

She proceeded.

Ananda, fortunately, could read. In a country where reading was not particularly encouraged for women, her mother had taught her, and she, in turn, had taught Diara. She continued to read the missive, her face lighting up when she was about halfway finished.

"Ah!" she said. "What lovely news."

"My lady?" Mathis said.

Ananda glanced at him. "It is an invitation to Diara's marriage to Roi," she said. "I was not sure when they intended to do it, but it seems that it is only a day or two away. I must tell my husband immediately."

With that, she dashed away from Mathis. He wasn't so excited by the news as she was. In fact, he was rather depressed. It wasn't as if he knew he had any chance with Diara, still, but news of her coming marriage somehow stomped out any embers of foolish hope he might have entertained. She was truly getting married, and there was nothing he could do about it.

Nothing but mourn what he'd hoped was his future.

Ananda wasn't oblivious to the fact, but much like her husband, she felt that Mathis wasn't a prestigious enough husband for their daughter, so his feelings in the matter were inconsequential to her. Diara was to be married shortly, and what Mathis felt or didn't feel didn't matter to her at all. All that mattered was that this wedding they'd hoped for, first with Beckett but now with his father, was imminent.

She ran all the way to the keep.

Once up the steps and into the cold and musty entry, Ananda went straight to her husband's solar. Without knocking, she burst into the chamber, the missive held high like a flag.

"Word has come from Lioncross Abbey, my husband," she announced. "The wedding is to be at the end of the week!"

Robin had been seated at his table, that vast and cluttered thing, studying a map of his southern lands. A cartographer from Nice had made the maps for him years ago, and they'd held up well. He looked up from the map without any outward reaction as his wife's words settled in his brain.

The wedding is at the end of the week!

He couldn't even muster the anger for her breaking into his sanctuary without knocking.

All he could feel was disappointment.

"So it comes," he muttered softly, sitting back in his chair. "They waited until after the funeral, just as Roi wanted to."

"Aye," Ananda said, rushing to the table and extending the invitation to him. "See for yourself. Lord Hereford has asked for the honor of our presence at the mass. We must leave immediately."

Robin looked at his wife, who was practically twitching with joy. Everything she had hoped and planned for her little girl was finally about to happen, and her happiness knew no bounds. That wasn't what Robin was feeling at all.

However...

He had known, at some point, that the announcement would come. Quite honestly, he had expected simply a marriage announcement, that the ceremony had already taken place and that his daughter was happily wed to the son of the Earl of Hereford. That was what he had been anticipating, so the fact that he was now invited to the wedding made the situation rather interesting.

The truth was that he was studying his maps for a reason. He was trying to determine the best location for a staged attack from his good friend to the south. His conversation with Riggs was still foremost in his mind even days after he had taken place. Nothing had changed. They had concocted a foolproof plan to rid himself of his daughter's new husband, and now, it was simply a matter of creating the situation that Roi, as his daughter's husband, would be morally obligated to engage in.

Robin had been planning to make amends with the already-married couple, but now he could simply do it at the actual wedding. What better way to lure Roi into a false sense of familial security than with a father-in-law who pretended to be incredibly grateful for the relationship? Robin knew that remaining distant and unhappy wasn't the way to solve his problem. Moreover, what son-in-law was going to want to fight for a man with whom he shared a bad relationship? Therefore, Robin was going to have to swallow his pride and pretend to be Roi's friend again.

But that was far from the truth.

He would never again be friends with a man who had gone against him. He would never again be friends with a man who shamed him in front of his own child. He would most definitely never again be friends again with a man who struck him in anger. It didn't matter that Robin had deserved it. He was never one to accept responsibility for his own actions, so understanding that he deserved what he received in the form of a flying fist had never been an option.

Now, he was going to do far worse to Roi than what Roi did to him, and in the end, his daughter would have a brand-new, controllable husband in the form of Cirencester's son. It was time to begin the performance that would convince the world that Robin was happy about the marriage, and that performance started with Ananda.

"Let me see the missive," he finally said, holding out his hand.

Ananda promptly handed over the envelope, and Robin read it, just once, before returning it to her.

"It is a joyous occasion," he said, forcing a smile. "Of course we shall leave immediately. Begin your packing and we shall leave at sunrise."

Ananda's face was aglow. "Our daughter is finally to be wed," she said, grasping his hand and giving it a squeeze. "To a de Lohr, no less. I cannot tell you how happy I am."

Robin kissed her hand and let it go. "As am I," he said. "To know that she is marrying my old friend brings me such comfort. Roi will be good to her. I pray she is worthy of him."

"But she will be," Ananda insisted. "She is young and strong. I can already feel those grandchildren in my arms."

With that, she rushed off, calling for the servants to bring forth the trunks from storage. Robin listened to her shouting as she faded away, off to pack for her daughter's wedding, off to experience what every woman dreamt of.

It was enough to give him a bad taste in his mouth.

Robin dutifully sent a servant for Mathis and Pryce, informing them that they would be escorting him and Lady Cheltenham to Lioncross Abbey on the morrow, to the wedding of their daughter. Leaving Eddard in command of Cicadia, Robin intended to take a hundred men with him in show of support for his new de Lohr in-laws. He gave normal orders for a normal event, giving no hint of what lay beneath.

But a good deal lay beneath.

The beginning of the end of Roi de Lohr.

CHAPTER TEN

"**H**AVE YOU SEEN Diara?"

It was after sunset at Lioncross Abbey, and Roi was back in the ladies' solar. His mother and eldest sister were there, too, with the lit tapers creating a warm glow against the backdrop of the neat but crowded solar as they both worked on garments.

Dustin looked up from the fabric in her hands.

"Nay," she said. "She never returned, so I assumed she had gone somewhere with you."

Roi shook his head. "She did not," he said. "I left her to go to your chamber, but I've not seen her since. I thought she was with you."

Dustin lowered her sewing into her lap. "I am sure she is around somewhere," she said. "Mayhap she was weary and lay down to rest. The past few days have been very busy for her."

Roi nodded. "Possibly," he said. "I will go and see."

"Everyone is gathering in the hall, Roi," Dustin called after him as he headed to the door. "Find her and bring her to sup. Your marriage is tomorrow, after all. We will want to celebrate tonight with you both."

Roi paused at the door. "There is a good deal to celebrate," he said. "But there is also a good deal to mourn. I find myself in a peculiar position."

Dustin wasn't unsympathetic. "I know," she said. "We will mourn Beckett forever. But you will only marry Diara once, so I do not think your son would mind if you celebrate your union tonight."

Roi thought on that. "You are right, of course," he said. "But I still feel as if something is missing."

"Something *is* missing, sweetheart," Dustin said softly. "But only in body. In spirit, he will be sitting next to you."

Roi nodded, but then he chuckled ironically. "That will be a little strange, considering I am marrying his betrothed."

"He would want you to be happy, and if it is with Diara, I do not think he would mind."

Roi hoped that was the case. Even if his son hadn't been interested in marrying, he still wondered how he would have felt about his father marrying the woman intended for him— and liking her.

His pale eyes glittered at his mother.

"You like her, don't you?" he asked.

Both Dustin and Christin, sitting next to her, nodded. "I do," Dustin said. "She is a sweet lass and she is eager to please. She will be good for you, Roi."

"She knows how to play chess," Christin said, a twinkle in her eye. "She brought the board in here from Papa's solar yesterday and was trying to teach the little girls. Have you played with her yet?"

"Nay."

"I suspect she might make a formidable opponent."

Roi simply grinned at his sister, indicating his joy at the

prospect. They all knew how competitive he was, so a new wife who could play board games would be of particular delight. With that, he left his mother's solar and headed to the wing where female and married couple visitors were housed. Single men were always kept in the knights' quarters or in another part of the house, and he made his way up the stairs to the level above.

A search of several chambers on that level, including the one that Iris was staying in, failed to produce Diara. Iris, now nursing a head cold, had no idea where Diara was but offered to help search. Roi declined the ill woman's offer because he wasn't particularly concerned, but he ended up searching other parts of the keep simply to see if she'd wandered around or was sidetracked by something. The entire third floor was void of her presence, as was the top floor.

He went back down to the entry level.

By now, he was becoming a little concerned, but not too terribly. He knew that she was somewhere on the grounds. He simply had to find her. But when a search of the entire keep and the abbey failed to turn her up, he went outside, into the night, to commandeer the help of a few soldiers. They knew what she looked like, so before the hour was up, Roi had about fifteen soldiers helping him search for her.

They looked everywhere.

At least, Roi thought they did. Two hours after he started his search for Diara, he was no closer to finding her and struggling not to get panicky. He came in through the kitchen yard, into the kitchens themselves simply as a back way into the keep. He'd come through the warm, steamy kitchens before in his search, but that had been early in the process and he hadn't asked any of the servants if they'd seen her. But on his second pass, he happened to ask if they'd seen Lady Diara and was rewarded with a few nodding heads.

They pointed out into the yard.

Now, he was getting somewhere. The cook, a big woman who had been making de Lohr meals for years, seemed to think that Diara might have gone into the stable because she never left the yard or came back into the kitchens, as far as she knew. The woman also happened to mention that she thought Diara might have been weeping, which concerned Roi even further. If he couldn't find her, then perhaps she didn't want to be found. But he was going to tear Lioncross apart until he did just that.

Find her.

The stable was dark and quiet at this hour except for a few oil lamps about, placed strategically so they were away from anything flammable. Horses were snorting, some were crunching the leftover grain in their buckets, and still others were lying down, sleeping. Roi's own horse, an enormous black stallion with white streaks in his mane, must have smelled his master, because he nickered softly as Roi passed by. Roi slapped the beast affectionately on his big arse and continued through the stable block, finally reaching the end. Still no Diara. He knew the soldiers had searched the stable earlier to no avail, so he was about to turn away when something caught his eye.

A ladder to the loft.

He had nothing to lose, so he quietly took the ladder, up into the darkness that was the hayloft, and poked his head up through the opening. It was fairly dark in the loft, with very little light penetrating from below, but it was enough to see a figure off to his right, several feet away and sitting against the roofline of the stable.

He struggled to see in the darkness.

"Diara?" he whispered.

The figure jumped as if startled, and Roi took it as an affirmative that he'd indeed found whom he was looking for. He climbed up into the loft, crawling over to the figure, only to see that there were two figures. Peering closely, he could see that Diara had her arm around Dorian, who was asleep with her head on Diara's lap.

"God's Bones," he muttered. "You scared the life out of me when I could not find you. What are you doing up here? And why is Dorian with you?"

Diara hadn't been asleep. She'd simply been dozing when Roi softly called her name, but was now focused on the man she'd been agonizing over for the past several hours. To hear his voice, soft and deep, was like a dagger to her heart. He sounded so concerned for her, and she loved that. She loved that he'd tracked her down, as if she was important to him.

And that's what was so heartbreaking about the entire situation.

"She was tending her horse in the stables," Diara whispered. "She and I have become friends. You have a very intelligent and clever daughter."

"Thank you," he said. "But why are you up here in the dark?"

"Because she found me," Diara said simply. "We spoke for quite some time until she fell asleep."

"That still does not tell me why you are in the loft," he said, looking around as if expecting to see others. "Are you playing a game of some kind?"

Diara thought on that question. Her hand was on Dorian's dark head, and she put her palm over the girl's ear, gently, to muffle the voices.

"I suppose I have been," she said, leaning her head back against the wall. "I've been playing a game all along, ever since we met. A game that pitted the reality of me against the reality of you."

Roi wasn't following her. "What reality?" he asked, no longer whispering. "Why are you up in the loft, and why has no one seen you for hours? What are you doing here?"

Diara looked at him. There were so many answers to those questions, answers that she didn't want to give.

But she knew she had to.

"I want to go home," she finally said, though her lower lip was beginning to tremble. "I wish to leave tomorrow morning."

"We are to be married tomorrow morning."

"Nay." She shook her head, tears filling her eyes. "Roi, we have been fooling ourselves. That is the game I am speaking of. The truth is that I am not meant for you. No one thinks so. If we go through with this wedding, eventually, you would come to realize what a mistake you have made, and I could not stand it. I could not go on knowing how miserable you were."

He frowned at her. "What in the hell are you talking about?" he said. "What do you mean that no one thinks you are meant for me?"

Diara was starting to weep. She was also still trying to remain still and quiet as Dorian slept on her lap, but it was a struggle. She was hurt and angry and filled with anguish, so much so that she didn't see any need to be evasive with Roi about her reasons any longer. He wanted the truth, and she would give it to him.

"When I was going to find the lace that your mother asked me to fetch, I heard Tiberius talking," she said. "I recognized his voice because of our conversation earlier in the ladies' solar. I do not know whom he was talking to, but I suspect it was his brothers. He told them that his Uncle Westley had informed them of the rumors he'd heard about me. Tiberius is under the impression that you are marrying a whore."

Roi flinched as if he'd been struck. For a moment, he simply stared at her, and she could see his eyes glittering in the darkness as he processed that statement. It was several long and tense seconds before he replied.

"Is that what Tiberius said?" he asked, his voice a rumble. "Exactly?"

Diara nodded. "He said that I was no stranger to spreading my legs, which is how I had managed to bewitch you," she said, wiping at her eyes. "He said that Odette was the only wife for you and that they should face the fact that their Uncle Roi was marrying a whore. Now that you know what your nephews and brothers are saying, I will not marry you and be subjected to that manner of vile abuse for the rest of my life. It is not fair to you and it is not fair to me. I want to go home tomorrow. If you will not take me, then I will simply go by myself, but either way, I am leaving. I came up here because I did not want to see your nephews again for as long as I remain at Lioncross."

By the time she finished, she was weeping softly. She couldn't even look at Roi, who so far hadn't moved a muscle. He was still on his knees in front of her. But suddenly, he was reaching down to pull Dorian off her lap. When Diara tried to protest, he grabbed her by the hand and practically yanked her onto her knees.

"You are coming with me," he said.

Diara dug in. "Nay," she said. "I'm not leaving the loft. I'm staying here until the morning, and then I am—"

"Nay, you are not," he growled, pulling her over to the

ladder. "You are coming with me and we are going to settle this once and for all."

Diara was beginning to pull at him, sobbing as she resisted. "I will *not* come with you," she said. "Don't you understand? I cannot do this to you, Roi. I cannot subject you to those rumors for the rest of your life. They have followed me, and I must accept that, but you did nothing to deserve it."

"Get on the ladder."

"Nay!" she shouted, bracing herself against the loft opening. "Are you listening to me? You cannot live your life with men whispering behind your back that you married a whore. I would not do that to you!"

He was already on the ladder, pulling her with him no matter how much she fought back. Finally, he grabbed both of her hands and held them still in a viselike grip.

"Look at me," he said calmly. "Diara, *look* at me. That is not a request."

She was a weeping mess, but she managed to lift her eyes to him. Once he saw that he had her attention, he pulled her hands to his lips and began to kiss them.

"When I volunteered to marry you in my son's stead, I did it out of duty," he said quietly. "I did not do it because I had any desire for a wife. I did not do it because of my personal regard for you. I did it because I felt I was morally obligated to do it. Do you understand that?"

She nodded, tears coursing down her cheeks. "Please, Roi," she begged softly. "Let me go. Let me go home and let us end this before either one of us is truly hurt."

His eyebrows lifted. "*Before* either one of us is hurt?" he said. "Lady, it is too late for that. I buried my son two days ago, and knowing you were in the chapel, feeling your presence, is one of the only reasons I was able to get through it without going mad because somehow, someway, you have gotten under my skin. I never thought I would feel this way again, the way I do when I look at you. The way my heart beats against my ribs at the sight of you. The way my soul takes flight when you laugh. The utter and complete joy I feel when I see you smile. All I know is that I cannot be without you. Please don't give me a taste of happiness only to take it away. It's like giving a man a glimpse of heaven and then denying him entry."

Diara was still weeping, but now with the thrill of his words. She stopped resisting him, and her hands moved to his face as he continued to kiss her fingers.

"When I look at you, I see a future I never thought I would have," she murmured. "Mayhap it is too soon to tell you that I love you, but I do. I have never loved anyone more in my life. I love the way you make me feel. I love the way you speak to me as an equal, and I love the conversations we have. You are kind and generous and compassionate. That is why I cannot marry you, Roi. I would never torture you with the horrible things men say about me. Can you not understand that?"

He pulled her to him, kissing her fiercely. "I think I loved you the moment you asked me if I had dreams, just like my son had," he said. "And the way I felt when I looked at you... I cannot describe it other than to say it made a grown man like me feel like a squire again. I was never giddy in my life until I met you."

"But..."

He cut her off with another kiss. "I understand what you are saying as far as the rumors of men," he said. "But I told you once and I will tell you again—I will kill anyone who speaks so terribly of you. I have shoulders big enough to bear your burden and I do it gladly, for it is something you should not have to deal with alone. I do not care what men say so long as you love me. That is all that matters to me."

"Papa?"

A small voice entered the mix, and they both looked over to see Dorian a few feet away, on her hands and knees, looking at her father and Diara apprehensively. When the young woman saw that she had their attention, she scooted over to Diara.

"Papa, you will marry her, won't you?" she said, laying her head on Diara's upper arm. "I do not want her to go away."

Roi smiled wearily at his youngest daughter. "Nor do I," he said, looking to Diara. "Mayhap if we both beg her to marry me, she will."

Diara found herself boxed in by a young girl with pleading eyes and a man who kept kissing her hands. This was the life she wanted, with people who adored her. But she was afraid—afraid those pleading eyes would turn away from her and she would lose this dream she was so afraid to believe in. Afraid that the rumors and gossip would finally break him down.

"Roi," she said softly. "You know I want to, but—"

He interrupted her. "You are so determined to protect me, come what may, that you are stripping me of my pride," he said. "I am a competent man, Diara. *Deedee.* I want to protect *you.* I want your burdens to be mine. I want to feel needed, because I most certainly need you. Can we not trust one another enough to know that nothing on this earth can separate us? Especially not foolish rumors?"

Diara could feel herself giving in. *Deedee,* he'd called her. That name had never meant so much to her as it did coming from him. She didn't want to leave him, anyway, and his pleading was succeeding in tearing down her wall of determination.

"Aye," she finally said. "I do trust you, I promise. But…"

He began to pull her down the ladder. "Then come with me," he said, not allowing her to finish. "Come with me because I am going to end this once and for all. Dorian, come with us, sweetheart."

Diara let him pull her down the ladder, down into the stables below. He had her by the waist, then by her hand, as if fearful she'd try to get away from him. He helped Dorian down the rest of the way, and his daughter latched on to Diara's other hand, which Roi thought was rather sweet. Truth be told, he'd always felt rather distant from his daughters. He'd identified so much more with his son. But he felt rather bad that Dorian was clinging to Diara, a woman she'd just met, and not to him. That told him a lot about how he'd treated her and her sister, though he really hadn't meant to.

A problem he would remedy after the more pressing one he was about to address.

He had some brothers and nephews to see.

○3

THE GREAT HALL of Lioncross Abbey Castle was full.

Clouds had moved in just after sunset and a light rain was beginning to fall. Inside the hall, the hearth was blazing and men were feasting on boiled beef and sauced mutton. The ale flowed freely, and somewhere, a soldier had a lute and strains of a song could be heard.

But Roi wasn't paying any attention to that.

He was focused on his family.

He entered the hall with Diara and Dorian in tow, pulling them through the crowd, heading for the dais where his family was sitting. The table was crowded with them—Curtis and three of Curtis' sons, with his mother and Adalia and Christin, and flame-haired Rebecca and her thieving boys. Further down the table sat Douglas and Westley, his de Shera nephews, and his youngest sister, Honey. His father sat right in the middle of everything, mostly listening to Curtis and his sons as they undoubtedly discussed something serious, because Christopher seemed quite intense.

But there were more people milling around the dais that he recognized.

People that had come for Beckett's funeral, including Roi's two knights, Kyne and Adrius, who had ridden in the escort party from Pembridge. There was also a local lord from the Welsh border, a Scotsman by the name of Jameson Munro. But mostly, he noticed that his eldest brother, Peter de Lohr, had arrived at some point during the day from his post of Ludlow Castle with his eldest son, Matthew. The only people missing from his immediate family were his middle brother, Myles, and his sister, Brielle.

He made eye contact with Peter as he approached the table. Peter hadn't been present at the funeral, as busy as he was, but even so, his presence now was most welcome. Roi had always had a close relationship with his father's bastard son, and he was glad to see him. When Peter saw Roi, his face lit up and he broke away from his conversation with Munro, but Roi didn't have time to greet him at the moment.

He was on a mission.

Without missing a step, he suddenly leapt onto the feasting table on the dais, nearly kicking his nephew, Arthur, in the head as he did so. Food scattered where Roi's big boots came to rest. As Arthur rubbed his clipped ear, Roi boomed at the entire table.

"Silence!" he roared. "All of you—shut your lips and be silent. I have something to say to all of you, and you will listen or you'll not like my reaction. Tiberius? Shut *up!*"

The table went deadly silent in an instant, including Tiberius, who had been drunkenly shouting at his cousin across the table. But he, and everyone else, looked at Roi in shock and surprise. Roi was more the silent, steady type, so this dramatic show wasn't like him at all. Roi was seething as he looked around the table, and that was clear to everyone.

No one would escape his wrath.

"It has come to my attention that some very unsavory things have been said about my betrothed, and I am going to put an end to it here and now," Roi barked. In particular, he focused on Westley. "West, you have been spreading gossip that you have heard from some lowly soldiers about Lady Diara, and I am here to tell you that if you ever repeat it again, I will cut your tongue out. Neither Father nor Mother can save you from my rage if you ever tell anyone again that you heard from some dimwitted soldiers that my betrothed has an unchaste reputation. Do you understand me?"

Westley's eyes were so wide that they threatened to pop from their sockets. "Roi," he stammered. "I... I..."

"Silence!" Roi shouted at him again. "You will not defend yourself, because you repeated the same rumor to me. Therefore, I know it to be true. You told Tiberius and Gallus and Maximus, and now Tiberius is going around telling people that I am marrying a whore."

All eyes turned accusingly to Tiberius, who suddenly took on a look of utter and complete fear. Before he could say a word, his mother stood up from her seat across the table.

"Did you say that?" Honey demanded. A petite woman with blonde hair and an iron fist, she glared at her youngest son. "Do not lie to me, Tiberius de Shera. Did you say such things about Roi's betrothed?"

Tiberius was in a world of trouble, and he knew it. Gallus and Maximus would give him no support in the matter because, in truth, they'd tried to be somewhat neutral about the situation. It was Tiberius who had run his mouth off.

"Uncle West said so," Tiberius said, climbing off the bench and backing away from a group of very angry people. "He said she easily spread her legs!"

Westley was on his feet. "I *never* said that," he fired back. "I will admit to telling you what I'd heard, but I never said that she spread her legs. I never said she was a whore."

Tiberius was going down, but he wasn't going to go down alone. "You said there were rumors that she was unchaste," he shouted. "It's the same thing!"

"It is not," Westley said angrily. "You're trying to put words in my mouth, and I will not let you do it. You're the one who is going around telling people she's a whore—not me."

Honey had heard enough. She flew around the table and grabbed Tiberius by the ear. Quick as a flash, she slapped him across the mouth—a fully grown knight—and yanked on his ear until he howled.

"I am ashamed of you," she said, dragging him down the table by the ear until he was within Roi's range. "Tell Roi that you are sorry and that you did not mean it. Tell him *now*."

Tiberius was young. Young, foolish, and defiant. With his mother yanking on his ear and his grandmother heading in his direction, he knew that he was in major trouble. More trouble than his uncle could ever give him. But he wouldn't apologize.

Not until he'd had his say.

"She was supposed to marry Beckett," he said, in great pain as his mother tugged. "Uncle Roi has no claim to her. She was supposed to bear Beckett's sons, and our sons were all going to grow up together. Don't you see? It's just not right!"

Dustin reached him and grabbed him by the hair. Between Dustin and Honey, Tiberius was in a world of hurt.

"So you called her a whore?" Dustin said angrily. "How could you do such a thing? You're a silly, foolish, stupid boy, Tiberius. Can you not see how happy she makes your uncle? That should be your only concern!"

Tiberius was fighting a losing battle. "But she belonged to Beckett!"

"Beckett never wanted her to begin with!"

Dustin hadn't meant to say that, even if it was the truth. Most of the family already knew it. She immediately looked to Roi apologetically as a gasp went up, mostly from the women at the table, and all eyes turned to Diara, who was viewing the entire scene with a good deal of horror. She was living her worst nightmare, slanderous rumors now being brought to light, but Roi had taken charge. He'd told her that he'd always protect her.

Now was his chance to prove it.

Before Diara could react in any way, Roi spoke.

"Beckett was unhappy with the betrothal, Ty, and since you were close to him, you know that," he said. "Why you should continue to state that Lady Diara belongs to him is beyond my comprehension. The truth is that Beckett was very displeased with the contract and had no interest in marrying at all. Stop acting like there was a love match, because there was most certainly not. Moreover, I fail to see how any of this is your concern. You have not only put your nose into business that did not involve you, but you spoke most unkindly of a woman who had never done you any harm. Is that the kind of man you are, Tiberius? A man who harms others and cares not for their feelings? Because if that is who you truly are, then I want no part of you. You are dead to me if that is the kind of man you are at heart."

Tiberius was feeling quite punished, literally, from all sides. His mother, his grandmother, and his uncle had publicly taken him to task. Arrogant as he was, he wasn't as stupid as his grandmother accused him of being. His brothers were virtually ignoring him, and Westley had already told him what he thought of him.

He knew he was done for.

He looked at Roi.

"I… I apologize," he finally said. "I suppose… I suppose things are changing, and I do not like it. Beckett is gone. He was the only one who understood me. And she… she was betrothed to him, and that means she belongs to him and I don't care what you say. But I'm sorry I said terrible things. I… I did not mean it."

Dustin let go of his hair, but Honey didn't let go of his ear. She dragged him over to where Diara was standing with Dorian cowering behind her.

"Apologize to her," Honey demanded. "You will never again shame me like this, Tiberius. Do you hear me? Apologize to this gentle woman."

Tiberius looked at Diara with a mixture of resignation and defiance. He hated apologizing. But he knew he had no choice.

"I apologize, my lady," he said quietly.

Diara gazed into the face of the young knight who hadn't

been particularly kind to her since she'd known him. She could have been gracious about it, but she didn't feel particularly gracious at the moment. This entire situation had her about as worked up as Roi was, but unlike him, she wasn't going to jump on the table and shout about it.

She was simply hurt.

"Words," she finally said. "Mere words, Sir Tiberius. You have been using them against me since we met, so you have simply uttered more words that mean nothing to me. Do you want to know where the source of those rumors came from? Mayhap Westley would like to know, since he has been spreading them so freely. You see, I fostered at Carisbrooke Castle. There were two unhappy and unattractive de Redvers daughters who were jealous of me, and they were the ones who started the rumors, rumors that have spread from soldier to soldier because they like to gossip about the nobles. I never did anything wrong. I was never unchaste. I was pious and obedient, but that did not matter to Lady de Redvers. She spread those rumors happily, hoping it would deter men from me and turn them towards her daughters. Now you know. You have continued a petty woman's petty scheme."

Most of the table heard her. That caused Dustin to grab Tiberius' hair again and swat him on the behind.

"Out of my sight," she hissed. "Get out of my sight. I do not want to see your face again until my anger has cooled. *Go.*"

The last word was spoken imperiously, and Tiberius left the dais, followed by his mother for good measure. Humiliated that his mummy was escorting him from the hall, Tiberius fled quickly. Before he was even out of the hall, Roi turned to the table, but mostly, he turned to Westley.

"You are my brother and I love you, but repeating that

gossip against a kind and decent woman makes me ashamed of you." He turned to the table at large. "And I am ashamed of anyone who listened to it and did not immediately dismiss it. You have all spent some time around Lady Diara, and I know you have seen what a fine, noble woman she is. She would make any man proud, and I must say, I feel wholly unworthy of her, and especially after this nonsense, she has every right to look at all of you as an undesirable group of in-laws. She has told me that because of your behavior, she wants to go home. She does not want to marry me. But I have begged her to reconsider because I have fallen in love with the woman and would be crushed if she were to leave. Mayhap you all can make up for your horrible behavior and plead on my behalf."

Dustin was the first one to step up, taking Diara's hands and looking her in the eye. "We are not such a terrible family, my lady," she said sincerely. "I am so sorry that your experience with us has proven otherwise. We are decent and kind, and we love one another deeply. I would like to think that was where Tiberius was coming from—a place of love for Beckett and Roi. A need to protect him against harm. He simply didn't go about it the right way. Mayhap in time you will forgive Tiberius, though I would not blame you if you did not. But do not punish Roi for a foolish nephew's loose tongue."

Diara smiled faintly, feeling the woman's genuine heart. And Dustin had a big one. But suddenly, there were two big bodies in front of her, gently pushing Dustin aside, and Diara looked up to see Christopher and Curtis standing there.

Christopher took her hand and held it.

"I am so very sorry," he said in a deep, quiet tone. "Please do not judge the entire family by the actions of a few. Westley is a good man. He is loyal to the bone. But he is very protective of his brothers, so I believe it when I say that he was concerned for the woman Roi was to marry. He heard the rumors, and naturally, he should be concerned. But he should not have repeated them the way he did. I hope you can forgive him."

Diara wasn't one to hold a grudge by nature, but she was still upset after the events of the day. She'd been wounded before by gossip, so she wasn't too keen to trust or forgive those who had tried to hurt her. Still, she was faced with Dustin and Christopher and Curtis, with Roi still standing on the table and looking at her anxiously. She knew none of this was his doing, and the fact that he'd stood up to his entire family, just for her, spoke volumes.

He was a man of his word.

"Of course I will marry Roi," she said, smiling weakly. "I would not dream of punishing him for something he had no control over. But for the rest... I have been hurt by nasty gossip for years. I am sure that I will forgive in time, but it is a wound that still must heal. Your kindness has helped more than you know."

Dustin smiled at her, patting her cheek, but Christopher made his way over to Westley, who had the appearance of a kicked dog. Once his father started talking to him in a low voice, that look only grew worse. Meanwhile, Christin and Rebecca had moved over to Diara, and Christin went so far as to put her arms around Diara's shoulders. It was a very nurturing, protective stance, one that bolstered Diara tremendously. She looked up at Roi, still on the table, who was now watching his father lecture Westley. Diara broke away from Christin, though gently done, and went to the edge of the table.

"Roi?" she said hesitantly.

Hearing his name, he snapped his head in her direction.

Quickly, he climbed off the table. "I am sorry if my actions upset you," he said. "But I felt strongly that I had to handle it in that manner. No questions, no confusion. I feel that it was the right thing to do."

She smiled at him to let him know that she wasn't upset by it. At least, not once she'd had time to digest it all. "You are a man of honor," she said. "I am grateful you thought enough of me, of the situation, to take it so seriously. I hope this is truly the end of it."

"It is," he assured her, his pale eyes glimmering at her. "I promise you, it is. You can see that everyone is very concerned about it. These are decent people, Diara. They simply had to be reminded of it."

Diara nodded. "I know," she said. "And I appreciate it. Do you think they would mind if we supped with them? Or should we go eat by ourselves?"

He chuckled. "Why would we do that?"

"Because you just berated everyone at this table. They may not want to eat with us."

He simply grinned. "How little you know, my lady," he said softly. "How little you know."

He was right.

As the group settled back down, Roi seated Diara at the end of the feasting table and made sure she was served the best of everything available. Dustin and Christin sat with them, along with Curtis and his sons, and eventually nearly everyone gravitated toward that end of the table. It was an apology, a salve to her wounded heart, and a show of unity for the future.

That was something Diara had never experienced.

For her, it was a night to remember. For the first time in her life, she was starting to feel accepted. As if she was part of something bigger, with people who wanted to embrace her. Rumors or not, it didn't matter. Roi had accepted her, and they would too. Odd how these people she had just met were turning out to be more of a family to her than her own.

And she was grateful.

CHAPTER ELEVEN

H E MADE HER wear the red dress.

Roi only had one request for their wedding day, and it was that she wear the red dress, the dress she'd worn at their first real introduction. It was such an exquisite garment in that deep ruby color, the color that symbolized love, and as she stood in front of the chapel of Lioncross Abbey as the priest from the village intoned the mass over her and Roi, she looked like a goddess.

Roi couldn't take his eyes off her.

The day had started at sunrise when Dustin and her daughters arrived to help prepare Diara for the day. Adalia and Dorian, along with Iris and a few of the younger girls, had also come to help because Dustin felt it was important that they all participate in such a major family event. Diara had been asleep when they had entered her chamber, and, quite literally, she had been pulled from her bed. Dustin ran a tight ship, and she had both the servants and her daughters jumping.

It was a big day.

A large copper tub had been brought into the room and filled with hot water and oils that smelled of flowers. Diara had been stripped of her night shift and plunged into the tub, where Dustin and the ladies proceeded to scrub her within an inch of her life. Her skin was washed with hard white soap, and her hair was washed with a solution of vinegar and flat ale. Diara had to grip the sides of the tub to keep from being toppled over as her new family enthusiastically scrubbed her.

Eventually, however, the scrubbing ceased and she was rinsed and rinsed again before being instructed to climb out of the tub. An enormous towel was waiting for her, and the buffeting she took from Dustin as the woman was drying her off was far worse than the scrubbing that had taken place in the tub. In fact, Dara found herself giggling through the entire thing because she was being pummeled in the nicest sort of way.

Then came the combing and the anointing of oils. Iris, still not entirely well from her illness, was put in charge of combing out Diara's hair while Dustin and Rebecca and Dorian were charged with rubbing oil into her skin to soften it. Diara simply sat there while several pairs of hands went to work on her from head to toe, even rubbing oil into her feet.

As she told Dustin, she felt like the Queen of Sheba.

Dustin had grinned at the comment.

But Diara suspected that some of this was to make up for what had happened the day before. Not that she minded, because she didn't. In truth, she was incredibly touched by all of the fuss they made. It had made her feel very special, a worthy bride for their precious son.

As Christin prepared the red dress while everyone else focused on the bride, servants were brought in to fan Diara's hair so it would sufficiently dry. With Iris combing and the servants fanning, her hair dried quickly enough, and Dustin used a hot iron, set in the fire, to tame the natural curl that she had. Her hair was pulled back, pinned back, and a garland of flowers was put on her head with a silken veil that Diara had brought from Cicadia. It had belonged to her mother, and Ananda had worn it on her wedding day. With everything set in place, the ladies escorted Diara out to the chapel, where Roi, the family, and several guests were waiting.

The moment was upon them.

Roi couldn't take his eyes off her when she arrived, and Diara blushed modestly throughout the entire ceremony. Roi couldn't stop staring, and she couldn't stop smiling. They were nearly to the end of the mass when the sentries took up the cry at the gatehouse, announcing the arrival of the Earl and Countess of Cheltenham.

Perhaps they had arrived late, but that didn't matter to Diara. She was thrilled they'd made it at all. She hugged her mother fiercely and embraced her father tightly, apologizing to the man for any disobedience or trouble she might have caused him, but Robin seemed overjoyed to see her. Not a harsh word passed between them, nor did any harsh words pass between him and Roi. Robin was the model father of the bride, gracious to everyone. He was everything Diara hoped he would be. The wedding mass was finished with her parents by her side, and with that, Diara became Lady de Lohr.

Then came the wedding feast.

Since Diara and Roi were married around midday, the feast started immediately thereafter and went on well into the night. Tiberius, back from his near-fatal beating from his mother, was the life of the party. As if nothing terrible had happened the night before. He drank, he sang, and he encouraged others to do the same. The only one who came close to his antics was

Peter's son, Andrew, but every time he got out of hand and his father would shoot him an appraising look, he'd settle down to avoid a fatherly scolding. But the process would repeat until Peter finally gave up and let his son have some fun.

There was plenty of laughter and singing to go around.

One of those singing was, in fact, Roi. He'd been roped into a few songs by Tiberius, Andrew, Douglas, and Westley, and every time he tried to leave, they'd grab him around the neck and make him stay. Diara sat at the dais with Iris and her mother, laughing at Roi's discomfort because he really wasn't much of an exhibitionist. She'd heard him sing several songs, not the least of which was a tavern song about an old whore named Rose. That song only came up once because when they realized it mentioned a whore, and because of the situation with Diara the night before, they quickly took that off their singing list. At one point, Roi pulled the soldier playing the lute over to the dais and had the man play a song for his new wife that soon had every woman at the table swooning.

In his surprisingly good baritone, he sang only for Diara.

Come roam with me, my love,
Come roam far with me,
Away from this hard world,
And love only me.

They said that you loved me,
They said that you cared.
They said that your strong heart,
Wasn't mine to be shared.

When he was finished, the table exploded with applause,

and that included Diara's parents. Roi reached out and took her hand, kissing it sweetly, but he was pulled away from the table by revelers who wanted to sing something more lively. Diara simply waved at him, deliriously happy with a husband, and a wedding, that was far beyond anything she could have ever imagined.

Her father, in fact, had been watching everything.

Sitting with Christopher and Peter and Jameson Munro, Robin was still under the impression that the sooner he rid himself of his de Lohr attachments, the happier he would be. He watched every man at the dais, the de Lohr relatives and sons and brothers, knowing that he was looking at the largest military might in England, but also knowing it only emphasized to him that he would never be able to control this bunch. He'd be a very tiny part of a much bigger picture, and that wasn't the life he wanted for himself.

He didn't know why he hadn't seen that before.

His greed to want the de Lohr ties had been his downfall. He thought it would bring him prestige. He thought it would bring him power. But he was coming to understand that the power wasn't his, and it never would be. Certainly, he was an earl—and he had a good-sized army and wealth—but the de Lohrs were in a league all their own, and it was nothing he would be able to compete with. Robin didn't like being a small fish in a big pond. He knew now, more than ever, that the de Lohr betrothal he'd begged for years ago had been a mistake.

He wanted out.

"Do you hunt?"

Robin was jolted from his train of thought by a question coming from Christopher. The man was seated next to him, cup of fine wine in hand, and Robin turned to him with a weak smile.

"From time to time," he said. "I prefer to spend my time traveling as opposed to hunting. I have lands in France, you know."

Christopher shook his head. "I did not," he said. "Where?"

"Near Caen," Robin said. "Something left to me by a distant cousin. Rich land, however. I enjoy spending summers there."

"I didn't realize you summered out of England."

Robin nodded. "I have for years," he said. "Ananda and Diara have never gone, and I prefer that. A man should have a place all his own, a place of peace. Chateaux Beuville is mine."

"What do you do for respite there?"

Robin shrugged. "I read," he said. "But I will tell you a secret—there is a lake on the property, and I like to fish. Seems like a rather common pursuit, but I enjoy it."

Christopher grinned. "I used to take my sons fishing," he said. "We would go to the River Arrow, which is not far from here. I can still see five young boys all lined up along the bank and Westley screaming because he cannot catch any fish."

Robin's expression flickered, suggestive of a man who was highly jealous over the fact that he had no sons to speak of. "Mayhap it taught him patience in the end," he said without enthusiasm. "I would not know about young boys. I only had a daughter, and she was raised by women."

"And she is a fine young woman," Christopher said. "We all like her very much."

Robin's lips twitched with a grateful, though insincere, smile. "Good," he said. "Though I am sorry for Beckett, I am grateful for Roi. He and I were great friends when we fought together in France."

Christopher nodded. "I know," he said. "He told me that

you command a fine army."

Robin shrugged. "I hope so," he said. "They are well paid. I pay men to train them well. But I am still wholly grateful for the de Lohr alliance. I have been having some trouble, you know."

It was the perfect lead-in to a subject Robin had intended to bring up all night. As he hoped, Christopher seemed interested in discussing it.

"Where?" he asked.

"South," Robin said. "From Cirencester."

Christopher frowned. "Fairford?"

"The same."

"What trouble?"

Robin sighed sharply, an act that conveyed great displeasure. "You know how the man has made his money," he said. "He and his family. They are bred from pirates and thieves, so they tend to steal and raid. Riggs Fairford is no different from his ancestors. The king tolerates him because he pays a great deal in taxes, so he'll do nothing about him."

"Is he becoming that much of a problem?"

Robin nodded. "A little," he said. "Though his activity comes and goes. Mayhap the next time he raids my border, a little show of force from my daughter's new husband might discourage them from more action."

Christopher pondered that. "Possibly," he said. "I do not know much about Fairford. I've never had any real contact with him."

"A viper," Robin said with mock disgust. "As I said... I am glad for our strong alliance, my lord. I am glad for Roi."

Christopher believed him. Robin had to refrain from patting himself on the back because Christopher seemed very much in agreement and understanding.

That would make what he had to do just a little bit easier.

And a little more believable.

The time would soon come.

ॐ

"MY FATHER AND your father seemed to be having a pleasant conversation," Diara said. "My father is in a surprisingly good mood."

Roi had just broken away from the group of drunken singers posing as his brothers and nephews. He had returned to the dais and claimed his seat next to the bride, taking her hand as he collected a chalice of what he thought was wine. What he discovered was that it was very watery wine. He took two big gulps before holding up the cup and looking at it strangely.

"What is this?" he asked.

Diara grinned. "I had the servants bring watered wine," she said. "I thought it might slake your thirst better. Did I do wrong?"

He looked at her, trying to scowl, but he kept breaking out in a grin. "You did not do this to slake my thirst," he accused lightly. "You think I am becoming too drunk."

She bit her lip to keep from laughing. "How dare you say such things," she said, pretending to be indignant. "I did not. And I do not want you drunk when we retire for the evening."

He broke out in laughter, pulling her against him and kissing her on the cheek. "You devious cat," he said. "I should have watched my cup. And I will *never* be too drunk, I promise. Don't you believe me?"

"Should I?"

"You should," he insisted. "I would never lie to you, angel. You do believe that, don't you?"

She smiled at him, stroking his cheek. "Of course I do," she said. "There is no question."

He smiled in return, kissing her on the cheek again. "Then may I please have wine with no water in it?"

She laughed softly and nodded, and he released her long enough to summon a servant and procure a big cup of rich red wine. He took a big swallow, eyeing his father and Robin across the table, huddled in conversation.

"And as for our fathers," he said, "it looks much better between them than it did the last time I saw them together. I am pleased that your father is behaving himself."

Diara couldn't disagree. "As am I," she said, looking around the table and noting Roi's daughters directly across from them. They were sitting next to Iris, seemingly playing a game with her using pieces of bread on the tabletop. "I do not know if you realize this, but I've never had a conversation with Adalia. She seems to have been busy with her cousins during her stay here. Is she a shy lass?"

Roi looked over at his two living children. "Verily," he said. "That is why she likes to spend her time minding the children. She is very good with them, but she has always been quite shy with people she does not know. Coming to know her will take a little longer than it will with Dorian, who seems to love you already. But when I look at them, sitting there like that… it's a little strange for me."

"Why?"

"Because they look so much like Odette."

Diara looked at him. "Then she must have been very pretty," she said. She hesitated briefly before continuing. "What was she like?"

He met her gaze. "She was quiet and obedient," he said.

"She had some of Adalia's shyness. Truthfully, she was a gentle creature. I never heard her raise her voice or become angry. And she was devoted to the children."

"Then she was a good wife," Diara said. "Is it difficult for you to speak of her?"

He shook his head. "It used to be," he said. "Not any longer. That part of my life is in the past, and I am looking forward to the future."

He meant with her, and she smiled at him. "As am I," she said. "Mayhap it isn't the best place to ask about Odette, but you have never spoken of her, and Beckett did not tell me much, either. But he did say that she died in childbirth."

"She did," Roi said. "With Dorian. And I haven't spoken of her because it is painful. It is simply because there hasn't been any opportunity to do so. We are only coming to know one another, and I did not want to bring my dead wife into the conversation. It did not seem right."

Diara understood. "And here I am, asking about her on our wedding day," she said, giggling when he grinned. "Mayhap not the most appropriate conversation, but in a sense, it is. I think that she would want you to be happy, wouldn't she? And I see no issue with keeping her spirit alive, especially for your daughters."

He leaned over and kissed her again. "A very wise and sensible view," he said. "I am coming very much to appreciate that about you, angel. To be so generous to the woman who preceded you is wise and magnanimous, indeed."

Her eyes glimmered. "As long as you do not compare me to her, I will embrace her memory because she is part of you and part of your children," she said. "But I imagine it might be difficult, in the beginning, for you not to compare us. She is the only other wife you have had. Unless there are others I do not know of."

Her message was serious, but she said it in such a way that he did not take offense. He wouldn't have, anyway, because he completely understood what she was saying.

"There are no other wives, unless I was drunk at the time and do not recall," he said, jesting. But he quickly sobered. "I will tell you this now so there is no doubt—I would never compare you to Odette. The two of you are a world apart. She was gentle and quiet, and you are vivacious and have fire in your spirit. My mother even commented on it, and I told her that I loved that about you. I think Odette would laugh at me because I've found a woman whose determination and spirit can match my own."

Diara pinched his chin gently. "And that is a good thing, is it not?" she said. "But why would she laugh?"

He snorted. "Because she knows that, deep down, I fear a woman who is stronger than I am," he said. "She knows I will acquiesce to you in all things. But know that it does not concern me at all. I welcome it."

He swooped in to kiss her again, but someone was tugging on his sleeve, and he looked over his shoulder to see Dorian and Adalia standing next to him.

"Papa?" Dorian said, rubbing her eyes. "I'm sleepy. Grand-mother told me to ask permission to go to bed."

It was getting late. Roi shifted his chair, turning in the direction of his daughters, and Dorian slipped past him, straight into Diara's lap. Though there were only six years between them, Dorian clearly felt comfortable with Diara as either a mother figure or an older sister figure. Sitting on Diara's lap, she put her arms around the woman and laid her head on her shoulder.

It was something that touched Roi deeply.

"If you want to go to sleep, you cannot sleep on Diara," he said, watching Dorian grin. "But I agree with you. I like her, too."

Dorian smiled up at Diara, who put her hand on the child's head in a motherly fashion. Meanwhile, Roi turned to Adalia, his eldest daughter who looked very much like Odette. She was petite, with dark hair and dark eyes, and a fragile-looking face. Roi reached out and took her hand.

"And you, my lady?" he said. "Are you sleepy, too?"

Adalia nodded, but she kept turning her attention to the room, now stuffed with soldiers and knights as the wedding celebration continued. Then she looked down the table to where Christopher and Robin were seated, and beyond them sat a couple of men she didn't recognize.

"Aye," she said in a squeaky voice. "A little. But I was wondering something."

"What?"

She discreetly pointed down the table. "Who are those men on the other side of Taid?" she said, referring to Christopher using the Welsh name for grandfather that the de Lohr children sometimes used. "Are they knights?"

Both Roi and Diara looked down the table. It was Diara who spoke. "Those are my father's knights," she said, returning her attention to Adalia. "They have served Cheltenham for many years."

Adalia nodded, but it was clear that she was shy when it came to Diara. Everything Roi had said about her was becoming obvious.

"Oh," she said timidly.

It seemed that the conversation was ending right there because she couldn't bring herself to ask more questions. But then she leaned over and whispered something in his ear. Diara noticed that Roi was trying not to smile.

"I do not know," he told her. "I do not know the man."

Adalia whispered again into his ear. Roi listened before shrugging.

"You will have to ask Diara," he said. "She would know."

Both Roi and Adalia looked at Diara, but Adalia was looking at her with genuine fear. Seeing that the young woman evidently had a question, Diara smiled at her.

"What may I tell you, Adalia?" she said. "I am happy to tell you what I know."

Adalia flushed a deep shade of red and looked at her feet. Roi took pity on her.

"She wants to know who the handsome knight is at the end of the table," he said. "She further wants to know if he is married."

"Papa!" Adalia said, mortified. "You should not have said that!"

Roi laughed softly. "Lass, if you want to know the answer to something, you must ask the question," he said. When Diara looked at him curiously, he gestured down the table. "She is speaking of Mathis. Is he married?"

Diara shook her head. "He is not," she said. "Would you like me to introduce you?"

That nearly sent Adalia bolting from the table. Roi grabbed her before she could get away, but she was so embarrassed that she was starting to cry. As Roi pulled her back to the table, Diara reached out and grasped the young woman's sweaty palm.

"I am sorry you are embarrassed," she said gently. "You needn't be, I promise. Your secret is safe with me. I will not say a word to him if you do not want me to. Does that make you feel better?"

Roi had his big arm around Adalia as she sniffled and wiped her eyes, but after a moment, she nodded shortly. Just once. But it was enough.

"Good," Diara said. "Would you like me to tell you what I know about him? Mayhap that would help. I do not want you to be sad or embarrassed. His name is Mathis de Geld and he has seen twenty years and nine. He comes from an old family, and they have a castle in the north that is said to have housed the kings of Northumbria, back in the olden times when England was several different countries. He is an excellent knight, he likes to train horses, and I know that he likes sweets. Whenever the cook at Cicadia makes sweet cakes with honey and oats, he eats most of them before I can get any. As you can imagine, that makes me very angry."

Adalia's tears were fading and she was becoming interested in what Diara was telling her. She dared to look up, at the very knight Diara was telling her about, and didn't seem quite so mortified.

"I was taught to manage the kitchens when I fostered," she said in her small voice. "The cook was from France, and she taught me many wonderful things. I can make sweets."

That was the most Diara had heard from her since she'd met the girl. "That sounds marvelous," she said, trying to keep the conversation going. "What do you like best? Sweets, I mean."

Adalia thought on that question. "I like the cakes with apricots and honey," she said. "I can make little cakes with apples and cinnamon inside."

Diara smiled encouragingly. "Then, much like your sister, you are very clever," she said. "This is just a thought, of course, but if you would like to make some of those cakes—if your grandmother will permit you to use her cook and kitchen— Mathis is not returning home for a day or two. Time for you to make the cakes and for me to take them to him and not tell him who made them. Only that an admirer has sent them. That way, you do not have to face him at all, but you can still show your appreciation."

It was a sweet little plan and one that had Adalia's attention. She wouldn't have to meet or see Mathis, yet she could send her regards via baked goods. She looked at her father, who nodded in wholehearted agreement with the plan.

"I think that is a brilliant scheme," he told her. "But you are of age now, Adalia. I should be seeking you a husband, but you never seemed very interested. If you'd like to make great bunches of treats, I'll send them out to every eligible knight in England. You'll have your pick of men rushing to Pembridge, lured by your cooking talents."

Adalia's cheeks turned a deep red, but this time, she smiled. She wasn't crying or embarrassed because her father, whom she didn't have much of a relationship with, seemed to be interested in her and in her future. That bolstered her bravery. Truthfully, they'd never really spoken of such things, and although it made her uncomfortable, it also interested her.

It was something they could both relate to.

"You jest, Papa," she said. "Food will not lure a husband to my doorstep."

He lifted his eyebrows. "You think not?" he said, incredulous. "Your mother lured me with a meat pie. I would wager to say that half of the men in this hall, if they are married, were ensnared into marriage with something delicious to eat."

"It is as good a talent to display as any," Diara agreed. "It is something a man enjoys. All men eat, so why not show him how fat and content he will be once he marries you?"

Roi continued to nod, squeezing Adalia's hand when she looked at him. "I think it is an excellent idea," he said. "Now, you must take Dorian to bed, and I will see you both on the morrow. We will discuss this plan more in depth. Would you like that?"

Adalia nodded. "I would, Papa," she said. "Thank you."

"It wasn't my idea."

He tilted her head in Diara's direction, and Adalia took the hint. She focused on Diara, smiling timidly at her for the very first time.

"Thank you," she said. "You have been most kind."

Diara grinned at her very shy, very timid stepdaughter. "It was my pleasure," she said. "I hope to help you with many such things in the future, if I can."

Adalia continued to smile, somewhat bashfully, as she took Dorian away from Diara and led her off the dais by the hand. Roi and Diara watched the girls disappear into a servants' alcove, which opened up on a direct path to the keep. When they were gone, Roi turned to his new wife.

"Thank you for that," he said quietly. "She's such a timid creature, but she's a good girl. Relationships aren't easy for her. This is the first time she didn't outright weep when discussing a man or a betrothal. And she did not mention joining the cloister again, so this is an improvement for Adalia."

Diara reached for her cup of wine, which was nearly drained. "Then if she is truly agreeable to finding a husband, that just made your life a little more hectic," she said. "You'll be sorting through marital offers for her from now until she marries."

"Her?" Roi said. Then he shrugged. "She's a beautiful girl, but she's not a spirited creature. You saw her. She will be difficult for a man to woo."

"Mayhap not," Diara said. "With instruction from your mother and sisters, I am certain she will know how to behave."

He looked at her. "Why them?" he said. "You are now her mother, and you are the most charming and witty woman I have ever met. Why can you not teach her?"

"Because I do not know her well," Diara said. "She might learn better from someone she knows, not a woman she hardly knows who has happened to marry her father."

He took her hand, kissing it. "You are the perfect teacher," he said. "Thank you for being so kind to my daughters. As I said, I've not been around them much... I should like to change that. With Dorian, I think I distanced myself because her mother died giving birth to her. Mayhap I blamed her a little, though I know it was not her fault. It was safer to distance myself and not feel grief every time I looked at her."

Diara reached up and gently stroked his hair. "That is completely understandable," she said. "Odette passed away and suddenly, you have two girl children to parent by yourself. Moreover, you said yourself that they went away to foster young. It seems that you've hardly been around them during their lifetime."

"I know," he said, subdued. "I have been fighting wars all my life. I've been in London with Henry or on the battlefields in the name of the king. I am a dedicated man with an excellent reputation, and it was simply easier to let someone else tend to my children. Even Beckett—I did not see him as much as I would have liked to, but he was my son and I naturally related better to him. I understood him. I never wanted to admit that my daughters have suffered my absence, but the truth is that they have. Even though they've been home for a couple of years, it is not as if I spend a good deal of time with them. Mostly, my mother does when she can."

"Do you want to spend time with them?"

"I would like to know them better."

"Then I will help you," Diara said. "I would like to come to know them too. We can do it together."

He smiled at her, thinking that sounded quite wonderful. He hadn't had a wife in so many years that he'd forgotten what it was like to have one. Someone who was part of him as he was part of her, someone to bring his troubles to or have a simple conversation with. Someone to be a family with.

Aye, he loved that idea with Diara.

He never thought he'd experience that again.

"I think I would like that," he said. Then he made a big show of yawning. "But I think that I am weary, too. Shall we retire for the night?"

Diara knew what that meant, and her heart began to race. She was excited, she was apprehensive, and everything in between. She nodded, smiling, which masked the quivering that had suddenly taken over her entire body. Roi leaned over and muttered something to his brother, Curtis, who was sitting on his other side. Curtis simply nodded, and Roi stood up, extending a hand to Diara.

"Come with me," he said. "And hurry. No farewells."

Diara put her hand in his but looked at him with puzzlement. "Why not?" she asked. "My parents are just down the table. And Iris is sitting across from us, looking at me."

Roi leaned down and lowered his voice. "Because the moment my brothers and nephews realize we are retreating to our marital chamber, they will try to follow us. It will turn into a battle, so come with me and come quickly."

Diara did. She bolted up from the chair and let him take her from the dais and behind a screened area that the servants used. Once they were there, they were out of the field of vision of nearly everyone in the great hall, and Roi took her quickly to a small door that led outside.

It was misting outside, with the clouds hanging low, and they ran nearly the entire way across the bailey with Roi helping her hold up the hem of her skirt so it wouldn't get muddy. They made an odd pair, running through the muddy bailey, but moving quickly saved her dress from becoming too wet and too dirty. In fact, the only things that were dirty on her person were her slippers, and that couldn't be helped. Once inside the keep, they quickly proceeded up the stairs to Roi's chamber on the family level.

The chamber was dark except for a banked fire in the hearth, and Roi left Diara standing by the door as he went to stoke the fire for a little more light. When the blaze began to perk up, he took a small straw of kindling, lit it, and went over to a bank of candles against the wall.

One by one, he lit the fat, yellowed tapers, before moving to another bank of candles and doing the same thing. Soon, the entire chamber was aglow, and Diara came away from the door, seeing that Roi's bed looked like something rich and luxurious. It was covered with silk drapes and silk pillows and a coverlet stuffed with feathers, and lying on the corner of it was a garment of some kind.

She held it up in the light.

"A robe," she said, fingering the elaborately embroidered fabric. "This is beautiful. Is it yours?"

He chuckled. "Does that look like it would fit me?"

She held out the sleeves before shaking her head. "You might be able to get one arm into the main part of it," she said. "But the sleeves would not fit you."

"Nay, they would not."

"Is it for me?"

Roi nodded faintly. "It is from my mother and father," he said. "While I went to Cheltenham to retrieve you, she went to Hereford and had this made. It's silk with rabbit lining."

Diara laid it back on the bed. It was pink, that color she positively detested, with a white fur lining. Truthfully, it was exquisite. It would have been magnificent had she not hated pink so, but she turned to Roi with her eyes alight.

"It's positively beautiful," she said. "Your mother was so kind to give this to me."

"I'm glad you like it."

She nodded, her smile fading as she looked at him seriously. "It's strange, truly," she said. "I have spent the vast majority of my life alone. I've never had many friends, as you know, and in my family, I am the only child. In the past few days, I've come to know this massive family you have, and it has given me a sense of belonging I've never experienced before. It's a crowded sensation, but a lovely one."

He went to her, taking the robe from her. "I hope it will become something you are always comfortable with and grow to appreciate," he said, holding up the robe. "Would you like to try this on?"

Still in her red silk dress, she put her arms through the

sleeves, which were big and belled. It was a delightful garment, and she turned to him with a grin, prompting him to wrap her up in his arms and hug her tightly. Their first true embrace as man and wife. It would have been an incredibly enticing moment except for one thing.

They began to hear singing.

Puzzled, they looked at one another to make sure they weren't hearing things. Clearly, Diara heard it, and so did Roi. They weren't hallucinating. Roi leaned toward the chamber door, but it didn't seem to be coming from there. Diara was already moving to the window, and he came up beside her in time to see several men gathered three stories below in the dark, misty bailey.

And they were singing.

There was a farmer and a whore,
A woman who demanded more!
Plow my field, she begged,
Plant your seed and do it again,
And the farmer used his plow on the sow!

They broke down into uproarious laughter at the lewd song, lifting their cups of wine to the married couple over their heads. As Roi waved his hands at them in an attempt to force them to stop, they launched into the second verse.

Aye, the farmer had a plow,
A plow that could topple a cow.
He used the whore, she cried for more,
But his wife came back from the store.
Now the farmer is nevermore, nevermore!

They were shouting more than singing by that point, howling at the bawdy song. Diara covered her mouth so they wouldn't see her grin as Roi, biting off laughter, continued to wave his hands at the group.

"Get out of here, you fools," he demanded. "Take your filthy plows elsewhere!"

They roared with laughter. Roi could see that the group was comprised of Douglas and Westley, Gallus, Tiberius, Maximus, and Andrew. There were also several de Lohr soldiers trailing after them from the great hall, who were now shouting up at the window.

"Take her by the hair and tie her to the bed, m'lord!" someone cried. "Women like it when you tie them up!"

Roi smirked, shaking his head at the group, turning to Diara and mouthing, *Nay, they do not.* She burst out laughing as Roi shouted down to the group again.

"If I have to leave this chamber to come down there to disperse the group, you will not be pleased," he warned. "It would be safer if you simply go back into the hall and stay there."

"Give her the flesh sword, Roi!"

That one came from Westley, who was quite drunk. But the entire group took up cries of "sheathe the flesh sword, sheathe the flesh sword!" and Roi slapped a hand over his face in disbelief while Diara giggled uncontrollably. At that point, Roi had had enough, and he shook a fist at the group below.

"Go *away*," he said. "That is not a request!"

As he reached for Diara to pull her inside, the group shouted up one last batch of encouragement.

"Demand the prick, Lady de Lohr!"

"Poke her, Roi!"

"Bury the matrimonial sword!"

That brought laughter from both Roi and Diara as he pulled his new wife into the chamber and dropped the oil cloth over the window opening. Diara was laughing so hard that she was wiping tears from her eyes, but just as she was calming down, she looked at Roi and started laughing all over again because he was smirking. He was terribly embarrassed. He opened his mouth to say something, but a faint shout caught his attention.

"Roi!" It was Douglas. "Shall I come up and give you some instructions? Shall I show you how it is done, brother?"

They could hear the laughter outside, and Roi rolled his eyes. "God's Bones," he muttered. "That group is enough to drive any man insane with rage. I am sorry, angel. They mean well."

Diara was still smiling. "They do it because they love you," she said. "I've seen enough mean-spirited men to know that they were not being malicious. They are simply happy."

Roi shrugged. "I suppose," he said, moving to the bed and sitting heavily. He puffed out his cheeks. "I did not realize how exhausted I was until this moment. It has been an eventful day."

She stood about a foot away, smiling at him. "Too exhausted?" she said. "Then mayhap you should go to sleep and we will continue this in the morning."

He looked at her for a moment before whipping out an arm and pulling her against him. "There is not a chance that will happen," he muttered, his face in her neck. "You and I have business to attend to."

Diara was quickly succumbing to his heated breath on her skin, his powerful body wrapping itself around her. "Business, is it?" she asked breathlessly. "What business could we possibly have?"

His lips were on her shoulder, but he couldn't help from

smiling. "You are about to find out."

It didn't matter that Diara had never really been in an intimate position like this. It didn't matter that she'd never gone beyond the kiss she and Roi had shared in the solar. Her mind might be naïve, but her body wasn't. It was responding, innately, to what it had been born and bred to do—respond to a man's touch. Everything about her was on fire as Roi kissed her, and she could hear her heart pounding in her ears.

"Show me," she whispered.

Roi didn't need any further prompting. Her request had him on fire, and he cupped her face in his two enormous hands, bringing her mouth to his. When his lips claimed hers, it was hungrily, as if he had never kissed a woman before until this moment. He'd been married before. He'd had women before. But not like this—never like this. It was as if Diara was the only one. As his tongue began to lick her, begging for welcome into her warm, delicious mouth, his hands moved from her face and went to work on her clothing.

The red dress came off, seemingly dissolving in his hands, and he had no idea why. He didn't think he'd pulled that hard on it, but he evidently didn't know his own strength. The entire thing began to fall away, and it took him a moment to realize that it was because Diara was helping him.

Inch by inch, the dress slid off her body and onto the floor.

Beneath that, she wore a shift, which came off as well, and in the dim light of a dozen glowing tapers, Roi found himself gazing at his wife's perfect, nude body. He couldn't remember ever seeing anything so completely arousing, but as he moved to pull her against him, he realized he was still wearing his clothing, and, almost frantically, it began to come off.

The tunic went over his head, and he tossed it to the ground before untying his breeches. He had to let her go in order to pull those off, and they ended up on the floor alongside the tunic. In all his naked glory, Roi returned his attention to Diara only to see that she was sitting on the bed trying to cover her chest with her arms. She seemed embarrassed, and probably cold, and he felt remorse that he hadn't shown more consideration. This was her first experience with a man, after all, and even though she was a strong and brave woman, she couldn't pretend that she was completely comfortable. Rather than try to move her arms, he simply pulled her into a tight embrace and covered her with his big body.

Together, they fell back on the bed.

He literally could not wait to get the woman on her back. It had been years since he'd bedded his wife, and he hadn't had a woman since she passed away, so his arousal was instantly quite stiff. Even his testicles were inflamed and swollen, as tight as an archer's bow, so he eased Diara down onto the bed and genuinely tried to control himself. He didn't want to act like a rutting bull, as if joining his body with her was all he cared about. There was so much more to it than that. But she was compliant, and his tender kisses told her without word how beautiful and desirable she was. Her arms went around his neck, her full and naked breasts against his broad chest. Roi could feel them, soft and round, and it was about all he could take.

He hungered for her in the worst, and best, possible way.

After he laid her against the bed, his hands began to wander. His right hand found her beautiful breasts, and he listened to her sigh with both surprise and pleasure when his palm closed around one. She stiffened a little, unfamiliar with the sensation, but he caressed her breast gently, toying with her nipples, until she began to relax again. He hoped she was enjoying it from the soft gasping she was emitting, but those sounds were driving him mad with lust.

His roving hands moved lower.

Every moment of exploration was better than the one before. Her skin was like silk beneath hands that had killed men, and he almost felt guilty for touching such virgin skin with those bloodstained appendages. But those same hands were as gentle as a kitten, and he worshiped every inch, every curve. He knew that he was unworthy of this beautiful creature, but he was willing to spend the rest of his life paying homage to her.

She smelled of flowers, pure and sweet, uninhibited and intoxicating. His hand moved down her torso and to her right thigh, grasping her behind the knee and pulling her legs apart so he could settle his big body between her legs. He began to drag his lips over her neck, tasting her beauty, feeling the warmth of her flesh against his tongue, but that only served to inflame his hunger.

Unable to hold off any longer, Roi rubbed his arousal against the pink flower between her legs, coaxing forth her warm wetness that would prepare her body for his entry. He could feel her wet heat, so he drew back and thrust into her, firmly but slowly, pushing his way into her body and taking possession of a woman who aroused him like no one else ever had. He could feel her tight heat around him, those honeyed walls that would give him life's greatest pleasure. His future son, if he had one, would be born here. It was a silken sheath meant only for him, and much as his brother had said, he was sheathing the matrimonial sword. When he thought of that, it brought a grin, but not laughter.

This was no laughing matter.

He was in heaven.

He drew back again, thrusting harder, making headway into her tight and virginal body. Beneath him, Diara groaned at the sting of possession, a sound somewhere between pleasure and pain. Roi took it as pleasure and thrust again, harder, listening to her gasp as he seated himself fully. Like her woman's center unfurling for him, her legs seemed to unfurl as well, opening wider to accommodate his enormous size. His hands slipped underneath her, holding her buttocks to him as he began to move.

Roi thrust hard, again and again, as Diara lay beneath him and softly moaned. Her hands touched him, timidly at first but with increasing confidence. The sensation was overwhelming to him, and he tried to ignore it, just a little, because he knew that if he gave in, all of this would be over well before he wanted it to be. So he focused on the feel of her in his hands, the feel of his body in hers, until her soft hands moved to his hips. When she dug in and he felt her nails prick him, his self-control ended. He spilled himself deep into her virginal womb, feeling every spasm, every twitch, down to his very bones.

Still, he continued to move. He was still hard. His thrusts grew gentler, longer, as he reached down to touch her where their bodies joined. It was enough to throw Diara over the edge, and her first climax washed over her. Her entire body stiffened, her back arched, and he held her tightly, suckling at her breasts, as a powerful release pulsed through her.

It was the most passionate thing he'd ever experienced.

Eventually, the squirming stopped. The thrusting stopped. Diara lay pinned beneath Roi's body, her arms around his neck and her legs wrapped around his hips. They simply lay there, the only sound being their heavy breathing. What they'd experienced together was everything Roi had imagined and everything Diara had hoped for. It was a coupling that drew them closer together, bonding them.

Filling them.

They had become one.

CHAPTER TWELVE

WHEN DIARA OPENED her eyes the next morning, it was to Roi staring at her.

Startled, she blinked a few times, trying to orient herself and quickly remembering where she was and whom she was with. And why. Very clearly, she remembered why.

She remembered everything.

"Good morn to you, angel," he purred.

With a smile, Diara wrapped her arms around his neck and pulled him down to her. In little time, he was sheathing the matrimonial sword again, buried down deep in the mattress where it was warm and musky and smelled of him. His flesh against hers, her legs wrapped around him, feeling his manhood as he brought her to a climax rather quickly. Roi followed, spilling himself with the greatest of pleasure, as his lips feasted on her neck and shoulder. He feasted on everything about her as Diara lay there and let him.

She let him do anything he wanted.

"I had not expected to do that," he muttered as he kissed her ear. "I thought it might not be too comfortable for you so soon after last night, but evidently, I was mistaken."

Diara laughed softly. "You were mistaken, indeed, my lord," she said. "Do not make that mistake again."

"Then I am to assume that you like the matrimonial sword when it is sheathed?"

Her laughter grew. Since nearly the moment they were introduced, Roi had had the ability to make her laugh, and she loved that. Even when it was slightly bawdy. She'd never known such genuine, unbridled joy.

"I do," she said. "Truthfully, I did not know what to expect, but you have made it easy for me. You are a thoughtful and considerate husband."

He smiled, stroking her cheek as he gazed down at her. "I awoke at sunrise to watch you sleep," he said. "You are so beautiful when you sleep."

She put a hand to her mussy hair. "Like this?" she said. "I must look like I was caught in a tempest."

"You look like an angel."

"You are sweet to say so."

"It is the truth."

The cry of a bird caught her attention, and she turned her head slightly, seeing that the oilcloth had been removed from one of the windows and the sun was streaming in. But she had no intention of getting out of bed, not with Roi so warm and cozy.

"How long has the sun been up?" she asked. "Please tell me we do not have to rise right away."

He glanced over his shoulder, at the window. "About an hour," he said. "Oddly enough, mornings are not my favorite time of day, which is not usual for a knight. Every knight I know is up before sunrise, tending his duties."

"But not you?"

He shifted so he was lying beside her and not on her, gathering her into his arms. "Only out of necessity," he said. "I prefer the dark. The twilight. The moment the day turns to night."

"Why?"

He shrugged. "There is a peace to it, I suppose," he said. "The twilight, I mean. But the dark... that is when I feel the most alive. That is when the earth is the most alive. Creatures and people and things move through the dark and there is an entire world we do not see. Twilight is the birth of that world. A rebirth of the day it was part of."

Diara's head was against his shoulder as she tried to picture the world that his words were painting. "That is interesting," she said. "I've never thought of it that way."

"No one does."

Her hand was on his chest, and she patted him gently. "Only you," she said. "That makes you unique. I think it also makes you a predator."

"Why would you say that?"

"Don't predators hunt at night?"

He turned his head so he was peering down at the top of her head. "You are the only prey I want to catch."

"You have already caught me."

He pulled her closer, kissing the top of her head, but before he could say another word, he began to hear voices from the bailey.

They were calling his name.

"God's Bones," Diara muttered. "Them again? Can they not leave us alone?"

Roi was torn between great irritation and great amusement. He let her go and rolled out of the bed, marching across the floor, stark naked, to the window.

"You idiots have angered my wife!" he shouted as he approached the window and subsequently hung out of it. "I am trying to convince her not to go down to the bailey and flog every one of you, so if you are wise, you will leave us alone!"

But the usual crowd wasn't down below—it was Curtis and a man Roi hadn't seen at the wedding or the subsequent feast. He found himself looking down at his cousin, Daniel de Lohr, the son of Christopher's only brother, David. David was, in fact, the Earl of Canterbury through his marriage, a title Daniel would inherit someday. He was also the liveliest and most emotional, humorous, and impulsive member of the de Lohr family. They used to call him the Prodigal Son because of his inability to stay in one place for too long until he married nearly ten years before. Then Daniel had settled down with his wife and children up in Yorkshire, which was why Roi was quite surprised to see him.

"Send her down!" Daniel called back to him. "I would like to meet this poor woman you have forced into marriage. I must tell her what she is in for with you."

Roi beamed at the sight of his cousin. "Danny," he said with delight. "When did you arrive?"

"Before sunrise, little prince," Daniel said, taunting him. "Uncle Christopher's precious little boy was still in bed, and I was told not to wake you, but it is more than an hour after sunrise and the day is wasting away. Pull yourself away from your new wife and get down here. I did not come all the way to Lioncross only to be saddled with your boring brothers for entertainment."

Roi laughed. "I must ask my wife," he said. "We have only just been married, you know. She may not want me to leave her anytime soon."

Curtis chimed in, waving a big arm at him. "Come down here, you gutless knave," he said. "The games are already being organized in honor of your wedding, and you do not want to miss them."

Roi wagged a finger at his brother. "I told you," he said. "No targeting my knees, buttocks, ballocks, or anything else I might need. Did you tell the others?"

Curtis nodded patiently. "I told them," he said. "At least, I did last night, but Douglas and Westley are still in bed, sleeping off the massive amounts of wine they consumed last night. So are many of the others. I'm not entirely sure we'll have an adequate amount of competitors for any of the games after that drunken orgy last night."

Roi rolled his eyes. "I am not surprised," he said. "Give me a few moments to get dressed and I shall meet you in the hall."

With that, he turned away from the window with the full intention of getting dressed and rushing down to see Daniel. But his eyes fell on the bed where Diara was sitting up, the coverlet clutched to her naked breast, and it took him a moment to realize that she was looking at him with a rather startled expression.

"I am sorry, angel," he said. "I've not seen my cousin, Daniel, in quite some time. May I go down and see him?"

Diara nodded, but she quickly averted her gaze. "Of course," she said. "You should go, right away."

He smiled gratefully and went on the hunt for his clothing. His tunic was on one spot, his breeches in another, and he had to walk to both sides of the bed in order to find everything. He went over to the big wardrobe against the wall to hang up the silk tunic he'd worn for his wedding and collect a more durable one that could handle the events planned for the day. But the entire time he was prancing around naked, he noticed one thing.

Diara wouldn't look at him.

He walked to one side of the bed and she'd turn her attention to the other. Then he'd walk back only for the same thing to happen in reverse. When he realized that, he could see that her cheeks were a dull red. It occurred to him that she was embarrassed to have a naked man parading in front of her, being that the lass hadn't even been kissed until a few days ago, and he thought it was rather sweet that she should be so prim. With his clothing in his hands, he sauntered over to the bed.

"Shall I send Iris up to help you dress?" he asked.

She had her head lowered. "I would appreciate that, thank you."

"My pleasure." He was standing right next to her, his flaccid manhood at the level of her head. "Which tunic do you think I should wear today?"

She only glanced up, sort of, to see what he had in his hand. "I… I like the blue one," she said.

He was fighting off a grin. "You did not even look."

"I did."

"Don't you like what you see?"

Diara began to catch on to the fact that he was teasing her, and she knew why. It embarrassed her to realize that he knew why she wouldn't look at him. From the moment he left the bed and crossed over to the window, she'd been confronted with perfect buttocks, a tight waist, impossibly broad shoulders attached to big arms, and legs that were rippling with muscles. Everything about him sang of perfection, and as she stared at his backside, becoming accustomed to his nude form, he'd suddenly turned around and she was confronted by his flaccid manhood.

That had sent the flames into her cheeks.

And he knew it.

"I like what I see," she said, still unable to look at him. "I like it very much."

"Then why don't you look at me?"

She sighed sharply. "Can I simply not take the time to get used to the idea?" she said irritably. "I have to lust over you like a dog over fresh meat right from the onset?"

He began to laugh. "I have lusted over you from the onset."

"But you have seen a woman without her clothing on before," she pointed out. "I've never seen a man lacking... attire."

His laugh deepened, and he took pity on her, pulling his breeches on and tying them off. "There, you coward," he said. "I am modestly covered. Will you at least look at me now?"

Diara lifted her eyes, fighting off a grin. "There may be a time when I demand you keep your clothing off, and then you'll be sorry."

"I doubt it."

The man gave her a cheeky wink and turned around, heading back over to the wardrobe, but Diara grabbed a pillow and threw it at him, hitting him in the back of the head. Chuckling, he picked it up and tossed it back onto the mattress before he finished dressing.

"Now," he said as he went back to the bed, "I will have food and a bath sent up to you along with Iris. Is there anything else you require?"

Diara shook her head. "Not that I can think of," she said. "But these games... What will you be playing?"

He shook his head. "I do not know," he said. "But send a

servant to the hall to fetch me when you are ready to come downstairs. I will escort you to the field."

"What field?"

He jabbed a thumb toward the south. "There is an open field on the other side of the road that leads to the gatehouse," he said. "We've held tournaments there in the past, so I'm assuming that is where these games will be held."

"Then I will bathe and dress quickly."

He bent over and kissed her. "Take your time, angel," he said. "We shall wait for you."

She put her hand behind his neck and pulled him down for another kiss. "I do not want to miss anything," she insisted. "I will be ready within the hour, I promise."

He smiled at her and touched her cheek affectionately before heading toward the door. Diara watched him, tall and strong and proud, her heart swelling with delirious joy at the sight of him. Her husband. *Her* Roi. No offense to Beckett, but she knew she'd married the right de Lohr.

Lifting the latch on the door, he paused and looked at her. "One more thing," he said.

"What is it?"

He appeared thoughtful. "I do not believe that I have told you that I love you."

Her lips broke out in the most amazing grin. "I do not believe I have told you that I love you, either."

"I do, you know."

"So do I."

Flashing her a toothy smile, he winked at her and quit the chamber, leaving Diara floating about five feet off the bed in euphoric delight.

CB

THE FIRST GAME was called, simply, "ball."

The object was to take an inflated pig's bladder from one end of the tournament field to the other and place it in a basket. There was a basket at either end and there were two teams, essentially just two groups of men, and each group was to protect their end and their basket from the other team, who would try to put their pig's bladder in it.

It was chaos from the start.

Diara stood at the edge of the field with the other de Lohr ladies and Iris, watching Roi, his cousin Daniel, Curtis, knights Kyne and Adrius, Gallus and Maximus, and a few soldiers as they took their ball and tried to plow through the other group of men, which was comprised of Westley, Douglas, Mathis and Pryce, Tiberius, a few guests, and a couple of soldiers. Roi wasn't the tallest de Lohr brother, but he was more than likely the most powerful, because his team gave him the ball every time and he essentially plowed through the opposing group like a runaway bull, with men hanging off him trying to bring him down.

It was hilarious and thrilling to watch.

Adalia and Dorian were also watching the games, with Dorian holding Diara's hand and Adalia essentially clinging to her grandmother. Mathis and Pryce were part of the opposition against Roi, and Adalia was particularly interested in watching that team but too shy to admit it.

Peter, Christopher, and his brother, David, were the field marshals for the game, calling for pause whenever Roi or someone else would go down. If a man dropped the ball and the other team picked it up, then that team would try to run it back the other direction. At one point, Roi was hit hard from the side by Westley, who lay on the field in agony next to Roi, who had only gone down to his knees. Westley's head was killing him from a night of overindulgence, and when he hit Roi and caused him to falter, Roi dropped the ball and went after Westley, throwing him in a chokehold and rubbing his knuckles across the top of Westley's aching head.

The crowd roared with laughter.

But the gesture caused Westley to jump on Roi's back every time he ran with the bladder in an attempt to bring him down. Given that Westley was a large man, he was successful more than once, which only made Roi grab him in frustration. Several times, they started to brawl, but Christopher and David broke it up, sending them to opposite sides of the field until the bladder was in play again and Westley would try to jump on Roi.

And the situation would repeat itself.

Unfortunately for Westley, Curtis was onto him. Curtis and Roi, the eldest brothers, stuck to each other like glue, and Curtis took Westley down when he tried to jump on Roi again. That brought Douglas, who would back Westley, and the de Lohr brothers were throwing punches, tripping one another, launching themselves at each other, and more besides. Peter got into the act, naturally siding with Curtis and Roi because they were the older brothers, and the game deteriorated into a battle between the de Lohr brothers, so Christopher finally put a stop to it and declared Roi's team the winners.

Westley didn't take kindly to it.

Sweaty, dirty, and sporting a cut above his right eye, Roi joined Diara on the edge of the field. She gave him a hero's welcome, hugging him and clapping, and the ladies around her joined in. Roi took a gallant bow, accepting a hug from Dorian, but Douglas and Westley crowded in and started to complain to Dustin, insisting that Roi had cheated. Diara and Roi stood together, shaking their heads at the annoying younger brothers.

"Are they always like this?" Diara asked.

Roi nodded firmly. "Always," he said. "I was nine years of age when Douglas was born and nearly twelve when Westley was born, so they have always been the little brothers. Any little thing and they would go running to my mother to cry and complain, like they are doing now. Some things never change."

Diara chuckled at the pair, who were trying very hard to convince Dustin that they were angels and that Roi was the devil himself. But watching them with their mother reminded Diara that her own parents were missing from the festivities, and she looked around, hoping she might have missed their arrival.

"I thought my father would be here, at least," she said, looking over her shoulder at the great walls of Lioncross. "I wonder if I should return to the castle and escort them over to the field?"

Roi looked over at the castle also. "Did you ask Mathis or Pryce where they are?"

"Nay."

"Roi!"

They both looked over to see Kyne waving Roi over to the middle of the field, and he obliged. As he headed over to a host of men standing around, Diara was increasingly focused on her missing parents. She mentioned it to Dustin, who offered to retrieve them, but Diara declined. They were her parents, after all, so she felt the duty should be hers. As the group of men decided what game to set up next, she scurried back across the road and in through Lioncross' enormous gatehouse.

The castle was virtually deserted except for a stalwart crew of soldiers manning the battlements, and one very old knight with a Teutonic accent commanding them. Diara headed for the keep, passing through the entry and realizing that the place seemed strangely empty with all of the de Lohrs out watching the game. In fact, it seemed eerily still because the castle was always full of people. It seemed so lonely without them. She was about to take the mural stairs to the guest wing where her parents were lodged when she heard something coming from Christopher's solar. Curious, she stuck her head in.

Robin was inside, alone.

He had his back to her, looking through something on a table against the wall. Puzzled, Diara stepped into the chamber.

"Papa?" she said. "What are you doing?"

Robin jumped, startled, and whirled to face her. He had something in his hand that he had yet to release, and to Diara, it looked like a missive. She pointed at it, but before she could speak, Robin interrupted.

"Looking for maps," he said. "You know I collect many maps. I wanted to see if Lord Hereford had any maps that included Cheltenham."

Diara wasn't hard-pressed to admit that she didn't believe him. Not for one moment. It was simply in the way he'd said it and his nervous body language. Furthermore, he had a strange look in his eye and was smiling far more than necessary.

Something seemed off to her.

"There are games going on to celebrate the wedding," she said. "Where is Mama? I thought you would both come out to watch the games."

Robin shook his head. "I am not one for games," he said. "You know that."

"But it is a celebration, Papa," she said as if she had to remind him. "It will be humiliating if the parents of the bride are not celebrating the wedding and isolating themselves from everyone. I realize that we did not marry when you wanted us to, but—"

He cut her off, rather sharply. "There is no humiliation to be had," he said. "I simply do not like games. Would you force me to watch them when I do not enjoy them?"

Diara was becoming impatient. "For my sake, you could make the effort," she said. "Papa, I know we've not had a chance to speak since your arrival, but you should know that I am very happy with Roi. I realize that I was unsure in the beginning, but I have come to know him, and he is a remarkable man. He's kind and thoughtful and he makes me laugh. He is a man to be proud of, so for my sake, will you please come outside and watch the games?"

Robin wasn't fond of the request. That much was clear. He hadn't been looking for maps, as he'd told his daughter. Simply put, he'd been snooping. With everyone over at the tournament field across the road, and he knew very well that they were over there, he had the run of the keep. He'd been able to read several missives between Henry and Christopher, between Christopher and some of his allies, and he got a general sense that Christopher controlled a world that Robin could only hope for. It served to underscore what he had feared—in the de Lohr world, he'd be a bug against a swarm of giants.

He wanted his own world to control.

More and more, he knew that only his daughter could bring him that.

But he had to proceed carefully.

"There is plenty of time to watch men chasing after one

another," he said evenly. "I've simply been enjoying the hospitality of Lioncross. The castle reminds me of another place I have visited. I believe you have visited it, also. Do you recall Totterdown Castle?"

Diara sighed heavily. "I remember," she said. "A big place that smelled of the dogs and pigs they kept in the hall. It was a horrible place."

Robin shrugged. "Horrible but big," he said. "Big like Lioncross' keep. It's also rich like Lioncross."

"Papa, I have no desire to speak on Totterdown Castle," she said. "Will you *please* come to the field with me?"

Robin looked at her with displeasure in his eyes. "Can you not spend just a few moments alone with your father?" he nearly demanded. "Must we only see one another when you are in a crowd of de Lohrs? As you said, I did not have the opportunity to speak to you at all during or after your wedding. During the feast, you only had eyes for your husband. I realize you feel that you can belittle and humiliate me now that you have married Roi, but let me assure you that your control of the situation is only temporary. Soon enough, you'll understand your place and you will give me the respect I am due."

Diara was looking at him with concern after that little diatribe. "Control of the situation?" she repeated, puzzled. "What does that mean? I have no control over anything. And if my attention is on Roi, it is because he is my husband. That is where my attention should be."

Robin realized he'd said too much in his irritation, but it was an effort not to say more. He very much wanted to because it seemed to him that his daughter's focus on Roi had somehow weakened her respect for him. He could pinpoint it to the moment back at Cicadia when he had wanted them to marry right away and Roi refused.

That had been the beginning of the end, for everything. He was rather hoping that had been an isolated incident and that the marriage was not at all a happy one for her, but he knew he'd been living a false dream with that hope. From what he saw at the wedding ceremony, the two of them were quite enamored with each other.

And that upset him deeply.

"This marriage does not displease you, I take it?" he asked.

"Nay, it does not," Diara replied. "I am very happy."

"You have *me* to thank for that."

"Thank you, Papa."

"You know that I will always do what is best for you, don't you?"

"Aye, Papa."

"You were not keen on this betrothal in the beginning, but I knew it was best."

"Aye, Papa."

"I will always do what is best."

"Aye, Papa." Diara watched him as he started to nose around Christopher's desk again. "Please come with me. You should not be here in Lord Hereford's solar, alone."

He cast her a long look. "Will you tell him that I was?"

"Nay," she said. "But leave with me now. I will not go until you do."

God, how he hated a woman who took a stand. Ananda had been his wife for twenty-three years, and she'd never once tried to assert herself like Diara was doing now. That infuriated him. He walked up to her, only slightly taller than she was, and looked down his nose at her.

"Marrying Roi has made you brave," he said. "But that will

not last."

With that, he headed out of the solar, leaving Diara trailing after him, puzzled by his behavior and what sounded ostensibly like a threat. Her father had always been ambitious and direct, but his behavior since learning of Beckett de Lohr's death had been... strange. Very strange. She couldn't put her finger on why he was being so odd. Something told her that there was more than met the eye, but she was at a loss as to what, exactly, that could be.

Perhaps she didn't want to know.

But something told her she'd find out soon enough.

CHAPTER THIRTEEN

T HEY WERE KNOWN as Executioner Knights.

Roi recognized them as they trotted up the road, heading for Lioncross' enormous gatehouse. There were three of them, traveling alone, but with men such as that, it was perfectly safe. They were perfectly capable of defending themselves against terrible odds. They could have probably taken on an entire army and emerged the victors.

Men who achieved the position of Executioner Knight did not do it because they were weak.

It was because they were the best.

In truth, these men were second-generation Executioner Knights. Their fathers had been some of the first men that William Marshal, Earl of Pembroke and the man known as England's greatest knight, recruited when he formed a circle of spies, assassins, and warriors that comprised the most elite group in all of England. Marshal used the men to keep England balanced.

They shadowed kings, killed enemies, fought off invasions—anything to keep their country strong. Their dedication was to the country above all, but they'd come into being during the time of King Richard but wholly during the reign of King John. After John's demise and the ascension of Henry III, they continued their duties even after William Marshal passed away. They were subsequently commanded by Marshal sons, and were now under the command of Anselm Marshal, a man who was in poor health and the last of his family. Rumor had it that command of the Executioner Knights would fall to Christopher de Lohr, one of the most respected men in all of England.

And a man who had been an Executioner Knight for more than sixty years.

Christopher had mostly been a warlord, though he'd worked closely with William Marshal as the man manipulated the politics and players of England. Peter, Christopher's son, had been a great Executioner Knight, now mostly retired due to his age, while Christin's husband, Sherry, and even Christin herself had been spies during their younger years. Truth be told, Roi had been involved with them in his younger years as well, as had Curtis. Douglas and Westley had avoided the service because Christopher had other duties for them, but Myles de Lohr—the great middle brother—was a fully fledged Execution-er Knight, and the main reason he wasn't at the wedding was because he was off on a mission.

Wherever there was need in England, the Executioner Knights—and the de Lohrs—answered the call.

These days, the sons of the original Executioner Knights were taking charge, and the three knights now taking a turn off the road and heading in their direction were the offspring of two of the original knights. Roi recognized Magnus of Lox-beare, his brother Aeron of Loxbeare, and Tiegh de Dere. Breaking away from the group of men organizing the next game, he waved them over.

Tiegh was the first man off his horse, grinning as he embraced Roi. He was tall and sinewy, with his mother's blond hair and his father's features. Tiegh was a likeable man, much like his father had been, amiable in every way but also deadly in every way. Next to him, Aeron reined his horse around and bailed off, moving to embrace Roi and congratulate him. He, too, was the congenial sort. But the last man to relay his greeting was Magnus, who was like his father in every way— surly, bad tempered, not particularly fun to be around, but a more professional and dedicated knight had never existed.

And he particularly liked Roi.

"Roi," Magnus said with satisfaction, reaching out to grasp him with both hands. "My deepest condolences on your son. Please know how heartbroken my entire family is on his passing."

Roi forced a smile. "Thank you," he said. "It has been difficult, of course, but for today, I have put my mourning aside. My mother says that Beckett would be happy that I have remarried, so I am focusing on the good. And today is very good."

Magnus grinned. "Is it?" he said. "Good. Then please accept my heartiest congratulations, old man. My father sends his regrets that he was unable to attend. He has sent us instead."

"I am sorry he was unable to come," Roi said. "I hope he is not in ill health?"

Magnus and Aeron passed glances. "He's not well," Magnus finally said. "In fact, he sent me with a message for your father. Where is he?"

Roi pointed back to the collection of men several feet away. "Over there," he said. "Shall I fetch him?"

Magnus shook his head, his dark eyes seeking out Christopher amongst the crowd. "Nay," he said. "I will find him."

Roi put his hand on the man's arm as he started to walk toward the group. "I am sorry for your father, Magnus," he said, looking to Aeron. "I am sorry for both of you. Maxton of Loxbeare is a great man. That is how I will always remember him and men like him, no matter how old they become or how failing their health. They will always be those men I grew up admiring."

Aeron smiled weakly. "He always liked you a great deal," he said. "Truthfully, he wanted to come very much, but my mother would not let him."

Roi understood that. He understood aging parents and the dynamics of such things. "May I ask what is wrong with Maxton?" he said. "Is it something to be cured?"

Aeron shook his head. "Nay," he said quietly. "Apoplexy. A few months ago, he awoke one morning and could not move one side of his body. The physics tell us that he will not improve. It is simply a matter of time until… Suffice it to say he will not improve."

Roi sighed sadly, putting his hand over his heart in a show of grief for the health of Maxton of Loxbeare. "I do not think my father knows," he said. "He's not said a word to me about it."

"He does not know," Magnus said. "No one really does. My mother did not want anyone to know, but my father is growing worse, so she has given me permission to tell your father. As I said, I come with a message for him."

Roi swept his arm in the direction of the group of men, and both Magnus and Aeron continued on to find Christopher. That left Roi standing with Tiegh, and he looked at the man, distress on his features.

"Please tell me that your father and mother are faring better," he said.

Tiegh nodded. "My father is in good health, thank you," he said. "My mother also. They spend their time with their grandchildren these days. My sisters have fifteen children between them, so the keep is full of screaming children. My father also wanted to come when he received the missive from your father about your marriage, but traveling is difficult for him these days. He is old, Roi. I volunteered to come instead because I wanted to see you and meet your new wife."

Roi smiled weakly. "And you shall meet her," he said. "I will go with you to take the horses over to the stables because she is in the keep with her parents. Her father is the Earl of Cheltenham, you know. She is the heiress, which means someday, the title will be mine."

He meant to boast because Tiegh was one of those people who boasted about anything and everything, so Roi wanted to gain the upper hand. But there was humor to it, especially when Tiegh appeared absolutely appalled at the prospect.

"To the devil with you, de Lohr," he scoffed. "I shall never bow down to you, even if you are an earl."

Roi chuckled. "Careful, lad," he said. "I may have to flog you in public for that."

"You will have to catch me first."

Laughing, they took the horses, including the two left behind by Magnus and Aeron, and headed across the road. There were soldiers at the gatehouse to take the animals for them, but Roi continued inside with Tiegh, crossing the bailey just as Diara and Robin were coming from the entry.

"Ah," Roi said as they met the pair at the bottom of the stairs. "Lady de Lohr, this is my dear friend, Tiegh de Dere. He has just arrived at my father's summons. Tiegh, this is my wife and her father, Lord Cheltenham."

Tiegh greeted Robin first, as was protocol. "My lord," he said to Robin, then dipped his head to Diara. "Lady de Lohr. It is a pleasure to meet you both. My parents send their regrets for not having attended the wedding, but they also send their warmest felicitations."

Diara came off the steps, taking Roi's arm. "Thank you, Sir Tiegh," she said. "From where do you hail?"

"Berkshire, my lady," Tiegh said. "I was born there."

"That is lovely country," Diara said. "I traveled through there once when I was a child. Remember, Papa?"

She turned to her father, who nodded. "I do, indeed," he said. "We stayed at a hunting lodge belonging to Lord Marlborough before continuing on to London. Who are your parents, Sir Tiegh?"

"My father is Sir Achilles de Dere, Lord Caversham," Tiegh said. "My mother is the former Susanna de Tiegh of Aysgarth Castle."

"That is in the north," Robin said. "Have you spent much time there?"

Tiegh nodded. "Enough, my lord," he said. "Though it has been a while."

"Do you hunt?"

"Indeed I do, my lord."

"Do you like games?"

Tiegh cocked his head curiously. "Games, my lord?"

Robin came off the steps, indicating the gatehouse. "Come with me," he said. "There are games to be had in the field across the way. Tell me of the hunting you have done at Aysgarth. Mayhap I should take a trip to the north if it is good."

They walked away, speaking of hunting and travel. Robin

was shockingly friendly with a simple knight. Roi and Diara watched them go for a moment before Roi moved to follow with Diara on his arm. But she wasn't moving, and he came to a halt, looking at her.

"Coming, my love?" he asked. "Two other friends have arrived along with Tiegh, so the coming game should be quite interesting."

Diara nodded, but her focus was on her father. "I will come," she said. "But... my father..."

Roi turned to watch Robin crossing the bailey with Tiegh. "What about him?"

Diara shook her head. "I wish I knew," she said, clearly puzzled. "I found him in your father's solar, Roi. I think... I think he was looking through your father's things. When I came in, I startled him, and he was not pleased with me."

Roi's brow furrowed. "Why should he want to go through my father's things?"

"I do not know," Diara said. "I do not know what he could hope to find. I do not think he stole anything, but he was definitely looking at your father's documents when I arrived. He said he was looking for maps, but something tells me that he was simply being curious about things that did not concern him."

Roi tucked her hand into the crook of his elbow, gently encouraging her to follow him. "I cannot imagine why he would do such a thing," he said. "I do not think my father has anything secretive or personal sitting out for all to see, but your father still should not have been rooting through his desk."

"He asked me if I was going to tell your father."

"Are you?"

"Nay," she said. "I told you. *You* can tell your father."

"If you think I should."

Diara sighed. "I'm not sure why I feel uncomfortable about it, but I feel that my father has not forgiven us for not marrying when he wanted us to marry," she said. "He can hold a grudge. I have seen it."

Roi shrugged. "Let him," he said. "I have what I want and there is nothing he can do about it, so if he intends to be petty, let him. I do not care."

Diara didn't say anything more, but she wasn't so sure that was a good thing. She knew her father and she knew he could be devious when the mood struck him. Devious about what, she didn't know, but perhaps she was simply being paranoid, since her last interaction with him at Cicadia saw her disobey the man. Not only disobey him, but lie to him as well.

Perhaps his behavior was just her overactive imagination.

Forcing thoughts of her father aside and smiling at her handsome husband, she held on to him tightly as they headed back to the field.

CB

IT WAS A strange, new world for Mathis.

He and Pryce had backed away from the group of de Lohr men, who were arguing about what game to proceed with next. In fact, they went to sit on the grass at the edge of the field. Pryce ended up lying down and dozing in the sun, while Mathis sat there and watched the happenings on the field and beyond. He could see the guests and women on the other side of the field, gathered together in conversation, waiting for the next game to begin. Because of the short time frame of the wedding, and the funeral that preceded it, not many people had been given the time to attend, but there were enough.

Bored by the view of the family and guests, and wishing he was anywhere but at Diara's wedding celebration, Mathis lay down and closed his eyes. When next he realized, a soft voice roused him.

"My lord?"

It took him a moment to realize he'd heard those words several times. At first, he thought he'd been dreaming them, but when he opened his eyes, a lovely young woman with dark eyes and dark hair was standing a few feet away with a basket in her hand.

He sat bolt upright.

"My lady?" he said, rolling to his knees. "How may I be of service?"

The young woman was dressed in blue, her long hair blowing gently in the breeze. She was also quite flushed, looking at him as if he had somehow startled her. She suddenly thrust the basket at him.

"I brought these for you, my lord," she said.

He looked at her curiously. "Me?" he said. Then he looked around as if making sure there was no one else she could have possibly meant. "Just… me?"

She nodded. "For you," she said. "I have been told you like sweets, and I made these myself."

Mathis was thoroughly perplexed. For lack of a better reaction, he reached out to take the basket from her. The moment it was in his grasp, she turned and began to run off.

"Wait!" he called after her. "My lady—please wait."

She came to an unsteady halt, turning to face him as if facing her worst nightmare. Mathis wasn't sure if she was just strange or awkward or both, but it was becoming comical. He walked up on her, trying to be gentle with the skittish creature.

"I do not even know your name," he said. "And who told you I like sweets?"

The young woman swallowed hard. "Diara told me."

"Ah," he said. "Are you a wedding guest?"

She shook her head. "Nay," she said. "She married my father."

Now, things were coming to make sense. Sort of. "You are Roi's daughter?"

She nodded. "One of them."

He smiled faintly. "I do not even know your name."

"I am Adalia."

"Lady Adalia," he said, rolling her name over his tongue. "That is a lovely name."

The red in her cheeks deepened, which was rather sweet, he thought. She was very young, however, and looked nothing like her red-haired father. Mathis knew that Roi had been married before, long ago, so he assumed the lass looked like her mother. But she didn't reply to his compliment, so he gestured to the basket.

"What did you bring me?" he said. "Moreover, did you bring this to distract me from the game? I'm opposing your father, you know. Did he send you to tempt me to keep me away from the field?"

He was teasing her, but she looked mortified. "Nay," she gasped. "I promise you that I would never do such a thing!"

He held up a hand to ease her. "I was jesting," he said. "I only meant that sweets and a lovely lady would accomplish the task. I would gladly be distracted."

Adalia calmed down a little when she realized he was gently humoring her. In fact, she actually smiled. "I could not be so clever, my lord," she said. "I would not know where to begin."

He smiled because she was. "I do not believe it," he said. "A lady as lovely as you? You must be very clever. You made these sweets, did you now? That proves you are quite clever."

He looked in the basket, which was covered by a cloth, pulling forth a small, round cake. Adalia craned her neck to see what he was poking at.

"They are oatcakes with currants and honey," she said. "My grandmother has citron trees, and I used that for the glaze on the top."

He didn't hesitate to take a big bite, chewing a couple of times before groaning in delight. "They are exquisite," he said, mouth full as he shoved the whole thing in. "Lady, you are masterful."

Adalia was back to flushing violently with his flattery. "I learned from a woman who came from France," she said. "While other girls were learning to dance and sing, I was learning to make sweets and breads and other things. I enjoy it."

Mathis' mouth was so full that he couldn't speak, so he held up a finger to beg patience while he finished chewing and swallowed.

"It shows," he said. "These are delicious. But may I ask why you chose to bring them to me? Did I do something to earn them?"

Adalia's smile faded and she began to grow nervous. "N-nay," she stammered. "You... you have done nothing. I... I simply thought... Good day to you, my lord."

With that, she raced off before Mathis could stop her. He watched her run to the other side of the field where the women were gathered, but he lost sight of her as she hid amongst the crowd. He was rather sorry he chased her off. Another hand abruptly appeared and plundered a sweet from his basket. He looked over to see Pryce standing next to him.

"Who was that?" Pryce asked, sticking a cake in his mouth and chewing. "God's Bones, these are good. Did she bring them?"

Mathis nodded. "She did," he said. "That is Roi's daughter, Adalia, but I am at a loss to know why she brought them to me."

Pryce tried to take another cake, but Mathis smacked his hand away and took his basket, heading over toward the other side of the field. He wasn't done with Lady Adalia, not in the least, but as he skirted the field, he saw Cheltenham and a man he didn't recognize approaching the field from across the road. Trailing behind them, he could see Roi and Diara.

He felt a little stab to his heart at the sight.

It was the stab of resignation, of acceptance. There was no longer a chance for him, so he accepted that. As much as he could, anyway. Most importantly, Diara seemed to be truly enamored with the man she'd married, and he would not begrudge her for her happiness. He was glad for her. In the end, that she was happy was all that mattered to him.

Taking a deep breath, he headed in Roi and Diara's direction.

They were talking and laughing about something as he approached, and he felt rather awkward for breaking into their moment, but he had something on his mind that required Roi's opinion. Diara was giggling about something, but when she saw Mathis, she held up a hand to him in greeting.

"Good morning to you," she called. "I am very sorry you are on the losing team of men. Mayhap if you ask nicely, Roi will allow you to be on his team."

Mathis smiled weakly. "I do not want to get in the middle of

Roi and his brothers, who seem to want to disable him," he said. Then he looked at Roi. "Did they manage to injure you?"

Roi shook his head. "They did not," he said. "But the day is still young."

"And they are quite determined."

Roi snorted. "Nothing has changed since we were children," he said. "But... it is enjoyable. It has been ages since we have played out in the open like this, like children."

Mathis nodded. "For me also," he said. "But speaking of children, I've come about one of yours."

Roi looked at him curiously. "Oh?" he said. "Which one?"

Mathis held up the basket. "Adalia," he said. "She brought these cakes to me and then ran off when I asked her why. I did not mean to offend her. I only asked her why she gave them to me."

Roi passed a knowing expression to Diara, who nodded her head when she realized what had happened.

"Do not be troubled," Diara said to Mathis. "It is my fault."

Mathis cocked his head curiously. "Your fault?"

"Aye," Diara said. "You see, last night, Adalia asked who you were. She must think you are very handsome, but she was mortified when I suggested an introduction. She is a very shy lass, Mathis. Very sweet but very shy. I told her that you were fond of sweets, so I believe that bringing you those cakes was her way of introducing herself. She was trying to do something nice for you."

The light of understanding went on in Mathis' eyes. "I see," he said, looking to the basket. "They are quite delicious. As I said, I did not mean to offend her by asking her why she brought them to me."

Diara watched him closely. "Would you be interested in a

formal introduction?" she asked. "Lady Adalia is a de Lohr, after all. She's very pretty and clearly talented."

Mathis could have throttled her. She was asking in front of the young woman's father, so if Mathis refused, he risked Roi's anger. He was only just dealing with a broken heart over Diara marrying another man and had no interest in entertaining his own romantic prospects at the moment, but he supposed it would do no good for him to lament that which he had lost for the rest of his life. Diara was gone, and he had accepted that.

Besides… Adalia *was* quite lovely.

It wouldn't kill him if they were formally introduced.

"Only with Roi's permission," he finally said. "I will do nothing without his permission."

Diara looked at Roi, who was looking at Mathis as if mulling the whole thing over. "Let me think on it," he said. "Mathis, you and I must speak before I do anything."

"Of course, Roi."

"She is my eldest daughter, after all."

"A fine woman."

"How old are you?"

"I have seen thirty years and five."

Roi grunted. "She has seen seventeen," he said. "She is still quite young."

"She is a woman," Diara said firmly. "You said yourself that you should be seeking a husband for her. Mathis is a most worthy candidate."

Roi looked at her with some exasperation. "I know the man," he said irritably. "Let me at least get used to the idea before you marry my daughter off tomorrow."

Diara laughed softly. "I apologize, my love," she said, properly contrite. "I will say no more about it."

"Thank you."

"Until tomorrow."

Roi rolled his eyes, sighing heavily as he turned to Mathis. "When are you returning home?"

Mathis instinctively turned to the crowd in the near distance, seeking out Robin as he spoke to a couple of men he was acquainted with but didn't really know.

"I am not certain," he said. "As soon as Cheltenham decides we must leave, but I have no idea when that will be. It could be tomorrow or it could be in a week. He's been fickle as of late, so I have no way of knowing."

Diara looked at him. Something he said stuck in her mind—*he's been fickle as of late*. That reminded her of finding her father in the hall.

"Mathis," she said slowly. "Has my father been acting strangely? Is that what you mean by fickle?"

Mathis shrugged. "Your father has his moments," he said. "The past week or two has seen him more short-tempered than usual. Ever since you and Roi departed Cicadia and Cirencester arrived."

Diara looked at him sharply. "Cirencester?" she said with surprise. "What did he want?"

Mathis shrugged. "Evidently, Beckett's funeral procession passed through his lands on the way to the marches," he said. "Since he was coming from Selbourne, the fastest route was through Cirencester. I do not know the details of the conversation, but I do know that he came to pay his respects for the loss of your betrothed to your father."

Diara grew tense, uncharacteristic for her. "There has to be more to it than that," she said. "Riggs Fairford has never done anything without an ulterior motive. What did he want? Money for allowing Beckett to pass through his lands?"

Mathis shook his head. "I do not know," he said. "But his visit must have done some good because after he left, your father was much happier and far more congenial than he'd been since he received the news that Beckett had died. After that, your father was eager to come when he received your wedding invitation."

Roi had been watching the exchange. Mostly, he'd been watching his wife nearly become irate over the visit of Cirencester. He patted the hand that was still clutching his elbow.

"See?" he said. "Your father has forgiven us our hasty departure."

Diara wasn't convinced in the least. "Then why was he in your father's solar, poking around?"

Mathis heard her. "What was he doing?" he asked.

Roi waved him off as if it wasn't a serious issue, but Diara answered. "When everyone was down here at the field, I found my father in Lord Hereford's solar, reading through his things," she said. "I thought it very strange that he should do so."

"I am sure he was simply being nosy," Roi said. "What harm can he do?"

Diara's gaze found her father near the field speaking with more men. "I do not know, but I do not like it," she said. "I told you that he can hold a grudge. What you did in his solar... he will not easily forgive that. I worry that he is... Oh, I do not know what I worry about. But I do not like Cirencester's visit."

"Why not?"

She shrugged. "Because I do not like the man," she said. "He's devious and immoral. He wanted me to marry his son, but my father would not allow it. Even he knows that Cirencester is not the most noble of families."

"Yet he accepted a visit from the man," Roi said. "And according to Mathis, the visit helped him a great deal."

"Possibly."

Roi could see that she wasn't convinced. He patted her hand again. "Stop worrying over your father," he said. "He will soon forget any imagined grudge. Right now, there are more games to play and more than I plan to win, so let us get on with it. Mathis?"

"My lord?"

"Let me introduce you to my daughter."

That seemed to switch Diara's focus from her father to Adalia, and she smiled weakly. "I thought you needed time to adjust to it?" she said.

Roi winked at her. "I have had plenty of time," he said. "Mathis, I hear your family comes from the north and lives in a castle that used to be inhabited by the kings of old."

Mathis nodded. "That is true," he said. "The ancient kingdom of Elmet. My family is descended from those kings."

"Is your father still alive?"

Mathis nodded. "He is," he said. "And before you ask, I am his only son. I will inherit Kongenhus Castle."

Roi's brow lifted. "Kongenhus," he repeated. "I do believe I've heard of it. Near Kendal?"

Mathis nodded. "It is."

"I always thought the name was strange."

"It means King's House in the old language."

"Have you learned enough?" Diara asked, interrupting them as she looked at Roi. "The man is descended from kings. Is he worthy of an introduction now?"

Roi snorted. "Mayhap," he said. "Mayhap not. Every father has the right to be selective when it comes to his daughter."

Diara assured him that Mathis was a fine prospect as they walked away, off to find Adalia. Mathis followed behind them, mulling over Diara's words to Roi. She had asked if the fact Mathis was descended from kings meant he was worthy of a de Lohr bride. Bitterly, he mused that it hadn't been good enough for Cheltenham. He'd lost the only bride he'd ever wanted, no matter whom he was related to.

But it was a new world now. He needed to embrace it. He wasn't entirely sure marrying the daughter of the man who married his only love would be a good match, for him emotionally, that was, but socially and politically, it would be an excellent one.

A new world, indeed.

And Mathis had to find his way in it.

CHAPTER FOURTEEN

Pembridge Castle
One Week Later

DORIAN WAS SCREAMING.

Roi had heard it from the bailey, and it caused him, Kyne, and Adrius to sprint in the direction of the sound, which happened to be somewhere near the kitchen yard. There was an area back there with a fishpond and the remnants of a garden that Diara had decided to bring back to life. Almost a week after their return from Lioncross and their wedding celebration, life at Pembridge was nicely settling in.

And what a life it had been.

Roi had been given a lot of time to think about the way his life had changed. It was difficult to put it into so many words, but the closest he could come was that it was as if the sun had risen over his darkness and all he could see was the light. Since Odette's death, he felt as if he'd been living in limbo—not sad, not happy, but simply existing. He'd sent his daughters away to foster and he'd buried himself in his duties. Anything to keep him distracted from the pain of losing his wife. But when he finally came to terms with that, he found himself in a colorless world where he had his reputation, his obligations, and a connection to the king that did nothing to fill the hole inside his heart.

A hole crying for joy.

He'd gotten used to living like that, but Beckett's death threatened to change everything. It threatened to break his carefully held control and plunge him from darkness into complete blackness. But a belligerent father had changed his life, and as much as Robin annoyed him, he had to admit that he was grateful to the man for forcing him into a marriage. Had Robin not been such a bully, Roi wouldn't have married Diara.

Now, he couldn't imagine his life without her.

He was still coming to know her, but every day was a new voyage of discovery that saw him fall more deeply in love with her. She was sweet and beautiful and, already, Adalia and Dorian adored her. Watching his daughters open up to a woman when such a role model had been absent from their everyday lives was truly something to see. Dorian wasn't so wrapped up in her horses, and Adalia had come out of the kitchens, now following Diara around and wanting to learn from her. More than that, she wanted to please her. Diara was very sweet with the girls, and it did Roi's heart good to see it. It was an absolute joy.

More than that, it was Diara herself who was the joy.

He'd married an angel.

From their wedding to the celebration afterward, the games that ended up going for two days that saw the de Lohr men, one by one, become injured or otherwise incapacitated, she had been a dream. He would have been fully enamored with the dream had his brothers not turned the wedding celebration into two days of beatings that somewhat took his attention away from her. They worked so hard to triumph over each other that they ended up injuring one another.

Curtis was the first one out with a twisted ankle, followed by Douglas, who was hit on the head when they played the game with a pig's bladder and sticks. The object was to hit the ball from one end of the field to the other while those on the opposition tried to prevent it, but those sticks they used did some damage. After Curtis and Douglas fell out, two of Curtis' sons received blows that took them out as well.

That upset Diara somewhat, and at her request, Dustin got involved. She didn't like seeing her sons and grandsons whipped and bleeding, either, but Christopher told her to stay out of it. That fueled her anger to the point of taking all the women inside with her so they would not watch the games except for Diara, who wouldn't leave Roi. She watched Westley go after her husband, presumably going after the ball that Roi was controlling, but he ended up hitting Roi in the neck. That brought Roi's anger, and he hit Westley so hard with his stick that it briefly knocked him unconscious.

With Westley dragged off the field, the de Shera brothers filled the holes left by Douglas and Westley, but Roi filled his holes with Magnus, Aeron, and Tiegh, which wasn't quite a fair match-up because they were unrelenting against the younger men. Tiberius was the first one to fall with a smashed foot, while Maximus, the biggest brother, was more of a challenge. Gallus remained in the game simply because he was intelligent and knew how to avoid trouble, but Maximus and Roi ended up in a stick fight that saw both sticks demolished. Fists and hands were used after that, and Christopher and David ended up breaking up a fight between them.

All the while, Diara watched anxiously from the edge of the

field.

It was encounters like the one between Roi and Maximus that had driven the games for two straight days until nearly everyone was battered, bloodied, and beaten. But they were also grinning and congratulating one another, which completely baffled Diara. Roi still chuckled when he remembered the scolding he received from her on the second night as she cleaned his wounds with witch hazel. The solution stung his cuts, but her words, though harsh, did his heart good because they told him how much she cared.

But she swore there would be no more games, and Dustin agreed with her.

The celebration of Roi and Diara's wedding was officially over.

Robin and Ananda were the first ones to leave and head home, taking Mathis and Pryce with them. On the very morning after the games, just before sunrise, their entire escort was prepared and ready to depart. Robin said his brief goodbyes to his daughter but seemed rather eager to leave. Ananda wept over leaving her only child, so very joyful that she was married. Ananda had mentioned grandchildren once or twice already, so Diara knew what was expected of her.

So did Roi.

He wasn't at all opposed to more children. In fact, he was quite eager to have children with his new wife. He had always viewed this marriage as being the opportunity to replace the son he lost, but it had become more than that. It was being proud of Diara bearing his children, children that were part of him and part of her. It was in knowing that this wonderful woman would be the mother of those children, and he knew that they would be extremely fortunate.

He knew that he was the most fortunate man in the entire world.

Therefore, the week back at Pembridge had been an astonishing one. When he wasn't thinking about Diara, he was talking about her. He could see in his knights' faces that he was becoming boring and repetitive talking about his wife all the time. But it had been difficult for him to contain himself, and, in fact, he'd been speaking to them about his desire to take Diara to France and beyond when they'd heard the screaming that was currently going on.

They went on the run.

As they closed in on the area behind the kitchen yard, an area next to the wall that had the fishpond, they started to hear laughter, too. More screams, more laughter, and they burst through the small gate that separated the pond from the rest of the yard only to see Dorian and Adalia pushing each other into the pond. Just as Adalia climbed out, Dorian would push her back in. They were both soaking wet. Standing a few feet away stood Diara, grinning at the antics.

"We heard the screaming," Roi said as he rushed in with Kyne and Adrius behind him. "What's amiss?"

"Papa!" Dorian cried. "The fish bite!"

With that, Adalia started screaming and leaping, trying desperately to get out of the pond of biting fish. She was also laughing in between screams, and it sounded like utter hysteria. But Diara went to her panicked husband, shaking her head.

"The fish do not bite," she said. "But they do nibble. Dorian found that out yesterday when she stepped in to pull some of the overgrowth out of the pond. She thought it would be fun to lure her sister in today."

Roi was breathing heavily from his run across the bailey,

putting his hands on his hips in a frustrated gesture as he watched Adalia pull Dorian in again and then push her down. Dorian started howling when fish lips began nibbling at her, and he was starting to see what was so funny about it. He watched his daughters play in a way he'd never seen them play before.

It was part of that newlywed happiness they were all starting to feel.

Happiness that Diara had brought to them.

"Now that I know what the screams are for, I shall ignore them," he told his wife. Then he eyed her. "Have *you* gone in there?"

She shook her head. "Nay," she said. "I am not so foolish as to—"

He cut her off by swinging her into his arms and carrying her to the edge of the pond as she shrieked and clung to his neck.

"Don't you dare, Richard de Lohr!" she cried. "Throw me in this pond at your own peril! You will have to sleep with one eye open for the rest of your life because I will not rest until you suffer such humiliation as you cannot imagine!"

He was nearly crying with laughter as he extended her out over the pond and she held fast to him. He really didn't intend to dump her into the pond, but it was quite humorous to tease her. The threats she was issuing at him were hilarious. Unfortunately, Adalia and Dorian didn't have the same restraint, and they yanked on his arms, causing him to go off balance. Diara went, bottom-first, into the pond as Roi toppled sideways. With a giant splash, the entire family was in the murky pond as Kyne and Adrius shook their heads at the antics.

Fortunately, the pond wasn't very deep, but Diara had gone

in over her head. She came up, sputtering, with leaves on her head, as the girls danced around her, splashing water. Roi was still laughing, trying to get up and help her up at the same time, but she shoved him away by the face and he fell on his backside. It was Kyne who extended a hand to her to pull her out of the pond while Roi sat there, up to his chest in the water, while his daughters splashed murky water on him.

"I am sorry, my love," he called after Diara as he wiped his eyes. "My dearest? I'm terribly sorry. I did not mean to toss you like that. Blame Adalia and Dorian. They are the enemy!"

Diara was soaked. She was also partially covered with stringy algae. She peeled it off her arms and tossed it at Roi, hitting him in the face.

"I hope those fish eat you," she said, pushing her wet hair out of her face. "I hope they strip your bones."

"Shall I just stay here, then?"

"Aye!" Diara said, half teasing, half angry. "Look at me! I'm covered in slime!"

"You are still beautiful," Roi said. "May I come out now?"

Diara was on the move, holding up her soaking skirts. She passed behind Roi as he sat there then she picked up some mud at the edge of the pond, flinging it on him from behind. It hit him in the back of the neck and the head, and immediately, he bolted to his feet.

"That is all I will take from you," he said, turning swiftly for her. "Be prepared to defend yourself."

With a yelp, Diara took off at a run. She was at a distinct disadvantage because her clothing was soaked and very heavy, and by the time she reached the kitchen door leading into the keep, Roi was on her. Picking her up, he slung her over one broad shoulder as he carried her through the kitchens, with her yelling and fussing all the way. The kitchen servants looked at them in shock, but Roi simply grinned.

"Send the bathtub and hot water up to our chamber immediately," he said. "Lady de Lohr is clumsy and fell in the pond. Had I not saved her, she would have drowned."

That brought a screech of outrage from Diara, who began slapping his behind. But she was laughing, and he was laughing, as he carried her up two flights of stairs, leaving a watery trail, until he reached their bedchamber. Once inside, he carefully set her to her feet.

She rushed him.

Roi was unprepared for Diara running at him and wrapping her hands around his throat. She was giggling as she did it, being playful about it, but when he stepped back, he ended up tripping and falling, hard, to the floor.

The giggles stopped.

"Roi!" she gasped, on top of him as he lay there. "Did you hurt yourself?"

He groaned. "I've broken something."

Diara pushed herself off him. "Where is your pain?" she asked seriously. "What did you fall on?"

He continued to lie there and grunt. "Everything," he said miserably. "Everything is broken."

Diara ran her hand against the back of his skull, looking for bumps or blood. "My love, I cannot help you if you do not tell me where it hurts," she said patiently. "Where is your pain?"

She was checking him all over for damage when he reached up and grabbed her, pulling her against him.

"Everywhere when I am not with you," he said, nuzzling her ear and cheek. "Every moment I spent away from you causes me excruciating pain. Even when I am in the bailey and you are out of my sight, my thoughts are only of you."

Diara was quickly succumbing to the man, as she had every night since their marriage, but it was still the middle of the day and Roi had ordered a bath. She knew the servants were on their way, and she didn't want to create a spectacle for them.

"I'm covered in pond scum," she reminded him, pushing against his chest as he tried to embrace her. "We both smell like dirty fish."

"I do not care," he said before finally slanting over her mouth and kissing her deeply. "I will kiss my wife no matter what she smells like."

Diara started to chuckle. "What about me?" she said, avoiding his seeking lips. "Am I not allowed an opinion in this directive? What if I do not want to kiss you because *you* smell like fish?"

"Then you had better learn to like fish, lady."

She continued to chuckle as he tried to pull her against him. The more he would pull, the more she would push, until he finally managed to move her arms out of the way and trap her. Once he did that, he had her, for she could no longer fight him off. But his victory didn't last for long because the door swung open and two male servants lugged in an enormous copper tub.

"By the hearth, please," Diara said, pushing herself away from Roi by using his head for a brace. "Fill it halfway and then leave me a few buckets of hot water, please."

Servants began moving in and out as Roi climbed up from the floor and went to a chair to remove his soaked boots. Diara supervised the servants as Roi's major-domo showed up, helping with the water brigade. His name was Finnick, and he had originally served at Lioncross before Roi brought him over to Pembridge when he took command. Finnick was quiet, efficient, and bright, and he and Diara had come to a somewhat symbiotic relationship since she arrived. Finnick deferred to her in all things, and they were still in the process of working out what his duties would be, but so far, it had gone smoothly.

He was a man who knew his place.

"Lady Dorian and Lady Adalia have had the same mishap in the pond that their father and I have had," she told Finnick as he passed by with an empty bucket. "Please find something they can bathe in because, between my lord and I, we are going to be using the big tub for some time."

Finnick nodded quickly and headed off to assist the younger ladies. Diara returned to the cabinet where she kept her bathing things, including soap and scrapers, razors, and more. When she'd come to Pembridge, Roi didn't really have anything other than a comb and a razor, so she'd been generous in lending him her soap. Actually, she'd insisted on it, and he started using it, afraid to smell bad for his new wife. He hadn't cared much how he smelled for the past fourteen years, but now he did. He had a wife he wanted to be worthy of, and he didn't want to smell like a stable.

When the servants were gone and the door closed and bolted, Diara set out the soap and oils and scrub brushes on a small table next to the tub and had Roi help her out of her sticky, heavy, damp garments. When they came off, all of them, she slipped into the hot tub and instructed him to do the same. The tub was big enough for them both, even if there wasn't a lot of room to move around, and he eagerly climbed in with her as she took a pitcher and poured water over them both, several times, before rinsing out the nasty water so she could scrub them both with the soap. As Roi relaxed in the hot water, Diara washed herself first, including her hair, before starting in on him.

He was more than happy to let her.

"I've been thinking something," he murmured, eyes closed as she washed his hair.

"What about?" she asked.

"That mayhap you would like to go to Paris," he said. "When we were married, I was thinking about taking you on a trip because you seemed so interested in talking to people from different places. Realizing that you've probably never been out of England, I thought you might enjoy a trip."

She stopped washing, forcing him to open his eyes and look at her. She appeared completely surprised.

"Paris?" she repeated. "Oh... *could* we? Do we dare?"

"Why wouldn't we?"

She shrugged and resumed washing. "Because you have many duties here that require you," she said. "You could not leave for a long period of time."

"Why not?"

"*Don't* you have duties that require you?"

He kept his eyes closed while she poured water on his head to rinse the soap out. "I am responsible for the southern border of my father's property," he said. "But before Beckett died, Henry had been demanding my return to London."

"Why?"

He lay back against the tub as she used the scrub brush and began to wash his arms and hands. "That is a question with many answers," he said. "Up until two years ago, I was in Poitou for the king. He had issues with his French neighbors, to put it mildly. That is where your father was, also."

She nodded as she used the brush on his dirty nails. "I know," she said. "I remember when he went there with his army. He came back to tell me that I was betrothed to Beckett."

"Right," Roi said. "I returned when your father did, but I remained in London at the head of Henry's council, along with a few others, while he argued with the Capetians for a while. But my father was having some trouble with a local Welsh lord, so I resigned my post and returned home to command Pembridge and hold the southern border of my father's property. That's when I brought Adalia and Dorian home."

Diara was listening with interest as she continued to wash him. "And Henry wants you to return?"

Roi nodded. "That has been my lot in life," he said. "A proctor for the king. With the legalities of treaties and such, he needs my knowledge of the laws. While I've been here at Pembridge, I've also been an itinerant justice. I hold court here about once a month to solve local grievances. I've even gone into Hereford to settle cases there as well. Beckett was being trained for the same work."

In all of the conversations they'd had since their introduction, he'd never really spoken of his work or background. Diara only knew what she'd heard and a few cursory things he'd told her. She picked up a rag from the nearby table, soaked it, and put it on his face to soften his beard.

"Then you are an important man," she said. "I had no idea I married a fighting scholar."

He grinned. "Every man has his strength," he said. "Some men's strength is their brute power in battle. For some, it is tactics or warfare. Still others are diplomats and masters at negotiation. For me, it is the law."

"Do you plan to return to London?"

"At some point," he said. "I am valuable to Henry, and he pays me well. Service to the king guarantees me a reward at some point—lands, titles, that kind of thing. Things I should like to pass down to our children."

Diara produced the slimy white soap that smelled of lavender and lathered up his beard. "You will inherit the Earldom of Cheltenham when my father dies," she said. "It is a wealthy holding."

"But that will go to one child, our eldest son, should we have one," he said. "I hope to have other children with you, and I should like to leave them something. And Adalia and Dorian—they must have dowries."

"You're ambitious, then?"

"Not ambitious," he said. "But I find it necessary to plan. I do not want uncertainty for the future."

At that point, he held stock-still because she was shaving him. His legs had kicked out at some point, and she was kneeling between them, carefully shaving him as he found her thighs. His hands moved up her legs, cupping her buttocks, and pulling her toward him slowly.

She finally snorted.

"Cease," she said softly. "You are only half shaved, and I would finish before you have your way with me."

He was trying not to smile or laugh, trying to remain still while she finished one side of his face before moving to the other.

"Sorry," he said, barely moving his lips. "I simply cannot help it."

"You'd better, or I might accidentally slit your throat."

He remained still after that, his eyes following her as she finished shaving him. Then she washed out the razor and set it aside, using the damp rag to wipe Roi's face of the remaining soap.

"There," she said, looking at her handiwork. "You look like a proper lord now."

His big hands completely covered both buttocks, and he pulled her against him, her naked flesh against his. "You have my thanks, wife," he said softly, instantly hard and aroused. "Now, it is my turn."

Diara wound her arms around his neck. "To do what?"

His answer was to slant his mouth over hers, kissing her passionately. Diara gave herself over to him completely, letting him have his way with her, and he took charge. His lips moved over her clean skin and to her damp, firm breasts before claiming her lips once more. The bath was growing cool, and he stood up, still holding her, and carried her over to the bed, where he laid her down atop the coverlet and had his way with her.

Twice.

As they lay there in clean, damp bliss, still wrapped around one another, they began to hear Dorian's voice as she argued with her sister. The family chambers were on one level, with Roi and Diara's chamber being right next to Adalia and Dorian's. The walls were thick, made of stone and two feet wide in some places, but the doors weren't good sound barriers. Dorian was upset about something, and tangled up in Roi's arms, Diara sighed heavily.

"Should I see what is amiss?" she asked, her face half pressed into Roi's chest.

He opened his eyes, staring up at the ceiling as he listened to his daughters argue. "Nay," he said quietly. "I will go."

"Are you certain?"

He gently let her go and sat up. "Aye," he said. "They are my daughters. I do not feel as if I've been a very good father to them. You've helped me to realize that I should pay more attention to them, whether or not you are aware of it."

Diara sat up beside him. "They do not think you are a bad father," she said gently, putting her hand on his head in a comforting gesture. "I certainly do not. Your children love you very much."

He looked at her. "That may be, but I have not been around for them," he said. "Watching you with them, seeing how you are with them... They are my family, Deedee. We are *all* a family. Losing Beckett has made me realize just how important my family is to me. And I want to be a better father to my daughters."

She smiled at him, and he kissed her before he stood up and went in search of his clothing. A week ago, Diara had been mortified at the sight of a naked man, but just a short time later, she'd relished it. The man had a spectacular form. As he pulled on his breeches, she got up from the bed and went to the wardrobe, finding the robe that Dustin had left for her on their wedding night. She pulled it on, tying the sash around her waist, as Roi pulled on a tunic.

There was a table near one of the windows with a small, polished mirror on it, and she sat in front of the table and picked up a comb, pulling it through her hair just as Roi opened the door to the girls squabbling in the corridor outside. As she combed her hair, she could hear him trying to negotiate a truce between two girls who hadn't had much fatherly interaction in their lives. But Diara smiled faintly as she realized that was about to change.

I want to be a better father to them.

She thought that Adalia and Dorian were lucky girls, indeed.

CHAPTER FIFTEEN

Totterdown Castle
Demesne of Lord Cirencester

"TELL ME WHAT he said again."

"The time is now, my lord."

Riggs Fairford clearly knew what Mathis meant, but Mathis had no idea. He was exhausted from a long ride that had started at Lioncross Abbey, escorting Robin and Ananda and Iris back to Cicadia Castle, but it ended at Totterdown when Robin demanded that he take a message to Cirencester. It wasn't even a written message, but a verbal one. Four very simple words—*the time is now.*

He'd had to repeat those words three times to Cirencester until the man seemed to understand them. In fact, his face appeared to light up with glee as he turned away from Mathis and paced the floor of a chamber in the keep of Totterdown that was barely habitable. There were holes in the wall, a floor that had some weak spots, and about a dozen dogs lounged over the place. For a family who was so legendary in their wealth, they certainly didn't show it.

"The time is now," Cirencester repeated succinctly. "That is very good news. You can return to tell him that I shall comply. Did he confirm that I should move my army to Colesborne?"

"Colesborne, my lord?" Mathis said, puzzled. "He said nothing about it."

Cirencester stroked his chin thoughtfully. "We already discussed that village, so I will assume that is what he means," he said. "It is the most logical place because it is in disputed land between Cheltenham and myself, so if I move my army in to claim the village, that will start the conflict. And then you will summon de Lohr, will you not?"

Mathis genuinely had no idea what the man was speaking of. Conflict? De Lohr? Something told him to play along and he'd get far more information out of Cirencester than he would out of his own liege because, clearly, Riggs thought that Robin had let his knight in on his plans. Mathis didn't even know there *were* plans until this very moment. Now, something told him to listen.

And learn.

Maybe he could figure out what in the hell was going on.

"If the conflict is big enough, de Lohr will come, my lord," Mathis said carefully, watching Cirencester as the man practically twitched with excitement. "He is obligated to."

"I know. That is why we have planned this conflict."

"When can we expect this… conflict?"

Cirencester looked at him. "You have heard it for yourself," he said. "Your lord says that now is the time. I will take my army, harass Colesborne, and Robin will be forced to summon Roi to defend his property. But I will need your help for the ambush."

Mathis was trying to make sense out of what the man was saying, but it was only growing more confusing. "Ambush, my lord?"

Cirencester nodded. Then he quickly moved over to a small table that was piled with clutter, throwing things aside as he searched for something. When he found it, he ripped it out from the bottom of a pile and went to Mathis, holding it out for the man to see. It was a map of Cirencester holdings.

"Look at the top of the map," he said. "That is where my lands join with Cheltenham, but only a sliver. Further to the west and it is Gloucester, so I do not want anything to happen on Gloucester lands or it will involve him. And he is not someone I wish to deal with."

Mathis was looking at the faded and stained map. "But an ambush, my lord?" he said. "Who are we ambushing?"

Cirencester tried to point to the upper-right portion of the map, made difficult because he was holding it open. "This is a heavily forested area," he said, avoiding a direct answer. "The king has used it for hunting before, so it is rich with foliage and streams and places where a man can be cut down and left, and it would take weeks to find his body. There is a place here, to the east of Colesborne, called the Withington Turn. I know this area. This is a road that goes deep into a vale with a stream. If we can lure Roi into that area, I will have men waiting to ambush him. It will appear as if he has been killed in the skirmish and no one will be the wiser, least of all his father. My only hesitation in this entire scheme is incurring Hereford's wrath, but in battle, anything can happen."

Mathis' mind was spinning with what he was hearing. Cirencester just explained the entire thing, evidently some scheme that had been brewing between him and Cheltenham. All of it to eliminate Roi de Lohr. But the question in Mathis' mind was—*why?*

Then it occurred to him.

The visit by Cheltenham last week. Robin's sudden change in mood. His aversion to Roi at the wedding and the festivities afterward.

All of it was pointing to a plot.

A plot he now had to pretend he was in on, or God only knew what would happen to him. Knowing Cirencester's history as a scoundrel and outlaw, he'd probably never make it out of Totterdown Castle alive. His heart began to race as a real sense of fear clutched at him. Steadying himself, he forced himself to be part of Cirencester's sickening conversation.

"There are a thousand ways to die in battle, my lord, and no one is to blame," he said evenly. "Hereford could not point the finger at you if his son were found facedown in a creek. And there are a thousand ways to direct Roi into that vale if, indeed, he answers the call."

Cirencester rolled up the map. "Of course he will answer the call," he said. "Cheltenham is his wife's father. He must answer the call, fortunately for us."

"And with Roi gone—"

Cirencester interrupted him, almost impatiently. "With Roi removed, Flavian becomes Cheltenham's heir and we shall all be one big, happy family," he said. "How long have you served Cheltenham, de Geld?"

"Nine years, my lord."

"Then you know how important it is for us to be allied by marriage," he said. "I have been stressing this to my good friend Robin for many years, but he chose to seek a de Lohr husband instead. But he has realized his mistake. A mistake we intend to rectify."

Now, it was clear. Everything. Mathis could see the big

picture, and it shook him. To his bones, it shook him. His liege was in on a murder plot, and now he was in on it too. He was an honorable knight, a man of character, and this went beyond anything he was capable of engaging in. But he knew he had to play the game, to convince Cirencester he was part of the plan, or his life was forfeit.

It was more important than ever for him to get out of there alive.

"Then I look forward to being of service on that day your son becomes Lord Cheltenham," he said. "If he has half the instincts his father has, then he will make a good earl, indeed."

Oh, but he was laying on the compliments. He had to. Men like Cirencester were led by their pride more than their heart or their minds. True to form, Cirencester fell for the flattery.

"I am simply grateful for the opportunity," he said, feigning humility. "You will return to Robin and tell him that I will move my army to Colesborne in two days."

"Aye, my lord," Mathis said. "Is there anything else?"

"Not now, but there will be when my son marries Robin's daughter. I'm sure there will be much to do then."

That statement made Mathis want to throw up. But he held himself in check, bowing swiftly to Cirencester and turning on his heel. As he headed for the chamber door, he realized that he was shaking. With fear, with anger, with a lot of things. He kept his focus straight ahead and tried not to run to the stables where his horse was being cooled off from his ride there. Cheltenham and Cirencester were about fifteen miles apart, less than a half-day's ride, but Mathis wasn't going home.

He was going to the Welsh marches.

He was headed for Lioncross Abbey Castle.

The last he saw Roi, the man was at Lioncross. That had

only been two days ago, so Mathis hoped—and prayed—that Roi was still there. Still enjoying his family, still enjoying his guests from the recent wedding. Nasty dealings were afoot, and Roi had to be informed that he had a viper in his family in the form of his wife's father. But strangely enough, Mathis wasn't doing this for Roi. He wasn't doing it for the man who had married the woman he wanted because, frankly, they'd never been close friends, so this wasn't a matter of friendship. He was doing it for one reason and one reason alone.

He'd seen the way Diara had looked at her new husband.

He knew there was love there. Because he wanted to see Diara happy, and keep her happy, he was going to help foil the plot to murder her husband.

For her.

Mounting his semi-rested steed, Mathis fled Totterdown Castle as if the devil himself was after him.

CHAPTER SIXTEEN

Pembridge Castle

T HESE WERE DAYS of sunshine and bliss.

That was the way Roi felt about them. After years of gloom, to wake up to Diara's beautiful face every morning was something out of a dream. Every morning since their marriage, he'd woken up before dawn and simply watched her sleep. It gave him comfort and joy beyond imagining. He'd never been so happy, or so in love, with anyone or anything in his life, and if that made him a foolish man, then he was content being foolish. Every single day, he thanked God for being utterly, ridiculously foolish.

It had been almost two weeks since their return to Pembridge, and life was settling into a delirium of wonderful normalcy. Diara was finding her place as chatelaine, Adalia was her shadow and enjoying every minute of it, and Dorian was still playing with her horses, but giving more attention to cleaning up the fishpond and restoring the garden that had languished for so long. She loved animals and plants and flowers. She even loved the biting fish.

Dorian, too, was growing up.

The latest with the youngest de Lohr daughter, however, was her desire for a new horse. Roi had taken Diara and the girls into the village of Pembridge, which was just to the east of the castle. It was a small village but a busy one, and it had a license for a market every Saturday. Roi wanted to introduce Diara to the villagers and for the villagers to realize there was a new Lady of Pembridge, but Dorian caught sight of a blond horse in one of the animal pens near the end of town and refused to leave it. It belonged to a merchant who wasn't too keen on parting with it for less than an exorbitant price, something Roi refused to pay. That had left Dorian in a flood of tears and Roi feeling like an ogre.

As Roi lay next to Diara, watching her sleep as the sun rose, he smiled when he thought of his dramatic younger daughter, who was positive she was going to die from the pain of not having the horse she wanted. Diara and Adalia had gone to visit the spice merchant as Roi remained with Dorian and tried to convince her that she would indeed survive. That only made things worse. Not even offering to buy her sweets from the only baker in town eased her wounded soul, and once Diara and Adalia had made their purchases, Dorian wept all the way home.

What she didn't know was that the next day, Roi's guilt had sent him back to the village for a round of intense negotiations for the mare, whose name was Brillante. He and the merchant finally settled on a price, and Roi had arranged to have the horse delivered today. When he heard the faint sounds of the sentries at the gatehouse, announcing an arrival as the sun rose, he quietly climbed out of bed and pulled his clothing on. Thinking that the golden horse had arrived, he peered out of the chamber window to the bailey—only to see that an unfamiliar horse and rider had arrived. Pulling his boots on quickly, he went downstairs.

Kyne was waiting for him.

The man had just come up the stairs of the keep and entered the cool, dim foyer as Roi came down. The two of them came together somewhere in the middle of the entry.

"Who comes?" Roi asked. "I saw a rider."

Kyne's response was to extend a missive to him, and Roi took it, noting the seal. He lifted his eyebrows in realization.

"Cheltenham," he said as he broke the seal and unfolded the vellum. "I wonder what he wants?"

Kyne didn't say anything. He waited until Roi had read the missive twice before speaking.

"The messenger says that Cheltenham is mobilizing his army," he said. "It seems that Cirencester has launched some sort of raid, and he's already burned two villages. What does the missive say?"

"It is a request for aid and says that I'm to proceed to the village of Colesborne to intercept Cirencester's army." But then Roi shook his head as if greatly confused. "Mathis de Geld told us that Cirencester visited Robin last week. Although he did not know the contents of the meeting, he said that Robin was not troubled when Cirencester departed. In fact, the man seemed rather happy. I cannot imagine that Cirencester arrived to threaten him and Robin was joyful about it. That makes no sense."

Kyne shook his head. "Nay, it does not," he said. "But why would Cirencester visit him and then attack him only days later?"

Roi pondered that dilemma. "Unless Cirencester gave him an ultimatum," he said. "But that would not explain Robin's jovial mood when Cirencester left. Unless…"

"Unless what?"

"Unless Cirencester somehow lied to the man," Roi said. "For example—what if Cirencester promised Robin something and then went back on his word?"

Kyne nodded. "That would explain the attacks," he said. "Now your wife's father is sending you a panicked missive for help. Mayhap his friend did indeed go back on his word."

Roi wasn't sure about any of it. "Robin certainly came to Lioncross without a care in the world," he said. "I never got any sense that he was concerned about anything, but then again, I did not spend any length of time with him. But Diara did. She said her father was behaving oddly. She found him going through the things in my father's study."

Kyne's brow furrowed. "Why?"

Roi shrugged. "I could not tell you," he said. "I forgot about it, in fact. I did not even tell my father what she told me."

"Then mayhap it was nothing more than a curious old man."

"True," Roi said. "That is what I thought."

Kyne gestured to the missive. "What are you going to do about that?"

"There is nothing else I can do but answer the summons," Roi said. "Tell Adrius. The two of you can muster about half of my army, and we'll ride to the southern border of Cheltenham's land and see what is happening between him and Cirencester. We'll head to Colesborne."

"Right away, Roi."

"And we should send word to my father and tell him what has happened," Roi said. "Send a messenger to him immediately and relay what was in Robin's missive. Tell my father that I am already moving out."

"It shall be done."

With that, the two of them parted ways. Roi was just heading up the steps of the keep when he heard his name being shouted, and he turned to see that the blond horse was being delivered. The merchant he'd haggled with was bringing the animal in through the gatehouse, leading it proudly. Finnick appeared on the steps of the keep, and Roi sent the man out to settle the horse while he continued inside to inform Diara of the situation and pack his belongings.

At this time of the morning, the keep was cold and smelling of smoke from the fires that had burned out overnight. Roi was nearly to the top of the stairs when Dorian suddenly bolted past him, nearly knocking him backward. When she realized the body in the stairwell was her father, she leapt on him, her arms around his neck as he held his balance and tried not to fall back down the stairs and take her with him.

"Papa!" Dorian shrieked in his ear. "I saw the horse in the bailey! You bought her!"

Roi patted her on the back. "Aye, I bought her," he said. "I was going to surprise you, but clearly, you have already seen her."

"The sentries woke me and I looked outside!"

"Then the sentries spoiled the surprise."

Dorian didn't care about any of that. She kissed him loudly and firmly on the cheek. "I love you, Papa!" she cried. "Thank you, thank you!"

She kissed him again, twice more, smacking him on the nose the second time in her haste. But she was giggling, gleeful, and frantic to see her new horse. She released her father and ran down the rest of the stairs far too quickly as Roi stood there and rubbed his nose where she'd hit him. But he felt good that he'd made her so happy. He hadn't done much of that during her young life. With a grin, he continued up the stairs and into the chamber he shared with Diara. As he opened the door, he wasn't surprised to find her up and dressing already.

"Good morn, angel," he said as he shut the door behind him. "Did you sleep well?"

Diara looked at him, smiling as she ran a comb through her hair. "You should know," she said. "You spend all of your time watching me. How did I sleep?"

He chuckled as he went over to her, taking her in his arms and kissing her sweetly. "It looked to me as if you slept very well," he said. "And I will not stop watching you even if you tell me to, so save your breath."

She giggled, pulling from his embrace and heading over to her dressing table. "I would never tell you what you can or cannot do," she said. "But watching me sleep is going to become quite boring after a time."

"Never."

She sat down in front of her table, setting her comb down as she opened up one of the several boxes on the table. "Have it your way, then," she said. "What do you have in your hand?"

Roi looked down to see that he was still holding the missive from Cheltenham. He'd been so caught up in the joy of seeing her that he'd nearly forgotten he still had it. He lifted it up.

"This is from your father," he said. "The messenger arrived early this morning. It seems that Cirencester is making trouble for him and he is asking for help."

Diara stopped what she was doing and turned to him. "*Cirencester?*"

"That's what he says."

She stood up from her chair and went to him, taking the missive and reading through it carefully. When she came to the end of it, she began shaking her head.

"That makes no sense to me," she said. "Cirencester has never given my father trouble in all of the years we have known him. They are friends."

"No longer, according to your father," Roi said, moving past her and going to the enormous wardrobe that had been part of the chamber when he first took possession of the castle. "He is asking me to bring my army and meet him in a village called Colesborne. You can see from the missive what else he says— that Cirencester has already burned two villages near their property boundary."

Diara was genuinely baffled. She sat on the edge of their bed, missive in hand, as Roi began to pull out pieces of clothing to pack.

"Did Mathis not say that Cirencester paid my father a visit before Beckett's funeral?" she said.

"That is what the knight said."

"And now Cirencester is attacking my father?"

Roi came over to the bed and began to lay things out. "Mathis told us of the meeting, but he did not know what was said," he replied. "It is possible that Cirencester threatened your father or tried to coerce him, but your father is a stubborn man. He must have refused, and now, Cirencester is retaliating. The only thing I do not understand is why he seemed happy after Cirencester's departure from Cicadia Castle. To me, that does not speak of a worried man."

Diara sat there, shaking her head, until she finally turned to him. "I do not like this at all, Roi," she said. "You do not know my father. He holds grudges. He becomes inflamed if anyone opposes him. You saw him when he went to Lioncross and bullied your father. You said so yourself."

"I did."

She stood up from the bed. "Something is very wrong here," she said. "Cirencester would never attack my father."

Roi looked at her. "Do you think it is someone other than Cirencester?"

"I don't know," she said, working herself up into a state. "Riggs Fairford is a wicked man, and his son, Flavian, is even worse. They were very upset when my father would not agree to a betrothal between Flavian and me, but that was so long ago. That is the only thing I can possibly think of that might make him angry enough to strike."

Roi appeared doubtful. "I cannot believe he would show his disappointment so long after the suit was refused," he said. "Moreover, you are married now. If they were still pursuing you, that is now ended. And wasn't all of that several years ago?"

"Before my father went to France."

"Then I am sure this has nothing to do with a rejected suit," he said. "Cirencester would not decide to attack your father four years after his suit was refused."

"But I have only been married for a couple of weeks."

That brought Roi pause. "You think that Cirencester may have held out hope for a betrothal until you were legally married, and now he is furious?"

Diara sighed heavily. "As I said, I do not know," she said. "But he visited my father before we were married and attacked him only after we were wed. Coincidence?"

"It has to be."

"Then if that is not the reason, something else must have

prompted the attack."

"Like what?"

She didn't have an answer, and because of that, she was close to tears. "I do not know," she whispered tightly. "But I do not want you to go."

He frowned, as if she had said something ridiculous. "I must go," he said, turning back to the wardrobe. "I am your husband and obligated to answer your father's call. You know this."

She didn't like the fact that he wasn't taking her seriously. "My father has not had trouble on his lands in almost twenty years," she pointed out. "And suddenly, he has an attack two weeks after I marry? An attack in which he summons de Lohr aid, no less?"

Roi looked at her. She was genuinely upset, but he thought it was more because he was going to face a skirmish and she was afraid in general. He thought that perhaps she was simply making up phantoms of suspicion where there weren't any. Removing a small leather satchel from the wardrobe, he tossed it onto the bed as he made his way over to her.

"This is the first time you've had a husband go to war, is it?" he said, his eyes glimmering. "I would have never known."

She didn't like being teased. "I know you think I am being foolish, but I do not have a good feeling about this," she said. "Nothing is making sense about my father, and it is frightening me. What about my catching him in your father's solar?"

"What about it?"

She threw up her hands in exasperation. "It was very odd."

"I think he was just being nosy, my love."

"He is up to something, and I do not know what it is!"

Roi didn't want to dismiss her again so obviously. Clearly,

she felt strongly about the situation, and he wanted to respect that. But he also thought she was simply being overdramatic because he was departing for a conflict and she didn't like that. Furthermore, she didn't like the fact that her father clearly hadn't forgiven them for refusing to marry when he wanted them to, so her paranoia had the better of her.

She was seeing trouble everywhere.

"My dearest angel," he said patiently. "Even if he is up to something, as you have put it, what harm can he do us? The man cannot touch the de Lohr empire, and he knows it. He would be foolish to try, although I do not know why he would try. He has everything he wants—you are married to a de Lohr son and he has his alliance. Why in the world would he be up to something that would harm us?"

Diara couldn't put her feelings into words. There was nothing tangible except for the fact that she knew her father and knew how he could be. But Roi had a point—her father had what he wanted. There was no reason for him to be scheming about something. Aye, that was all quite logical, and she knew that.

But she still had a suspicious feeling deep in her belly.

However, she didn't want Roi to think he'd married a fidgety, silly bird. She wanted him to see her as she really was, as she had been since their introduction. That was the true Diara, a woman of reason and strength, but when it came to her father and his questionable character, she was nervous.

But she couldn't prove anything.

"You are correct, of course," she said, forcing a smile. "I suppose that I am simply nervous that you are going into battle and we have only been married a couple of weeks. I was hoping we would have more time before I bade you farewell as you headed to an armed conflict."

He smiled at her. "There is no need to be concerned," he said. "I am taking five hundred men with me and Adrius. I will leave Kyne here with you, to command in my absence. I will be well protected and I will be very careful, I promise. But you must let me do what I was born to do and what I am trained to do. You married a knight, Lady de Lohr. You must let me be what I am."

She nodded quickly. "Of course," she said. "I did not mean to suggest you become less than you are."

He went to her, taking her in his arms and kissing her gently. "You did not suggest that at all," he said. "This is the first time we have been separated, and you are understandably uneasy. I do not want to leave you, either, but your father has asked for help. How would you feel about me if I refused?"

"Upset, I suppose."

"Exactly," he said, releasing her. "I will, therefore, go and see what this is all about, but I am sending a missive to my father to have his men join me. Your father will have thousands of men on his doorstep in a few short days."

"Good," Diara said, relieved. "Then you will have help."

"I will have a lot of help," he said. "Now, pick up the clothing I've laid out and come with me. My saddlebags are in the armory, and I would like your assistance."

Diara nodded quickly, though she ran to her dressing table first and braided her hair quickly to get it out of the way. "I would be honored to help you," she said as her fingers flew. "Is there anything else to bring from this chamber?"

Roi looked around. "I do not think so," he said. "Mayhap an extra pair of boots."

"Shall I get them?"

"Nay," he said, already moving for the wardrobe. "I will get the boots. You get the clothing."

Diara tied off her hair swiftly, a lovely blonde braid hanging over her shoulder as she rushed to collect his clothing off the bed. They headed from the chamber, Roi taking the lead as he led her down the stairs and out of the keep, crossing the bailey just as Dorian was taking a ride on her new horse, bareback, waving to her father and stepmother as she did so. Diara waved back, casting Roi a long look to remind him that he'd denied his daughter that particular pony only a couple of days ago.

Her husband's sheepish smile had her laughing all the way to the armory.

CHAPTER SEVENTEEN

Lioncross Abbey Castle

"**W**HO IS HERE?"

"Mathis de Geld. Cheltenham's knight."

Christopher was in his solar, surrounded by several men who had attended Beckett's funeral and Roi's wedding, and had subsequently remained at Lioncross because Christopher requested it. Nearly everyone else had departed, including the de Shera brothers, but there was business to discuss, and the solar was full of some of the most elite knights in England. Therefore, the announcement of the arrival of Cheltenham's knight was not something Christopher had expected.

"What does he want?" he asked.

The young knight from the gatehouse, a member of the de Royans family, shook his head. "He would not say, my lord," he said. "Only that it is urgent."

Christopher's eyebrows lifted in surprise as he looked at his brother, seated next to him. David seemed rather surprised, too. Christopher returned his attention to the knight.

"Admit him," he said simply.

The knight departed the solar. When he was gone, Christopher stood up from the heavily cushioned seat he'd been planted in. His bones were old, his body worn, and comfort was something he dreamt of these days. He'd spent so many years on a hard saddle that all of the seats in his solar were heavily cushioned, as if a group of delicate ladies regularly sat about the place.

"I wonder what de Geld is doing here," Christopher muttered. "Did he not just leave with Robin a few days ago?"

David, who had been a stellar knight in his day, nodded. "Right before Roi and his new wife headed home," he said. "If de Geld is here, he must not have spent much time at Cicadia. Mayhap Cheltenham forgot something?"

There was no real concern in the tone of their conversation. An urgent message could mean many things. Christopher was moving for the wine at the table under the lancet windows, but his eldest grandson and namesake, Chris, stood up and waved him off.

"I will bring you a cup, Taid," he said. "Sit down. Uncle David, do you wish for some wine also?"

David nodded, and Chris began to pour. Other men came to the table, namely Magnus and Aeron, who were still there along with Tiegh. Curtis' other sons, William and Arthur, were in the chamber also. So was Daniel, lounging in a chair next to his father, as well as Peter and Andrew. In truth, they'd been discussing Anselm Marshal's failing health and how the man was literally on his deathbed. Christopher received regular communication from Farringdon House, the Marshal townhome in London, and the last information he'd received hadn't been good. It seemed that the control of the Executioner Knights was about to change hands, but further discussion would have to wait.

They had a visitor.

Mathis appeared in the doorway of Christopher's solar, looking worn and weary. He was sweaty and dirty, and the first thing he did was look around the room. He looked at every man's face, and an expression of concern suddenly rippled over his features.

He was missing someone.

"My Lord Hereford," he greeted Christopher. "Where is Roi?"

Christopher looked at the disheveled man, who was usually more composed than what he was seeing. Already, he was on his guard.

"He is back at Pembridge," he said. "Why?"

Mathis sighed heavily and dropped his chin into his chest, as if that wasn't an answer he wanted to hear. But after a brief and faltering moment, he lifted his head once again and looked Christopher in the eye.

"You must send him word right away, my lord," he said. "I thought I would find him here, still. I have information…"

He abruptly stopped, looking at the other men in the room, clearly reluctant to continue, but Christopher urged him on.

"Continue," he said. "These men are trustworthy, and the information will not go beyond these walls unless you want it to. What is so important to Roi?"

Mathis looked at Christopher, something painful flickering in his eyes. "He is not to go to Cheltenham or Cirencester under any circumstances," he said. "I have just come from Riggs Fairford, and the man proceeded to tell me that Lord Cheltenham has been plotting Roi's death."

"What?" Christopher nearly shouted. Suddenly, men were bolting from their seats and the mood of the room grew thick with tension. "What are you saying, de Geld? Slow yourself and tell me what has happened."

Mathis lifted a weary hand to remove his helm. "Cheltenham does not know I am here," he said. "In fact, he does not even know what Cirencester is planning. He only knows that something will be planned, as I was supposed to return to him with Cirencester's scheme. But I came here first because you must know what will happen, my lord."

"Then tell me what you know," Christopher demanded. "Tell me from the beginning."

Mathis took a deep breath to steady himself. "It all started, I believe, with a visit from Lord Cirencester," he said. "Riggs Fairford came to Cicadia Castle right before Roi and Lady Diara were married. I even told Roi about the visit, but I did not know the contents or the reason for Cirencester's visit. When I returned home with Lord Cheltenham after his daughter's marriage, he immediately sent me to Cirencester's seat to give the man a message."

Christopher was hanging on every word. "What message?"

"'The time is now.'"

Christopher was expecting more. "Is that it?" he said. "What does that mean?"

Mathis nodded slowly. "I, too, wondered," he said. "I had no idea what those words would even mean to Cirencester, but Fairford thought I already knew. He thought that Cheltenham had already informed me of his scheme. According to Cirencester, he is to pillage some of Cheltenham's villages where his lands border Cheltenham. It is meant to look like a raid. Cheltenham will then send word to Roi, requesting his assistant, and then Cirencester is to set up an ambush and kill Roi. It is supposed to look like the man was simply killed in a skirmish."

Christopher was beside himself. "For what purpose?"

Mathis sighed heavily. "Because he wants to marry Lady Diara to Lord Cirencester's son," he said. "I do not know why, only that the two of them have come to some sort of agreement. They evidently want to be allied by marriage, and Roi stands in the way. I do not know any more than that, only that Roi is not to answer any such summons from Cheltenham for aid. It is a trap."

"How soon is this to happen, de Geld?"

"It is imminent, my lord," Mathis said. "Cirencester told me that he was moving his men to begin the raids in a couple of days, and that was over a day ago. I have ridden as hard as I could to get here, hoping Roi would be here so I could tell him personally."

"Christ," David muttered, turning to his brother. "If the raids are to take place in the next day or two, it is possible that Cheltenham has already sent Roi a request for aid."

Christopher looked sick. "And Roi would, of course, answer it."

Daniel was out of his chair, heading for the door as Curtis and his sons followed. But Curtis paused at the door as the others rushed past him. "I'll send the fastest messenger I have, Papa," he said. "I'll find Douglas and Westley, and we will ride for Pembridge immediately."

"Wait," Christopher said quickly. "If Roi has already mobilized and has left Pembridge, someone needs to intercept him. Send someone straight for Cirencester's lands to stop him."

"Colesborne," Mathis said. "That is where the raids will occur, where the ambush will be set."

Christopher nodded, swiftly returning his attention to Curtis. "Do you know where that is?"

Curtis nodded. "I think so," he said. "East of Gloucester, I believe."

"A moment, please," Mathis said, stopping the motion for the moment. "I know exactly where it is. More than that, I am supposed to be there to help with the ambush. I will ride for Colesborne. If Roi hasn't left Pembridge yet, then you must stop him."

"But what if he *has* left?" Curtis wanted to know.

"Then I will be there to intercept him," Mathis said. "I will find him before Cirencester does."

"Andrew and I will go with him," Peter said, stepping forth. "I'm also taking as many men as I can muster with me, men who can ride swiftly. Roi may need us."

Peter was a fine knight, even at his age, as was Andrew. But Christopher had to admit that he felt better with Andrew covering Peter's back. Peter may be a seasoned knight, but he was older. Reflexes tended to dull with age. But it gave Christopher great comfort to know Peter, Andrew, and Mathis were riding to intercept Roi, if necessary.

"Good," he said. "If Roi has already left Pembridge, it will be up to you three to stop him from reaching Colesborne. But if he has not left—if you do not find him—do not engage Cirencester or Cheltenham's men. Return here immediately."

They had a plan. The problem was having enough time to execute it. Christopher waved everyone on, with a sense of urgency nipping at their heels. Curtis, Daniel, and Curtis' sons were heading to Pembridge, while Peter, Andrew, and Mathis were heading for the horrible location of Colesborne. Everyone was moving, trying to save Roi's life. When the group filtered out, Christopher turned to David in complete bewilderment.

"Cheltenham bullies Roi into a marriage and when he finally agrees and marries the man's daughter, Cheltenham plans to kill him?" he said, aghast. "Only a madman would do such a thing. The question is why?"

David was at a loss. "I do not know," he said. "Mayhap he had planned that all along."

"Explain."

David shrugged. "We all know that Cheltenham is an ambitious man," he said. "I've never liked him, but fortunately, I've not had many dealings with him. However, now he is proving deadly to the House of de Lohr. His daughter would be Roi's widow, and she would inherit his wealth. She would take that into a marriage to Cirencester's son."

"And Cirencester's son becomes the next earl."

"That is reason enough to kill a man, isn't it?"

Christopher sat heavily in the nearest chair. The thought of a man he had wined and dined plotting to kill one of his sons was absolutely horrifying to him. It was also enraging. Once he overcame his shock, the fury began to take hold. The Christopher de Lohr of old was not a man who would take such a thing lying down. The Christopher de Lohr who served King Richard in the Levant, who actively fought against Richard's brother, John, and who had been one of the deadliest knights in England's history, wasn't going to take any of this lying down. As far as he was concerned, Cheltenham had committed an unforgiveable sin against him.

The man was going to pay.

His attention moved to the three knights who were still in the chamber. Magnus, Aeron, and Tiegh were Executioner Knights. They were spies and assassins, men who did the dirty work necessary to keep England strong.

Or avenge enemies.

And that gave Christopher an idea.

"Good knights," he said in a voice that was a little more than a growl. "It is possible that I require your services."

Tiegh stood up. "My lord?"

Christopher sat back in his chair, letting the rage of revenge fill his veins. To keep his family safe, he would do anything.

Anything.

"As you have heard, the Earl of Cheltenham has plotted the death of my son," he said. "I am an old man. I have seen many things. I have tolerated many things. But the one thing I will not tolerate is a man who plots to destroy those I love. Robin le Bec is a poor excuse for a warrior and an even poorer excuse for an earl. Now, he threatens my family. This I cannot abide."

"How may we be of service, my lord?" Tiegh said.

"He must be dealt with."

"How, my lord?"

"I think you know."

Now, the knights were catching on. Magnus, who had been standing by the windows, watching the activity in the bailey, came away from the window and moved in Christopher's direction. He was sharp, like his father, but more than that, he was deadly as well. Maxton of Loxbeare would kill on command with complete ease. No questions, no mess, no conscience. He was one of the finest assassins to bear the Executioner Knights moniker.

And Magnus was like his father in every way.

"Even if you thwart his attempt to kill Roi this time, there *will* be a next time, my lord," Magnus said. "Roi will live the rest of his life fearful that his wife's father will eventually succeed in killing him."

"Exactly my thoughts, Magnus."

"That is no way for a man to live, my lord."

"Indeed, it is not."

"For Roi's health and happiness, you must protect your son."

"Any way I can."

"Give the word, my lord, and it will be our honor to protect Roi for you."

That was what Christopher had been waiting to hear. All three of them were standing in front of him, their expressions serious as well as composed. There was a serenity to them, suggesting that they knew exactly what was coming and were relishing the opportunity to have a hand in it.

That was what the Executioner Knights did.

This was their battlefield.

"It is my suspicion that Cheltenham will not lead his army into a skirmish," he said. "If he is not present at Roi's death, he can say with a clear conscience that he was at Cicadia Castle when Roi was killed. That eliminates him as a suspect."

"It gives him plausible deniability, my lord."

"Precisely," Christopher said. "Therefore, I believe you can find Robin le Bec at Cheltenham. If he is not there, of course, you know where to find him—near Colesborne. But I would go to Cicadia first."

Magnus nodded sharply. "How far is it?"

Christopher pointed to the road outside the walls of Lioncross. "Take the road all the way to Gloucester," he said. "Cheltenham is just beyond Gloucester, to the east. You will not arrive until tomorrow at the earliest."

"Understood, my lord."

Christopher lingered on the trio for a moment before averting his gaze. "Go forth," he finally whispered. "No trace."

The three knights slipped from the chamber, heading out to collect their horses and ride to Cicadia Castle. Knowing that he had just sighed Cheltenham's death warrant didn't bother Christopher in the least. If it was between Roi's life and Robin le Bec's, there was only one choice Christopher could make.

Only one choice he *would* make.

He turned to David.

"God help us if Roi has already left for Cirencester's ambush," he muttered.

David sighed faintly. "Let us pray he has not," he said. "The lads… they will get to him in time. I would not worry."

Christopher rolled his eyes. "That is an impossible bit of advice," he said. "Of course I am going to worry. But I will tell you one thing, David."

"What?"

"I do not regret sending Loxbeare and de Dere to eliminate the root of the problem."

David snorted softly. "If you had not asked them to do it, I was going to do it myself."

Christopher looked at him, his eyes glimmering dully. "Don't you think you're a little old?"

David pursed his lips wryly. "I would not be so smug if I were you," he said. "I'm still younger than you are."

"At our age, that means nothing."

They started to laugh at one another, an unexpected moment of levity in a situation that had them both on edge. But as the laughter died away, Christopher fixed on his brother.

"It's not just Cheltenham, you know," he said quietly. "Cirencester is a threat as well. He may be moving on Cheltenham's orders, but he is most definitely a threat. His son is the one who would benefit the most from Roi's death."

David thought on that before standing up and moving for the door. Christopher watched him go.

"Where are you going?" he asked.

David looked at him. "To tell the other Executioner Knight that very good point," he said. "Let the Loxbeare brothers and de Dere handle Cheltenham. I would say Peter might be interested in taking care of Cirencester himself. For his brother."

Christopher nodded faintly, feeling sick and saddened by the entire situation. "For his brother," he whispered. "And David?"

"What is it?"

"Do not tell Dustin," he said quietly. "If one of us must shoulder the burden of worry before we have any news, let it be me."

David understood. He left the solar to speak with Peter and the others, and everyone who was bound for Cicadia, Pembridge, or other points east was cleared out of the bailey within the hour.

The long wait, for Christopher, had begun.

CHAPTER EIGHTEEN

Near the village of Colesborne

H E HADN'T ARRIVED yet.
Cheltenham, that was.

Riggs found himself outside of the village of Colesborne, literally waiting for another army to show up and fight him off. Robin's knight had returned to Cicadia Castle, undoubtedly, to tell Cheltenham to muster the army and move south, but so far, the army hadn't shown up. Riggs was burning and pillaging at will, but it was more of a show than anything else, simply to scare the villagers and create chaos.

Cirencester wanted to make a lot of noise more than he really wanted to damage anything, so his tactics had involved things like opening corrals to scatter livestock or cleaning out chicken houses. If he saw a decent horse, he had his men grab the horse and run with it. It was really just harassment, but it was meant to look like trouble.

Trouble that the de Lohr army would fall right into.

It was just him and about eight hundred of his men. His son, Flavian, had remained at Totterdown Castle because Riggs didn't want the lad involved in a fight. He wanted to keep his son safe while he wrangled an earldom for him. Riggs had even waited three days before taking his army up north, time enough for Robin to send word to Roi about a battle that hadn't started yet, so if Roi had received word over the past couple of days, he was surely on his way.

Riggs was unaware that the message had already gone out, days ago.

At the Withington Turn, as he'd told Mathis, the road led down to a river crossing that was thick with trees. Riggs was already putting archers in those trees because the best thing to do would be to lure Roi into that area and let the archers take him out. Riggs knew that his knights, well armed as they were, still wouldn't have a chance against a knight of Roi's ability, so the safest thing would be to use the archers. A neat, clean job of taking down a de Lohr knight with the least amount of risk.

That was the plan.

Of course, Mathis couldn't lead Roi into the area. There was a chance they'd hit Mathis with an archer barrage, and Riggs wanted to keep Mathis safe. The future Earl of Cheltenham would need a knight like that. Therefore, it made the most sense to keep his army near Colesborne until Roi showed up, and then have the man chase the Cirencester army down the Withington Turn and into the area where the archers would be waiting.

Then they would have him.

Therefore, three days after Riggs sent Mathis back to Cicadia Castle, the Cirencester army spent most of the time simply harassing the village and the outskirts. For fun, they lit some fires that spat black smoke into the air, like a beacon for the de Lohr army. Riggs wanted to make it easy for Roi to find him, and he was doing everything he could short of sending out invitations. The fires and harassment went into the fourth day, all day, and through the night. But on the morning of the fifth day since Mathis had delivered those fateful words—*the time is now*—an army was sighted at dawn coming from the west.

When Riggs was informed by his scouts, he knew the moment of triumph was upon him. Cheltenham still hadn't arrived yet, but that didn't matter. Roi had come, as they'd planned, and Riggs couldn't wait for Robin to show himself.

The time *was* now.

ᘓ

WHEN ROI ARRIVED at the village of Colesborne, he wasn't any clearer about the situation than he had been when he first received Cheltenham's request for aid.

Something seemed off.

In the first place, Colesborne was not nearly as destroyed as the missive had led him to believe. There had been some burning on the edge of town, and the street of merchants had been mildly looted, but nothing crucial. The villagers seemed scared more than anything, and they were very clear that the Cirencester army was on the east side of the village, out in the heavily forested areas, but the Cheltenham army was nowhere to be seen. Roi and the men he'd brought with him made sure the village was secure and helped put a couple of fires out, but for the most part, the damage wasn't too terrible.

Very strange, indeed.

"For a raid, I would say there is very little damage," Roi said to Adrius. "What in the hell is Cirencester doing?"

Adrius looked around. "I would not know," he said. "But I was thinking the same thing. This was not a raid."

"Nay, it was not," Roi said. "It seems like it was simply annoyance. No one is dead, nothing is stolen. The man at the end of town said one of his horses was taken by the army but that it returned to the corral on its own, unharmed."

Adrius pushed his helm back and scratched his forehead. "This makes little sense," he said, looking around. "And where is Cheltenham in all of this? Should he not be here?"

Roi shrugged. "I would assume so," he said. "But this situation is so bizarre... who can tell? The villagers said the Cirencester army is to the east, so mayhap he's there. If they are engaging, then that is where we should go."

Adrius agreed. He had the sergeants round up the army, which was mostly helping villagers at that point, but barked commands had them all mounting their horses and following Adrius and Roi as they charged to the other end of town in search of Cheltenham's army. Once they cleared the village outskirts and the hedgerows cleared, giving them a view of the meadows and fields around them, they could see an army to the east.

They were simply standing around.

Roi and Adrius looked at one another, baffled, but the moment the other army caught sight of the de Lohr men, they began to yell and run. They leapt onto their horses, tearing off in a panic, and the natural response from Roi was to follow. They chased them across two big fields and onto a narrow road that angled downward. It was surrounded by heavy trees, a green canopy overhead, but Roi continued after them.

Some of the men were branching off from the bulk of the fleeing army, taking off in different directions, and a few of the de Lohr men went off after them. But most of the de Lohr army was close on the heels of the retreating army, and by the time they hit a forested area where the road leveled off and crossed a large brook, Roi could see that they were closing in on the retreating army.

But that was when the sky let loose.

It was raining arrows.

Roi was hit almost immediately, a powerful bolt that hit him in the back, just below his left shoulder blade. It wasn't enough to knock him off his horse, but he knew that he was in trouble. He cursed himself for being stupid enough to chase the fleeing army through an area that was ideal for an ambush. It had all happened so quickly that he hadn't given it much thought, but given the strangeness of the situation, he should have.

Damn… he should have.

They had to get out of there.

Roi had whirled his steed around, bellowing orders to his men to go back the way they came, when another bolt hit him in the chest. That one was enough to topple him from the horse, and as he went down, he could see Adrius going down as well with a bolt through the neck.

Suddenly, a puzzling skirmish had become deadly.

Roi wasn't one to panic, but he hit the ground hard, feeling genuine fear because he was wounded and without his broadsword, which was still on the horse when it darted away. He was in the stream, face-first in the freezing water, but he managed to push himself up and get clear of the water. There was chaos all around him while his men fought for their lives as the trees came alive with men bearing swords. Hand-to-hand combat commenced. Even the retreating army was returning now that Roi and his men had been ambushed. They were being attacked from all sides.

Roi knew they were in trouble.

He could feel the bolt in his back. He didn't know how bad it was, but he couldn't get to it. He could, however, get to the one in his chest, and the moment he ripped it out, he was sorry. It had nicked a lung, and now he had a sucking wound that was causing him to feel faint because he couldn't catch his breath. Slapping a hand against it to try to seal the hole, he staggered over to Adrius, who was lying on his back bleeding to death.

Reaching out, Roi grasped him by the arm and began to drag him away from the fighting, which was quite heavy and quite vicious. A few of his men saw what he was doing, and they immediately rushed to Roi to protect him and Adrius. It was common, in any battle strategy, for the enemy to remove the knights and commanders of the opposing army at the beginning of a battle in the hopes of splintering the army. That was exactly what the ambush had done—taken out the command. Roi thought they might have a chance to get clear of the fighting when a barrage of arrows let loose on his group and the men protecting him all went down, leaving Roi standing there alone, still gripping Adrius' arm.

He looked up to see an armored man and several men with loaded crossbows moving swiftly in his direction.

"Stop," the man called to him. "Stop what you are doing and I will call my men off. If you try to get away, I will be forced to kill you."

Roi was in a bad way. The fighting had moved off toward the west as his men tried to flee, so there were pockets of fighting. From what he could see, he'd lost a few men in the initial arrow barrage, but for the most part, they seemed to be holding their own. They were outmanned—he could see that— but they were giving it one hell of a fight.

But for Roi, that fight had ended.

He dropped Adrius' arm.

"At least let me tend his wound," he said quietly but firmly. "Show us that mercy."

The man drew closer to him, and to Roi, he looked vaguely familiar. He couldn't put his finger on it, but he'd seen that man before. Roi didn't take his eyes off him as the man peered down at Adrius.

"There is no need to tend his wound," he said. "He is dead."

Roi sighed faintly, daring to look down to see that, indeed, Adrius was dead. The man was lying there, blood coming out of his neck, his mouth, and his nose, staring up at the sky. A good knight, so wastefully taken. That realization inflamed Roi, but it was a rage tempered by fear. Fear that he was the next to die, and he very much didn't want to. He wanted to go home to his new wife and live a full life by her side. He'd finally found the love of his life, and the thought that he was going to be brutally taken from her made him sick to his stomach. Not for himself, but for her. He knew how badly she would take his death. But here he was, facing down his own mortality and wondering how in the hell he got here.

He still didn't know what was going on.

"Who *are* you?" he finally asked, sounding exasperated. "What is this all about?"

The man looked at him for a moment before answering. "What is your name?"

"Richard de Lohr," Roi said without hesitation. "Now that I have told you my name, what is yours?"

The man's face lit up as if he'd just met an old and dear friend. "It *is* you!" he said. "I was hoping that you were part of that army, but I could not be sure. Finally... Roi de Lohr, in the flesh."

Roi was having trouble breathing, trouble standing, and it was taking every bit of strength he had to stay upright.

"Your name," he said again, decidedly unfriendly.

But the man held up a hand as if begging patience. "We've not been formally introduced," he said. "But I know all about you. I know about your family and your father, the great Earl of Hereford and Worcester. I know that the House of de Lohr controls nearly everything on the Welsh marches. I know the greatness you come from. I also know that you married Diara le Bec."

Roi was at a distinct disadvantage. The man did look familiar to him, but he still couldn't place him. And he didn't like the fact that the man had mentioned Diara by name.

"How would you know about my marriage?" he said, pressing his hand hard over the hole in his chest. "*Who* are you?"

The pleasant expression from the man's face faded. "I am the last man you will see on this earth," he said. "You see, you took what belongs to me. Now, I am rectifying that situation."

Roi had no idea what he was talking about, mostly because his mind was starting to muddle from blood loss and the inability to breathe. "Be plain," he said. "I've no time for this. Tell me what you want and be done with it."

"Why are you in a hurry to die?" the man said. "You will not leave this place alive, de Lohr. But I wanted you to see the face of the man who took your life. I want you to understand what it took to come to this moment in time. You see, this was all planned for your benefit. The battle, the ambush—it was all meant for you. You have asked who I am—can you not guess? You married the woman meant for my son."

The light went on in Roi's mind. Now, he knew who the man was before him, and he wasn't surprised. But he still wasn't clear on what was happening and why Cirencester had evidently lured him into a trap.

"Cirencester?" he muttered.

Riggs' eyebrows lifted. "Then you know you married a woman who did not belong to you."

Roi wasn't feeling fear at the moment so much as he was feeling rage. He looked around, seeing a few of his dead soldiers on the ground several feet away, seeing Adrius dead at his feet.

Disgust washed over him.

"You set this up to trap me?" he said. "You knew I would come to Cheltenham's aid, so you did this to trap me? To kill me?"

Riggs was back to looking pleased with himself. A faint smile creased his lips. "There was no other way to do it," he said. "Robin and I agreed—"

Roi interrupted him, shocked. "Robin is in on this, too?"

Riggs nodded. "Of course he is," he said. "He realized that he'd made a mistake by betrothing his daughter to you, and since he knew you would not break the betrothal, because what man would when an earldom is involved, this was the only solution. Now, my son will marry Lady Diara and inherit Cheltenham. It's all quite simple."

Roi was feeling sick. Sicker than he already was. In fact, his body was beginning to tremble and he was finding it difficult to stand. To realize that Robin was in on this scheme brought back all of the things Diara had said—how she thought her father was acting strange, how she'd warned Roi about him. How she hadn't wanted Roi to answer her father's call for aid. She'd been trying to warn him, and he'd brushed her off. Her paranoia had turned out to be true. He'd thought she was just being a nervous bride.

As it turned out, she'd been right all along.

Now, he was going to pay the price.

"You two planned this between you," he finally said, trying to keep his balance because his legs were trembling so. "Why in the hell did Robin push a betrothal with the House of de Lohr if you had already made the offer between Diara and your son? I do not understand any of this."

Riggs shrugged. "When your son died, his procession passed through my lands," he said. "That is how I knew Lady Diara's betrothal was no more. When I went to Robin, my good friend, to convey my condolences, he was regretting the betrothal between you and his daughter. He agreed that it was a mistake. I offered to help him fix that mistake… for a price."

"Your son's marriage to Diara."

"Exactly."

Roi shook his head in disgust, but it threw him off balance and he pitched down to one knee. His breathing was growing worse because he was having a difficult time keeping the hole in his chest covered up. It wasn't a horrible sucking wound, because he'd seen those, but it was bad enough. Just enough to cause him problems.

And he had problems aplenty.

"If you were a man of honor, you would give me a sword and at least give me a fighting chance," he said, wondering how long he could draw this out before they killed him outright. "You used a coward's tactics by ambushing me from the trees. A worthy man would have challenged me with a sword, but I can see that was too much for you. I wonder if your son is as cowardly as his father is."

Infuriated, Riggs marched up on him and kicked him in the other knee, causing him to fall heavily on his buttocks. He came in again for another kick, but Roi grabbed his foot and twisted, throwing him to the ground. Wounded and all, Roi pounced on Riggs and gave him a good beating with three or four strikes to the face before Riggs' men pulled him off their lord. One man grabbed Roi by the bolt that was sticking out of his back, yanking on it with the intention of pulling him away, but he ended up pulling out the bolt completely. In agony, Roi was thrown onto his side while Riggs' men kicked him and stomped on him, but Riggs call them off.

"Enough!" he bellowed. "Get away from him. I'll slice that bastard to pieces!"

With that, he withdrew his broadsword. Roi knew that because he could hear it sing as it was unsheathed. He was without a sword, but he did have daggers on his body. The problem was that between his back wound and the chest wound, he was beginning to see stars. His eyesight was starting to dim, and he knew that he wasn't going to stay conscious much longer.

Still, he had to fight.

He had a perfect life now, and he wasn't about to give it up.

With the greatest struggle, he pushed himself onto his back in time to see Riggs bearing down on him. Immediately, he unsheathed a dagger he knew was at his waist, but when he'd fallen, he must have damaged the sheath because he couldn't get it out. That meant his boot came up, and he kicked Riggs in the groin area, causing the man to cry out in pain as he stumbled back.

But it was only momentary.

Fury had Riggs regrouping. He lifted his broadsword over his head and moved in to make the kill. Roi could see it coming and thought quickly—he could try to roll away and get to his feet, or he could fall forward into the man's legs and hopefully send him off balance. All he needed was the opportunity to get the broadsword away from him. He knew that if he did, by sheer willpower alone, he'd have a fighting chance. All he could see or think or feel was Diara, a vision before him that was keeping him alive. She was feeding his fighting spirit. He simply couldn't leave her.

But then something strange happened.

Suddenly, men were charging through the brush, in his direction, and an arrow sailed right into Riggs' midsection. He opened his mouth to scream, but another bolt went into his mouth, through his head, and emerged on the other side.

He was dead before he hit the ground.

The men with him scattered. Battered, wounded, and close to passing out, Roi tried to get up, to face whoever was attacking them through the bramble, but he couldn't seem to make it. He grabbed at the daggers on his thigh, managing to unsheathe one of them, holding it up and preparing to slash anyone who came near him. He was going to fight to the death, damn it, and to hell with anyone who would try to take him down. They would leave their share of blood on the ground.

"Roi!" Someone was beside him, grasping him, holding his wrist so he didn't slash at him. "Let the dagger go, Roi. It's me. It's Peter. Let it go, man. You're safe. I will not let anyone harm you, I swear it."

Roi was quivering violently. The dagger fell to the ground, and he looked up at his eldest brother, so shocked that he could hardly believe what he was seeing.

"Peter?" he gasped. "My God… is it really you?"

Peter smiled at him, but the concern on his face was obvious. "It is really me," he said. "But there's no time for talk. We need to get you out of here, old man."

Roi was trying to get on his feet but he couldn't seem to manage it. "What are you doing here?" he demanded weakly. "How did you find me?"

More men were swarming around him, and Roi could feel arms around him, lifting him up, moving him away from the carnage. They began running with him, through the brush and bramble.

"Everything will be fine, Roi," Peter said steadily, slashing bushes out of the way as they moved. "We need to tend your wounds. You're safe now."

Roi could see his nephew, Andrew, helping to carry him. There were other de Lohr men, probably more than a dozen, all of them carrying him away from the blood and chaos. In truth, Roi could hardly believe it. He was still back there on his knees, preparing to fight for his life.

But he wasn't.

Peter had saved him.

"It was an ambush," Roi said breathlessly. "Cirencester wanted to kill me. He wants Diara. He wants my wife."

"I know," Peter said. "We were told what was happening."

"You *know*?" Roi said. "How do you know?"

Peter was trying to keep an eye on the fighting around them, making sure they took Roi some place safe before they set him down. "Cheltenham's knight," he said. "None of this would have been possible had Mathis de Geld not come to Lioncross to tell us about the plot. Papa sent us all to find you—some of us went to Pembridge, some to this godforsaken village of Colesborne. But we found you. Thank God we found you."

They'd reached a crest on a hill, away from the pockets of fighting, and Peter had the men lay Roi down, very carefully.

Roi grabbed at his brother, weakly.

"Mathis?" he repeated. "Robin was in on the plot, Peter. Mathis serves Robin!"

Peter looked around, catching sight of Mathis on the road cutting down a Cirencester man. "I do not think he wants to serve him any longer," he said. "Were it not for him, you would now be dead. We owe him everything, Roi."

Roi understood. Sort of. He was so exhausted, so muddled, that all he could do was nod faintly and close his eyes. As Peter and Andrew worked on him to seal up the hole in his chest with the field kit they'd brought with them, they noticed the tears that had begun to stream down Roi's temples. Stricken with sorrow at the sight, perhaps indicative of the real fear Roi had been subjected to, Peter cupped his brother's face with one hand, touching his forehead to Roi's.

"You will be fine," he whispered. "We will patch your wounds and take you home today. You needn't worry, Roi. I promise you will heal."

Roi's voice broke. "I just want to see my wife again," he said. "I did not think I was going to."

Peter felt great pity for his brother, one of the strongest men he'd ever known. "You will see her again," he said softly. "I swear you will."

"Peter?"

"What is it?"

"Thank you," Roi whispered. "For my life… thank you."

Peter kissed his forehead, but Roi didn't feel it. He was in a haze and fading fast. He could feel Peter and Andrew moving him around, stripping off his tunics and protection to get to the wounds, packing the holes with clean linen soaked in wine. As he lay there in limbo with the darkness calling softly to him, he happened to open his eyes. There was a shadow over him, and he swore, as he lived and breathed, that he found himself looking at Beckett.

His son, blond and handsome, with that cheeky smile he remembered so well, was gazing down at him. Roi's face lit up as he beheld his beloved son. He even lifted a hand, trying to touch him. But Beckett was beyond his reach.

He simply smiled down at his father.

"'Tis not your time yet, Papa," Beckett said, his voice as faint as the wind through the trees. "Go home now. Go home and love."

With that, he was gone.

Blissful unconsciousness finally claimed Roi.

CHAPTER NINETEEN

Cicadia Castle

H E WAS PACING the floor like a nervous cat.

It had been almost five days since Robin had sent Mathis to Cirencester with those fateful words—*the time is now.* But Mathis had yet to return, and Robin was becoming more impatient by the day. He couldn't imagine what had kept Mathis from returning right away. Everything was hinging on Cirencester's plans, and Robin didn't even know what those plans were other than they'd discussed everything happening at the village of Colesborne. That was where he assumed Cirencester would strike, and that was where he had told Roi to join him.

But he wasn't even at Colesborne.

He was still at Cicadia.

But not for long. It had all started a day ago, when a man traveling from the south told the gatehouse guards about some raids near Colesborne. People were being burned out, he said, and Eddard was at the gatehouse when the reports were given. He immediately went to Robin and told him. Pryce, in command with Mathis away, sent scouts to the southern end of the Cheltenham property to see what was going on, but the men hadn't returned yet. By the end of day, Robin grew agitated and impatient, so much so that he ordered Pryce to muster the army.

They were moving south.

Robin began to suspect that something must have happened to Mathis. Perhaps the man was set upon as he traveled and was now dead in a ditch somewhere. That was the only explanation for Mathis' absence, because he knew the man was dependable and loyal. He'd served Cheltenham flawlessly for nine years, so Robin trusted him completely. He was quite concerned for Mathis, but more concerned that he had no idea what Cirencester was planning beyond the raid at Colesborne.

Robin was in quite a state about it, but he didn't plan on riding with his army. That way, he could tell Christopher that he hadn't been in the field when Roi met his end. Surely Hereford couldn't blame him if he wasn't even there.

He'd let others do his dirty work for him.

And he didn't feel the least bit guilty about it.

Standing at the window of his solar, overlooking Cicadia's small bailey, Robin watched the big gates swing open as Pryce and Eddard began to move the wagons inside to load them. Because the bailey wasn't large enough to store the wagons necessary to accompany the army, they kept them stored in outbuildings nearby. Men were moving in and out of the gates as preparations were underway, reminding Robin of the last time he'd moved his army out. That had been to France those years ago, when he'd practically forced Roi into a betrothal between their children. Odd how that memory should pop up. Roi couldn't have known that when he'd agreed to the betrothal, he'd essentially signed his own death warrant.

Courtesy of an ambitious and immoral friend.

"Where is the army going, my husband?"

Jolted from his train of thought, Robin turned to see Ananda standing in the doorway. She was dressed in dark colors, as she always was, her graying hair covered by a wimple and her blue eyes curious. Robin had sought her advice on many things over the years, but this was something he didn't want her to know about. He didn't need any advice about what he intended to do.

"Trouble," he said, turning away from her. "Nothing that concerns you. Go about your business."

But Ananda wouldn't be brushed off so easily. "Will you not confide the trouble to me?" she asked. "You are sending your entire army out. It must be serious, indeed. May I help?"

Robin sighed sharply. "I told you that it did not concern you," he said. "Yet you pester me. You have grown too bold, Ananda. When I tell you that something is none of your concern, I mean it."

"I am sorry, my husband," she said, though she didn't mean it. "Would you prefer it if Iris and I went into town? It would remove us from underfoot. It seems there is a good deal going on, and it is possible that you would like the women removed."

Robin spun around to face her. "My preference would be that the women of my home leave and never come back," he snarled. "I have already gotten rid of one of you. Now I am still saddled with Iris. And you. I do not care where you go or what you do. Leave me alone!"

Ananda backed off. Truth be told, Robin had been unpredictable for a couple of weeks now, ever since Roi and Diara left Cicadia for Lioncross. That seemed to be when Robin became snappish, and Ananda had no idea why. She knew that he'd been distant the entire time they'd been at Lioncross for the wedding, and she had seen her husband muttering to himself now and again. If she didn't know better, she'd say the man was in trouble, but without his confidence, she could not help him.

Truthfully, she wasn't sure she wanted to.

Ananda had been forced into a marriage with Robin those years ago. She tried to be a good wife, a helpful wife, and Robin would let her from time to time. But the reality was that she'd married a petty, bitter, vindictive man whom she wasn't particularly fond of. Moments like this, when he was snappish with her, reminded her of the fact. Long ago, she'd been in love with a good man, a simple knight, but Robin had seen her in a marketplace one day and bullied her father into a betrothal. That seemed to be what he did best, because he'd done the same thing to Roi de Lohr.

After all these years, she still couldn't figure him out.

She didn't want to.

Quietly, she left the room.

Robin knew when she was gone because he heard the door shut softly. He was glad. He had his own issues to deal with and didn't need Ananda trying to push her way into his business. Too many things were in the balance at the moment, and he needed all of his focus so he could be ready to move in the direction that was best suited for him. Somewhere to the south, a battle was happening. Or not happening. Roi de Lohr might be there. Or he might not be. If the man wasn't killed in this skirmish, Robin would have an entirely new set of problems to deal with.

He had to think.

To plan.

Above all else, he had to survive.

There were a lot of men in his small bailey now, moving in and out of the gates. It wasn't exactly optimal for a castle to have to mobilize both in and out of the bailey, with the gates wide open, but they had no choice. They could hardly fit all of the men inside the bailey as it was. Robin continued to watch the activity, pausing only to pour himself some wine. He drank as he watched, losing track of time. He ended up drinking two full cups. By the third one, he was starting to feel slightly drunk. But it was of no matter.

Drink was the only thing he looked forward to these days.

As he continued to watch the activity, he heard his solar door open—it was unmistakable because the iron hinges squeaked horribly. He was preparing for another onslaught from Ananda, so he downed all of the wine in his cup in frustration and threw it to the ground.

"I told you to leave me alone," he growled as he whirled to face her. "I do not want you to—"

Robin stopped dead, looking at three men he'd never seen before. Or had he? They seemed strangely familiar, but he couldn't remember where he'd seen them. One was standing near his fine table, another near the wine pitcher, and the third one was by the door.

He cocked his head curiously.

"Who are you?" he asked. "You have not been announced. Where did you come from?"

The man near the wine table was the closest one to him. He was enormous, with shaggy, dark hair and piercing, dark eyes.

"Your gatehouse is open," he said. "We simply walked in."

Robin focused on the man. "So you have," he said. "But I have seen you before."

The man nodded. "You have," he said. "At your daughter's

wedding. We are allies of Christopher de Lohr."

Suddenly, it dawned on him. Robin looked at the man by the door and remembered that they'd shared an entire conversation. He pointed to the man.

"De Dere, is it?" he said. "Tiegh de Dere. You are from Berkshire."

Tiegh nodded. "I am," he said. "And we did have a long talk about hunting in the north."

"I recall," Robin said with some enthusiasm. But then it occurred to him that Christopher de Lohr must have sent these men, and he had no idea why. "But why have you come here, to my home? I do not understand."

Tiegh's reply was to throw the bolt on the door, locking them all in the solar. It was the man with the shaggy hair who took over the conversation at that point.

"My name is Magnus of Loxbeare," he said quietly. "You have met Tiegh, but our third companion is my brother, Aeron. We have come because you have done something quite despicable. A little matter of planning Roi de Lohr's death. We know about it, and so does Lord Hereford. That is why we've come."

Robin was drunk, but not so drunk that he didn't understand Magnus' words. It took him a few moments to process them, but once they sank deep, his eyes widened.

"Roi's death?" he repeated, suddenly nervous. "Who told you such things?"

Magnus' dark eyes never left him. "It seems that you and Lord Cirencester have done some plotting," he said. "Your plan is to lure Roi into an ambush and kill him, making it seem as if he has been killed in battle. Then you plan to marry his widow to Cirencester's son. Do not deny it, for we know it to be true.

We have come to tell you that your plan has been thwarted. And you, my lord, shall be punished."

"I do not know what you are talking about."

"I think that you do."

"Get out or I will call my knights."

"They cannot hear you. No one can."

Robin went into panic mode after that. He tried to rush to his table where he kept weapons, but Magnus was in his way, so he darted back toward the hearth, where there was a shovel and a poker. He grabbed the iron poker and wielded it with both hands.

"Get back," he said. "Get back and leave me. I will kill you all if you come near me!"

Magnus didn't back away. Neither did the others. In fact, they began to close in on Robin.

"It is my pleasure to tell you, Lord Cheltenham, that your vile life is over," Magnus rumbled. "You have plotted against the wrong family. Did you think de Lohr would do nothing when he discovered your scheme? A threat against Roi is a threat against the entire de Lohr family. And threats must be eliminated."

Robin screamed like a woman, slashing wildly with the poker. "Leave me alone!" he cried. "You cannot harm me! I will have you killed, do you hear? *I will kill you!*"

Magnus glanced at Aeron and Tiegh, briefly nodding his head. "Not before we kill you first," Magnus said. "The end has arrived, my lord."

Robin was still slashing the poker as Tiegh came up on his left, Magnus on his right. Tiegh grabbed the poker and lashed out an enormous hand in the same motion, grabbing Robin around the neck. He squeezed hard enough to crush the man's windpipe as Aeron yanked the poker away. Magnus went in for the kill, grabbing Robin's flailing hand and planting a dagger in it. Wrapping his own hand around the one holding the dagger, he rammed the blade between Robin's ribs and straight into his heart. As Robin gasped and pitched forward, Magnus made sure he fell face-first onto the floor, hand still on the dagger, making it appear that he'd stabbed himself in the heart.

And with that, Robin le Bec's life was over.

But it was all in a day's work for the Executioner Knights. Tiegh unbolted the door and stuck his head out into the entry, making sure the area was empty, before slipping out with Magnus and Aeron right behind him. Together, the three of them rushed out into the bailey, mingling with the troops and losing themselves in the grounds before departing Cicadia the same way they'd arrived.

Through the open gatehouse.

There were so many people going in and out that no one thought anything of a few random men they didn't recognize. No one gave it a second thought. But back in the keep, Robin's strange screams had been heard by one person.

Ananda.

In truth, she had been going up the stairs, still stinging from Robin's harsh words, when she heard the door hinges squeak. Thinking that he might be leaving his solar, she peered down the stairwell only to see strange men enter his solar and close the door. Curious, she went to the door, putting her ear against the panel to hear what was being said, and she heard everything.

Absolutely everything.

Ananda heard the conversation, Robin's screams, and the subsequent scuffle. Fearful that the knights might try to do her harm if they knew she eavesdropped, she slipped away, hiding in the gap under the stairwell, until they departed the solar and fled outside. When she was certain they were gone, she timidly went to the open solar door and peered inside, only to see Robin lying facedown in a pool of blood.

For a moment, Ananda simply stood there and absorbed the scene before her. She realized that she wasn't sorry. She wasn't even shocked. She knew what had happened and why. But all she could manage to feel was relief. Pure, unrestrained relief. It was a day she never thought she'd see, the day that she had been reprieved from her life sentence of marriage to Robin le Bec. If she ever saw those men again, she would thank them profusely for the gift they'd unknowingly given her. It was all she could to keep from shouting with joy.

It was the day of Ananda's emancipation.

Quietly, she closed the door to her husband's solar and went about her business, just as he had asked.

Let someone else find the body.

She was finished.

CHAPTER TWENTY

Pembridge Castle

I T WAS A waiting game now.

Daniel, Curtis, Douglas, Westley, Chris, William, and Arthur had come to Pembridge and left. They'd only left the day before, heading out with about six hundred troops, a mix of men from Lioncross Abbey and the remains of those left behind at Pembridge. Unfortunately, they had to explain their arrival at Pembridge when they'd come seeking Roi, and Diara had told them that he'd gone to the aid of her father. The men had very nearly panicked over that news, and their behavior, in turn, had upset Diara, so they were forced to tell her everything.

Absolutely everything.

Now, all that she had feared had become reality. Her father's meddling, his odd behavior—it all became clear as Curtis calmly told her what Mathis had told them. Diara wept as she realized what her father was trying to do. She knew, as she lived and breathed, that it all had to do with the scene back at Cicadia when Roi had struck her father in the face. Before Roi left to answer her father's summons, she'd tried to tell him that her father wasn't the forgiving kind and that he held a grudge against those who went against him. She'd even begged Roi not to go. But not even Diara thought her father would go this far.

The man was trying to kill her husband.

It was beyond belief, but in the same breath, she really wasn't surprised. Diara had seen her father turn against men who did not obey his wishes. Curtis and Daniel were adamant that they needed to leave for Colesborne to help Roi, so she let them go. Kyne remained with her, still in command of the castle, but Curtis and his brothers, cousin, and sons took a large contingent and rushed out of Pembridge.

Rushing to save her husband.

Diara hadn't stopped weeping for days.

Now, it was morning of the fifth day since Roi had departed, lured by the false missive sent by her father. Curtis and the others had been gone for a couple of days, and Diara couldn't eat or sleep. All she could do was watch from her window, for any sign of a returning army. Sometimes she wandered the bailey, hoping she would be there at just the right time when the army came through the gatehouse. Kyne watched her walk around, and sometimes, he would join her and try to calm her fears. But he knew it was useless.

Truthfully, he was fearful himself.

But this morning, Diara made it down into the fishpond area behind the kitchens. Roi had had a stone bench put in before he left because sometimes they'd come down and sit, watching the fish or watching Dorian as she tried to make the area thrive again. It was her pet project, this pond and the surrounding garden, and Diara sat on the bench, watching the fish, remembering the time when Roi threw her into the pond without meaning to.

It had been one of the better moments of her life.

"Diara?"

She heard her name, and looked over her shoulder to see Adalia entering the area. Diara forced a smile when she saw Roi's daughter, holding out a hand to her.

"Come and sit with me," she said. "I have been thinking about all of the fish we will put in this pond once Dorian has it clean."

Adalia took her hand and held it as she sat down next to her. "I do not like fish very much," Adalia admitted. "I like to watch them swim, but I do not like to eat them."

Diara grinned. "I do not like fish, either," she said. "Have you noticed that we've not had any fish for supper? It is because I cannot stand the smell of it."

Adalia smiled timidly. "Nor I," she said. "I would rather have chicken."

"I would, too."

"I do not even like goose."

"I cannot stand it. Too oily."

As they giggled over their mutual dislike of fish and roast goose, Dorian entered the area, looking as if she was armed for a trip into the lion's den. She had on gloves and boots and a long tunic of canvas that Diara helped make for her. She was also carrying several gardening implements. When she noticed her sister and stepmother sitting there, she threw down the tools in her hands.

"I am cleaning out the plants today," she announced. "All of those plants in the pond that are making the water so green. I am removing them."

Diara nodded. "That is very brave of you," she said. "The pond will be wonderful when you are finished with it."

Dorian picked up something that looked like a hoe. "Do

think we can get more fish when Papa returns?"

The mirth faded from Diara's face. "I think so," she said. "Adalia and I were just speaking on the fish we would put in the pond. I do not like to eat fish. Do you?"

Dorian shook her head. "I would rather feed them and watch them swim," she said. "I do not like to eat creatures that I can pet."

"But you eat beef and mutton," Diara pointed out.

Dorian curled her lip. "I know," she said. "But I do not like to. I do not like to eat anything with eyeballs."

That brought a smile from Diara. "Then you do have a quandary," she said. "You know that some people even eat horses."

Dorian's eyes widened. "They are horrible people," she said. "Horses are our friends. They are not meant to be eaten."

"How is Brillante?"

Dorian smiled broadly at the mention of her blond horse. "She is very sweet," she said. "I love her very much. But... but when we saw her in the village, she had a companion. Another horse who was her companion. I think she is missing her."

"Oh?" Diara said. "I did not see another horse."

"I did," Dorian said. "A little red pony. When is Papa coming back? I want to ask him if I can have Brillante's companion. She needs her."

Diara lifted an eyebrow. "*She* needs her?" she said. "Or you need her?"

Dorian shrugged and stepped into the pond, hoe in hand. She wasn't going to answer that particular question, and Diara knew it, so she looked at Adalia, winking to let her know that she was onto her sister. Adalia knew, too. Dorian was learning to manipulate her father, and it was fun to watch. Adalia watched her sister for a moment as the girl began ripping out overgrown plants before turning her attention to Diara.

"When *is* Papa coming back?" she asked softly.

Diara's smile faded. She had avoided telling the girls anything about Roi's situation because she hadn't wanted to frighten them, but the truth was that they weren't babies. They were young women, and sometimes, young women had to face harsh facts. As much as she was trying to protect them, she probably wasn't doing them any favors by not being honest with them. They hadn't really asked about their father until today, and now, she had a direct question.

She simply couldn't avoid it any longer.

"I do not know," she said honestly. "He has gone to… There was a skirmish that he has been asked to… The truth is that I simply don't know. He has gone to fight in a skirmish. That is why his brothers came here. Now, they've gone off to help him, so I really do not know when he will be back, but hopefully it will be soon."

That was about all she could get out. She hoped it would satisfy Adalia, but she could tell by the expression on the young woman's face that the wheels of thought were turning. Unable to look at Adalia anymore, she turned her attention to Dorian, who had plucked a fish out of the pond to admire its colors, when Adalia spoke softly.

"There is trouble, isn't there?" she asked.

Diara looked at her. "Why would you think so?"

"Because my uncles were here, and I know they were upset," she said. "I heard them speaking of an ambush. Did they mean my father?"

Diara didn't want to lie to her. "I do not know, sweetheart, truly," she said, unwilling to commit to something as horrible as that word. "We will know soon enough."

"Are you afraid?"

Diara wasn't sure how to answer that. She looked at Adalia, seeing an earnest question. After a moment, she simply nodded her head.

"Aye," she whispered.

Adalia squeezed her hands to give her some comfort, and it nearly undid Diara. Here she was, trying to comfort Roi's daughter, but the daughter was comforting her instead. As she struggled to regain her composure, she heard someone call her name and turned to see Kyne standing in the open gate.

"My lady?" he said again, quietly. "May I speak with you?"

Diara nodded and stood up, directing Adalia to remain with her sister to make sure she didn't get into any trouble as she went to Kyne.

"What is it?" she asked politely.

Kyne motioned for her to follow. Diara did, walking beside the silent knight, feeling a good deal more apprehension than curiosity with every step she took. He wouldn't look at her and he wouldn't talk to her. They headed out of the kitchen yard, and she was about to ask him where they were going when she caught sight of another knight standing several feet away.

It was Westley.

Diara's breath caught in her throat. She stumbled to a stop. She tried to take another step but couldn't manage to do it. The only thing she could do at that moment was feel complete, unrestrained horror.

If Westley was here and not the entire army, his reasons for coming could not be good.

"Oh… God," she breathed, her hands flying to her mouth. "Sweet Jesus. Why… why is he here? Why is Westley here?"

She was starting to panic, and Kyne reached out to grasp her as Westley bolted in her direction. The knights both reached out to steady her as Westley took her hands and forced her to look at him.

"Steady, Lady de Lohr," he said. "I've been sent ahead to prepare you."

Diara broke down, falling to pieces right before their eyes. "Prepare me for *what*?" she wept. "Where is Roi?"

"He is coming," Westley assured her. "Truly, it's not so terrible. But he will need a comfortable bed to recover in, and he has sent me ahead to tell you. He did not want you to be worried when you saw that he had been injured."

That didn't help Diara in the least. She was sobbing. "*Injured*?" she cried. "What has happened to him?"

Westley was genuinely distressed to see how upset she was. "I'm sorry," he said. "I did not do this very well. I wanted to tell you in private that we found Roi. He had been injured in a skirmish. But he is alive and he is coming home. He simply needs some time to recover, but he *is* alive, Diara. I swear to you, he is alive."

That did absolutely nothing to ease her. She wept for an entirely different reason now, knowing her husband was injured but alive. He was coming home, in what condition she didn't know, but at least he was heading home. Diara wept for another solid minute, struggling to catch her breath, while Kyne and Westley desperately tried to comfort her. But just as quickly, she took a deep breath, stopped her tears, and wiped furiously at her face.

"He's alive," she said, more to herself than to them. "He's coming home and he's alive."

"Aye," Westley said, still deeply concerned. "But please do

not tell Roi that I made you cry. He will kill me."

That had Diara bursting out into laughter. "If you are worried about that, then he must not be too seriously hurt," she said. "I promise I will not tell him. But the next time you come to prepare me for something like this, the first words out of your mouth should be that my husband is alive and will be fine, given time."

Westley nodded. "I will try to remember that," he said. "But hopefully, there will not be another time."

Diara couldn't disagree with him. She continued to wipe at her eyes, composing herself as best she could. "Now," she said, trying to focus on what needed to be done. "I will go to the keep to ensure that our bed is ready for him. Is there anything else he needs?"

"Only you, I am sure," Westley said. "He has been talking about you, without stopping, since we found him."

Diara wanted to ask him so much more, but that would have to wait. She knew that Roi was coming home and that he would be well again, and that was all that mattered. She broke away from Kyne and Westley, rushing back to the keep and sending Finnick into a fit when she gave him the news. The man whipped the servants into a frenzy, all of it directed at preparing the master's bedchamber for his return. As she turned to head to the kitchen to talk to the cook about preparing food that was easy to digest, she caught sight of a few soldiers coming in through the gatehouse. Soldiers meant army.

The army had returned.

She made a run for it.

Westley, in fact, was at the gatehouse and had to hold her back. Diara fully intended to go charging into the ranks to find her husband, but that would only get her trampled, so Westley held on to her as the bulk of the army passed beneath the gatehouse. The wagons, slower, were tagging along behind. Once Diara caught a glimpse of the wagons, Westley lost his grip on her.

She ran like the wind.

The first wagon contained food stores, but the second wagon contained several de Lohr brothers, sitting on the bed and on the sides of the wagon, and right in the middle of them was Roi. When Diara caught sight of him, she cried out, and, startled, he turned to see her trying to vault onto the wagon. Douglas was there and lifted her up, straight into Roi's open arms.

Actually, it was only one arm, since the left one had been bandaged into position so it couldn't move. Both of his wounds were on the left side, so the physic that traveled with the de Lohr army bandaged him up tightly so he couldn't move the limb. But he didn't need that arm to hold Diara, who had her arms around his neck and her face in the side of his head, weeping softly at the joy of the reunion.

Truth be told, Roi shed a few tears himself.

"They told me what happened," Diara wept. "I'm so sorry, Roi. Sorry my father did this to you. I'm so very, very sorry."

He kissed her repeatedly, on the cheek and on the hair, holding her so tightly with his one arm that he was squeezing the breath from her.

"You tried to warn me," he said. "I should have listened. I am so sorry that I did not."

She pulled back to look at him, running her hands over his face to reacquaint herself with him. He was dirty, sweaty, and his lip was swollen from where he'd clearly been hit, but he'd never looked so good to her.

"In a world where my father is a normal man, you would have been perfectly correct not to listen to me," she said. "But he is not a normal man. He's horrible and vindictive, but this went beyond anything I believed he was capable of. I will never speak to him again as long as I live."

Roi didn't say anything for a moment. He simply pulled her into his embrace again, but his gaze was on the men riding either on or around the wagon. Each one of them knew the truth of what had happened. Directly behind the wagon, Magnus, Aeron, and Tiegh were on their horses. They'd joined up with the de Lohr army after their task at Cicadia was complete. Therefore, Roi knew everything.

It was important that Diara knew everything, too.

Almost everything, anyway… and gently told.

"Angel," he said, loosening his grip so he could look at her. "Though I survived the battle, your father did not. For your sake, I will mourn him if you want me to. But you must know that he is no longer with us."

Diara looked at him in shock. "He… My father is dead?"

"He is."

She stared at him for a moment, digesting the information, before finally shaking her head. "I do not know what I feel," she said, though she was blinking away the tears. "He was so wicked to you, Roi. I can never forgive that. And if his wicked actions brought about his own end, then it was deserved. How can I mourn the loss of such evil?"

He stroked her cheek with his thumb. "I will do whatever you want me to," he said softly. "He tried to cause my death, but he is also your father. I realize that puts you in a difficult position."

She shook her head before he finished speaking. "Nay, it

does not," she said. "My father and I... I am not a fool, Roi. I know he only paid me attention because he thought he could make a fine marriage match and profit from it. That is the truth of it. I wasn't a daughter to him as much as I was a commodity. While I will mourn the loss of my father, I will not mourn the loss of the man. Does that make sense?"

He nodded. "It does."

"What of my mother?" she said. "Does she know?"

Roi nodded. "She does," he said. "Would you like to go to her? I will understand if you do."

Diara looked at him for a long moment. It was clear that she was thinking about something, because she had a way of looking at Roi that very nearly gave him a peek into her mind's eye.

And she had such a brilliant mind.

"Nay," she finally said. "I do not want to go to her. I do not want to go to Cicadia at all, but you are the Earl of Cheltenham now, and Cicadia Castle is your property. Mayhap... mayhap I will invite my mother to stay with us, if she wishes, and Iris can come with her. I have missed Iris."

"You could have sent for her anytime, you know."

Diara nodded. "Aye, I know," she said. "But we were just coming to know one another, and I was just coming to know Adalia and Dorian. I wanted that time with you, and with them, without Iris interfering. We are a family, after all. We needed to be with one another."

He stroked her hair gently. "A sweet sentiment and one that is appreciated," he said. "But at some point, your father must be buried. Will you want to attend his funeral?"

Diara sighed faintly. "I am his only child," she said. "Yet I am not sure I want to be there. He tried to kill you, Roi. I simply cannot forgive him for that."

He didn't push her. She could make her own decisions and he would abide by them. There was much more he wanted to tell her—about Cirencester's demise, perhaps even a general description of the battle and the situation, but that would have to wait. He simply didn't feel like bringing that into their world right now because he was safe, he was home, and that was all that mattered.

And he had the men around him to thank for that.

Brothers, cousins, nephews, and colleagues. Some of the best men England had to offer, in both skill and character. He owed them everything and he knew it, but for the new Earl of Cheltenham and his countess, his life, as he saw it, was just beginning.

Roi de Lohr had been given a second chance, and he wasn't going to squander it.

But the one person who had made it all possible was back behind Magnus, plodding along on his exhausted steed. Roi could see about half of Mathis' body, and he motioned to Douglas to bring the man forward. Mathis heard his name being called and reined his beast next to the wagon.

"Mathis, if it were not for you, I would not be here," Roi said as Diara turned to look at her father's former knight. "I realize I've been surrounded by a dozen de Lohrs, all of them grimly determined to ensure that I survive, but the real person to thank in all of this is you. You did not have to do what you did. You could have gone along with Robin's plans, and I would now be moldering on the ground somewhere. If you would like to remain in the service of Cheltenham, as the commander at my garrison of Cicadia Castle, I would be most grateful."

Mathis looked weary and worn. Diara pushed herself off

Roi and moved to the edge of the wagon, holding out her hand to Mathis, who took it after a moment's hesitation.

She squeezed his hand tightly.

"Thank you," she murmured. "For saving his life. I know none of this has been easy for you, but for the fact that you decided to do what was right and good, I can never thank you enough. I owe you everything."

Mathis smiled weakly, giving her hand a squeeze before letting it go. "You've not known much happiness in your life, Lady Cheltenham," he said, using her title for the first time. "I've known you for many years, and I have seen the things you've had to endure, and you have always done it with grace. The rumors of your time at Carisbrooke, the attitude of your father... I've seen it all. When I realized what was happening between your father and Fairford, I knew I had to do something about it. I did not do it for any great loyalty towards the House of de Lohr, but I did it because I knew, if Roi perished, that you would not recover. Every person hopes they meet that person who makes them feel whole. I believe you have met yours. I could not stand by and watch you lose him."

The tears were back in Diara's eyes. "And I will be ever grateful for it," she said. "If I can ever return the favor, you know I will."

He lifted a dark brow. "Will you, my lady?"

"Of course. Anything."

Mathis' eyes took on a gleam. "Enough to convince your husband to allow me to court his daughter?"

Diara broke out in a big smile. "Enough even for that," she assured him confidently. "In fact, while I take Roi into the keep, I believe a certain young lady is behind the kitchens at the fishpond. I know she would be more than happy to see you."

Mathis chuckled, but he was grateful. Perhaps he was unable to marry Diara, but in the end, they had a good understanding of one another. He appreciated the bond they had built, and that was something he never wanted to lose. He wanted to be in her life any way he could be.

Even if that meant only as a friend.

As the wagon came to a halt in the bailey and several men went to help Roi out of the wagon bed, Diara simply backed away and let the men do the work. She remembered telling Roi once that she'd never really had much of a family and, suddenly, she had a big one. Men who had risked their lives to save Roi, to pull him from the jaws of death. It was only later—much later—she was told just *how* close to death he had come.

That made her more grateful than ever for those who had come together to save him.

It was the best possible outcome of the tale of the widower who had no intention of remarrying until he agreed to fulfill the betrothal of his dead son, marrying a woman half his age, but in that marriage, Roi de Lohr was reborn.

Theirs was a love story for the ages.

EPILOGUE

Three years later
Lioncross Abbey Castle

"**I** CAME AS quickly as I could," Roi said. "What has happened?"

He had just entered the keep of Lioncross only to be met by his brother, Myles. He was like the rest of the de Lohr men— big, blond, well built—only Myles had luscious blond hair that fell past his shoulders, something every woman he met envied. His wife particularly liked it. He had his mother's hair because in her youth, she had a cascade of gold down her back, well past her buttocks. That wasn't where his similarities to his mother ended, because he was her son in every way, except for one.

Myles was a trained assassin.

Roi knew that his presence at Lioncross meant something serious.

"Steel yourself, man," Myles said, looking over Roi's shoulder at the woman in the bailey behind him, being greeted by their mother. "Many things are afoot. But why did you bring your wife? I told you that I would need your full attention."

Roi turned to look at Diara with a toddler in her arms and

an enormously pregnant stomach. "Because she wanted to come," he said simply. "I will not leave her at Pembridge, not when she is due to deliver our son any day. Besides, she wants him born at Lioncross like I was and like his brother was. I could not, and would not, leave her behind, so you'll simply have to accept it."

Myles didn't look pleased. "I hope she does not become upset when we take all of your time."

"Diara is not like that, and you know it," Roi said. "She will let me do what needs to be done and not complain about it. Now, what's this all about?"

As if on cue, a blond toddler suddenly darted up the stairs, screaming because his grandmother was coming for him. Roi grabbed little Rex de Lohr before he could get away from him, kissing his son's cheeks loudly as the baby cried and tried to push away. Chuckling, Roi set him on his feet, and the first thing the child did was run straight into Christopher's solar. They could hear a faint cry go up as Christopher caught sight of his beloved grandson.

"You know Papa wants to see him," Roi said. "He's an old man, Myles. Let him enjoy his grandchildren while he can."

Myles knew it was futile to resist. He shook his head in resignation. "I know," he said. "And Rex is welcome, you know that. But I still laugh when I think of that name."

"What name?"

"Rex."

Roi stiffened. "And why not?" he said. "Roi means 'king.' Rex also means king. It is well and good that a son be named after his father, and well you know it."

Myles held up his hands in surrender. "I know," he said. "But I had a dog named Rex. Now I have a nephew named

Rex."

"Be very careful or I will name my next horse Myles and beat it constantly."

Myles started laughing. "You would, too."

"Of course I would."

At that point, they were interrupted by Diara as she entered the keep along with Dustin. Myles bent over to kiss his sister-in-law, a truly radiant beauty that had her husband more enamored with her every day, on the cheek. The entire family had seen Roi change from a serious, rather lonely man to a doting husband and father with the introduction of a wife he adored.

It had been good to see.

"Lady Cheltenham," Myles greeted Diara. "It is agreeable to see you again."

Diara lifted an eyebrow at her brother-in-law. The man wasn't much for pleasantries and probably didn't have a flattering bone in his body. She'd never once heard him give a compliment, which was something of a running joke with the family.

"Agreeable, am I?" she said. "Be careful with your sweet words, Myles de Lohr, or they will swell my head. Where is your wife?"

"Unable to come, my lady."

"I am sorry," Diara said, sobering. "She is well, is she not?"

"Very well," Myles said. "But I would not let her travel. Our child is due very soon as well. And what are you to name Roi's latest offspring? Queen? Prince? Peasant?"

Dustin, who had been standing next to Diara, swatted Myles from behind. "Cease your taunts," she said. "I will not let you harass her."

Diara chuckled at her protective mother-in-law. "Not to worry, Naina," she said, using the name for Dustin that her grandchildren had given her. "I'll have my revenge when he least expects it. And since you are asking so nicely, Myles, I will tell you that this son will bear the name of Beau, the name of a man who was a dear friend to us when we traveled to Lac du Lausanne before Rex was born. I am telling you this so that you will not give your child the same name. I will be furious if you do."

Myles shook his head. "I promise that I will not call my son by the same name," he said. "But what if it is a girl?"

"How can it be a girl if I am to name him Beau?"

Myles looked at Roi, who simply shrugged. Such was the logic of a pregnant woman. Inside the solar, they could hear Rex laughing loudly about something, which drew the women. As they followed the sounds of the happy baby, Myles prevented Roi from going after them. When Roi looked at him curiously, he shook his head faintly.

"Not yet," he said softly. "There are things to discuss before you go in there."

"For example?"

"Papa is no longer in command of the Executioner Knights," Myles said softly. "He has turned that duty over to Peter. Peter not only controls everything now, but Anselm Marshal willed Farringdon House to Papa before he died. Papa has given it over to Peter."

Those were some serious changes. "Farringdon House has been a Marshal property for over fifty years," Roi said. "That is the heart of the Executioner Knight operation."

Myles nodded. "I know," he said. "But no one knows that it is a de Lohr property yet, so given that you spend a good deal of time in London with Henry, you should be aware."

"Absolutely. Henry must not know, for he's not said a word."

Myles shrugged. "I suppose it does not matter who the townhome belongs to, at least to Henry," he said. "But it is a valuable property and Peter will be there frequently. He's in the solar, Roi. He wants to ask you to consider returning to the Executioner Knights."

"As an operative?"

Myles merely nodded, leaving Roi to consider the possibilities. But that was short-lived because he had news of his own.

"I am too old," he finally said. "Moreover, there is something you should know. Henry has offered me the appointment of chief justiciar, Myles. You know what that means."

Myles' eyes widened. "He has?" he said, astounded. "Roi, that's astonishing. You'll have more power than the king in a position like that. Head of the judiciary system and the laws."

"I know."

"Your word will be law."

"I am well aware."

"You'll have your own court and counselors."

"I will, indeed."

Myles was clearly impressed. "Will you accept?"

Roi grinned. "Of course I will," he said. "How else do you think I will be able to work in concert with Peter and the Executioner Knights, making sure England remains safe and secure for all of us? If there is a problem that laws cannot fix, then the Executioner Knights can."

Myles, who wasn't one to easily smile, was nearly beaming at his brother. "Chief justiciar," he repeated in awe. "God's Bones, Roi. Papa will be so proud."

Roi sobered, humbled by his brother's praise. "I've had a different path than most of you," he said. "I'm a knight, and a skilled one, but I'm not a warlord. I've been more of a scholar, and I always wondered if Papa was somehow disappointed by that."

Myles frowned. "Are you mad?" he said. "You are a better knight than any of us. And as for Papa being disappointed... go in there and tell him what you just told me. The man will be beside himself with glee."

"I hope so," Roi said. "I feel that I can do England—and our family—much more good as justiciar than as an Executioner Knight. We all have our roles to play in life, and this is mine."

"Agreed," Myles said. "When will you assume the role officially?"

Roi lifted his eyebrows. "After Adalia's wedding," he said. "That is coming this summer, after the baby is born. But with Iris marrying Kyne a few months ago, Adalia has a serious case of wedding fever, and she can hardly wait. Mathis is at Pembridge more than he is at Cicadia, and he is excited, too, though he will not admit it."

"You still have not officially moved into Cicadia?"

Roi shook his head. "It is my seat, but I prefer Pembridge," he said. "Diara prefers it there, too. She said that she never had a happy childhood at Cicadia, so she wants to raise our children at Pembridge. Adalia will make a fine chatelaine at Cicadia when she marries Mathis, so let her make her own good memories there."

"And Dorian?"

Roi chuckled. "She has her eye on Eddard de Vahn," he said, shaking his head in disbelief. "He serves me at Cicadia, you know. Have you met him? He's difficult to miss. Smells like a stable. I think that is why she is fond of him."

Myles started laughing. "I think I have met the man," he said. "Hair the color of straw?"

"That is him."

"Is there any way you can keep downwind of him?"

Roi put his hand over his face, snorting. "The problem is that he is an excellent knight," he said. "But I've a mind to send him to my property in France, Chateau de Beuville, simply to get him away from people who don't like his smell."

"But Dorian does."

"She does, indeed."

"Then it sounds as if your daughters have found their true loves."

Rex picked that moment to bolt out of Christopher's solar with Dustin in pursuit. Roi watched them scurry down a corridor, listening to his son scream and his mother's calm voice. Diara emerged from the solar as well, standing in the doorway as she watched her husband's mother chase down her skittish toddler.

But Roi only had eyes for his wife.

Somehow, Myles' words had particular resonance at the moment.

"Mayhap," he said softly. "For I have certainly found mine."

When Diara caught his eye, smiling adoringly at him, there was no doubt in Roi's mind that the feeling was quite mutual.

True love always was.

⁂ THE END? ⁂

Children of Roi and Diara
Adalia (Odette)
Dorian (Odette)
Rex
Beau
Evan
Daphne
Rose
Lucan
Alex
Willow

KATHRYN LE VEQUE NOVELS

Medieval Romance:

De Wolfe Pack Series:
Warwolfe
The Wolfe
Nighthawk
ShadowWolfe
DarkWolfe
A Joyous de Wolfe Christmas
BlackWolfe
Serpent
A Wolfe Among Dragons
Scorpion
StormWolfe
Dark Destroyer
The Lion of the North
Walls of Babylon
The Best Is Yet To Be
BattleWolfe
Castle of Bones

De Wolfe Pack Generations:
WolfeHeart
WolfeStrike
WolfeSword
WolfeBlade
WolfeLord
WolfeShield
Nevermore
WolfeAx

The Executioner Knights:
By the Unholy Hand

The Mountain Dark
Starless
A Time of End
Winter of Solace
Lord of the Sky
The Splendid Hour
The Whispering Night
Netherworld
Lord of the Shadows
Of Mortal Fury
'Twas the Executioner Knight
Before Christmas
Crimson Shield

The de Russe Legacy:
The Falls of Erith
Lord of War: Black Angel
The Iron Knight
Beast
The Dark One: Dark Knight
The White Lord of Wellesbourne
Dark Moon
Dark Steel
A de Russe Christmas Miracle
Dark Warrior

The de Lohr Dynasty:
While Angels Slept
Rise of the Defender
Steelheart
Shadowmoor
Silversword
Spectre of the Sword
Unending Love

Eliza Knight):	Veque
Savage of the Sea by Eliza Knight	The Sea Devil by Eliza Knight
Leader of Titans by Kathryn Le	Sea Wolfe by Kathryn Le Veque

Note: All Kathryn's novels are designed to be read as stand-alones, although many have cross-over characters or cross-over family groups. Novels that are grouped together have related characters or family groups. You will notice that some series have the same books; that is because they are cross-overs. A hero in one book may be the secondary character in another.

There is NO reading order except by chronology, but even in that case, you can still read the books as stand-alones. No novel is connected to another by a cliff hanger, and every book has an HEA.

Series are clearly marked. All series contain the same characters or family groups except the American Heroes Series, which is an anthology with unrelated characters.

For more information, find it in **A Reader's Guide to the Medieval World of Le Veque.**

ABOUT KATHRYN LE VEQUE

Bringing the Medieval to Romance

KATHRYN LE VEQUE is a critically acclaimed, multiple USA TODAY Bestselling author, an Indie Reader bestseller, a charter Amazon All-Star author, and a #1 bestselling, award-winning, multi-published author in Medieval Historical Romance with over 100 published novels.

Kathryn is a multiple award nominee and winner, including the winner of Uncaged Book Reviews Magazine 2017 and 2018 "Raven Award" for Favorite Medieval Romance. Kathryn is also a multiple RONE nominee (InD'Tale Magazine), holding a record for the number of nominations. In 2018, her novel WARWOLFE was the winner in the Romance category of the Book Excellence Award and in 2019, her novel A WOLFE AMONG DRAGONS won the prestigious RONE award for best pre-16th century romance.

Kathryn is considered one of the top Indie authors in the world with over 2M copies in circulation, and her novels have been translated into several languages. Kathryn recently signed with Sourcebooks Casablanca for a Medieval Fight Club series, first published in 2020.

In addition to her own published works, Kathryn is also the President/CEO of Dragonblade Publishing, a boutique publishing house specializing in Historical Romance. Dragonblade's success has seen it rise in the ranks to become Amazon's #1 e-book publisher of Historical Romance (K-Lytics report July 2020).

Kathryn loves to hear from her readers. Please find Kathryn on Facebook at Kathryn Le Veque, Author, or join her on Twitter @kathrynleveque. Sign up for Kathryn's blog at www.kathrynleveque.com for the latest news and sales.

CPSIA information can be obtained
at www.ICGtesting.com
Printed in the USA
LVHW020137290423
745602LV00003B/205